BOB HAYES

THE CLAN OF THE WOLF

ZHÒH - The Clan of the Wolf

Published in 2016

by Bob Hayes

Printed in Germany

Kriechbaumer Druck GmbH & Co. KG

Ehrenbreitsteiner Straße 28 / 80993 München

ISBN: 978-0-9867376-1-9

COLLƧ

At the far end of the grey lake

beneath damp mountains

A worked chert flake shines

from its cobbled bed

At last, the black blade

has carved its portal

through compacted centuries

Here, two makers meet

touch fingers chilled

from working the valley's perpetual mist -

Pass it on

Erling Friis-Baastad - Wood Spoken

TABLE OF CONTENTS

TO AVA AND CAROLINE

PROLOGUE

THE WOLF

Porcupine River — 14,000 years ago

The boar grizzly weaves through a high stand of willows at the bend of a flooding river. Huge ice blocks tumble downstream, slamming into the shore before twisting back into the racing flood. An ice pan crushes through willows and stunted poplar trees before it shatters.

The bear stops to watch as a lone caribou, perched precariously on a tilted ice floe, passes close to shore. He raises his nose in mild interest, but his instincts warn him the water is too dangerous. The prey disappears down the river in a jumble of lurching ice slabs.

An overturned boat surfaces, the wooden gunnels and ribs crushed. The wreck enters a roiling eddy of grey slush and then disappears, spitting back to the surface far downstream. A lifeless body covered in caribou-skin clothing floats behind the wreckage.

The boar stands over the twisted roots of a fallen poplar. With his long claws he rips away the bark, tearing into the rotted wood. He drops his head, uncurls his tongue and licks up a colony of dazed ants. Suddenly, a familiar scent floods his brain; he feels both excited and uneasy. The smell of wolf mingled with the lure of dead flesh calls to him. The bear enters a shallow ravine, stepping into a small creek that cascades noisily down to the river. He slips up the creek until he is standing in high willow shrubs at the edge of a familiar sage-grass meadow. The smell of danger is here.

"*Sik-sik-sik-sik!*" A ground squirrel, surprised by the bear, screeches as it scrambles into its burrow. The bear stands quietly, every muscle relaxed, not breathing — listening, smelling. Finally, he steps out onto the meadow, his thick snout lifted in the air. Wolf smell is here - the smell of enemy. Their resting beds are scattered everywhere, strewn with wolf hair, scat and bones. A white-crowned sparrow lands, picks up a twist of hair and flies back to her nest in the shrubs. Her mate is singing, his clear whistles and buzzy trills drowned out occasionally by a brisk, cool wind.

The bear finds a leg of horse still fresh with the bitter tang of wolf saliva and rolls it over, stripping away the dried flesh wedged beneath the hide. A hole in the centre of the meadow draws his attention. He stands on a mound of freshly dug soil and shoves his wide head inside the hole. The den is filled with the milky, humid scent of young wolves. A faint shuffling is coming from the darkness below.

The bear raises his head and looks around the meadow for the big ones, but none are here. He tears into the den, kicking the cool soil under him with his powerful legs. Soon, the excavation is wide enough to stand inside. He disappears, dislodging small rocks and gravel as he digs deeper. Suddenly, the tunnel opens into a wide chamber brimming with wolf scent. Pups are scrambling in every direction as he smashes the roof of

12

the den. The boar drives his forepaw down, instantly killing two. He snatches a third as it scrambles under his legs.

The last pup, a female, is jammed under the lip of a boulder at the back of the chamber. She squeezes into a narrow tunnel just as the boar slams his long canines into the dirt. She wiggles farther down the hole, where she runs into a surprised ground squirrel straddling a nest of newborn young. The squirrel screams defiantly at the intruder but quickly reconsiders and bolts from her burrow, screeching across the meadow before disappearing into an abandoned hole.

The bear shakes and wrenches the rock, but it will not budge. He gives up and collects the three dead pups in his jaws, laying them neatly together in the trench. His knife-sharp claw flays the skin from the tiny bodies. Each morsel of pup is eaten in a few bites. The bones are dropped in a neat pile.

A noise suddenly breaks the silence of the meadow. Something is moving through the willows along the river. The bear walks out of the meadow, in no mood to defend himself against the big ones. He glances briefly in the direction of the approaching sound before disappearing behind a curtain of greening shrubs.

THE GIRL

Bluefish Hills

The girl moves along the edge of a small creek crusted in a slick apron of early autumn ice. Beneath her feet, the ground is a red carpet of dwarf arctic willow and cranberries. She slips her fingers under the low, leathery leaves, scooping a handful of red berries into her leather bag. From somewhere upstream, she hears her mother mimic the ascending whistle of a grey-headed loon: "*Kwao - kwao kwao.*" The girl cups her hands and whistles a grey-cheeked thrush - a soft, rolling series of flute-like notes rising at the end - answering that she is safe.

The girl cranes her neck to look for her family. Her mother moves in and out of view, bent over in her own rhythmic picking. The girl is following the trail of berries through low shrubs across a broad meadow. She is moving into a light wind, the way her father has taught her to travel: smelling the air, listening, looking for killing beasts. She is startled to see lion tracks at the edge of a small pond. Dead leaves fill the pugmarks, telling her the beast passed by some days ago. She knows she must move quickly to her father if she sees a lion, a wolf or a bear. He is walking the open plain ahead, his spear bobbing along the brown horizon. Her brother is in front, hunting ground squirrel with a rock sling. *Sik-Sik* is fattest in autumn. It is the girl's favourite meal. She is about to deliver her bag of berries to her mother when she senses something watching her. Her eye catches a light-coloured shape just as it disappears behind a low rise. Her heart stops.

Lion!

She puts the bone whistle in her mouth, about to blow the killing-beast warning, when it appears again.

Wolf.

She feels a mix of relief and apprehension. She knows long-ago stories of people killed by wolves, but she has seen so many in her life she feels a sense of kinship. Like humans, wolves follow the same herds of grasseaters. The wolf comes into view. From its broad head and heavy shoulders, the girl can tell it is a male. It is young, not yet an adult. The wolf leaps into the air, driving his forepaws into the ground. Each failed lunge is followed by a shrill "*sik-sik-sik*" as ground squirrels escape, chattering, into burrows.

The wolf is only a few feet away when he spots the girl. They stand facing each other, their eyes locked in mutual surprise - each waiting for the other to make the first move.

Finally, the girl breaks the silence. "*Zhòh dinji*, I do not wish you harm," she says. She is strangely unafraid. She can hear the words but does not know they are from her own lips.

The wolf turns his head slightly at the unfamiliar sound, his yellow eyes studying this upright animal making strange noises. The girl slowly reaches into her parka and pulls out a sliver of dry meat to offer to the wolf. He steps back, recognizing the smell of caribou but keeping his distance.

She quickly forgets the wolf might be dangerous; she steps forward as the wolf inches back. Rolling the meat in her hand, she drops it at the wolf's feet, moves back and watches. He cautiously nudges it with his nose and then bolts it down. The girl takes another piece and tosses it. He devours it and looks at the girl for more. As she holds another piece out in her hand, he stretches his neck, snapping the offering from her outstretched fingers, grazing the tip of her thumb with a flashing canine.

"I share my meat," she says, her voice quiet and soothing as she offers more. Soon her pocket is empty and she stands with her arms by her side. The wolf searches her hand, not understanding where the food has gone.

Overwhelmed by a sense of trust, she extends her empty hand to him. A familiar fear is telling her to stop - to pull back - but

15

the trust becomes stronger. Her fingers brush the fine white tips of the wolf's shoulder hair. He brushes his nose against her hand as her fingers glide softly against his head.

Slipping into a semi-trance, she is suddenly aware of the wolf's mind. She remembers her father telling her that only Wolf is smart enough for a human's soul to enter into. The wolf is greeting her in a language she has never heard but somehow understands.

"I know your voice," the wolf claims. "You speak my tongue."

The girl replies in a voice that is thin and strange in her own ear. "I am a spirit-traveller; I know wolf tongue."

He is looking into her eyes. "All living spirits speak but not all hear."

"I am child of Bear Band. I am with my pack. My mother and father and brother are here." The girl waves her arm slowly toward the creek.

The wolf suddenly looks at something behind her. His eyes are dark, alert and tense, no longer soft. She can feel fear surging through his heart, so intense it is as if it is her own heart.

A hunting dart whistles past her head. The wolf leaps back as the long weapon sinks into the ground a few inches from him. He spins away, retreating quickly to a low ridge a few hundred feet away.

Her father's distant voice breaks her trance. "Naali! What are you doing!" Moments later he is standing in front of her. "Wolves are dangerous. *Zhòh* can kill you. You fed it!" He cuffs her across the back of her head, knocking her fur hat to the ground.

She glances up at him. "He was hungry," she explains as she stoops and picks up the hat. He cuffs her again.

"Never feed killing beasts. You know the rule. Would you feed bear or lion?"

"No," Naali replies, raising her hand to block another blow, but her father is finishing the lesson.

"Why do you think we have signals?" His voice softens a

16

little.

"I know. I will not do it again."

"Why did it come to you?"

"I do not know," she lies.

She wants to tell her father the wolf came to speak to her, but she knows better. She looks out on the open meadow for the wolf, but he is gone.

"Come," her father says, touching her shoulder gently. They walk toward her mother, who is watching.

"Look - natl'at," the girl proudly says, holding her sack of cranberries open so her mother can see. Her brother approaches and shoves his fingers into the sack, pulling out a handful.

"Wolf girl," he mutters under his breath as he fills his mouth with the juicy berries.

"I am Naali," she says, glaring hard at him as she empties her sack into her mother's.

Her father inspects the stone tip of his dart for damage. "Zhòh would have made fine parka trim," he says. Naali silently follows her mother along the creek, collecting natl'at and thinking about the wolf.

The Boy

Hole-in-Rock Camp

Through the narrow slits in his caribou-skin visor, the boy can barely make out the shape moving on top of a snow-covered knoll. It is too small to be a grasseater, or bear, or wolf. The knoll is in the middle of a wide ravine surrounded by a long circular ridge, broken here and there by small cliffs. Brilliant sunlight reflects off the spring snow, obscuring everything. He squints, trying to identify the shape.

Nehtr'uh - wolverine!

Dropping onto one knee, Kazan props his spear against a boulder, takes off his backpack and pulls out a sun-bleached caribou hide. He unfolds it, slipping his head through a hole in the centre. The white skin falls below his knees.

I am snow. I am invisible.

Kazan removes his bison-fur mitts, letting them hang free from the rawhide thongs slung around his neck and fed through the arms of his caribou-skin parka. He reaches over his shoulder and pulls a throwing board the length of his forearm from a hunting quiver strapped to his back. He inspects the leather finger loops and the spur end he will attach the long hunting dart to. The dart foreshaft is mammoth ivory, tipped with a deadly stone point. The willow aftershaft is bevelled to the ivory with sinew and fletched with two ptarmigan-wing feathers. He notches the projectile into the stick and practises a sweeping arm and wrist motion, as he has done countless times before. Adjusting his visor, he moves slowly up the knoll, the dart poised for hurling.

His heart is racing. He has never darted a wolverine. *Nehtr'uh* is unpredictable and very dangerous. It is small, but he knows it can kill a human. Its fur is the finest, with long hairs that shed frost better than any other animal's.

18

Kazan imagines what his father would say now: *"Nehtr'uh -* wolverine. I hunt you for your skin. Your spirit may travel on."

He looks up, planning his approach. The knoll is icy. He must take care not to slip and give his approach away, but his nerves feel jagged.

He must strike the wolverine quickly with the dart. If it sees him coming, it will spin and turn, making an almost impossible target. If he misses, the wolverine might come for him. He touches the antler club hung from his waist belt, suddenly feeling unsure about the hunt. As he works his way up the knoll he loses sight of the top and his target, and his apprehension grows. He takes off the cape and stuffs it carefully into his pack. Kneeling down, he waits, listening to the drumming of his heart.

There is no wind. His shadow is behind him; it will not give him away to the sharp-eyed wolverine. Raising the throwing stick to his shoulder, Kazan peers along the dart shaft. He continues uphill, ready at any instant to throw. His heart is bursting with excitement, his fingers trembling. Gripping the stick, the boy takes a deep breath and runs the last few steps uphill. As he reaches the top, he drops his arm back, aiming at the moving shape at his feet.

The boy slides to a sudden stop - ten feet away, the massive head of a grizzly bear is turning toward him, its skull broader than Kazan's shoulders. As it turns, its small black eyes fix vacantly on him. It explodes out of the ground with a deafening roar, showering slabs of snow and ice everywhere. The boy stumbles backward and falls just as the bear shakes off the snowy blanket and charges.

Kazan freezes, every muscle in his body unable to move. The bear is nearly upon him when everything slows. Strangely, his mind is calmly processing rich details of everything that is happening. The bitter taste of bear fills his mouth, pressing on his tongue. It is coming at him so slowly it is as if time has stood still. Every detail of the bear is revealed.

Long snout, narrow face: *shih tri'ik*. It is a female, and she is coming…

19

Her black hump is shimmering in the brilliant sunlight. The hairs ripple and sparkle as if on fire. Her heavy, milk-laden teats quiver under her thick belly.

Cubs… there are cubs here.

The sow's eyes lock on his. Her ears are flattened against her neck, her mouth is open, her thick legs churning through the snow.

She is roaring but he hears nothing coming out of the twisted, gaping mouth. His mind races to remember something - anything - that might save him.

Cover my head...

But Kazan is unable to raise his hands from the snow. He is frozen. He will be crushed, his body shattered by the huge beast hurtling at him. The bear is almost upon him when a blurred shape suddenly appears, snapping at her head.

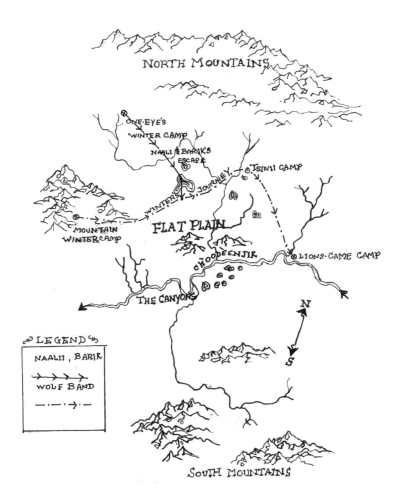

NORTH MOUNTAINS

ONE-EYE'S WINTER CAMP

NAALI & BARIK'S ESCAPE

TSINII CAMP

WINTER'S JOURNEY

MOUNTAIN WINTER CAMP

FLAT PLAIN

CHOODEENJIK

LIONS-CAME CAMP

THE CANYONS

N

S

LEGEND

NAALII , BARIK

WOLF BAND

SOUTH MOUNTAINS

21

PART 1

KHAII: THE DARK DAYS

Long-Nose Camp

The humans were moving slowly over the dark plain through a maze of bare ground and drifted snow. It was midday, but the Arctic sun was well below the horizon, offering only a lingering twilight of pale blues and dim pinks. A thick veil of falling snow made it impossible to see far ahead. Like the rest of the band, the boy in the rear was near exhaustion. He peered through the falling snow at the moving shapes ahead.

Kazan was at the end of the line to ensure no one fell behind or got lost in the snowstorm. He was 13 summers and already towered over all the men except his father. Unlike the short, thickly built hunters, he moved easily through the snow thanks to his tall, light frame. Otherwise, he looked like the rest of them. His heart-shaped face was framed by high, thick cheekbones. His broad, flat nose and brown eyes were hidden beneath a thick mop of jet-black hair.

A sudden wind blew and he turned his face into the wolf-fur trim of his hood, protecting his eyes from the stinging snow. He was wearing a caribou-skin parka - the long hair of the hide worn inside for the greatest warmth - and sheepskin pants, the thick white hair heavily stained and knees worn by the constant chafing of windblown snow. His mukluks were made from the lower leg skin of caribou, bound tight around his legs with leather cord. Despite the layers of fur, the cold had penetrated through to his light clothes. To stay warm, he had to keep moving. When the wind stopped, Kazan brushed his hood back. Through the falling snow he saw his father, Khon, at the front of the loaded sled, harnessed to a long tether.

Khon pulled down the hood of his caribou-skin parka and loosened the leather harness. He was tall and powerful, but today he felt old and tired. He was *Khehkai* - Chief - and like everyone, he was starving. Behind him, four men rested against the sled, their harness hanging loosely. In the morning, they had led the way, breaking trail and hunting as they went. When the snow began to fall they had turned back to help the women pull the heavy sled.

Chii Tsal, Khon's brother, watched him, ready to pull on the harness when he signalled. Beside him were the three youngest and strongest men, their heads bowed as they caught their breath. Four women were behind the sled. Two carried infants in packs wrapped in warm sheepskin blankets. Karun, Chii Tsal's wife, did not carry a baby. When Khon saw her he was suddenly struck with a deep sadness. She was staring off into the falling snow. Her infant daughter had died two nights ago. She and Chii Tsal had wrapped the little body in hare skins, laid her down on the frozen ground and covered her with snow. Chii Tsal had placed an antler dart foreshaft beside her so the infant would know grasseaters in the spirit world. He had sprinkled ochre pigment on the antler shaft to bring her spirit luck. When the burial was finished, the band had left without saying a word. No one looked back and no one spoke her name again. A child was not to die before her parents. It upset the order of spirits. It was a bad omen. They had covered her in a high snow mound, but Khon knew killing beasts would find her before spring. He grieved the death of every child, but a female was the future.

Is the child's death the omen of the end of our people?

His eyes turned back to his band.

Tarin, *Danach'I'* - Old Man - was limping along the trail, leaning on a long walking stick. Eyak, *Shanaghàn* - Old Woman - walked a few steps behind him. She clasped a blackened

23

wolverine skull that held a smoking willow root. Khon watched her feed shaved wood chips into the fire cup. She blew lightly on the smouldering coals, bringing the fire to life. A wisp of smoke rose above her and mingled with the thick snowflakes that fell from the grey sky.

Assan, Khon's first wife, walked behind Eyak. She was followed by their daughter, So'tsal, and Khon's second wife, Dèhzhòo. Aron and Korya, children of Chii Tsal and Karun, walked a few paces behind, their short legs struggling through the deep snow. Kazan, Khon's son, was last in line. He lifted Aron, his five-year-old cousin, over a deep snowdrift, setting him gently back onto the trail.

Satisfied he had seen everyone, Khon turned his attention back to the sled. With practised eyes he surveyed the heavy load. Everything was cinched tight with thick rawhide cord. On top of the load were long willow poles to frame two tents, spears and throwing darts of various shapes and sizes. Below were the tent skins. Wrapped inside them were all the worldly goods of the Wolf Band: fur sleeping beds, clothes, flint blades, bone utensils, scrapers, skull cups, woven baskets, flake-knapping tools, burins, microblades, hammerstones, stone points, bladders, tent floor skins, willow-root nets, rawhide snares, mammoth ivory awls and bone needles, bags of dried medicine plants, bear bladders filled with bone grease, mammoth ivory and elk antler beams for making foreshafts, dried berries and the last bag of dry meat, almost empty.

Khon turned and leaned into his harness as he waved his arm. The heavy sled slid ahead on the smooth elk skins and stopped after a few feet. He waved again and it inched forward. He peered into the stark grey horizon ahead, imagining what the Flat Plain looked like in summer: the sun circling high above the horizon... herds of caribou, bison, mammoth, horse and elk... multi-coloured carpets of tundra flowers... birds singing and ground squirrels chattering from every direction... flocks of geese, swans and ducks filling the blue skies. *Shin*, summer - time to hunt

24

newborn grasseaters. *Shin* - when grasseaters grow fat and Wolf Band grows strong.

But it was not summer. It was *Khaii*, the Dark Days. The winter sun had sunk beneath the horizon and would stay down for a moon. The frozen Flat Plain they travelled was dark and empty - as empty as his shrunken stomach. The starkness was magnified by the complete absence of animal life. It was as if the world had emptied. They had been travelling more than a moon and had not seen any *nin* - animals - larger than hare.

The sled crawled ahead. Khon's mukluks ground into the snow. He heard the hoarse exhaustion in his voice as he shouted "Pull... pull!"

A gust of wind blew snow in his face, blinding him. He buried his face in his hood and waited for the squall to end. Pressing his mitt against his face, he slowly rubbed his frosted cheeks back to life. His nose had been frozen so many times he could no longer feel it. He inhaled carefully, gauging the coldness of the air.

Too cold to be travelling.

But there was no choice. They had to find grasseaters or the band would starve.

Khon stopped suddenly as an enormous shape appeared through the veil of falling snow. He fell to his knees and waved the others down. The men untied their harnesses and gathered their spears. Crouching, they moved toward him.

"Long-Nose," Khon whispered as they gathered. He pointed into the whiteness ahead. They smelled the death in the air.

The view ahead cleared briefly, revealing the carcass of a bull mammoth half covered in drifted snow. The bull was on his side, the head resting on two long, curved tusks. The men crept forward, jabbing their spears into flank hairs the length of their arms. Khon waded closer and brushed the snow from the tusks, each longer than a man. He imagined the hunting points, sewing tools and dart foreshafts they would fashion with the ivory.

He turned to wave to Kazan in the rear and made a cutting motion with his hands. His son scrambled through the snow to the sled and untied the straps. Pulling off his mitts, he dug down into the load, lifted out a small leather sack and brought it to his father. Khon removed a fistful of black obsidian flakes each the size of his hand and gave one to every man. They sliced through the long mammoth hair, flaying the thick skin back and exposing the pink flesh. Kazan longed to join the men, but they were hunters. He was not. Until he had killed his first grasseater he could only watch and learn their ways.

Khon held his nose close to a pink patch of mammoth flesh. He shook his head in disappointment.

Chii Tsal smelled it next and shook his head. "Spoiled," he said flatly.

The others took turns pressing their noses to the flesh, shaking their heads in agreement. The mammoth's long hair and thick skin had kept the flesh warm after the beast had died, spoiling the meat. Here was more food than Wolf Band could eat in a year - but it was not fit for consumption.

Khon climbed up on the tusks and peeled back the neck where the flesh had cooled in the frigid wind. It was not exactly fresh, but it did not smell bad. The men followed Khon up onto the massive head of the mammoth while the women and children gathered around. Khon sliced off a piece of meat and tasted it. He nodded, pointing at the neck and grinning.

Chii Tsal slapped him on the back, shouting, "It is good!" Then he jumped down and began slicing open a leg to salvage the giant long bones for bone-grease.

Assan looked up at her husband and smiled. She placed her arm around Eyak's thin shoulders. "The meat is good," she said. „We will camp here." The old woman nodded silently and then turned to unload the sled.

As the men went to work butchering, the children spread out to search the area for fire dung. The women erected two dome tents, each one big enough to hold ten people. The roof was formed by a circle of bent willow trunks covered by a patchwork of caribou and elk skins. The centre top was left open to form the chimney. A caribou skin was draped across the door. The inner skins were painted with red and blue dyed imprints of eagle feathers; the seams were sealed with berry pigment. Skins of various shapes and sizes were scattered on the cold ground.

Soon small fires were warming the two tents. The entire band gathered in Khon's family tent and waited with great anticipation for the mammoth meat to roast.

A Daagoo Warning

Kazan sat in a heap of furs at the back of the tent savouring his mammoth meal with Aron. A wall of parkas, mukluks and pants were hung on long cords around the tent walls. Everyone was stripped to light caribou-skin garments. Gilgan was breastfeeding her baby, Jak, while Teekai sang softly to her infant, Yukaih. The chatter of men's and women's voices was mixed with the giggling of children and the crackle of burning coals. The men, never idle, were splitting the mammoth ivory into long shafts for making dart foreshafts, knapping flint into points, or stripping worn fletching off willow aftershafts and tying on fresh ptarmigan flight feathers. Each man worked his projectile to suit his own arm, binding the fore and aftershafts together with ochre-dyed sinew for good hunting luck.

The men sat nearest to the fire, Tarin to the right of Khon. He was the smallest of the six adult men, barely reaching Khon's chest. Old Man's back was bent from nearly five decades of hard life on the tundra-steppe. He had a pronounced limp, his leg broken long ago by a crushing bison kick that abruptly ended his life as a hunter. Dat'san, Jovan and Yogh - the youngest of the six - sat right of Tarin. Chii Tsal sat alone, farthest from Khon.

Behind the men, women were busy preparing the meal. Eyak moved around the fire with practised ease, despite the thick cataracts that left her almost blind. She stoked the bed of hot dung while Assan sliced and stuffed fresh meat and handfuls of cranberries into an elk-stomach bladder suspended over the fire. Using a piece of hide, she carefully picked stones from the hearth, dropping them slowly into the broth until it was steaming. Dèhzhòo, Khon's second wife, served the piping hot broth in cups made from the skulls of wolverine and fox. Kazan sat eagerly awaiting another serving, listening to the men.

Khon held up a piece of meat. "No fat," he pronounced, turning it in his fingers. "The Long-Nose starved. It was only with luck we found it before all the *nilli* was spoiled." He broke the flesh

28

apart with his fingers, chewing it slowly. "Tomorrow we finish butchering. The meat is little and will feed us for only a few days. The legs will render bone grease, but the marrow is gone." He paused thoughtfully. "This is the only grasseater we have seen since the snows fell. It is a bad omen that it has starved. Are there any living grasseaters on this Flat Plain?"

Kazan saw his father look to Tarin, but Old Man said nothing. Glancing up from his cup, Tarin considered his reply. He had expected to be asked for spirit advice, but he would rather have finished eating first.

"Life is movement," he said dryly. Tarin was Medicine Man, a dream-traveller. He had a special gift of connection with the underworld of animal spirits. In dreams he could locate grasseaters. When he woke he sometimes remembered the way, how far to travel, how many in the herd. In his most powerful visions, he could coax animals toward hunters using spirit tricks. But those powerful days were long ago. As he grew older, his ability to dream-travel had weakened. Now when he dreamed, the best he could do was sometimes know the direction to send hunters. He had not lured a grasseater toward hunters for a year.

Lately, his dreams had failed to show grasseaters. In fact, Tarin had not dream-travelled during the winter journey. He had not felt the presence of grasseaters anywhere on the great Flat Plain. The few fresh animal tracks they had crossed disappeared beneath an endless carpet of windswept snow and ice. It was as if every living beast on the face of the earth had vanished. They had embarked on a dangerous winter journey and had not found a single living grasseater. Tarin was about to say this when he was suddenly overcome by such a disturbing vision that he heard his own voice screaming out.

Around him the tent walls are awash in blood. The stains swirl and twist, forming a shape he does not recognize. It spins around wildly, flashing across the ceiling, swirling behind him, racing into the fire, whipping the flames into a spinning vortex flaring up the chimney of the tent.

Tarin's eyes raced around the tent, expecting to see the shape standing, waiting for him. But there were only the relaxed faces of his band waiting for him to speak. He glanced into the fire, his face flushed with confusion and fear. He considered his words carefully.

"We must go now. We must leave this place," he said. There was a dark and ominous edge to his voice. Before he could say more, a ptarmigan landed on the tent and in a rapid, drum-like voice called *tuk-tuk-tuk-tuk...* Everyone glanced up at the ceiling. There was a long silence.

"It is bad luck for *Daagoo* to land on a *nèevyaa zheh* while humans are living inside," Tarin exclaimed. He stood up, his eyes fixed on the source of the sound. "*Daagoo* is warning us. We must leave here."

Khon, warming his hands by the fire, listened to the ptarmigan calling. "*Daagoo* is an omen. But it also eats berries dug out of the snow by grasseaters. *Daagoo* could be announcing that animals are close," he said, watching the faces of his band mates for reaction.

When Kazan heard the bird's staccato call, he put down his food. There was something important happening. He moved in closer to hear.

Tarin turned around slowly, his eyes locked on the dome as he listened to the winds racking the tent.

It is here - there is a powerful danger here.

His throat went dry and his heart was beating wildly. He had felt such a disturbing premonition only once before. It was long ago, but the memory rushed back as though only moments had passed.

He was a young man kneeling on a gravel bar beside a blue rushing river as he prepared a meal. He had snared a hare and was roasting it over a fire when he was overwhelmed by a disturbing chill. He looked up and down the shore, certain

30

something was there, but he but saw nothing. The wind blew and ragged clouds filled a darkening sky. Then the premonition of his own death struck. It was coming, spreading though his mind - death. It was sliding through the river cobbles, reaching for his feet. Tossing the hare into the fire, he slung on his pack, grabbed his spear and ran. As he was climbing the bluff, he glanced back and saw what had made him so frightened. A bear - the largest he had ever seen - was beside his fire, sniffing the air. It turned and looked directly at him. He froze, not daring to move a muscle. The great bear walked toward him, its pace quickening with each step. Tarin scrambled up the bluff as fast as his shaking legs could carry him. He ran until he was standing on the bank of a fast-flowing creek surrounded by low willows. Splashing through the stream, he tossed his pack on the far side. Then he waded upstream to a black pool beneath an overhanging thicket. Sinking down, he waited, submerged to his neck in the frigid stream. When the great bear finally appeared, it startled him so that he nearly shouted out in surprise. It leaped the creek in a single jarring bound, landing next to his discarded pack. It circled, sniffing at the pack with great interest. With a single blow of its forepaw, the beast shredded it, sending the contents everywhere. The bear turned and looked up and down the creek, raising its nose into the air. Tarin held his breath, sinking down until only his eyes were above the rushing current. He stared into the bear's eyes and did not blink. Just when he was sure it had seen him, it left the creek and disappeared. He stayed submerged, certain the beast was waiting out of sight to ambush him.

Tarin could no longer feel his legs and arms and could not stay in the water any longer. He stumbled from the stream, stripping off his wet clothes and stretching out on the ground to warm his frozen body in the sun. He told no one about the great bear. He was afraid that the telling of the story would bring bad luck to his band.

Now he felt it again, a chilling premonition of death: a

warning to leave the ground he stood upon. This time he would speak.

He rapped the ceiling with his fist, sending the ptarmigan flapping off. "We must leave," he said with authority. "The ground is cursed by a bad spirit," he added, casting his eyes to the floor. His voice was thin, quaking. "I do not know what shape the bad spirit takes, but it is here." Tarin swayed momentarily and Khon steadied him as he settled back down on the tent floor.

Eyak, Old Woman, broke the awkward silence. "We have just made night camp. The tents are standing and there are warming fires in both. There is mammoth to butcher. We are all tired. Before we can leave, we need meat to make us strong. Teekai and Gilgan are hardly making milk for their babies. Without milk, Jak and Yukaih will die."

She waved her hand around the tent, looking at her band. "If we leave without taking all the meat, more of us will die. We have lost one child," she said, glancing at Karun. "We cannot lose another." Old Woman looked at Tarin and then sat down.

Chii Tsal rose to his feet and cleared his throat. "Wolf Band has never walked the Flat Plain. It is bigger than we thought. We are *Nantsaii*, the first humans in the world. But here we have no mind maps to guide us. We have not scouted this ground in summer to know it. We travel without ancestors' eyes to show us." He was becoming excited. His voice rose above the winds outside.

"We have not killed a grasseater since the snow came. We scavenge a dead mammoth. We are hunters - not ravens! We are Band of the Wolf! We hunt grasseaters! It has always been our life. But we have not killed a grasseater since the snow came!" His voice dropped. "Our girl-child has died on the Flat Plain." Chii Tsal paused to look at Karun. His heart was filling with grief, which increased his desperation.

"The Flat Plain is no place for Wolf Band," Chii Tsal added, waving his hand around the tent. "There is little wood. There is no place to find shelter from the winds. There are no

32

grasseaters!" He turned to face Khon. "We should have stayed in the mountains," he said defiantly. "The Flat Plain gives nothing - no grasseaters, no wood, no shelter. We should have waited for grasseaters. We all saw the many caribou and elk antlers cast in the mountain valleys. It was a winter place for grasseaters." His dark eyes narrowed. "We should not have left winter camp."

Kazan felt the tension bristle inside the tent. Chii Tsal was accusing his father of a decision the entire band had made. Grasseaters had not come to Mountain Winter Camp. The men had hunted the mountain valleys every day, in every direction, but nothing came - no caribou, mammoth, horse, elk or bison. The women waited patiently in camp, but the drying racks remained empty. The snows fell and still no *nin* came. Without fresh meat, they would starve. They had chosen to leave or to die, and had discussed their situation over many evenings. In the end, not one person disagreed. They would travel in winter in search of grasseaters. Everyone knew the great risk of travelling in winter - even the children. They would have to find dung and wood for fires as they travelled, and find ridges to camp out of the blistering winds. And they would have to find and kill grasseaters.

"Chii Tsal, have you forgotten you agreed to leave Mountain Winter Camp?" It was Eyak again, and this time her voice was bristling. Chii Tsal's face reddened.

"Wolf Band chose to travel the Flat Plain," Eyak said, looking at Khon. "We all knew we had never travelled this way before. It was a band decision."

Khon had anticipated his brother's criticism. Whenever times became difficult, Chii Tsal was quick to blame any troubles, big or small, on his leadership. Chii Tsal was not as clever and did not understand the changing moods of the band or the difficulties of leading a group of people. Chii Tsal was a powerful man and a good hunter, but he was not a chief. His decisions were often rash, driven more by temper than thought.

Khon looked at him. "The past leads only to the ground

we are standing on. To this place. The past cannot be changed," he said, feeling his confidence grow. "What we do now is what matters. We cannot change the path we have travelled, but we can choose where it leads. There are no grasseaters behind us. We waited for them at Mountain Winter Camp, and our meat racks stayed empty." He paused, hoping to smooth over the harsh words his brother had spoken.

"You speak truthfully, Chii Tsal. We travel during the Dark Days when we should be in warm tents with plenty of fire dung and meat to keep the chill from our beds. We should be sharing stories to pass away the long nights instead of thinking about hunger. We all chose to make this winter journey. We left nothing behind in the mountains." He raised the piece of meat again. "Leaving without taking all the *nilli* will bring bad luck to Wolf Band. Wasting food is not our clan's way."

Chii Tsal's eyes dropped. "My empty stomach has spoken the words," he said curtly, rubbing his hands and staring into the fire. But there was no apology in his voice. He stood and walked out of the tent without looking at anyone.

Khon was watching everyone. He saw the discomfort in their faces, their bowed heads, their downcast eyes. A lively discussion was good, but criticism led to dangerous division in the very fabric of the band. Any hard feelings among members spelled trouble. Everyone - every man, woman and child - was needed to survive. The men hunted and killed grasseaters. The women tended the camp, tanned hides, made stone knives, cooked meals, healed cuts and raised the children. The children snared small animals, collected fuel and picked berries. Each person had a role in the band, as important as the next. Mutual cooperation meant the survival of all. Every game, every story, every meal, every hunt reinforced the importance of living in harmony as a unit. The surest way to destroy the bond that held the band together was to openly criticize another member.

"A single blade of grass is weak, but a bundle cannot be

broken," Khon said, seeing unease grow on their faces. "Wolf Band is strong when we stand together."

He raised his voice, drowning out the wind battering the dome. "We hunt not only to eat." He kicked lightly at the skins covering the floor. "The hides are old and the hair is thin. Winter is when skins are thick and hair is full. We hunt grasseaters for food and for hides to make beds and cover our tents."

Tarin stood suddenly, his voice sharp and shrill. "We camp beside a dead mammoth. Lions and wolves will smell death and come. We cannot stay here."

Kazan saw Tarin was deeply disturbed. He had never seen Old Man so agitated.

"We will leave," Khon said agreeably. "But first we must finish the butchering. The mammoth *niilii* will give us strength to pull the sled."

Khon looked at the men and women. They were quietly nodding their agreement. "Then, it is so," he concluded. "We leave after butchering is done."

Tarin opened his mouth to speak but stopped. He glanced at the faces of his band. Let them enjoy their meal in peace, he decided, lifting his skull cup to his lips, savouring the broth.

Has this dark spirit come from my empty stomach? From too many days of only bone-grease broth?

He was not convinced. Something had entered the tent - a spirit warning, an omen. He did not know what shape it took, but he knew the fear in his heart was real.

Chii Tsal came back into the tent with a slab of meat on his shoulder; he had dug it from the snow cache. Everyone clapped and shouted as he presented it, redeeming himself for his earlier outburst. Khon watched him stride across the tent and drop the meat down with great ceremony. They glanced at each other and nodded a new peace. When the meal was finished, the families of Chii Tsal, Dat'san and Jovan moved into the adjacent tent.

Kazan slid into the comfort of the fur bed next to So'tsal and lay there thinking of Tarin's warning. What had Old Man seen? It was something dangerous, Kazan knew that much. Lions were the most dangerous beasts. They killed humans, usually ambushing a lone person. They rarely attacked a band. Most times they avoided humans on the open tundra-steppe. When they did approach, the women made high, shrill noises and the men shouted and waved their spears, clapping the shafts together, and the lions moved off. Wolves were less dangerous. Kazan knew they sometimes killed people, but such stories were always about someone alone. Kazan lay back with visions of lions, wolves and mammoths filling his dreams.

Khon Worries

Yogh shook Khon awake and slid into his own sleeping skins beside his wife, Teekai. He was sound asleep by the time Khon climbed out of his bed. It was his turn to watch. The warmth had left the tent, the cold creeping back in, wrapping the sleeping humans in its bitter grip. The storm outside was worsening. Khon listened carefully for sounds of life as gusts of wind battered the tent dome. Stoking the fire with a thick slab of mammoth dung, he gazed into the flames and worried.

Everything was changing rapidly. The grassland was disappearing, replaced every year by more willow shrubs. The once great herds of horses were smaller every year. As a boy, he remembered hunting herds that stretched across the plain as far as he could see. Now there were only small scattered bands. Mammoths, a common sight when he was smaller, were even rarer. They had not killed a Long-Nose in more than a year.

The winters were warmer and the snow deeper. He recalled the cold winter days of his youth and the clear blue skies, the calm nights filled with so many stars they were as bright as day. Now the winds always blew, bringing clouds and snow. Some days it warmed enough that the snow melted. The land was changing, and his people were struggling to stay alive. The band weakened with each passing day, and he was powerless to stop it.

Chii Tsal is right, he thought. We scavenge like ravens, picking at leftovers. We are dart hunters, spear hunters!

He felt uneasy about the evening. It had been a long time since he had taken part in such a hard conversation. Had hunger brought out Chii Tsal's anger, or was he losing his place as chief? The young men - Yogh, Dat'san, Jovan - were faster runners and they hurled their darts farther. Still, none could match his accuracy, and none could plan a hunt better - not even Chii Tsal.

Khon's skills had earned him Dèhzhòo, his second wife. Assan was at the end of her childbearing days. During the summer she had come to him and told him he should take a second wife. He chose Dèhzhòo, Anik's younger sister, who was nearly half his age. She was strong and attractive, and a hard worker. Khon was relieved they had not yet made a child. The winter journey was difficult enough. It would be too much for a woman with child.

Khon's thoughts turned from his wives to his younger brother. Chii Tsal had been growing openly critical of his leadership for some time. Was it time to step aside? He had been chief since Kazan had taken his first step. It was a long time to lead a band. Was Chii Tsal right? Should Wolf Band have stayed at Mountain Winter Camp? Were grasseaters now there, wandering through the abandoned site? Like everyone, he had expected the journey to be short. They had always found grasseaters. He thought about Tarin's warning of an omen.

Old Man was a medicine man, but that did not mean things he said were certain to happen. Lately, he had said things that did not come true - and what had he actually said? The ground was bad. Privately, Khon was losing confidence in Tarin's ability to make medicine. He laid his hands on the frozen ground beneath the skins. He felt nothing but coldness.

Animal spirits were often confusing, and Tarin was becoming more muddled and confounding. Was he too old? Had he lost his power to talk to animal spirits? Khon stroked his full belly, annoyed that he did not better understand the ways of the medicine man. He climbed back into his bed and dozed lightly, one ear listening to the wind battering the tent.

The Smoking Beast

The pack is moving along the frozen plain, hugging the edge of a broad stand of snowbound willows. The wolves are travelling blindly in a heavy winter storm. The low light casts a soft, dull hue through the curtain of falling snow. The adult male is leading. He is silver-blue, with long white guard hairs covering a heavy layer of black under-fur. Blue pushes through the deep snow with his chest, his snout gliding over the surface, continually testing for fresh scent of prey. A dozen white wolves following in line carve out a deep trail in the snow. Blue's mate is behind him. Unlike those of Blue and their offspring, her eyes are not yellow but grey. Grey-Eye stops to shake off the snow collecting on her back. The land is silent except for a light wind blowing through the willows encircling the broad plain. It is snowing so heavily their trail disappears in minutes.

Blue stumbles into the trail of prey before he sees it. He presses his nose into the tracks. The scent of horse fills his nostrils. He pushes his snout in deeper, sniffing and feeling for signs of direction and freshness. He moves his nose carefully to the edges of the track, where the leading edge of the horse's foot has compressed and hardened the snow slightly. Blue moves to the next trail. The horses are moving onto the open plain. The wolves spread out through the tracks, wagging their tails and burying their snouts into the sweet aroma of prey. They move onto the plain, their pace much quicker now.

A maze of deep drifts slows the progress of the herd of small steppe horses. They are moving into a strong wind and cannot smell the danger silently closing in from behind. The wolves move quickly in the trails and soon close the gap. The first horse to die is trailing the herd. Blue first sees the startled horse as he collides into it. The tiny stallion rears up and plunges headlong into a high drift. Blue grabs him by the neck, tearing into his jugular vein with a powerful bite. He shifts his grip

39

around the windpipe and pulls the stallion down to the snow, cutting off air to the horse's starving lungs. The other wolves rush past and vanish into the storm. Ahead, there is a clattering of many hooves on ice.

The horses have sensed the approaching danger and are galloping blindly through a series of frozen ponds. A young stallion slips and falls on the slick ice, unable to regain his feet. He is spinning in a slow arc on the ice, his legs splayed out. A yearling wolf reaches the ice first and hears the soft whinny of the stallion ahead. The second horse dies.

The storm lifts and reveals a dark line of heavy shrubs blocking the herd from escaping. The front horses hesitate, sensing a dangerous trap ahead. But there is no time to turn around. They charge into the shrubs and leap headlong into a drifted wall of snow and willow, sinking to their withers. The horses kick and scramble ahead, their forelegs churning into the soft, yielding snow until some smaller ones sink under the whiteness.

A stallion swings back onto the plain in a desperate bid to escape. The dark shapes of wolves appear from out of the snowstorm. Two wolves slam into the stallion, driving him off his feet into a deep drift. He staggers and tumbles over backward, kicking at his attackers.

Grey–Eye leaps onto three horses that have collapsed onto each other. She kills the two floundering on the surface and drives her head into the snow, finding the soft neck of the third struggling to resurface. A yearling female launches onto the back of a stallion entangled in the shrubs, riding him down into the snow. He kicks her off but she clamps onto his neck as the stallion drags them deeper into the willows. In a desperate attempt to shed his attacker, the horse pummels the wolf's flank with a flurry of stunning kicks, crushing her tail bone with a sharp blow. She yelps as the thick hooves pound her flank but holds on until the horse is still. The wolf stands on the dead

40

stallion's chest and watches a few horses retreat onto the open plain. As they disappear into the darkening squalls, she turns her attention to feeding, barely noticing her aching tail after the excitement of killing. Around her, dead and dying horses are scattered through the blood-stained drifts. The pack spreads out along the edge of the plain and feed through the night.

The storm has passed when the moon rises over the flat horizon. The yearling with the broken tail howls and is answered by a yearling male resting nearby. Moments later, Blue

and Grey-Eye answer, and soon the entire pack is howling. After a few minutes of the chorus, Broken-Tail leaves the horse kills and heads out onto the moonlit plain, followed by one of her sisters. They find an old mammoth trail in the snow and follow it along the edge of the willow stand. The air is suddenly filled with the smell of danger. The wolves stop as three shadows silently appear out of the shrubs. The lions walk onto the plain and roar, their long tails swinging excitedly. Behind, a mammoth carcass is sprawled in the willows, the white tusks shining in the moonlight. The wolves, no match for the huge cats, retreat, and the lions melt back into the shadowy shrubs.

The two wolves swing farther out on the plain through a maze of drifts and windswept open ground, where they stumble upon another dead mammoth and an unfamiliar smell. Behind the carcass, there is a strange light and smoke rising. As they move closer, the wolves hear muffled sounds coming from a jumble of glowing skins. Broken-Tail quietly circles the smoking beast while her sister watches. Suddenly the hide opens and a strange shape covered in skins walks out on two legs. Its head is covered in long dark hair. The wolves, having never before seen such an animal, slip back into the darkness.

The two-legged creature moves to a snow pile, digs out something and disappears back into the smoking skins. There is a loud noise followed by silence. The wolves slip behind the mammoth, nervous about the noise, the strange light and the unfamiliar smells everywhere. Broken-Tail sniffs at the carcass, but she is well-fed with horse and decides to leave it.

The grey dawn is breaking when the two yearlings head back to rejoin the pack. As they approach the horse kills, the wind begins to blow. Broken-Tail raises her head and howls, waiting for the invitation to return. Grey-Eye, ever watchful of her wandering offspring, comes out to greet them. She notices one is holding her tail differently. As the two wolves press against her side, she smells strange scents in their fur.

Another Long-Nose

By morning, the winds had stopped but the snow continued to fall. Assan woke, filled a caribou bladder with snow and spun it over the fire, melting the snow for water. She reached over and shook Kazan and So'tsal awake, who crawled out from warm beds, their tousled hair covering dark, sleepy faces. So'tsal looked up at her absentmindedly as if she did not know why she had been so rudely woken. Assan pointed to the fire. Without a word, Kazan and So'tsal pulled on their coats and sheepskin pants, tied on their mukluks and slipped out of the tent into the dim light of morning.

As she watched her children leave, Assan looked down on Khon and Dèhzhòo. He and his new wife were wrapped under a mountain of bison furs, still asleep. They had been married the past summer and it had taken some time for Assan to get used to the young woman sharing her husband. Dèhzhòo was the younger sister to Anik. She was twenty summers and a good worker. Dèhzhòo knew the women's ways, and she was attractive. Khon was worthy of two wives, an honour the band gave him in recognition of his long leadership and his hunting skills. Chii Tsal had argued that he, too, should have a second wife, believing himself the best hunter of Wolf Band. Assan watched with amusement and no small sense of pride as Chii Tsal's lobbying failed to find support among the women. Besides, they told him, there were no other unmarried girls. Was he interested in Eyak, the old woman, the only unmarried woman? They all laughed - Eyak the loudest. Chii Tsal soon gave up his quest.

Dèhzhòo's marriage to Khon was also a silent acknowledgement to Assan. She was past her safe childbearing time and would soon join the ranks of the Elders. Dèhzhòo's union to Khon brought no jealousy to her heart. It was the way of the *Nantsaii*, the first clan on the earth. The strongest men had two or three wives so they could sire many offspring into the world. Assan

43

thought of her two children. Kazan would be a man soon; So'tsal already was a young woman, nearly old enough to be mated. Assan and Khon had made good children, and now it would be Dèhzhòo's turn. Assan looked down at the jumbled furs. She had not been under furs with Khon for a long time and she had not missed it.

She reached down and shook the bed gently. Khon's broad face emerged and he nodded, rubbing his dark eyes with the back of his hand. As he slipped out of the furs, she handed him a steaming broth in his wolverine-skull cup - the morning ritual they had shared for most of their lives.

Assan poured another skull cup and brought it to Eyak, who was still sleeping. Old Woman woke, smelling the cooking food, but did not rise. Her hand reached up and touched Assan's face, and she smiled. Then she sat up slowly and took the broth with her twisted fingers, barely able to see the steaming cup.

"Thank you, young sister. I can live without my eyes but not without your hands," Eyak said, sipping at the hot brew. Assan saw she was weakening, her hands barely able to clasp the cup. The long journey and the scant meals had taken most of her strength.

I will be Shanagàn if she dies.

The thought disturbed her. She had never considered it before. She was thirteen summers younger than Eyak. Assan's mother had died giving birth to her, and it was Eyak who had raised her. She had taught her about medicine plants and how to hammer stone blades from chert, strip sinew through her front teeth and weave carry baskets and fish nets from willow roots. It was Eyak who had helped her through the birth of So'tsal and Kazan. And it was Eyak who had taken the dead child from her womb one summer ago. Assan looked at Eyak's wrinkled hands holding the skull cup, saddened she was nearing the end of a hard life on the tundra-steppe.

Assan returned to the fire, filled a handful of skull cups

and continued pouring broth for the rest of the people waking in the tent. The mammoth flesh would delay the inevitable shrink of the sack of dry meat, but only for a few days. When the winter journey was one moon long, she had begun to worry about the supply of dry meat. As they moved over the Flat Plain, the women and children scavenged any bone they found, smashing them into pieces and boiling the mash. When the mash cooled, the women separated the bone fragments and stored the rendered fat in bear stomach bladders.

It was now two full moons since they had left Mountain Winter Camp, and there was barely four days of dry meat left. The mammoth head meat would last three days. The women had discussed how to ration the food and decided to mix the meat with the mammoth bone grease. If they were careful, they could make the food last another moon.

As the other women joined her around the cooking fire, Assan watched the band savour the thin results of their broth recipe. Their faces were gaunt and their clothes hung loose from thinning bodies. Since the winter journey had begun, the men and women spoke less and rarely laughed. She hoped the broth would keep the hunger away long enough to find grasseaters. Eyak is not the only one who will not see the spring, she thought.

Khon drained his broth. Shifting toward the fire, he held his cup out, silently waiting a refill. She gently pushed his hand away.

"The morning is wiser than the evening, and night is wiser than a man begging food," she said, a faint smile lifting her lips. All the women laughed, and Assan's heart warmed. She poured him a half cup of broth, waving him away to join the men.

Chii Tsal was already outside surveying the grey dawn. He nodded silently to Kazan and So'tsal as they left the tent carrying dung packs. They were walking past the mammoth carcass when Kazan noticed the wolf tracks.

"Zhòh," he said, pointing to a narrow trail in the snow. He

called to Chii Tsal, who came over for a look. "Two young females - the tracks are small," he said. "They are confused and unsure. Look. One wolf came to the carcass and did not feed. The other did not look at it. They are full, or afraid." He put his mitt into the trail. "Feel the edge - still soft. They came before dawn." Kazan reached down and rubbed his hand in the track.

"Young wolves do not walk alone," Chii Tsal said. "Their pack is close. Keep your eyes open. Come back if you see *Zhòh*. They will be as hungry as humans." He waved the children on and walked back to the tent.

Kazan moved ahead, his spear pointed in front of him as he watched the horizon for movement. The storm had scoured much of the snow away during the night, leaving behind broad patches of open ground in a sea of hard-packed drifts. He found a thick slab of mammoth dung frozen into the ground, pried the disc free with the end of his spear and dropped it into So'tsal's waiting pack. As they continued collecting, Kazan kept the camp in sight, sticking willow markers in the ground in case snow or fog came. So'tsal whistled to signal she had also found dung. He dislodged it and filled his pack with the elk dung pellets. They worked together until both packs were full. By mid-morning there were waist-high dung piles stacked beside both tents.

The wind had picked up and now the children were cold and hungry. They slipped into the warm tent, removed their heavy outside clothes and took a meal near the fire. When they were done eating, they headed farther out on the plain while the men butchered meat and bone from the mammoth. As they moved farther from camp it began to snow. Kazan drove sticks into the snow, marking their way back.

When they had full packs, he and So'tsal stopped to rest behind a high snowdrift. Kazan scanned in all directions, hoping to see grasseaters. Through the falling snow, he saw a dark line stretching across the horizon. He stared at it for a long time, not sure what he was looking at.

46

"*K'àii'* - willow," he said finally, pointing his spear. "Look. There is wood." So'tsal stood up and looked. Suddenly, a loud roar pierced the snowy silence.

"Lion!" she gasped.

He pulled her down behind the drift, watching the fear grow in her eyes. "It is close. Stay down." He crawled up on the drift and peered over the top. In the distance, a dead mammoth lay on its side, partly hidden by high shrubs.

"Long-Nose," he whispered, not taking his eyes off it. He watched for a long time, but nothing moved. He could not see the lion, and he began to worry.

"Is it dead?" So'tsal asked just before the lion roared again. Kazan listened carefully as the sound faded, trying to figure distance and direction.

It is upwind and cannot smell us.

He pointed his spear toward camp. They crawled from drift to drift, careful to keep out of sight. As they followed the stick markers, Kazan looked back often but did not see the lion following. He hurried toward the men who were on the mammoth's head while So'tsal ran to the tents to tell the women of their find.

Kazan climbed up the tusk and stood on the mammoth's back. His father, bent over slicing off meat, did not notice him. As Kazan touched his arm, Khon turned and noted the excitement in his son's eyes.

"Lion!" Kazan said, trying to sound calm. "A mammoth - dead! Willows - high willows!" he added excitedly.

"Kazan! Slow down. A lion? Long-Nose? Wood? Where? How far?" Khon asked, pulling down his hood.

Kazan caught his breath and pointed his spear over the line of markers barely visible in the snow.

"You saw a lion?

"It roared. It is with the mammoth. I could not see it."

Leaping down, Khon shouted and the men collected

47

around him. "Kazan. Tell them what you have seen."

Kazan suddenly became nervous. He had never talked to all the men before. He repeated what he and So'tsal had seen.

"Show us," said Chii Tsal. They collected their hunting packs and weapons and followed him. The snow stopped falling just as they reached the place where they had seen the dead mammoth. The clouds lifted, revealing shrubs that stretched across Flat Plain as far as they could see.

"*Dachan* - wood! Enough for many winters," Khon exclaimed.

"There!" Chii Tsal said, pointing to the mammoth. The men crouched down and silently watched.

Tarin turned to Kazan. "You saw a lion?"

"We heard it." He pointed to the fallen mammoth. "Over there." He hoped he sounded convincing.

"Not wind? Not wind blowing in willows?"

Kazan thought Tarin sounded upset. He shook his head. "No. It was a lion. It roared." But he was beginning to feel uncertain.

As the others watched the mammoth, Khon looked around and caught a fleeting movement on the Flat Plain behind them. "Grasseaters," he whispered, hardly believing his eyes. A band of horses came briefly into view before vanishing behind a wall of high drifts. The herd was moving away and had not seen them. The men looked at each other, barely able to contain their excitement. The wind favoured a flank attack; the grasseaters would not smell them approach. The mammoth and the lion were quickly forgotten as they silently prepared the stalk.

Yogh, Jovan and Dat'san - the three fastest runners - took off, sprinting short distances and hiding behind the drifts to stay out of sight. Khon, Tarin and Kazan followed well behind. The horses moved slowly, stopping to paw snow and graze the exposed tufts of grass. The hunters separated as they neared the band. Yogh crawled directly toward the herd while Dat'san and Jovan

48

continued to move parallel to the moving horses. When Yogh was within range, he stood up and walked casually toward the horses, his head bent down, his eyes fixed on the ground. The closest stallion raised his head and stopped chewing on the grass. He had not seen humans before and did not sense danger.

Yogh slowly raised the throwing dart to his shoulder, careful not to look at the stallion. He stopped and casually swung his foot back and forth, like a horse pawing snow. The other horses raised their heads and watched with mild interest. Yogh lowered his head and moved a few steps closer, his lowered eyes fixed on the stallion's forelegs. He was watching for any movement, gauging the distance, feeling the wind. He saw the stallion's legs tense; it was about to turn and run. Yogh skipped forward and threw the hunting dart with all his strength. The stallion watched the flying projectile sail over its back and sink into the frozen snow. It bolted, and the rest of the herd followed.

Dat'san and Jovan were a few hundred feet ahead, waiting behind a drift. They heard the horses fast approaching. As the herd came into range, Jovan stood up and launched a dart. The leading horses swerved, and the rest of the panicking herd turned with them. Dat'san waited until they were broadside and quartering away through the drifts. He sprinted forward, launching his long dart just ahead of a mare at the rear of the herd. It plunged deep into her shoulder behind the neck, striking with such force she was driven off her feet. Dat'san and Jovan unleashed their clubs, leaping through the drifts until they fell upon her. Yogh arrived moments later to watch them finish the mare off. Then Chii Tsal and Khon appeared, grinning, followed by Kazan and then Tarin hobbling on his staff.

The men slipped off their mitts and rubbed their fingers through the mare's tawny mane, silently thanking Horse Spirit for the kill. Chii Tsal tied the mare's legs and wrapped a rawhide cord around the centre of his spear. The men took hold of the shaft and pulled the horse toward camp. When the tents came into sight, they stopped and began the butchering.

They skinned the legs first, severing the quarters from the horse's body. Dat'san made the first cut, slit open the belly and reached into the gut to remove the blood-rich heart, liver and kidneys. He dropped the organs into a skin sack and wrapped it with a rawhide thong. Then he cut out the lungs, discarding the organs, and reached into the neck, severing the windpipe and lopping off the tongue. With the top of the windpipe in his grasp, he hauled the entrails out of the body. Khon spread the organs on the snow and began cleaning the stomach and intestines.

Kazan had never killed a grasseater, but he had watched many die at the hands of hunters. He knew every step of the butchering process: where to make each cut, how to push the fingers down to separate hide from flesh, where to slice the richest meat from the backbone. As he watched, he longed to plunge his hands into the carcass and be part of the hunt's last step.

Dat'san opened the stomach, releasing a sour mist of digested grass. He dug out a handful and tasted it, then offered the others a handful, stuffing the fermented mash into a skin bag. Meanwhile, Tarin split the ribs along the backbone with a stone axe. He rolled and tied the rack with a thong, lifted it onto his shoulder and headed for camp.

Khon collected the blood from the gut, filling two stomach bladders. Chii Tsal broke the skull open and removed the brain as Yogh rolled the gut casings into a ball and dropped it into a sack.

As the men filled their packs, Kazan looked down on the snow at the dark shadow of blood where the horse had been. One by one the men left with their loads and Kazan followed behind, catching up to his father.

"I will be a hunter," Kazan said, trying to sound confident. Khon glanced at him and nodded. They caught up to Tarin, who stopped before entering camp.

"A grasseater will not take away the bad spirits," he said. "We are camped on bad ground. I have told you, but you do not listen." He stared into Khon's eyes and continued toward the tents, the horse ribs bobbing on his shoulder. Kazan saw his father's face darken.

I Am Vadzaih *caribou*

Kazan is dreaming caribou. He is kneeling at the bank of a rushing river, a faded caribou skin loosely draped around him. It is a bright, sunny morning, but a thick fog shrouds the river. He shaves kindling from a dry willow with a stone knife and watches the slivers piling up between his knees. Pulling up a handful of dead grass, he cradles it under the shavings. From a small sack he removes a short stick with a dull point and a piece of wood with a groove cut down its length. He begins rubbing the short stick against the groove in a rapid plowing motion. As the wood dust heats, a small black coal begins to smolder. He carefully introduces the coal to the tinder, coaxing the fire to life. A small flame grows and sends a thin white smoke curling into the air, filling his nostrils. He raises his head.

They are coming.

The caribou slowly appear through the fog. The bulls come first, their broad antlers wrapped in summer velvet. They jostle and push each other but are reluctant to cross the fast-flowing river. Kazan reaches into his pack and pulls out a twisted belt of dried caribou hooves. He shakes the belt, mimicking the clicking sounds of walking feet, and waits patiently for the bulls to enter the water and begin swimming toward him. As they approach, Kazan fastens a small set of caribou antlers on his head. He stands slowly, holding his spear out of sight. As the first bulls arrive, the fire ignites at his feet, enshrouding him in white smoke. The bulls scramble up the bank on both sides, barely a spear length away. They do not look at him as they pass. Soon, cows with calves follow, pouring onto the shore. He grips his spear and waits, listening to their thick breathing as they stream by, some close enough to touch. The river fills with thousands of glistening brown bodies, their antlers swaying above the rushing water. He stands still, watching the herd pass, but does not raise the spear. The fire is cold when he turns around to watch the last ones disappear.

I am Vadzaih.

Laying Snare

Kazan woke to the aroma of cooked horse. The tent was already moving with life, the air warm and comfortable. Dat'san was squatting nearby, braiding strips of the mare's tail into a long rope. Chii Tsal and Khon were unwrapping a bundle of thick rawhide snares, carefully checking their condition.

Last night, the men had decided to build a snare set and drive the herd of horses into it. All except Tarin had agreed to the plan. He told them to move camp before any snares were set. The hunters disagreed, saying they would lose a day and the horses could be lost on the windblown plain. Setting snares took patience and skill in hiding the loops from the watchful eyes and sensitive noses of grasseaters.

When the snares were ready the men packed and left the tent. As Khon opened the tent flap, he nodded for Kazan to follow. Kazan scrambled for his parka, eager to be part of snaring.

"Watch and learn," Khon said. "The grasseaters must not sense there is anything wrong. It is important that everything is in place and the wind is right."

The men spotted the horses in the distance and skirted around them to a narrow band of shrubs that separated the two large meadows. Chii Tsal and Khon went to work laying the snares, anchoring each around the base of a shrub. They hung the nooses at shoulder height, using branches to disguise the loops from the horses' sharp eyes. Moving slowly and methodically through the shrubs, they took great care not to brush the willows with their clothes and leave scent.

Out on the meadow, Kazan pushed a long line of willow sticks into the snow while Yogh followed behind him, tying short pieces of hide to the top of each branch. Dat'san and Jovan did the same, forming the other fence. As the teams moved closer to the line of willows, the fences gradually pinched into a V-shaped funnel, closing at the snares.

When it was finished, Kazan looked out on the plain. The strips of hide were blowing in the wind, as if they were people moving. His excitement grew as he anticipated the hunt. With luck, the hunters would kill many and he would be close enough to watch the snaring of the horses.

It was nearly dark when the men headed back for camp. Ahead, a flock of ravens lifted into the fading light. The black birds circled, scolding them with their raspy voices. Ravens on the open plain meant one thing: something was dead.

"Wolves," Khon said as he picked up a shattered leg bone of horse and inspected the break. Poking his knife into the hollow centre, he pulled out a thin string of pink marrow. He ate a little and then offered some to Kazan, who quickly accepted. The bones - even the broken ones - were food. They spread out in the willows and began digging in the drifted snow, excavating half a dozen heavily scavenged horse carcasses. Soon they had dug out a few pack-loads of bones.

"The wolves caught the horses here," Jovan said to Kazan. "They drove them into the deep snow from the open plain. We will do the same tomorrow. We will be wolves." Jovan hoisted his pack and followed the other hunters to camp.

Behind them, two lions moved across the plain. The cats stopped when they reached the human trail, sniffing at the strange scent. Circling the tracks, they roared a few times and followed the smell across the tundra-steppe, their ghostly forms swallowed in a sea of moonlit drifts.

The Calf

The wolves linger on the horse kills for a few days before they head out onto the plain. On the second day of travelling their hunger returns. They cross fresh tracks and follow the trail to a large group of bison feeding along the shore of a small, windswept lake. Dark horns sway in the twilight as the bison push the deep snow away with their broad heads, grazing on the exposed grass and sedge.

Grey-Eye settles down on the lake ice, watching. The others wolves join her and are soon scattered around her, asleep. Some time later, she stands and walks toward the herd. Blue and Broken-Tail follow.

The herd stops feeding as the wolves circle, checking for a limp, wound or nervous movement to exploit. Blue trots directly to a group of bulls, rushing them and turning away at the last instant. The bulls merely look at him and snort as they swing their tails in the air. He continues testing, halting his attack a step away from the bulls' legs. Grey-Eye and Broken-Tail join in, darting and lunging at the legs, watching for an opening to the calves hidden behind. The bulls suddenly rush out, their heads low and tails snapping behind them, snorting clouds of vapour. Broken-Tail tries to slip around the bulls, but she is blocked by a bristling wall of horns. Grey-Eye darts between two bulls but cannot get to a calf. Blue circles and tries the other direction only to be met by a group of angry cows.

The bison are becoming agitated by the constant harassment and leave the meadow in a tight group, heading for a nearby ridge. A small band of cows and their calves falls behind the main herd. Blue charges for a faltering calf as she runs to catch up to her mother, but Grey-Eye and Broken-Tail overtake him. The cow suddenly turns back and charges, driving them off, but misses Blue coming in late. He snatches the calf's back leg, knocking her to the ground. Somehow she struggles free and scrambles to safety behind her mother.

Blue and Grey-Eye surround the pair, lunging and diving at the stunned calf. The cow suddenly bolts for the herd and the calf follows her. Blue knocks the calf down again, but a group of bulls have heard her bawling and arrive before he can finish her. The bulls surround the desperate calf, snorting their fury at the pesky wolves. The three wolves retreat to the lake and join the rest of the pack.

After a short sleep, Grey-Eye stands, stretches and walks toward the herd scattered along a moonlit ridge. Once again Blue follows his mate. They locate the cow and wounded calf standing at the bottom of the ridge. Grey-Eye slips by the cow and lunges for the calf, but the cow is ready. She swings her head at Grey-Eye, grazing the wolf's shoulder with her sharp horns. Grey-Eye rolls away just as the cow's massive forelegs slam down in the snow behind her. Blue sees the new opening and attacks, bowling the calf over once again. He grips at her shoulder but his teeth slide harmlessly off as a dozen bulls arrive, driving the two wolves back.

The calf is in shock, bawling loudly. Her upper leg is bleeding and there is a fresh wound on her neck. Blue and Grey-Eye circle her, but the bulls form an impenetrable wall. Exhausted, the wolves walk to ridge and lie down. The hunt is over.

The next morning the bison are gone, leaving only a few blood-stained tracks in the heavy trails. The wolves leave the plain and skirt the edge of the willows, eventually arriving at their recent horse kills. Ravens rise from the drifts and circle noisily above them.

There are many smells here: raven, fox, wolverine - and a strange scent Grey-Eye has never known. The horse kills have been dug up and the holes are filled with the strange odour. The wolves dig into a few kills, finding few bones. Blue is nervous about the scent and leads the pack into the shrubs and up a narrow creek past patches of open water, heading toward a low mountain shrouded in darkness.

Wolf Leg

The mare pawed into the soft snow to expose the tufts of grass. Her male foal pressed his nose into the craters, chewed down the dry grass leaves and turned his face from the blowing wind. Behind them, a stallion scented the approaching line of humans; the mare raised her head at his snort of alarm. They were moving on the horizon toward the herd, shepherding the nervous horses toward the shrubs. More humans appeared, and the horses began to trot. Soon the herd had moved into the narrowing funnel with no chance of escaping onto the open plain. The lead mare grew apprehensive as she saw the band of willows approaching. Shrubs were a dangerous place, where lions and wolves waited in ambush. Beyond the line of shrubs, she saw the meadow, and safety. Her foal was behind her when she galloped forward, aiming for a narrow opening between the bushes.

As the mare entered the band of shrubs, a snare brushed her nose. She swung her head as the noose slipped down her shoulder and dropped to the ground, still open. The foal stepped into the noose and it caught, slamming him into the snow. He tried to stand but the snare held fast. He gave a whinny and the mare turned to see her foal kicking frantically in the snow as the willows shook.

Kazan was running for the snares with Khon, Jovan, Yogh and Dat'san, waving his arms and shouting. The horses were jostling each other, spooked by the foal thrashing in the willows ahead and the humans closing in from the meadow. A dart flew and the horses bolted for the shrubs. A stallion was immediately caught around the neck and the snare was torn from the shrubs. Another stallion was caught and pulled off his feet. As he kicked and twisted the noose slowly tightened. The snare set was chaos. Willows were shaking and snapping, snow was flying and horses were twisting, leaping and falling. Kazan was running behind his father. Around him spears and clubs were flashing, horses were dying. Kazan saw Chii Tsal explode out of his hiding place in the snow and leap onto the struggling foal, killing it instantly with his club. Suddenly, Kazan found himself alone, facing a panting stallion. The snare had missed his neck, catching the horse high on the thigh. As the horse stumbled backwards, the noose slid down his leg and fell harmlessly to the ground.

Kazan hesitated, uncertain what he should do. He had never killed a grasseater. The horse backed farther into the shrubs and stopped. He looked at Kazan and charged straight for him. At the last moment he leaped and Kazan closed his eyes, blindly driving his spear up. The shaft snapped, slamming into his head and knocking his hat off. He fell to his knees, stunned by the powerful blow. The noises faded as he slipped in and out of consciousness. Kazan fought the blankness with all his will, swooning as he fell on his face into cool snow. Then he was being pulled to his feet.

"Your hunt! Go! Go! Watch his legs!" It was his father's voice.

Kazan's mind cleared, even as he staggered, as he realized this was to be his kill — his alone. He ran. Ahead, the stallion stumbled on a patch of ice and fell, blood streaming from the deep wound to his gut. Kazan pulled his club from his belt and slid into the sprawled horse. The stallion whinnied and kicked as Kazan clubbed his head until he was still. Kazan looked down at the horse's bloodied head, vaguely aware of his own heavy breathing. He had killed a grasseater. A grasseater!

His father was shouting. Kazan turned.

"Watch his feet!"

The stallion suddenly kicked out with lightning speed, grazing Kazan's knee with a flying hoof. He jumped back and slammed his club down again and again until he could not recognize the head as a horse's. Dat'san shouted from the willows.

"Wolf Leg! You are Zhòh vitth'àn."

Kazan raised his hand weakly, suddenly filled with an

58

elation mixed with gnawing sadness. He dropped his club on the ice and wandered back to the snares in a mild state of shock. He had killed a grasseater. His leg was nearly broken. As he walked into the shrubs, Kazan slowly realized the hunt was a great success; even more than the hunters could have hoped. Five dead horses lay sprawled through the shrubs. Jovan and Chii Tsal had already started butchering. Dat'san was kneeling in the snow, unwrapping the snare from the neck of a mare.

"A flying horse," he said, gripping him heartily on the shoulder. "You killed a flying horse! You are *Zhòh vitth'àn* - Wolf Leg!"

Kazan was overwhelmed. He had killed his first grasseater - the greatest moment in a young hunter's life. He turned to see his father lifting his broken, bloodied spear out of the snow.

"Always watch grasseater feet. A broken leg is the end of a hunter," Khon said firmly.

The hunters touched their spears together and ran their hands through the manes of the horses, giving thanks to Horse Spirit. Kazan gazed out over the darkening plain. His life had changed forever. He was a hunter. He had chased down a grasseater and killed it.

I am Zhòh vitth'àn - Wolf Leg. I killed a flying horse.

Death in the Snow

The otter swims up the icy creek, moving from one patch of open water to the next, slipping under the shelf ice in search of swimming food. He is young and looking for a place to winter and find a mate. He arrives at a dark pool at the head of the snowbound creek. The pool is fed by a complex of warm springs that bubble out from the base of a low mountain. As he submerges himself in the inky water, a school of grayling appears, their broad dorsal fins flashing silver in the moonlight. He attacks using his thick, muscular tail for propulsion, twisting downward, his razor−sharp teeth latching onto the back of a fish. The otter surfaces with the thrashing grayling in his jaws, his teeth sunk in the fish's head. As he tears into flesh, he senses vibrations in the water moving toward him and rolls away just as big otter suddenly surfaces, slashing into his side. The young otter releases the fish, somersaults and snaps at his attacker. The big otter has disappeared but is coming back under him. The young otter dives, barely escaping a bite that glances off his shoulder.

He swims for the shore and scrambles onto the ice. Digging in with his claws, he glides over the glassy surface on his belly. The big otter slides out of the water but does not pursue the young interloper.

The young one is bleeding, leaving a spotted trail of blood across the ice. He heads for deep, soft snow, sliding his way up the mountain slope, stopping often to lick at the wound on his side. Tunneling into a drift, he digs himself a resting bed and licks at the wound until it stops bleeding. He dozes in the snow den until it is completely dark. Under the cover of night, he moves uphill, crossing a cascading creek with patches of open water. He follows the creek up the mountain, stopping at a rocky shallow. Slipping into the stream, the otter turns over small stones in a futile search for small fish or insects. Near the top of the mountain the creek ends. The snow is deep here. He digs a resting bed in a drift and falls asleep.

Below, the wolf pack moves over the dark plain until it comes to a snow-filled creek. Grey-Eye takes the lead from Blue, following the narrow watercourse upstream. They move quickly along the creek ice, passing by stretches of open water until they arrive at an open pool. As the wolves pass by a stand of willows they surprise a flock of ptarmigan bedded in the snow. The birds erupt out of the snow, disappearing out over the pond. The stained ice surrounding the pool smells of otter and dead fish. The wolves scratch at the ice, licking at the scents, but soon abandon the pool and head up the mountain slope. When they reach the top they bed down for the night. Before he goes to sleep, Blue looks down the mountain. Far out on the plain a strange light shines.

In the morning, Blue is woken by a hare hopping among the sleeping pack. He lifts his head, startling the small intruder. It disappears along the ridge, oblivious of its fortunate passage through danger.

The pack slowly stirs, stretching and shaking night frost from their coats. The young gather around Blue and Grey-Eye, licking at their mouths and nudging their parents. They are all hungry. Grey-Eye leads the pack off along the ridge top as light gathers on the horizon.

Not far along the ridge, the wolves cross the scent of otter. Two pups follow the trail down the slope to a large drift, while the rest of the pack stand and watch with interest.

The otter senses something moving over him and awakes. He turns on his back in the snow bed and waits, his teeth bared. A leg punches through the snow near his head – a furred foot lands on his shoulder. He lunges upward, delivering a flurry of lightning bites, tearing into a soft belly. The female pup leaps back, yelping and snapping blindly at the snow. She crawls from the bloody snow as the other pup jumps into the drift. In seconds, his loins are shredded, too.

The two wolves stumble out of the bloody drift, yowling and barking as they stagger back up the trail, where the male falls into shock. The female is wailing, a loop of her intestine hanging loose from her torn belly. She crumples in front of her mother, whimpering and moaning as she licks at her bleeding guts. The pack silently watches the young wolves slowly die.

Grey-Eye approaches their sprawled bodies. She nudges the female; she does not stir. Otter scent is everywhere. Grey-Eye walks to the blood-stained drift, sniffing cautiously at the snow. Returning to the ridge, she stands and howls. The other wolves sniff at the dead pups and join her mournful call.

Meanwhile, the otter has left the drift and is sliding quickly down the mountain. Part way down, he crosses a small creek, slips under the ice and surprises a sculpin. He eats it in a few bites and continues down the creek.

A Lion Inside

The sky had cleared and the night had turned bitter cold. The fire burned low as everyone huddled deep in their beds. Kazan slipped in and out of a restless sleep. His breath formed a thick layer of frost on the fur surrounding his face. As it melted, it dripped down, waking him often. He was chilled and pulled the furs over his head. At the far side of the tent he heard Tarin's familiar, muffled snoring.

How can Old Man sleep so deeply when it is so cold?

A shadow moved. Kazan saw Yogh unloading an armful of wood on the fire.

Yogh is on watch.

Yogh stood and stepped over him, opened the tent flap and went outside. Kazan heard the dull crunch of mukluks on the hard snow, followed by the familiar sound of urinating. When Yogh finished, Kazan heard him blow into his hands, warming his fingers. The boy slipped back into sleep, lulled by the familiar sounds.

Yogh was about to raise his spear and return inside the tent when he suddenly froze. Every nerve in his body was instantly alive. Next to his mukluk was a fresh pugmark in the snow.

Lion!

Something moved behind, raising the hairs on his neck. He turned his head slowly. There was nothing. Then his eyes were drawn to the mammoth carcass. He knew every detail of the shape of the land surrounding camp. Something was in front of the Long-Nose. Yogh's eyes strained in the dim light, watching for movement. Slowly the dark shape formed. Something twitched - an ear? A yellow eye blinked. Yogh swallowed hard as he made out the head of a lion crouched on the snow. Then he heard something shifting behind him again.

Two lions!

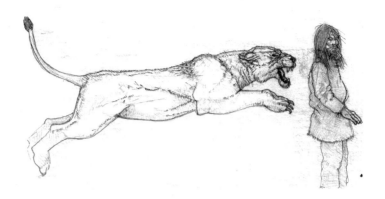

He knew he would die if he called out or moved suddenly. The lion in front was in a crouch, poised to spring. He saw it was much closer than he had first thought. The one behind was near, but how close? His only chance was the tent.

From the corner of his eye, Yogh saw the dim glow of the fire beneath the tent door, urging to come inside, to come to the safety of his band. He was about to dive for the door when the air compressed against his back like a sudden windstorm. The ground shuddered beneath his feet. Something huge crashed into his back, driving every molecule of air from his lungs. He heard the sound of his bones breaking as his back and neck shattered. He was flying. Everything turned white and static and Yogh was suddenly hotter than he had ever felt in his life. Then the night turned as bright as a summer day.

Kazan woke suddenly.

Had the tent shook?

He listened but could hear nothing. Looking around he saw Yogh had not returned.

He is still outside.

Kazan buried his face back under the furs and dozed off. A little later he woke to something heavy pressing down on his bed. Half asleep, he reached out to push it off. As his fingers brushed against the thick curved claw, his heart shuddered.

A lion was standing over him. Its face was pressing down

64

on the furs, licking at the ice that had formed from his breathing. Kazan froze in fear and disbelief. The lion's head hovered inches from his face, pushing down at the furs. He held his breath and closed his eyes, a scream in his throat waiting to be released. Then the weight lifted and the lion was moving across the tent. He decided he must have been dreaming.

Lions do not come into tents!

But he was awake. And the lion was there, inside the tent - stepping over the sleeping bodies.

Am I the only one awake? I must warn everyone!

He was about to shout, but something stopped him. He knew that if he shouted, the lion would attack him. He watched the dark outline of the beast moving in front of the smoldering fire. The only sounds he heard were Tarin's staggered snoring and the soft crackle of the embers. The lion halted and stood over Old Man. The snoring suddenly stopped. Kazan tried to scream, but his throat seized and no sound would come.

Before Tarin fell asleep, he had taken a piece of caribou sinew from his medicine sack and laid it in the fire. He watched as it shrank and curled under the heat, leaving only a charred knot on the coals. How the sinew offering burned told him things about dreaming. It had mostly burned, which was a good omen. It meant if he dream-travelled, the place he saw would be close.

Now he was dream-travelling for the first time in many moons. It was a remarkably vivid dream. He was high above a vast plain, looking down like a bird. The land below was flat and filled with grasseater tracks in every direction. Caribou began to appear - only a few scattered animals at first, and then more and more until there were thousands of *Vadzaih*, all moving for a low hill. Behind the rise, two tents were nestled in a stand of strangely shaped trees. Tarin could see people running with spears and darts. Suddenly the dream shifted and he was standing on the shore of a grey windblown lake.

Daadzaii - loon - is swimming on the surface. It turns and

65

looks directly into Tarin's eyes and dives beneath the rolling waves. Tarin's mother is standing beside him. She is telling him the story every human on earth knows by heart.

"The earth flooded long ago," she says. "There was no land. The creator needed soil to make a place for humans to live. Creator told Daadzaii to dive to the bottom of lake and bring back mud. Loon dove until its lungs were nearly bursting for air." Her voice thins until Tarin can no longer hear her words. He waits for the story to continue, but his mother is no longer there.

Suddenly, Daadzaii surfaces. In its beak is a tree branch full of small green spikes. He tries to remember the name of the tree that is always green, but he cannot. He looks around for his mother. She will remember the name. Suddenly the sky roars. He looks up and watches blackness blotting out the light, smothering the lake and the ground around him.

Tarin woke screaming as his ribs snapped and shattered. He punched blindly upward, striking a mouthful of huge teeth. Jaws gripped his skull and he instantly knew the shape of the beast he had feared would come. Before he could draw breath and scream again, the jaws snapped down, shattering his skull and filling the lion's mouth with blood and splintered bone. Tarin's final thought was of *Daadzaii's* lungs bursting as it swam for the surface, the last of the air streaming from its beak in a thin trail of bubbles.

The lion gripped Tarin by the head, lifted him from the bed, stepped over Kazan and disappeared out of the tent. It had happened so quickly Tarin's screams were still ringing in Kazan's ears. There was an eerie, terrible silence followed by quiet whispering.

Teekai was calling out softly, "Yogh. Where is Yogh?"

All at once everyone flew out of their beds. In the chaos of screams, cries and shouts, Khon quickly counted heads in the darkness: Eyak… Assan… So'tsal… Dèhzhòo… Teekai and the baby, Yukaih - the women and children were alive. He glanced around the shadowy tent. Kazan was standing next to the door

66

holding a spear, a look of shock on his face.

Tarin is dead. Yogh. Where is Yogh?

"Yogh!" he shouted. "Are you there?" No answer. The tent suddenly fell silent. He raised his voice so the other tent could hear. "Chii Tsal! Lion! Lion!" Moving toward the door, he pushed open the tent flap.

"Yogh?" he whispered, stepping into the moonlight. As his eyes adjusted to the light, he glimpsed two shapes moving away on the plain.

Two lions...

He scanned the camp but knew it was hopeless. Yogh was dead. Tarin was dead. He knelt down and touched a heavy blood spot in the snow. "Yogh's last place on earth," he said in a broken voice. "Stay close," he whispered to Kazan.

Jovan, Dat'san and Chii Tsal came running from the other tent.

"Tarin and Yogh," Khon said. "There were two lions. One came inside and took Tarin. The other killed Yogh here." He pointed to the bloody spot. They stood for a long time looking out over the moonlit plain without speaking.

Khon turned to Chii Tsal. "Bring everyone to this tent," he said. Then he braced for the confusion and fear he knew waited inside.

Teekai was in shock, silently swaying back and forth. Eyak's arm was around her, holding her up. Khon watched, but in his heart he knew there was nothing anyone could say or do for the young woman. Yogh was dead - her husband and the father to Yukaih. Khon embraced Assan, Dèhzhòo and So'tsal, burying his face in Assan's hair. Kazan joined in, wrapping his arm around his mother. He looked at So'tsal, her eyes filled with tears of disbelief and terror. Suddenly, he was struck with shame.

I should have warned everyone!

He had been too afraid to shout and bring the lion on himself. Kazan looked to the tent door, his eyes fixed on the blood streak.

I could have warned them.

He glanced at his father's fallen face, wanting to tell him of his shame, to tell him how he had frozen with fear. But Khon's eyes were darting around the tent, his mind clearly on more important things. Kazan turned and stared into the fire. When he looked up again, the tent was filled with people.

Windblown

Eyak was huddled deep in the furs, her arms around Teekai and Yukaih. The young woman had cried all night, but now she was sleeping. Old Woman had not slept at all, worrying about Wolf Band. Like all the women, she was born into the band and she would stay until she died. Men born into the band left to find a mate in other bands and stayed away. In that way, blood was always mixed, keeping the clan strong.

She lay in her bed, remembering a time long ago when three young men arrived from the Raven Band. Khon, Chii Tsal and their oldest brother, Kuhl, had travelled with their father, Kott. After a short visit, he left them with Wolf Band. Following tradition, three boys born in Wolf Band were promised to Raven in exchange. Over the next year, the three brothers were tested and evaluated for their physical strength, patience and hunting skills. Each boy was being judged for his potential as a husband to a Wolf Band woman. Eventually, the three were matched: Khon to Assan, Chii Tsal to Karun, and Kuhl to Eyak.

A year later, Kuhl suddenly died of a fever. Eyak had almost no memory of him, except that he was broody and distant, with little interest in her. Luckily, he had left her childless. His brothers, on the other hand, were well-matched. Khon was a good mate to Assan. He had excelled as a hunter and showed strong leadership whenever he was offered the chance. Chii Tsal was younger and tough but lacked the awareness of others. Still, he proved to be a remarkably strong hunter. Both brought good children to Wolf Band.

Tarin had come to the band a summer later. Eyak was married to him soon after he arrived, but the union was brief and forgettable. No children came and they soon drifted apart, finding separate lives in the band. Even in the early days of his arrival, Tarin showed he had a special medicine. He was an animal dreamer, a spirit-traveller. No one would call him Medicine Man

69

because it was bad luck to speak of such powers. No person in the band was held in higher esteem or respect than the others, regardless of skills or special powers, including the chief. It was bad luck to speak of one's skills at the expense of others. That way, all people were seen as equal, reducing the likelihood of jealous conflict. Of course, natural skills were recognized. The faster men chased down grasseaters. The better hunters spoke first when hunts were being planned. The most experienced women taught others their ways of sewing clothes or making knives. The strongest women pulled the sled. In this way, each person found a role that served the band. Cooperation was the key to survival.

Eyak slipped her arm away from Teekai, climbed from her bed and dressed quietly to avoid waking the grieving girl and her baby. She moved to the fire while watching Teekai sleep. Yogh had been a promising young hunter and a good mate and father. His death meant the band would have to care for Teekai and the baby until Teekai found a new mate. And that would not happen until they met another band and sent word for a suitor across the tundra-steppe. Wolf Band had been travelling east into country no humans had ever walked before. It had been two summers since they had seen other people. Eyak worried they were heading to the end of the earth, where they would never again see other humans and mix Wolf Band blood.

The entire band had stayed the night in Khon's family tent, afraid the lions would return. Most had not slept. The men went on watch in pairs, bundled in their sleeping beds, their spears cradled in their laps.

Khon had been awake all night, thinking about what had to be done. As morning light brightened the tent he rose and dressed, watching Eyak and Assan preparing the morning meal. He stepped outside and saw the dark shape of the mammoth's carcass looming ahead. Last night, the men had gone out on the plain and tracked the two lions a short distance; they found the cats' trail had come straight to Khon's tent. They did not visit the dead mammoth.

They came here to kill us.

Khon considered what this meant.

They do not fear us. They made two easy kills. They did not feel the pain of a spear or hunting dart. They will come back.

As Khon turned for the tent door, a brisk gust blew at his back. He looked toward the rising sun and saw a high bank of pink clouds swirling on the horizon.

A storm comes.

He turned down his parka hood and went inside.

The morning meal was silent and sombre. After they had eaten, Khon called for a meeting, but most of the band was still in shock and few spoke.

"I do not know a story about lions coming inside a tent," Khon said, expressing what was on everyone's mind.

"It has not happened," Eyak replied as she cleaned skull cups. "There are no stories." She looked at the blood smear. "Tarin was shaman. Only he could cleanse the lion spirits from this tent."

"The lions will be back," Khon said. "They do not fear us."

Assan went to the bloodied skin door, unlashing the rawhide thong attaching it to the wall of the tent. "The door is bad luck. It is covered in the blood of Tarin. It must be replaced. His blood must be cleaned from the tent wall."

She pulled out a piece of caribou skin from a large bag and began cutting a new door flap. When she was done, she untied the blood-stained one while Karun sewed the new one on. Meanwhile, Anik scrubbed the bloody tent skins.

Khon looked at Teekai as she bent her head over her child. "Teekai," he said softly. "Yogh was a hunter, a good husband. You are Wolf Band and will always be." He touched her shoulder. Teekai wiped away her tears and nodded silently. Eyak bent over and clucked softly into Yukaih's ear.

When the women were finished the repairs, Khon stood. "It is time to move," he said, reaching for his parka. "We take down Chii Tsal's tent and then this one." There was a murmur of agreement as the band began to dress for the cold. Wind suddenly buffeted the tent, setting the poles to creaking and the skins rippling in the gusts.

Kazan followed the men outside. He staggered back as a gust of wind slammed into the tent. The grey sky was rapidly fading to black. He could barely hear his father's voice over the wind.

Khon was standing between the tents, waving and shouting to everyone to get back inside. Chii Tsal ran for his tent but was knocked to the ground by the gale before he could reach the entrance. Then the full and terrible fury of the storm hit.

Huge columns of snow rose high into the air. Powerful surface winds tore into the snow, peeling away snowdrifts. Kazan crawled on his hands and knees, the wind shrieking in his ears. Someone's hat flew by, then a spear tumbled by in a swirl of snow and ice. Behind him, the tent was swaying, about to lift into the air. He crawled for the door, rolled inside and saw hands desperately gripping the poles to hold down the tent. Chii Tsal scrambled into the tent as Dat'san and Khon wrapped cord to the top of the poles. The three men fell to the floor, pulling down on the cord with all their weight.

"Take a pole!" Dat'san shouted to Kazan. He ran to the nearest one and gripped it as the tent skins rose and sunk like a living, breathing beast. Assan was beside him holding down a pole, her face grim and full of fear. He glanced around and saw the women were clutching the poles.

"Hold on!" Assan shouted. "Hold on!"

A huge gust nearly flattened the dome, and Kazan and his mother dove for the bottom of the skins and pushed down.

"Do not let the wind in!" she screamed. The tent billowed and shook but somehow they held it on the ground.

They could hear the other tent being torn apart. Skins ripped and split as the dome collapsed in the gale. It sailed into the air and tumbled over the frozen plain, the poles snapping like kindling.

Suddenly Khon was pulling Kazan to the door. "The meat!"

They scrambled from the tent into a maelstrom of snow and ice. Kazan followed Khon, who was on his knees crawling toward the snow cache, barely visible ahead. When they reached the cache Khon saw the snow was all but gone and meat sacks were missing. He gripped Kazan by the hood, hauled him forward and shoved a heavy sack into his hand, and then another, until there were four. Khon tied the sacks together, wrapped his waist belt around the load and shouted "To the tent!"

They turned as a blast of wind hit Kazan. The sacks slid away, but Khon jammed his mukluk and pulled the meat sacks back. They crawled, holding the load downwind, until they made it back to the tent, shoving themselves and the sacks inside.

"Poles!" Assan shouted at them as they entered. They each grabbled a pole and pulled down.

"How many?" Assan asked.

"This is all," Khon replied.

"Two sacks are missing."

The storm raged all day and into the night. It was pitch black when the winds finally dropped enough for them to let go of the poles and secure the tent to the ground. Eyak built a hot fire; soon the tent was warm enough for them to shed their frozen mitts.

The men went outside to survey the damage. Everything they had was gone, scattered across the Flat Plain. Chii Tsal said nothing. His tent had contained their summer clothes, a meat sack, cooking tools, hunting darts, packs. All that remained were a few shattered tent poles and the fire pit filled with blowing snow.

Dat'san and Chii Tsal went in search of the tent. They returned carrying a handful of poles and a half-empty sack of meat.

"Gone," Dat'san said shaking his head as he tossed the bundle of willow poles down. "We could see nothing else. The skins are gone."

Khon turned to Chii Tsal. "It is good luck you slept in our

73

tent last night. Your beds and winter clothes are not lost."

"There is no good luck on this bad ground," Chii Tsal snapped. "We should have listened to Old Man."

The men returned inside the tent, where Eyak met Khon at the door.

"No one is hurt," she said, touching him gently on the shoulder.

"We cannot leave in this wind," Khon said to everyone. "We wait for the storm to end."

"We need food," said Assan, almost cheerily. She went back to the fire and began directing So'tsal and Dèhzhòo. "Bring snow to melt, and kindling." Soon a hot meal was steaming over the flames. Few spoke as they repaired torn skins and broken poles. The storm had destroyed a tent, taken half of their stock of fresh meat and the weapons of three hunters. Yet, somehow, battling the windstorm had dulled the loss of Yogh and Tarin. They had all worked together to save Khon's tent and won. Losing both tents would have been a disaster and certain death for some. For the moment, they forgot the marauding lions. They had saved a tent, much of the band's clothes, half the weapons and all the sleeping beds. There were enough skins to make a new tent and there were good willows nearby to make new poles.

When they finished eating, Assan saw the despair in Teekai's eyes. Dèhzhòo had slipped between Khon and Teekai and was cradling Yukaih, singing softly in his ear.

Assan went to Khon and whispered in his ear. "Tell a story - a hopeful story."

Khon cradled his skull cup, warming his hands as he drank broth. He considered what he could do or say at such a hard time. He thought about it for a while. There was something, but he knew it would be risky. Normally, Tarin would perform the shoulder-blade ritual. He had never done it. If it did not work, the band would fall further into bad luck and despair.

Khon motioned to Dat'san, the best artist in the band.

Khon picked up the shoulder blade of a caribou and a piece of charcoal from the fire. He asked Dat'san to draw a rough map of Flat Plain on the blade with a line marking their route. When Dat'san finished, Khon placed the shoulder blade by the fire and waited for it to heat. They all gathered around and watched intently as the blade began to smoulder. When the bone eventually cracked, it would show them the direction to grasseaters. A hush filled the tent. Kazan moved closer to the fire to watch the ritual. As the blade began to smoke, he looked at Khon. His father's eyes were closed and his lips were pursed. Kazan could feel the anticipation in the crowd. The blade was burning now, about to ignite. When it suddenly cracked it caught everyone by surprise.

The blade split exactly along the charcoal line - in the very direction they were moving. Khon's slowly opened his eyes and grinned. Taking a piece of hide in his hand, he wrapped it around the broken blade. "Grasseaters are ahead!" he said, raising it over his head. There was a chorus of laughter and shouts. The blade was showing them the location of grasseaters! They were heading to good hunting ground.

"The blade has split in two pieces!" His voice rose higher with excitement. "It is a good omen. There will be good hunting!" He glanced at Assan, who was smiling.

The tent was full of laughter and shouting. Chii Tsal smiled as he embraced every hunter; even Khon. The hunting would be good again. Khon watched as his band celebrated, wishing he believed the results of the ritual as much as the others. He remembered more than one time the ritual had failed.

He thought of another story, hoping the telling would also bring luck. He waved his hands and motioned everyone to sit.

"I will tell a _Googwandak_ - the story of my first grasseater hunt." He leaned forward and waited for the crowd to settle. "Long ago our fathers learned to hunt Long-Noses from their fathers." He reached over and took a spear leaning against the tent wall. "Spears cannot pierce the skin of the big Long-Nose, but they can

75

pierce a calf's skin. Hunting the big mammoth is dangerous. A hunter hides and waits until a calf leaves its mother's side. He must get close to the calf and stab it, and escape before the angry mother comes. All of the herd will defend the calf, so a hunter must watch carefully in all directions. That is why Long-Nose hunting is the most dangerous. There can be no mistake. Each step must be carefully planned: how the hunter conceals himself to reach the calf and where to escape when the Long-Noses come. If he wounds a calf the herd will stay and watch over it. Sometimes the mother will wait many days for her dead calf to stand up. But, one day, the herd must leave the calf."

Khon paused, scanning faces. He had told the same story many times, knowing it always raised the spirits of the listeners. "My father, Kott, took me on my first grasseater hunt. I was a boy as old as Kazan. We went to a river far from here, hid in the bluffs and waited. A little later the Long-Nose came. We waited until a calf was alone and close to the bluff. My father ran and I followed him, catching the surprised calf. We speared it in the ribs. It cried out and the mother charged, shaking the ground beneath our feet as we ran. We had luck and escaped down a gully and hid behind a big rock. Other Long-Noses heard the calf crying above and came to help. They were angry and stamped the ground and blew their long noses so loud it hurt our ears. But my father had chosen the hunt well. The bluff was too steep for Long-Nose. We waited behind the rock for two days until it was quiet on the top. Then my father went up to see the calf."

Kazan knew his father's story by heart and waited excitedly for Khon's next words.

"The mother was waiting and nearly caught my father under her foot, but he rolled down the bluff and twisted his leg. She roared and charged again.

"My father shouted for help. I was afraid to go, but I did not think. So I ran to him. The mother was coming, pounding her great legs on the ground and making terrible noises from her long nose. My father climbed on my back and I carried him down the ravine. The mother followed us until the ground was too steep for her to walk. She stayed on the ridge, roaring day and night. One day the herd was gone. We climbed up and found the calf and brought back a feast to *Deetrù* Band."

Khon ended his story to a chorus of clapping and shouts.

Kazan had stopped listening when Khon was describing how he carried his father to safety. He was imagining *his* first hunt - running for a Long-Nose calf, his spear in his hand, leaping over willow shrubs and boulders, dodging the great bulls, sinking his spear into the bawling calf, and escaping. Then he remembered Tarin - his body hanging from the jaws of the lion. Suddenly Kazan no longer felt brave. More stories followed as Kazan wondered how he could ever be as brave as his father. He could not even open his mouth and warn his band.

The stories ended and everyone moved to their beds. Chii Tsal and Jovan took their beds outside to watch for lions until late into the night, when Dat'san and Khon took over the watch. It was still dark when Kazan was woken by voices.

"The lions do not know humans," his father was saying. "They do not fear us yet." He paused. "I did not see the lion until he moved to Tarin."

"You were awake?" Dat'san asked.

"Assan woke me. It is lucky no one shouted; the lion would have panicked and killed many more." His voice softened and there was a long pause. "We are but guests in this life."

Kazan sat up, surprised by what his father was saying.

They were awake! They did not shout a warning!

He suddenly understood.

If I had shouted, others would have died.

"Tarin lived a long life," Dat'san was saying. "I hope my life will be long and end so quick."

Kazan waited for more conversation, but they fell silent. His guilt began to ebb. He had done the right thing. He had kept quiet.

His father had not warned Tarin. Now Kazan understood why - it was more dangerous to attack a lion in a crowded tent than let it take one of them. He wondered if it had been him - would his father watch as the lion took his only son? He fell asleep and did not dream. The lions did not return that night. In the morning, light returned to the world.

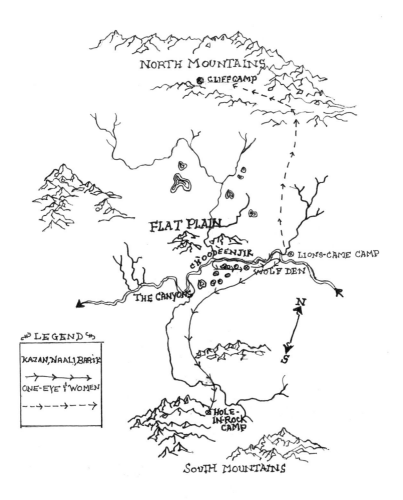

NORTH MOUNTAINS

⊗ CLIFF CAMP

FLAT PLAIN

CHOODEENJIK

⊗ LIONS-CAME CAMP

WOLF DEN

THE CANYONS

N

S

⊗ HOLE-IN-ROCK CAMP

SOUTH MOUNTAINS

LEGEND

KAZAN, NAALI, BARIK
⟶ ⟶ ⟶
ONE-EYE & WOMEN
--⟶ --⟶ --⟶

79

PART 2

SREENDYIT: GETTING LIGHT

A Meeting of the Clan

Sunlight, spreading its brilliant pink glow across the sparkling white mountain slope, breaks above the horizon for the first time in more than a month. Blue wakes and stretches, turning his face to the glimmering rays. He stands and surveys his sleeping pack. He sees that Grey–Eye has left her sleeping bed. She is standing on a boulder silently watching the mountain, her ears cocked forward. She whines softly and suddenly barks a sharp warning. The other wolves rise quickly and listen. There are other wolves howling, far off but moving closer. Blue looks in the direction of the howling and spots a pack moving across the mountain, weaving its way through the willows, heading straight for his pack.

Blue and Grey–Eye run out to meet the approaching wolves, barking hoarsely. The young wolves scramble to their feet and follow their parents, uncertain what has caused all the excitement. As the two packs meet, the leaders collide into each other. Blue bites into the shoulder of a big dusky male with a ripped ear. Torn–Ear twists and clamps his teeth into Blue's thick neck. Grey–Eye bowls a snow–white female over, gripping her by the back of the neck. The female kicks and rolls, trying to get on top, but Grey–Eye's grip is strong and holds. She is pressing her canines deep into the female's neck when she recognizes the scent.

It is her sister, Black–Foot. The memory is vague, but the scent is unmistakable, and so is the dark band of hair on the forefoot. Grey–Eye instantly releases her grip and stands in front

80

of her sister. Meanwhile, Blue, struggling under a pile of snarling wolves, breaks free of the melee. He sees his mate circling a female, their heads down and eyes locked.

Suddenly there's a different kind of excitement. Wolves are sniffing and jostling one another. Grey-Eye and Black-Foot are swarmed by a mob of young. Soon they are all leaping and smelling, barking and growling. Blue approaches Torn-Ear. They cautiously circle, gradually trading scents from a safe distance.

The meeting of the packs continues through the day and night. Eventually the wolves settle down to rest on the mountain ridge. The adults, tired of the stimulation, find resting places away from the young wolves, who play well into the night. One by one, they dig beds in the snow and fall asleep, exhausted from a day of romping and wrestling.

The next morning, Grey-Eye wakes and moves toward Black-Foot, nudging her sister's shoulder. Black-Foot stands and stretches as the wolves resume their sniffing and wrestling, bowling into each other, rubbing shoulders, gnawing on necks. Before long the packs are restless and eager to travel. Black-Foot heads down the mountain with her wolves while Grey-Eye takes her pack in the opposite direction, leaving behind a field of empty snow beds, scat and urine.

Strangers on the Tundra-Steppe

The entire Wolf band stood on the tundra-steppe and watched the rosy fingers of the sunrise. Far away, snowy mountain peaks were bathed in a soft blue hue. The light spilled over the horizon, shimmering through morning frost and shrouding the breath of the hooded onlookers in misty halos. The women were singing, their voices carrying far out onto the windless Flat Plain:

From down under the sky,
I come to earth shining
Light that ends Khaii and brings warmth to the earth.
Sree shares her light so snow will melt and grass will grow,
And Wolf Band will grow strong on the flesh of the land.

So'tsal was the first to notice the strangers standing in the distance.

"*Dinjii kat - people,*" she muttered almost matter-of-factly, pointing to the two figures standing a few hundred yards away. Everyone turned and the singing stopped.

"*Tr'iinin,*" whispered Assan. "Two children."

Khon scanned the horizon, expecting other people to appear, but there were only two. Neither carried throwing darts or spears. They were dressed in caribou-skin parkas cut long at the waist. Their pants were sheepskin, their mukluks made of the leg skin of caribou. He nodded to Chii Tsal and Dat'san. They walked toward the children, skirted around them and disappeared into the grey margin between the plain and sky. A little later Chii Tsal and Dat'san reappeared, avoiding the two children and rejoining Wolf Band.

Chii Tsal shook his head, catching his breath. "Their tracks come from a big lake. They are only two - no others. They were running."

Khon raised his hand, motioning the strangers to come forward. At first they hesitated, glancing at each other as if speaking, then they walked slowly toward the band. When the
82

children were close they stopped, their fur-trimmed hoods hiding dark faces.

The boy appeared to be fourteen or fifteen summers. He was short with a smooth-skinned face. His mouth was thin and tight. High cheekbones framed two brown eyes that refused to look at them. The girl was younger, twelve or thirteen summers only, Khon guessed. Her angular face gave her a hard look older than her years. Her black hair was tied back like the women's. Khon noticed her eyes: blue like a mountain stream in summer. He had never seen eyes of such colour. She looked directly at him and he felt a strange uneasiness, as if his thoughts were being read.

"Welcome," he said in his friendliest voice. "Where is your band?"

"What name is this band?" the boy countered.

Khon smiled, waving his arm at the crowd of staring faces. "Wolf. We are Wolf Band." There was a long silence. The boy looked as if he was about to say something, but the girl answered before he could speak.

"*Shih* - we are Bear Band." She looked into their watchful eyes for a sign of recognition but saw nothing. From her parka she drew a necklace featuring a carved ivory figure of a bear. "*Shih.*' The women leaned forward, inspecting the carving.

Eyak came forward and touched the necklace, turning the tiny ivory figure over in her fingers. It was a bear-woman: a woman's head on the body of a bear.

"*Shih.*" Eyak nodded.

Khon pressed the girl for more. "Where is *Shih* Band?"

She shook her head.

Kazan was standing behind the crowd. He moved closer for a better look at the two strangers. The boy was staring hard at the girl, his eyes darkening. She did not seem to notice.

"Where are you travelling?" asked Kohn. The boy and girl glanced at each other. He could see they had no idea.

"Who are you?" the boy asked.

"Khon."

"I am Barik," the boy said, touching his chest lightly with his thick mitt of bison fur. He pointed at the girl. "Naali, my sister."

"Where is your mother, your father?"

"Dead."

"How?"

"Killed."

"How?"

"A *nanaa'in'* - a bushman," Naali answered. She sensed Barik's impatience and waited for him to speak.

"He killed our father, stole our camp and took us. Then he killed our mother. He would have killed us. We burned the camp and ran." He looked back and pointed to the north. "He followed us across the plain but he did not find us."

Kazan looked into girl's face, noticing her blue eyes for the first time. He turned his attention to the brother. He was taller and a little older but still a boy. Unlike the girl, who seemed calm, he was uneasy, constantly shuffling from one foot to the other, glancing up and down at them but never looking into their eyes. Then the words the boy had spoken struck him.

They burned a bushman's camp and crossed the Flat Plain in winter. With no weapons - a boy and a girl, alone!

Kazan had never seen a bushman. He had heard the frightening stories of how they stole women and children and made them slaves. In every story, the bushman always killed the children. He wondered if he would have been afraid on such a journey. He had never spent a night away from his family tent.

I would be very afraid.

"The bushman is as big as a bear," Naali was saying. She touched her left eye and moved her finger down her cheek to her mouth. "There is a scar here and his eye is gone." She looked down on the ground, biting her lip. "One-Eye. Our mother called him One-Eye." Tears welled in her eyes.

Khon shook his head. "We do not know any bushmen. We

have heard of *Shih* Band but have not met them for many years. Your father and mother, what were they called?"

The boy pulled his hood away from his face. "Our father was called Gilt. Our mother was Saran."

Eyak looked at him. "I know a Gilt. He was born of the *Daagoo* band. Is it the same one?"

Barik nodded.

"None here are of the *Shih* or *Daagoo* band," Assan said. She pointed to each man. "Khon and Chii Tsal are Raven. Dat'san is Otter and Jovan is Blackfox. There were two others: Yogh was Otter and Tarin was Bluefish. They were killed by lions." She pointed to the tent. "The lions came here - to the tent."

"You had luck of *Shih* to not meet them," Chii Tsal said, but the children did not respond.

"Come," Khon said, waving them to the tent. "There is fire. You have been cold. What food we have we will share. We will leave this place today. You may follow or make your own trail." He motioned everyone back to the tent.

As they approached the dome, Kazan lifted the door flap for Naali and Barik to enter. They did not look at him as they disappeared inside. Before Kazan followed, he gazed out on the Flat Plain, half expecting to see the bushman standing on the horizon, watching him with one eye. He saw only blowing snow.

There was barely room in the tent for the additional children. Eyak motioned to Naali to sit beside her. As she sat, food materialized in her hand from someone. She nearly fainted at the aroma of the braised horsemeat. She realized she had not eaten in days as she eagerly scooped the steaming meat into her mouth. When she was done, a girl some years older brought her tea.

"I am So'tsal," the girl said, smiling as she melted back into the crowd.

Naali leaned back and noticed a boy watching her. As their eyes met, he glanced down at his food, his face reddening. He was about her age, but he was much taller than the men in the crowd. She had never seen such a tall boy. Suddenly she felt tired, more tired than she had ever felt in her thirteen summers. She leaned back on the wall of the tent and closed her eyes as images of their escape from the bushman filled her thoughts.

Naali Remembers

One-Eye the bushman swung the club, instantly realizing the blow would be too much. The antler beam cracked into the woman's skull just behind the ear; she had turned too late to avoid the strike. He lunged forward as she crumpled, catching her before she collapsed onto the fire pit.

An anguished roar escaped from his throat. He looked at the girl and boy staring wide-eyed from the back of the tent as he settled her gently onto the floor. Naali scrambled forward, her hands reaching for her mother. The bushman swung his arm and she went crashing into the tent wall.

He heard the boy moving for him and instinctively gripped the club. Barik slammed into him, grasping for his thick neck, but before his fingers could touch him the boy was sailing across the tent. One-Eye lunged for him and slammed the club down inches from his howling face. The girl was screaming, too, her hands pressed hard down on her mother's skull. Blood was oozing through her fingers. With one hand the bushman snatched the boy off the ground and flung him into the tent wall. Barik glared back and screamed, his eyes filled with hatred. Then he turned away and held his mother in his arms.

Naali stripped off her caribou-skin shirt, wrapping it tightly around her mother's head to staunch the bleeding. Saran was breathing unevenly, her eyes flickering. She couldn't hear Naali's whisperings; she had sunk into a coma. The girl touched the ivory-figure necklace on her mother's heaving chest. The figure depicted a bear-woman, arms at her side and belly protruding far in front. Bear paws with long claws reached to her knees.

The bushman clutched his antler club, stunned by what had just happened. The woman had poured him a cup of tea and spilled it on his mukluk. He had felt the familiar hot flash and sparkling points of light, and the next thing he knew his hand was swinging the heavy club.

He recalled how he had killed her husband. He had found them just before the snows came. They were collecting berries. He smelled their fire first. They did not see him moving along the creek. He easily subdued the man and the boy and tied them together. The woman and girl tried to run, but he caught them and dragged them back. The woman screamed; the girl remained silent. He untied the man and stripped off his clothes. Brandishing his club, the bushman silently pointed to the horizon. The man looked at his family for a moment and ran. The next morning, he caught the man moving behind the tent wielding a horse bone. He was blue with cold, his hands and feet already frostbitten. He speared him through the chest, lifting him high into the air. He threw him to the ground then clubbed him until there was only shattered bones and flesh. Dragging the woman and children out of the tent, he showed them what he had done as a warning of their fate if they tried to run. That night he was living in their tent. He made a small cut on his arm and bound it in a piece of skin, adding another scar to his arm.

He had not intended to strike the woman like that - the blow was too hard, and he had meant to hit her only with his hand. He felt a glimmer of regret - a distant emotion from somewhere in his past - but the feeling soon vanished. He looked at the girl. She was staring hard at him through her tears. Her eyes were the strangest he had ever seen. Blue, like the sky.

The bushman felt uneasy whenever she looked at him, suddenly self-conscious about the heavy scar that ran from his forehead down through his empty eye socket to the corner of his twisted mouth. The girl was sitting at the back of the tent with her mother cradled in her arms. She was looking at the bushman. Unable to match her gaze, he shifted his eyes to the floor. He wondered why she made him so uneasy. He felt anger surging up, the urge to strike her down. But he needed the two of them.

A little later the woman's breathing became broken, her chest barely rising. Naali and Barik were holding her when a final shudder vibrated through her body. They had been in and out of a light sleep all night, taking turns compressing the wound and tending the fire. Naali felt Saran pass and pressed her lips to her mother's forehead. She began to silently weep as Barik wrapped his arms around both of them. Naali saw One-Eye was lying awake, watching the end of Saran's life. He rose and stood towering above her. Then he kicked her, pointed to the fire and left the tent. Naali removed the necklace from her mother's neck and slipped it around her own. She knew what she must do.

A few days earlier, Saran had taken Naali aside while they were collecting wood kindling. "*Ch'ihlak Ch'indèe* - One-Eye - he is a bushman, a *nanaa'in'*. He lives alone. He will keep us until he no longer needs us. He will grow tired of this tent and he will kill us. That is bushman way. They kill and steal and share nothing. You have seen the scars on the arm. Each cut is for a human he has killed. He will add three more and think nothing of it. It is *nanaa'in'* way."

Naali and her mother moved through the shrubs, splitting

off the dead branches and piling them onto an elk hide spread out on the snow behind them. When it was full of wood, Saran signalled to Barik, who came and pulled it back to the tent. Naali and her mother continued collecting wood in silence.

"*Geh*," Saran said, pointing to a white hare lying under a bush with a snare around its neck. It was still alive. Naali picked it up, gently loosening the noose she had made from twisted caribou sinew. She whispered soothing words, patting the hare's long ears. Then with a sharp twist, she snapped its neck, stuffed it into a sack and reset the snare.

Her mother crouched down with her. "When the next snow falls, we must run. He will kill us before spring. He will not want us slowing him down. He cannot let us live to tell others about the one-eyed bushman. We take only our beds and some dry meat. We burn the camp." She looked out on the Flat Plain stretching as far as they could see. "That is where we go. The snow will cover our trail. It is the only way. Say nothing to Barik until it is time. He will not want to leave the tent. He does not understand *nanaa'in*."

They walked back to the tent, stepping by One-Eye's deep tracks. He was out hunting grasseaters as he did every day. Naali silently asked *Shih* Spirit for the same gift she had asked for each day since the bushman killed her father and taken them:

A killing beast will find the nanaa'in and kill him.

The Burning

Naali had not believed her mother's plan could work. One-Eye would surely find them. He was big and strong, and he could run faster than any man she had ever seen. She had watched him chase down a big bull elk, refusing to give up even as the animal began to outdistance him in the deep snow. After he had missed with his hunting dart, the bushman pulled his club and ran through the snowdrifts like a stampeding bison until he was out of sight. Late that night, he walked back into camp pulling the elk carcass behind him. But Naali knew her mother's warning was true, her concern real. The bushman would kill them. Living in the same tent, waiting to be clubbed to death in her sleep, was more unbearable than being killed for running.

A few days after they buried Saran under a high mound of snow, Naali woke to the sound of snow blowing against the tent and saw One-Eye's bed was empty. She pulled on her mukluks, pushed the door flap open and looked out onto a fresh blanket of knee-deep snow. One-Eye's tracks were already invisible. Filled with a sudden anxiety, Naali swallowed hard. Was this the day to run? The day she would die? Her hands were shaking as she slipped back into the tent. She could barely hold the kindling as she made a fire. Her hands shook as she nudged her brother awake.

"We are leaving," she said, slipping her caribou-skin parka over her head. She could hardly believe she had the courage to say the words.

Barik rubbed his eyes and sat up in his bed. He looked at her, not sure what she meant.

"Where are we going?"

"Away. To the Flat Plain."

"What? There is nowhere to go." He laughed, then saw she was serious. He sat up straight. "This is our winter shelter," he complained.

Naali said nothing as she pulled on her mukluks and wrapped the rawhide laces around her pant legs, hoping that putting on her outside clothes would quiet her pounding chest. If she made the next move, there would be no going back. She looked at the rising flames. Barik climbed from his bed and looked outside.

"It is snowing," he said sharply. Naali stuffed dry meat into her pack. "We cannot leave," he said, his voice ringing. "It is snowstorm!"

"I am leaving," she answered, not looking at him.

"But he will catch you."

"He has already caught me - and you. He killed our mother and father. You saw the scars. He will kill us before spring. He will cut his arm two more times." She rolled and tied her sleeping bed and slung it over her back. Slipping her club into her waistband, she looked at him, trying to hide her fear and trepidation.

"This was our mother's plan. If she were alive she would be standing here now - not me. Come, or stay," she said dispassionately, hoping desperately she would not be leaving alone.

He hesitated, looking around the tent. "If we work hard he will not kill us. He needs us. We bring wood and kill small animals. The tent is our shelter. We only need to bring him hares and wood!"

She untied a bladder of warm water that was suspended over the fire. Tying the top, she stuffed it into her pack. Then she moved to the fire, adding an armload of kindling until the flames roared.

"What are you doing?" he asked as she gathered a heap of skins from the floor. She threw them on the flames and watched them ignite. Barik stood frozen as the skins flared. It was suddenly as bright as a summer day. The floor around the fire erupted in flames, and the tent was a blazing inferno. Barik raised his hands to his face and staggered back in disbelief.

"It is our mother's plan," Naali shouted as she walked out of the tent. "Come!"

Barik stuffed his clothes and fur bed into his pack and scrambled out of the smoke-filled tent. He ran for Naali and shoved her hard into the snow.

"You have killed us!" he screamed as he kicked at her. She climbed to her feet and faced him.

"He will kill us if he catches us!" she screamed back as tears streamed down her cheeks. She turned and stumbled on through the snow, not caring if he followed.

What have I done? The bushman will find us and he will kill us for burning the shelter!

Barik stood watching the tent turn into a firestorm as a great cloud of black smoke rose high into the snowy sky.

He will see the smoke!

He stood there, uncertain which way to go.

Would the bushman believe me if I ran to him? Would he believe it was her idea?

There would be no shelter. The meat would be gone. The bushman's bed was burning in the fire. Everything was gone. He had witnessed his anger too many times. This time it would be like nothing he had ever experienced.

He began to run, hoping the smoke could not be seen in the snowstorm. Naali was not far ahead, pushing her way through the drifts, falling down every few steps. She looked back, certain Barik would not be following. But he was there, barely visible behind the heavy veil of snow. Exhausted and unable to break trail further, she waited for him to take over. His eyes were dark and distant as he moved silently past her, slamming his shoulder into her chest and pushing her into the snow again. She stared at her brother's back as he plowed through.

"You burned it!" he shouted. "Remember when he catches us. You burned his tent and his bed. You tell him!"

The snow was falling so heavily they could see only a few feet in front of them. Naali constantly looked back. If One-Eye were coming she would not know it until his club struck her. She and Barik traded off breaking trail in silence as the snow piled up around them. Their pace was painfully slow until they reached a small lake covered in ice. As they began moving faster, Naali felt a faint glimmer of hope. Even the bushman would have trouble moving through the deep snow. If he did not find their trail they might escape.

"Our trail will be lost on the ice," she said, hoping Barik was over his sulking. He did not reply.

The Wrath of One-Eye

One-Eye was following fresh caribou trails, sinking to his thighs in the soft snow. He ploughed through the drifts, sweeping his mitt over the tracks. The snow edges were soft. The animals were close. He raised the spear to his shoulder and peered into the falling snow, listening. Somewhere ahead he heard the quiet shifting of snow, an antler brushing snow, a soft breathing. He squatted so that only his head was visible, pulled up his hood and waited.

Vadzaih were moving his way. He heard a grunt. Directly in front, a head was bobbing up and down in the whiteness. The calf had not seen him. He carefully slid his spear on top of the snow. The calf was almost within reach. It froze as One-Eye slowly stood. He lifted the spear, ready to plunge it into the calf's neck, when a rack of antlers appeared beside him. The cow stopped chewing lichen and looked at him, her eyes wide with surprise as he drove the spear into her ribs. She fell over onto her side as he lunged forward, swimming through the deep snow to reach her. The cow was now on her back, frantically kicking. He grabbed for a leg but missed. Her broad hooves pummelled his shoulder, sending a shower of snow in his face. He reached for his antler club and smashed at her head until she stopped moving. The calf had not moved and was still looking at him, shocked with fright. In a single motion the bushman yanked the spear from the cow and drove it into calf's pounding heart.

Wasting no time, he began butchering. When he was done he stretched out the skin of the cow, lashed both carcasses inside, tied the bundle to his center of his spear with a leather strap and began pulling the load back to camp.

The blizzard was so heavy he could barely stay on his trail. More than once he strayed off course into a tangle of shrubs. Twice he found himself back at the meadow where he had killed the caribou. As he finally approached camp it was completely dark.

He smelled the smoke before he saw the remains of the tent. Blackened poles leaned over smoking skins. The smell of burnt hair filled his nose and lungs as he untied his spear from the load and circled what was left of his camp.

His first thought was that they were both dead, caught in a freak fire. Standing back, he reached into the smoking hides with his spear, searching for their bodies. He moved around the wreckage, carefully turning over the remains. They were not there! As he stared at the ruins he suddenly understood. They had burned the tent and run. He looked for their trail but found only a sea of trackless snow in all directions. Then his foot slipped and his mukluk slid into a slurry of slush and ash. He pulled his foot back, but it was too late. Moisture seeped into his mukluk. He knew the grave danger of wet feet.

Running to the nearest shrubs, One-Eye snapped off an armful of willow branches, kicked out a snow pit and knelt down, his wet foot already cooling. He pulled out a stone blade from his coat and began shaving thin slices from the branches. He found the firesticks inside his parka and soon had a fire burning. One-Eye stood beside the rising flames, stamping his feet up and down.

He shook his head furiously, screaming into the black sky as snow fell on his face. Unwrapping his mukluk, he saw his toes were turning blue. He rubbed them over the flame until feeling returned. He turned his mukluk inside out and placed it on a branch by the fire, and he did the same with his icy hare-skin sock. When they dried, he quickly pulled them on and began shoveling snow into a pile. After the pile had hardened, he dug a tunnel into it the length of his body. Unloading the caribou meat, he unrolled the frozen hide and held it to the flames. When the skin thawed, he shoved it into the tunnel and then returned to the fire.

The wind began to blow. He sat warming his foot until the fire was nearly out. He crawled into the tunnel, lay down on the caribou skin and wrapped his arms around his chest. He tried to sleep, but the bitter cold repeatedly woke him. He listened to the wind, thinking.

I will find them. I will find them and burn them alive.

Blown Away

Naali woke in a startle. Dim light was shining through the wall of their snow cave and her heart raced. It was dawn and they had overslept. She slipped out of her sleeping skins and crawled outside. The storm had ended. She looked back from where they had travelled, half expecting to see the bushman. The Flat Plain was a bleak grey-white curtain in all directions. She went back into the tunnel and shook Barik awake.

"It is light," she said, pulling her bed out and tying it into a bundle. She dug into the bag of dry meat and stuffed a few slices in her mouth. Barik emerged and looked around. She chewed the meat and swallowed a mouthful of cool water from the bladder she had put in her sleeping furs. She passed the bladder to her brother. He drank a few mouthfuls and handed it back.

"He will have trouble finding us," she said, looking at the deep carpet of snow. But she was not fooling herself or Barik. He would be coming for them. He was already coming for them. She remembered how the bushman had killed their father.

Will he make me watch Barik die first?

Barik tied his sleeping bed, snatched a handful of dry meat and headed out onto the Flat Plain, using the dim light on the south horizon for guidance. Naali threw her bundle on her back and felt a sudden chill along her spine.

He is coming. I feel him.

They walked all day through drifting snow and across windswept ground before stopping to make a snow tunnel. They managed to collect a few handfuls of dung and built a small fire. The next morning, they both woke early from hunger. Their water was gone, so they ate snow and a small ration of dry meat.

"The sun is returning," she said, pointing to the brightening horizon, hoping a conversation would brighten their spirits. Barik was still not talking. She put on her pack and began walking south. They were in the middle of a large windswept lake when snow

98

started falling. The sky darkened and the wind increased, sending plumes of spindrift high in the air. When the snowstorm arrived they huddled together on the ice, holding their parka hoods closed. There was no point in trying to move in the storm, so they sat with their backs to the wind and waited for it to pass. As darkness fell, the storm grew. It was sucking the heat from their still bodies; without shelter, they would freeze to death.

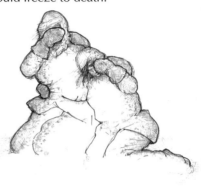

Suddenly Barik gave a shout. Naali turned to see his outstretched hand disappearing into the darkness.

He is blowing away!

She dove to catch him but missed. Then she was sliding, too, spinning helplessly down the lake and gaining speed with every second. Her foot suddenly crashed into something and a hand gripped her shoulder. Barik rolled over on Naali, pressing his face into hers. The wind was so strong she could barely make out his words.

"...belt!"

She understood. Reaching for her belt, she unwrapped it carefully from her waist. She looped it through his belt, tied it back around herself, closed her eyes and buried her head in his parka. They lay together on the ice, hoping the savage winds would end before they froze to death.

A Close Encounter

One-Eye had left the smoking ruins before dawn. By midmorning he had found their trail. By midday he was standing by their first snow tunnel. It was nearly dark when he reached their second. He dug it out, squeezed in, wrapped the caribou skin around himself and slept.

The next morning, he lost the trail. They had gone onto a large unsheltered lake. He looked for them along the shore. When the wind came up, he was blinded by driving snow. Finding shelter under a bank on the lakeshore, he took a piece of raw meat from his pack and waited for the storm to pass. The winds increased as night fell, and he had no choice but to move. Without shelter he would freeze. His swung his spear ahead and walked through the darkness until he reached a turn in the shore where the wind shifted to his side.

He was travelling uphill when his foot struck something hard. A lion suddenly roared - so close he felt the air tremble. He swung his spear at the sound and saw something move in the blackness. The roar was behind him. He stood still and waited with his spear poised, certain the beast was circling closer.

It roared again, but this time from farther away. Once more it roared and he knew it was moving off. One-Eye stood for a while listening to the raging winds. He shifted his foot and kicked the hard thing again. He looked down and saw a small human skull, the empty eye sockets staring up at him. The face was gone and a long tuft of black hair blew against his leg. He knelt and saw an arm severed at the shoulder.

The lion has killed them.

One-Eye felt resentment. He had come to kill them. Now they were dead. The anger grew until he raised his face to the sky and screamed. He retreated blindly onto the lake, bracing his spear on the ice to keep from falling. Far off he could hear the roar of the lion fade into the blistering wind.

100

Naali and Barik were sprawled on the ice in the inky blackness, holding each other tight.

"...freezing," Barik shouted over the winds. "...need shelter." They crawled into the wind until they came to a drift surrounded by black ice.

She heard it first: a sliding, scraping sound coming toward them. She touched Barik on the shoulder - it was the clatter of wood on ice. A human shape suddenly appeared so close she could reach out and touch the sliding boot.

One-Eye!

She held her breath, certain he must have spotted them. When she raised her head again he was gone. They lay on the snowdrift for a long time, hardly believing their good luck. He had not seen them.

"Go!" Barik whispered, and they continued crawling upwind, finally finding the end of the lake. Nearly frozen, they dug into a drift and fell into the tunnel exhausted.

Barik's voice was filled with resignation. "He is here. I told you... he would find us."

She did not answer. The storm had saved them from certain death, but he was here, searching for them. He was too strong.

He will find us.

Naali crawled deeper in her bed, eventually sinking into a dreamless sleep and not caring if she woke.

Talking Lion

Naali woke with Barik's hand pressed on her mouth, his eyes shimmering with fear as he silently shook his head. Something large was moving beside the drift. Holding her breath, she waited for the spear to plunge through the snow and end her life. They lay in the tunnel, still and silent, listening, until Barik mustered the courage to peer out. Slowly he swept away the fallen snow from the entrance and poked his head out in the dim light of morning.

There was a lion pugmark in the fresh snow. He slid back inside. He mouthed the word "Lion," his face ashen. She shrugged in disbelief.

Why does it not dig us out?

A crunching sound approached again and stopped. They waited in terror for claws to tear into the snow, but nothing happened.

It made no sense. The lion must have smelled them. It must have known they were hidden in the drift. They lay there for a long time, and then the sound moved off. Barik whispered, "It is leaving."

He rolled out of his bed, wrapped it in a bundle and crawled out of the tunnel. Naali followed. She was about to stand when Barik's hand suddenly stopped her. She froze, her eyes fixed on his hand inches from her face.

He was looking at a lion asleep on a small hill, so close he could hear its thick breathing. At its feet was a human skull, a patch of black hair still attached, and scattered bones everywhere. The lion was sleeping with its head turned away from them.

They were partially hidden behind the drift; the lion would not see them without turning its head. Barik crouched down, careful not to make a sound. Taking small steps, he shuffled backward, beckoning her to follow him. As she crawled along, an enormous roar split the morning silence. Naali turned to watch the huge beast stand up, its eyes on them. Its long tail flicked excitedly behind its massive body. A deep growl turned her legs to jelly, but she kept her eyes on the lion's as a strange warmth slowly swept over her.

The lion roared again and shook its head, but Naali did not feel fear. In a semi-trance, she stood as high as she could. Her own voice startled her, at first soft and then becoming louder and more confident as the words came. She was speaking a language she had once heard coming from her own tongue; she recalled the face of a wolf speaking to her as the smell of cranberry filled her senses.

"Lion beast, we wish no share of your kill. We are children of Shih, a beast as powerful as lion. Shih will be grateful if you let us pass unharmed."

The lion roars, shaking its massive head. Naali stares into its eyes, refusing to look away. She sees the human skull between its legs and her confidence falters.

Her voice breaks and she knows the lion has heard the change.

"You have made a kill of my kind. We are not here for the bones. We wish only to pass safely."

The lion is looking at her, its eyes searching for a weakness, for a hint of fear and a reason to hunt the small human. Naali senses the lion's indifference and fights back panic. She is slipping into a blankness as the words unravel around her. Her tongue is twisting and she is losing contact with the lion's spirit. As it takes a step toward her she is struck by a cascade of sparkling light shredding the smothering darkness. Naali stands as high as she can and raises her hand.

"I am a spirit-traveller; I know lion tongue. I wish to pass unharmed."

The lion is swaying. "The one behind. I wish to kill it."

"He is my brother. I ask you not to eat him."

"What will I receive in exchange?"

Naali scrambles for an answer. "You have fed on our kind.
You are not hungry. There is little on our bones for such a powerful
killing beast."

The lion lies down on the snow and turns its head away.
"Go, before I feel hunger."
"We are leaving. Shih is grateful."

She stepped back as the lion closed its eyes. Naali and
Barik walked until they lost sight of the lion, then turned and ran
onto the windswept plain. Barik was astonished by Naali's
encounter with the lion. He did understand what had happened,
what she had said, why they were now alive and running. She had
spoken to a lion in a tongue he had never heard. He glanced over
at his sister. He had thought her strange, but he had never heard
her speak to animals.

She made a lion sleep! Even the most powerful medicine
man cannot make a lion sleep!

He wondered who had taught her such powerful
medicine. How had she learned to speak lion tongue? No one in
Bear Band could have taught her such spirit power. He would have
known; he would have seen the change in her.

Naali was running across a small pond, leaping over knee-
high drifts. Ahead, dawn was breaking on the horizon. She felt as
light as a snowflake. As she ran up over a low rise, slivers of bright
pink light suddenly blinded her.

Sree - the sun! It is Sun Day. The sun returns today!

When her eyes adjusted to the brightness, she saw
mountain peaks shining blue-gold far off in the distance. Around
her the snow on the Flat Plain sparkled. She stopped running. Tears
of joy streamed down her face. Barik was standing looking at
something. Then she heard the voices. They were singing the Sun
Welcome song.

The sun is singing…

Naali heard someone singing to a baby. She looked
around the crowded tent and saw people crawling into their
104

sleeping beds. The fire was glowing hot and bright. She could hardly believe she and Barik were alive, warm inside a tent, stomachs filled with fresh meat. Only last night they had watched as One-Eye passed by them in a storm. In the morning, she had spoken to the most dangerous killing beast on earth - in a language she did not know. It had heard her and let them pass. She did not know where she learned animal tongue, spirit travel, but she knew she must have medicine power. Naali recalled the first time with the wolf. She had felt the same sense of calm, the same bright points of light that flashed as the animal words came. She had heard many stories of spirit-travellers from *Shih* Band but never expected she would know such power.

Now she and Barik were safe, surrounded by people who were not *Shih* Band, not kin. The chief, Khon, had invited them to stay. She saw their food was desperately low, yet he still invited them to join. She thought of One-Eye. He was out on the plain somewhere.

Is he watching the tent now?

She climbed into her bed and wrapped the furs around her shoulders, listening to the familiar sounds of people preparing for sleep: beds being made, a baby crying, dung being loaded onto the hearth, low whispering, a child's muffled laughter. She was suddenly struck by a deep longing. She missed her mother and father, her *Shih* band. She lay her head down and looked at Barik beside her, but he was already sleeping. Above her, firelight danced across the tent ceiling as she fell into a deep and peaceful slumber.

Barik Considers the Future

Barik was not sleeping. He was thinking about Wolf Band. He had listened to the men and women during the evening, quietly evaluating their strengths and weaknesses - measuring who was strong, who was not. He had done this since he was a child. It had become second nature. Knowing weakness enabled him to exploit other boys for his advantage. He was smarter than most and could easily coax and coerce them into unknowingly doing work for him. He was sure he could have done the same with One-Eye, until his sister ruined everything.

Since he was a small boy he had tried to imagine himself as a hunter, the only role for a male in a band of humans. Men hunted grasseaters. There was no other path to follow. Men lived and breathed hunting from morning to night, and they dreamed of killing animals when they slept. Fathers began instruction as soon as a boy could walk. By the time he was ten summers, he had built countless child-spears and hunting darts. He practiced dart throwing until he could hit skin dummies as he stood still, walked and ran from every direction. He learned to navigate by the night stars, track animals across windblown snow, recognize the smell of most beasts on the tundra-steppe and the songs of every bird. He could twist snares of caribou and elk sinew and catch ground squirrel. He could run down young hares in open pursuit.

To become a hunter, every boy must learn to live and breathe grasseaters - become the animal in his own mind. His father taught him to always think about what had made a hunt successful or not. He watched and listened to the men and knew their knowledge came from endless discussion and storytelling about their hunts. Sharing knowledge about the shifting shape of the land, wind, weather or change in the behaviour of prey helped guide a hunter's future decisions. He was fourteen summers now and had already watched many hunts made by his father. He had been preparing to make his first grasseater hunt when the bushman came and killed his father.

The strange thing was that he did not care so much that he had not yet killed a grasseater. Thinking day and night about hunting had only bored him. He liked the idea of being a chief, but he would let the other boys be hunters. He had raided their snares and stolen their ground squirrels when he had only a handful of his own sets. It was remarkable how easy it was to fool them all.

It was not that he minded killing things. In fact, he enjoyed it - especially if the animal suffered. Once, his father had beaten him for burning the ears of a hare. Barik promised he would never do it again, but he secretly continued cutting their ears off, burning ground squirrels in their holes and skinning fish alive. A voice would come to him at night and tell him to do these things. At first he resisted, knowing it was bad luck to make animals suffer. As he got older, the voice became impossible to ignore.

Barik was beginning to understand One-Eye, the best hunter he had ever known. Although the bushman was very dangerous, Barik saw he was not smart and could be influenced, even manipulated — until his foolish sister had torched the tent and sent them running for their lives in the dead of winter. That had ruined everything.

Naali… his little sister. She was becoming stranger by the day. He realized he did not know her. She would become a young woman soon and he would know her even less.

His thoughts turned to the lion encounter that morning. How had she learned to spirit-travel? Speaking with animals was an ancient skill only shamans possessed. Was she a shaman? Shaman were old men and women, not girls who have not had their first bleed. His anger rose when he recollected how she took over their meeting with the band in the morning, leaving him only to fill in details.

I am the older brother. I should have spoken - not her, not a girl-child.

He closed his eyes and evaluated their chances of survival.

107

The band had little food, and he could see from how gaunt they looked they were near starvation. They travelled the Flat Plain during the Dark Days when they should have been resting in a winter camp. Hunger was making decisions and, so far, Wolf Band had seen only trouble and bad luck.

But what choice did he have but to stay? There was no going back to One-Eye. He would never believe the tent-burning was solely Naali's doing. He closed his eyes and felt a familiar darkness descend around him. As he lay there, he heard the voice in his head whispering something. The same voice that told him to torture hares, skin fish alive. He tried to push it from his head, but it did not leave.

Eyak Chooses Her Place

Khon told Naali and Barik they were guests of Wolf Band until they could be returned to *Shih* Band, their own people. They accepted the offer, knowing there was no other way. They were children and would never survive the tundra-steppe alone. Barik had yet to kill a grasseater. They had no weapon, shelter, food or tools of their own. It was a simple choice: stay with Wolf Band - or die.

They packed their sleeping beds and broke camp along with the others the next morning. The band slowly crossed the Flat Plain as the light lasted longer with each passing day. They hauled the camp through meadows of waist-deep snow and over lakes covered in deep hard drifts, they wove around broad stands of willow shrubs, but they did not cross a single grasseater trail. At night the women sewed skins for a second tent, using all of the remaining raw hides. The men continually fashioned new stone points or shaped and smoothed hunting darts, waiting for the day they could be useful again.

One day Eyak stumbled in the snow and could not continue. She had been slowing down, arriving at camp later each evening. The band stopped moving while the women gave Eyak warm broth and words of encouragement. She rose and continued walking, but the next day she collapsed again. As she lay on her back staring blankly into the grey sky, Assan knelt down next to her. This time, there were no encouraging words.

"Rest here, Eyak," Assan said as she removed the old woman's pack. Her sister's breathing was uneven, and when Old Woman tried to stand her legs simply gave way. The other women gathered around, aware something important was happening.

"We must make camp here," Assan said to the men. But it was still early and they had travelled only a short distance.

Eyak spoke. "No, you keep moving. I will rest here and follow." She waved them on toward the horizon. "I will come," she said, but there was little confidence in her voice. Assan glanced at Khon. He was watching Eyak kindly. Assan understood what her sister was saying.

Eyak has chosen her last place on earth.

Everyone felt the gravity of the moment as they silently stood by, their eyes on Old Woman. She had been part of their lives for as long as they could remember. Kazan saw the sorrow on his mother's face.

Are we are leaving her here to die?

He felt a sudden pang of loss. He had never known a day Eyak was not part of. She had held him when he had cried. She had healed his cuts and scrapes; poured him drink and served him his food everyday.

We cannot leave her here.

Khon pulled a bladder of broth from inside his parka and handed it to Eyak. "Drink, *Shanagàn.* Come soon, when you are strong. Our trail is easy to follow. There will be food and shelter waiting for you." He touched her head gently and tightened his harness.

One by one the women approached Old Woman. They caressed her cheek and murmured words of encouragement. Assan was last. She bent down, raising her sister's face to hers and kissed her wrinkled forehead. "*Shanagàn,* my sister," she whispered. "You have always made my life easier. You will always be in my heart. Come when you are strong. I will have a tea to warm your bones."

Eyak reached into the neck of her parka, pulled an ivory necklace out and dropped it into Assan's hand. Assan looked down at the carved ivory figure of a wolf and gripped Eyak's hand, not wanting to let go.

"You are cold. I will bring you another coat," she said as she turned to the sled.

"No." Eyak raised her hand and reached inside her pack for a small sack. "Take the medicine. I have told you all I know of

110

medicine ways."

Assan hesitated. "I will carry it for now. You will rest here and follow. We will find grasseaters and make camp."

Eyak nodded as she looked into Assan's eyes. "Go."

Assan smiled a last time. Then she turned and without another word walked away. The others slowly followed.

Kazan waited until the others were moving. He turned to Eyak, holding back the tears filling his eyes.

"You will be a hunter," she said, turning her eyes away. He kissed the top of her hat and walked away. When he looked back, Eyak was sitting up with her arms wrapped around her shoulders. A little later snow began to fall, and when he looked again he could no longer see her.

Eyak unfolded a small caribou skin from her pack and laid it on the snow. She sat on it, crossed her legs and closed her eyes. She was not afraid.

It is time.

She removed all her clothing until she was sitting naked. As she drank her broth, a sudden chill overwhelmed her. Soon she was shivering uncontrollably, the feeling in her arms and legs gone. She looked at her hands resting on her lap; she was no longer able to raise them to her shoulders. Her mind slipped in and out of a dreamless sleep. Sometime later Eyak woke and saw her clothes covered by the falling snow.

Why are my clothes there?

She tried to reach for her parka but her arms would not respond.

In a dreamy fog, she suddenly realized she was alone. She vaguely remembered watching the band disappear into the whiteness. Which way had they gone? Why had they left her here?

"I must follow... I am *Shanagàn*..." she whispered. She heard the wind blowing but she could not feel it. She felt only peaceful warmth surging through her, as if her skin were on fire. Then the dream came:

She is a young girl. Her mother is sitting beside her, showing her how to make stone knives. The tent is warm and Eyak can feel the pleasant heat of the fire across the small of her back. There is a gentle softness to her mother's calloused hands as she slowly turns the stone flake in Eyak's fingers.

"This is where to strike. Feel the spot. Raise the stone. Strike down on it, quick."

Eyak's fingers press down on the flake, feeling the depression.

"It will break when you hit it right."

Her mother takes the other hand and places the stone in it. Eyak knows how to strike with a stone. She has watched her mother make knives many times, but this is the first time she will try it. Eyak raises her arm and looks up at her mother, who nods. She strikes but misses the spot; her blow glances off the unbroken flake. Her mother is smiling.

"Again."

Eyak raises her arm and strikes once more, her eyes fixed on the surface of the flake. This time a sharp "Ping" rings through the tent. The other women stop what they are doing and look at her. She is holding up a shard of broken chert.

Her mother's voice is strong, proud. "That is the sound of making a blade."

Eyak woke a last time and opened her eyes. She was lying on her back covered in falling snow. She tried to sweep it from her face, but her body was peacefully still and calm. Old Woman stared into the deepening blackness and dreamed no more.

Ts'îivii

The death of Eyak seemed to add an enormous emotional weight to the band. They rarely spoke as they pulled the sled, their grief over the loss of their *Shanagàn* overwhelming. Their night camps were sombre places filled with silence and sorrow. Eyak had been so much a part of their daily lives the men and women were at a loss as to what to do or say. She had been one of the strongest voices at their evening meetings, ready to give advice and share her knowledge on any topic. Her hands were a constant presence around the cooking fire, her tongue ever testing steaming meals.

As the sun rose earlier and fell later each day, the band's mood began to improve. They were moving east, and a low hill began to appear out of the plain. Their excitement increased each day until one evening they were standing at the bottom of the knoll. It was low, but they knew the view of the Flat Plain would be a great advantage for hunting grasseaters.

The men collected their hunting weapons and walked single file up the slope through the heavy snow. When they reached the top they spread out, checking the views of the surrounding plain. Kazan was looking west to their travelled route when he heard Dat'san shouting; he was pointing down at something on the other side of the hill. He ran over, expecting to see a herd of grasseaters. But Dat'san was not pointing to grasseaters. He was looking at a thin stand of stunted trees nestled at the base of the knoll. The trees were green, like summer willow. The colour looked out of place against the white winter landscape they knew.

"*Ts'îivii, Ts'îivii!*" Chii Tsal shouted as he joined Dat'san and Kazan. The other men arrived and descended into the trees, inspecting the trunks straight and thick as a man's arm, wide branches covered in slender green leaves and the tops higher than two men. Kazan watched his father cut away the bark and chew a

113

knot of frozen sap. Kazan did the same, spitting out the unpleasant taste of the pitch as it met his tongue. He followed Khon through the trees, watching him rub the trunks with his mitt.

"It is *Ts'íivii* – spruce," he said, turning to his son. "I have not seen the always-green trees since I was a young boy." He waved Kazan over closer and pointed to a trunk. "Our fathers made lion spears with *Ts'íivii*."

Kazan watched a thin smile break across his father's weathered face. "We will camp. There is good luck here. Do your young bones feel the good luck?"

Kazan nodded but felt only the excitement in his father's voice.

A little later the tents were sitting among the stand of spruce, the fires billowing smoke high into the star-filled sky. Inside the tents, the air was warm and comfortable. Despite the small food rations, the conversation was animated and enthusiastic for the first time since Eyak's death.

Chii Tsal said that finding a stand of *Ts'íivii* was a great gift. Although most of the band had never seen always-green trees, they knew about spruce medicine from long-ago stories. As fuel, the always-green wood burned hot and fast. The sticky pitch was good for starting fire. The trunks made strong and light spears, and poles for racks.

When it was Assan's turn to speak she talked about the tree's medicine. Her mother had told her the sticky gum healed wounds. A tea made from the cones and tips of the branches stopped coughing, sore throats and itching. Boiling the green tips inside a tent kept sickness away. The talk went long into the night.

Khon described in detail how lion spears were made from spruce. "A lion spear is longer and stronger than our hunting spears. It is sharpened to a thin point and fire-hardened for days until it cannot break. Here is a story of the lion spear."

Khon sat down and began. "My father told this story from his father. A long time ago, there was a hunter who made a lion spear. One day he saw a great lion approaching and he shook the spear at it, shouting 'Come and taste this lion spear. I made it for you.'

"It came closer and circled the hunter. Seeing an easy kill, the lion spoke to the man. 'I will kill you, but before I do it, you will run for your life. If you are faster than I you will live. If not, you will die in my jaws.'

"The man pretended he was afraid and ran. The lion cannot stop from chasing anything that runs and charged. It was almost on top of the hunter when the man turned. He drove the base of the lion spear into the ground, the tip pointing up, and he waited with both hands on the shaft. The lion was so excited about the kill it did not see the waiting spear. It ran into the sharp point so fast the spear went in its chest and out its back."

A great cheer rose from the band.

Khon continued. "The man stepped aside as the lion fell at his feet. He pulled his spear out of its chest and pushed it into the beast's mouth. Then he said, 'The bite of a spear is more powerful than a lion's teeth.'" Khon paused as the tent erupted in shouts and laughter. "That is a story my father, Kott, told to me and I tell it to you so you will remember." Khon smiled, pleased how well his story was received by the appreciative audience of hungry stomachs.

As Naali listened, she noticed Kazan looking at her. She had seen him looking at her before, glancing away when she met his eye. He sat among the men, which meant he was a hunter. But he was a boy, no older than she. He was already much taller than all the men but for his father. She had noticed how easily he could move through snow while everyone else struggled on shorter legs.

He walks like a wolf.

Naali looked for her brother. Assan was talking to him, rolling a spruce cone in her hands. Barik took the spruce cone from her and looked down at it, nodding with interest. He had hardly spoken to Naali since they had joined Wolf Band; he was

115

always talking to the others, especially the women. Like Naali, he willingly did his share of camp chores.

Why will he not speak to me?

Naali turned her attention back to the conversation in the tent. Khon was speaking. "*Ts'iivii* are a gift we cannot pass up," he said, lifting a green bough. "This is a good place for Winter Camp. There is wood and shelter for tents in the trees from the winds of Flat Plain. The hill gives us a view of the land. Only grasseaters are missing. It is time to wait for animals to come to our hunting darts. The always-green trees are a good omen - the first we have seen since before the winter came. We do not have a medicine person to say more. It is a good place to camp." He sat down, waiting for others to speak.

Each hunter spoke, agreeing the hill was a good viewpoint to see out onto the plain.

Assan spoke next, saying they were getting too weak to travel farther and the trees were an omen. "I do not know the ways of grasseaters, but we cannot search for their spirits. We do not have the strength. The always-green trees are telling me we must wait."

"How much meat is there," Chii Tsal said, his eyes on Naali and Barik, "now that we have two more mouths to feed?"

Assan raised her hand and spread her fingers wide. "Five days if we are careful. There is bone grease but little meat." She tried to sound optimistic, but they all knew it was too little. If grasseaters did not come, they would starve here.

"There are *Geh* and *Daagoo* trails here," Barik offered. "We will snare hare and ptarmigan while we wait for grasseaters." Kazan looked at him, wishing *he* had spoken about snaring. But Kazan had never talked at a meeting of the band. He wished he had Barik's confidence.

By the end of the evening, they had chosen to stay and wait for grasseaters to come to the hill where *Ts'iivii* was telling them there was good luck awaiting Wolf Band.

116

Dream-travelling

The dream is vivid, revealing details of a shimmering snowy landscape bathed in a yellow light. Naali sees the ground below as if she is a bird flying high in the sky. She flies out beyond the hill, the vast plain a patchwork of shrub tundra and grass meadows. Soon grasseaters begin to appear. There are small bands of horses at first, and then many caribou are moving across the windblown plateau, away from the hill with the always-green trees.

She is uncertain what to do. She remembers dream-travel stories, how dreamers coax grasseaters to waiting hunters. She does not know how to turn animals around, to make them go the way she wishes them to. Voices swirl, some vaguely human and some animal. A voice speaks but she does not understand the words. Then she remembers.

Long ago caribou and humans were close. Each Vadzaih had a human heart and every human had a caribou heart. Because of this, humans and caribou always knew what the other was thinking. She finds a word that is clear and understandable in the swirl of noises. The grasseaters are talking about lichen, winter food — Vadzaih zhii. There are so many Vadzaih speaking she becomes lost in a confusion of voices. She tries to enter their thoughts but they are too busy chewing on lichens. She is about to give up when she sees an old cow standing apart from the others. Naali scoops a handful of thick lichens from the snow and shows it to the cow.

"There is a much lichen over there," she says, pointing to the hill in the distance. She can feel the caribou's heart beating beneath her own parka. The cow knows what Naali is thinking and she is suspicious.

"If I go there humans will kill me."

"We need only a few grasseaters. There are many in your herd. Like Vadzaih, humans must eat, too."

"You say the hill has much lichen."

117

"I have never seen lichen so thick."

"If I go, how will I not be killed?"

Naali knows Vadzaih cannot be lied to because each shared the other's heart.

"Go first and then move to the back of the herd when you reach the hill. You will not be harmed."

The cow is convinced and moves toward the hill, calling to the others to follow. She is old and they listen to her.

Naali's spirit enters the cow and sees the world through the animal's eyes. She sees the hill and the smoke rising high into the air behind the ridge. On the hilltop people are standing up, looking down at her. She slows and lets the herd pass, watching the caribou moving up the slope. The cow turns away and Naali can no longer see the hill.

Naali woke in a sweat, her heart pounding. She was out of her bed but still burning up in the cold air. She looked up to the ceiling. How long had she been dreaming? She held her breath and listened, expecting to hear a great herd of caribou bearing down on camp. But there was only silence. She was exhausted from the powerful dream. As her body cooled down, she slipped back inside her bed, a faint taste of lichen on her tongue.

The Prophecy

Kazan, wrapped in a thick bison robe, was sitting on top of the hill watching the morning light gather on the horizon. Khon was beside him, asleep. Kazan's excitement built as he scanned the plain. He was hoping to be the first to see grasseaters. He heard something moving and turned to see Naali standing behind him. He nodded to her and then turned his attention back to the plain. She stood there for a long time without speaking as he grew more nervous. He had not spoken to her since she had joined Wolf Band.

Naali broke the awkward silence. "They are coming."

Her voice woke Khon and he turned to her. "What? What comes?" he asked sleepily.

"*Vadzaih.*"

Khon rubbed his eyes and looked over the plain. There was nothing but snow and ice and windswept ground.

"Where?"

"There," she said, pointing north.

"I see nothing," Khon said, getting to his feet.

"*Vadzaih* come," Naali said calmly as she turned and walked back to camp.

Khon and Kazan stood and watched the Flat Plain as the light gathered. They walked around the hill, checking the different views below, but they saw nothing moving. Finally, Khon shook his head and motioned Kazan to return to camp.

That afternoon Kazan was standing in the trees checking snares when he heard whistling coming from the top of hill. He looked up and saw Chii Tsal shaking his spear above his head, signalling the other hunters to come quickly.

"Grasseaters!" Kazan shouted to no one. He scrambled through the trees and ran through camp, passing Naali, who was looking up at the hill.

She said grasseaters would come!

119

The women had heard Chii Tsal's whistling and were looking up at him. Kazan grabbed his throwing darts and ran for the hill. When he reached the top he could scarcely believe his eyes. Hundreds of caribou were milling around Chii Tsal, who was kneeling over a dead cow. Chii Tsal pulled a hunting dart from the cow's neck, hooked it into his throwing board and threw it again, hitting a second cow. Kazan raced forward and hurled his dart, but in the excitement it went wide. Caribou continued to mill and prance about on the top of the hill, their eyes wide and noses lifting in the air.

As Kazan fixed a second projectile, a dart whistled by his head and slammed into a calf, driving it off its feet. Khon ran past him, pulling another hunting dart from his quiver. The herd suddenly panicked, streaming down the slopes in every direction. Kazan gave chase, leaping down the hill through the deep snow in long strides. Near the bottom he caught up with a straggling bull and knocked it down with a dart. As the wounded animal struggled to escape, Kazan killed it with his club. He ran back up the hill, exhilarated by his second grasseater kill. On his way up, he saw Barik following a cow carrying a dart deep in her side. When he reached the top of the hill, Barik was clubbing her.

"A good kill," Kazan shouted as he ran by. "Your first grasseater!"

Barik looked at him strangely. "How would you know a good kill? How many grasseaters have you killed?"

Kazan stopped running, surprised by the remark. Pretending he had not heard the insult, he helped Barik turn the carcass over for butchering. Then he quickly left, feeling both embarrassed and angry.

The hunters had been busy. Six caribou lay on the snow. They whooped and shouted, embracing each other. They called to Kazan and Barik and embraced them, congratulating Barik on his first grasseater kill. Then the butchering began. Kazan returned to his kill at the bottom of the hill and drew his knife. He looked
120

toward camp and saw Naali still gazing up at the hill.

She had dream-travelled grasseaters. She knew.

Eagle and Fox

The white fox is moving up the ridge through a broad meadow of powder snow. She stops, her ears cocked forward. Soft sounds are coming from somewhere under the snow, close. She stands completely still, watching the trackless snow ahead. Every muscle in her body is poised. She waits patiently, trying to pinpoint what is barely audible. She feels vibrations beneath her and springs into the air, driving her feet down into the snow. A flock of snow-white ptarmigan erupts from hidden beds, filling the sky with their beating wings. The flock glides low over the ground, twisting and turning, landing far down the mountain slope. The fox has a mouthful of feathers but no bird. She walks into the beds, sniffing the small craters that moments ago were filled with prey. She pushes her nose into a pile of dung, still warm and moist. Leaving the empty beds, she continues hunting the snow to the top of the ridge.

As she reaches the crest, a great force smashes into her side. She tumbles down the slope, caught in a frenzy of feathers. Thick talons dig into her spine and her backbone snaps under the pressure of the eagle's grip. She twists her head around, but the eagle's foot is clamped on her head, holding her snapping jaws away. The talons slowly tighten, breaking her ribs and puncturing her lungs.

The eagle and fox roll and tumble down the mountainside, coming to a stop at the base of a large boulder. The paralyzed fox lies sprawled on the snow. The eagle flaps its wing, shifting its grip until the fox is no longer breathing.

On the other side of the boulder, a wolf pup is wakened by sounds from the slope above. He looks up to see something tumbling toward him. He stumbles back a few steps and barks as the thing comes to rest. A fox is lying motionless on the snow, an eagle standing on its back as it flaps its wings. The eagle covers the fox with its wings and fluffs its head feathers up, staring at the pup in defiant ownership.

The pup watches the bird until his curiosity wins out. As he approaches, the eagle releases the fox and hops on the snow to face him but soon loses its nerve. It flaps its wings and skips over the surface of the snow until it finds lift. As it gains elevation, it catches a breeze along the mountain slope and soars high, circling the fox.

The wolf gently nudges the dead fox, gripping the limp body in his jaws. He carries it to the boulder and drops it between his feet. Turning the carcass over, the wolf opens the gut and pulls out the liver, warm and rich in blood. Not far away, his pack is sleeping, oblivious of the pup's private meal.

Hours later Blue and Grey-Eye are moving down the dark mountain. As they pass the pup, they smell the fox. He stands ready to follow them, but Blue turns him back with a low growl. When the pup wakes the next morning, he finds his parents are gone. He joins the other wolves as they wait.

Two days later Blue and Grey-Eye return. The pack greets them excitedly, leaping and jumping onto their backs. Both adults growl and snap at their young with affection. There is a new scent on Grey-Eye that excites a young male. He approaches his mother, but Blue stands in front of him and growls. The other wolves circle their parents, sniffing at the exciting scent, eager to

123

begin travelling again. But Blue and Grey-Eye are exhausted from days of mating. Inside Grey-Eye's womb, a new litter of young is beginning. She slips behind a rock, lies down and sleeps in peace. Blue finds a quiet place beside her. The wolves return to their snow beds and wait patiently to be taken to prey.

Naali Reveals Her Power

For three days the caribou came in waves. The hunters could hardly keep up with the killing, butchering and processing of meat and skins. On the fourth day the herd moved off to the east, disappearing onto the high plateau. Khon stood alone outside his tent in the early light of dawn, taking stock of the hunt. The meat was stored under snow mounds around the camp. Slabs of frozen hides were stacked beside makeshift racks already heavy with skins curing over smudge fires. White smoke coiled high in the air, wafting through the trees. He pulled down his hood and surveyed the camp. It was the greatest hunt of his life. Last night Chii Tsal had named it Came-to-a-Hill Hunt. They had been saved from starvation. Still, Khon's jubilation was mixed with unease.

How had the girl known grasseaters would come? They had not seen them anywhere on the plain that morning. His eyes were still good, and Kazan's were sharper than most. They could not have missed seeing such a large herd. But Naali had known they were coming before she saw them - in a dream, perhaps. It was the only explanation.

Khon considered what this meant. If Naali could dream-travel, she had a special gift. She could locate animals and speak with their spirits. But how could this be? She was a still a girl, the same age as Kazan. How could she know dream-travel? Tarin had not dream-travelled such a large herd of grasseaters. They had come to the hill as she had said they would. The girl has great power, he thought.

Khon knew stories of other medicine women who could dream-travel, but all were older. He decided he would have to get to know Naali better.

The band was finishing their morning meal, the relief of enough food written on everyone's faces and in the bright voices that filled the tents. Naali was busy collecting bowls when Khon motioned her to follow him outside. She slipped on her parka and found him kneeling by the drying racks, stoking the embers of the smudge fire. She waited for him to speak.

He stood and looked past her, his eyes fixed on the top of the hill. "How did you know?" he asked.

Naali looked up at him, hesitating. She could hardly believe what she had done herself. How could anyone else understand? Collecting courage, she replied, "I dream-travelled."

"You dreamed this?" he said, pointing to many racks of grasseater skins.

She nodded.

"You dream-travelled and brought grasseaters to the hill?"

She nodded again.

"How did you bring them here?"

"I spoke to a cow *Vadzaih*. I said the best lichens were here, on the hill. She led the others to them."

Khon was astonished. He had never before asked details of a dream-traveller. "How did you speak to her? What language?"

"I do not remember the dream language. When I am awake I cannot remember the words."

He nodded, and Naali saw Khon was not challenging her. He believed her.

"I could not keep them all moving. Some turned back. There were too many," she added, matter-of-factly.

Khon was delving into shaman ways he did not understand. He was a hunter, not a medicine man. He did not need or want to know more about the underworld of animal spirits.

"I do not dream-travel, but I have seen its power. But none stronger than Came-to-a-Hill Hunt."

He looked down at her, nodding at the tent. "The band must know, but this is not the time." He turned and disappeared inside the tent. Naali watched him go. Somewhere beyond the hill a wolf howled, and then another one answered far off. Came-to-a-Hill Hunt had been found.

The processing of animals went on for two moons. Assan organized the women in teams cutting and drying meat, collecting brains for use in tanning, scraping and washing skins, stripping sinew, and boiling bones. They cut meat in long strips, hanging the pieces on racks above the smoking fires. The women turned the strips twice a day, wrapped the dried pieces in hides and stamped them into thin jerky. The best skins were tanned with hair on for winter clothes. They smoke-tanned the hides to a nut-brown colour for men's clothes, while the women's clothes were not smoked and left the natural white colour.

Came-to-a-Hill Hunt killed many grasseaters, but it took its toll on the store of hunting weapons. Every hunter lost throwing darts in the deep snow, and other darts broke when wounded or dying animals fell. Replacing darts took many days as men collected willows, honing and scraping the wood into smooth, light aftershafts. They split long strips of mammoth ivory and carved new foreshafts. Broken stone points were replaced with new ones until the cache of weapons was replenished. They cut spruce for spears, carving the shafts for balance and strength. Khon and Chii Tsal selected long, straight trees and built lion spears, hardening the tips in hot coals for several days.

Both Barik and Kazan killed three grasseaters each during Came-to-a-Hill Hunt. Kazan was a faster runner, but his throw was not as powerful as Barik's dart delivery. The two boys did not speak, sharing nothing of their hunts.

Kazan grew more interested in Barik's sister but was too shy to speak with her. She had become a part of the team of women processing the skins and meat and spent little time with the men. He asked his father how she knew about the grasseaters, but Khon refused to speak about it. He suspected she must possess spirit power, but he had no idea what that meant.

A few days after the hunt, Kazan spoke to her for the first time. He was checking snares when he saw her coming up his snow trail, heading for camp with an armload of willow. As she approached, he pretended not to notice her and bent down to search for a snare. She stopped in his path and stood in awkward silence.

"Are you checking snares?" she asked, knowing the question needed no answer.

"Yes."

"Good luck."

He nodded weakly and watched her pass by. When she was a few steps away he suddenly said what had been on his mind since the first morning of Came-to-a-Hill Hunt. "How did you know grasseaters were coming?"

Naali turned and look at him. "I dream-travelled," she said, adjusting the load of wood in her arms.

"Did you bring them — to the hill? Did you dream-travel with them?"

She paused. "It was a *Vadzaih*. I helped her."

Naali waited for another question, but Kazan was now lost for words.

"Do you believe me?"

"Yes." He reached out and took the load of wood from her and they walked back to camp without speaking. Kazan's heart sang like a robin in spring.

The Den

Grey-Eye lowers her head into the frozen ground, inhaling faint smells that bring back the memory of pups she has raised in the dark hole. Her last litter is standing behind her, now fully matured. Inside her womb, new pups are growing, and the need to prepare a birth den dominates everything she does. The sloping meadow is close to the river for drinking, and she has a good view of the shore in all directions. She begins excavating the old hole, scraping and trimming the entrance so it is just wide enough for her to squeeze into. Grey-Eye squirms her way down the narrow tunnel until she reaches the birthing chamber. She lies down in the comfortable scent of her dark home and soon falls asleep.

When she wakes a little later she finds her pack has left. She circles the snowy meadow, recalling resting areas where her pups played in other summers and the low scrape in the ground where she slept many days in the warm sun. A bleached caribou skull lies on the ground among ragged tufts of meadow grass. She sniffs it and then moves toward the river, turning over a bison leg partly covered in snow. She remembers both kills the same way she remembers every kill she has made in her life. Satisfied with her den choice, she finds her pack's scent and follows it to the river ice, where they are sprawled out. Broken-Tail walks out to greet her, licking at her face with affection. Grey-Eye's tail instinctively rises, signalling she is still the dominant female, as she walks by. The other wolves stand, waiting for their mother to join them.

Nehtr'uh Melts

The snow beneath Khon's mukluk was soft and wet. The days had suddenly turned warm - much too warm. The south slopes were already melting, and much earlier than he could remember. He was standing among the hunters at the top of the hill. The sky was cloudless and the Flat Plain shone silver-bright as far as he could see. It was so warm none of the men wore their mitts. They had talked the previous night and agreed they must move immediately or be stranded in the spring on ground they did not know.

Khon turned, pointing north to a large range of snow-white mountain peaks. "That way is ice and snow. We do not know those mountains for grasseaters." He shifted to face east, where a rolling plateau stretched far on the horizon. "We have never scouted there and know nothing of grasseater summer ground." Khon looked west over the Flat Plain and shook his head. "We found no grasseaters on Flat Plain and cannot return there." Finally, he looked south toward a distant range of mountains. He looked at Chii Tsal.

"It is the only way," Chii Tsal said. "We scouted beyond the *Ch'oodèenjik* River last summer and found many herds of elk, bison and caribou. There are shrubs and mammoth bones for building shelters. That is the way."

"To reach *Ch'oodèenjik* we must go up onto the plateau," Chii Tsal said, pointing east. "We will travel during night when the snow is hard-crusted and the skins can slide easily. If we have good luck, we can reach the river before the ice is running." He carved a rudimentary map in the snow, showing the route. "After we cross we must travel fast to the mountains before summer comes. *Nehtr'uh* shows us the land will stay warm until next winter."

When the warm days had begun, Chii Tsal had carved a snow sculpture in the shape of a wolverine and placed it next to
130

the fire. As the first drop melted off the nose, he toppled it into the flames - an annual ritual the band performed to keep the land cold for fast travelling. But *Nehtr'uh* failed to bring back cold days. As the days grew warmer, the band grew more anxious to move from the Flat Plain.

They were caught on the Flat Plain because it had taken much longer than they had expected to deal with the outcome of Came-to-a-Hill Hunt. They had killed too many grasseaters.

Chii Tsal showed his growing impatience. "The more we speak the later we cross *Ch'oodèenjik*." He lifted his spear to his shoulder and went down to camp. The men watched him disappear. Chii Tsal had warned them they needed to break camp more than a moon ago or they would miss the crossing. But they could not leave good meat and skins behind. Wasting a grasseater was unthinkable, bad luck. No one could have known the warm days would come so early.

The men walked together to the far side of the hill, plotting their route. Once they reached the high plateau, their course would swing directly south toward the Porcupine River. Kazan studied the planned route, but his mind was elsewhere as they walked down the hill.

Kazan knew enough about band ways to understand they could not have left sooner. The Wolf band used everything: the meat, the bones, the hide, the hair, the blood and the organs of every killed animal. He turned his face to the sun. Soon the chorus of bird song and the drone of mosquitoes would fill the spring air. He hurried along and fell into line behind his father, who was in deep thought as the hunters arrived in camp.

They broke camp, and by early evening the snow had hardened enough to support the skin sleds. They travelled through the long evening light, stopping the next morning when the sun had softened the snow and the sled slowly bogged down. It took two long nights to reach the plateau and better snow. In many places they had to carry the sleds over open creeks and sinking

131

bogs. On the plateau, the trail of Wolf Band swung toward the low hills of Porcupine River.

Zhòh is Born

Grey-Eye bites the slick membrane off with her incisors, freeing the female and the last of her six pups from the birth sack. She swallows the bloody membrane and licks the sticky fluid from the pup's body. When she is finished cleaning, Grey-Eye lifts the female onto her milky belly, where she squirms among her five suckling brothers. The female pushes them aside until she finds her mother's teat. Thick warm milk flows into her mouth.

Grey-Eye sleeps lightly in the dark of the cool den, waking now and again to retrieve a pup that has slid off her belly or re-position one that cannot locate her teats. She licks at their rumps, stimulating them to defecate, and eats the tiny feces, keeping the den spotless. One day she wakes to find a dead pup beside her. She eats it and falls back asleep.

In two weeks the pups' eyes are fully open. They stumble around in the dark on wobbly legs, exploring the corners of the chamber before returning to the warm comfort of their mother's abdomen. The female pup is the first to venture out of the tunnel and outside. She stumbles out of the hole and is blinded by the bright light. Broken-Tail, her yearling sister from the previous litter, promptly nudges her back into the safety of the den.

Some days later the pups have grown and have all made their way out of the den. They are mobile and full of play. The female nips at her brothers and dodges their playful attacks, unaware this is preparing them for a life among their own kind and learning the early skills of killing. Broken-Tail appears on the meadow from the willows, regurgitating a mash of freshly digested meat. The pups scramble for the smelly offering, scarfing down the meal.

A little later the female pup is basking in the sun when she is woken by a sound. Springing to her feet, she looks apprehensively toward the river. The ice shifts, grinding and twisting until it convulses with a thunderous crack. It shatters, and suddenly everything is moving. She scrambles down the den with the rest of her yelping littermates.

One day the pups are following Grey–Eye across the meadow. A pup stops and pushes his head into a ground–squirrel burrow as a shadow flashes above. Grey–Eye turns to see an eagle swoop down, snatch the pup in its thick, yellow talons and fly off. She runs after it but the eagle is already flying low over the river with the hapless pup dangling beneath. Grey–Eye quickly collects her four pups and sends them scurrying down into the den.

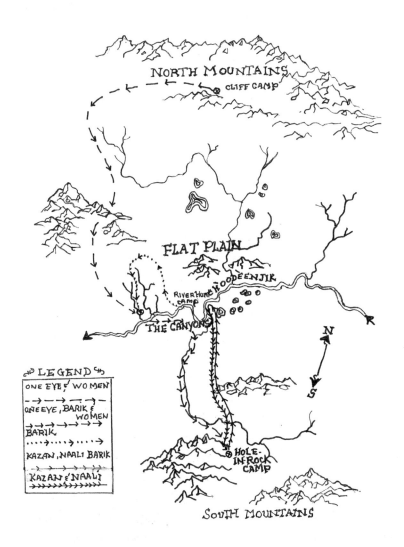

NORTH MOUNTAINS

CLIFF CAMP

FLAT PLAIN

OODEENJIK

RiverHunt
Camp

THE CANYONS

N

S

R

LEGEND

ONE EYE, WOMEN

ONE EYE, BARIK &
WOMEN

BARIK

KAZAN, NAALI BARIK

KAZAN & NAALI

HOLE-
IN-ROCK
CAMP

SOUTH MOUNTAINS

PART 3

DAII: BREAK-UP

Running Ice

They knew the *Ch'oodèenjik* was running ice before they saw the river. Wolf Band was moving up a steep ridge when a flock of ducks flew low over the top. Black ducks - *Njàa* - were the earliest waterfowl arrivals, timing their return to the first open water. When the band reached the top of the ridge they saw the brown, ice-choked *Ch'oodèenjik* flowing in the broad valley below.

All eyes were on the running river as they voiced their collective disappointment. Khon searched for ice bridges to cross, but there was only flowing ice as far as he could see. The mountains, and their destination, were far off, shimmering in the misty spring air, and out of reach until the river ice cleared so they could safely cross. Dejected, the silent band descended the valley to the river shore, stopping at the mouth of a smaller river that joined the *Ch'oodèenjik*. The band shed their harnesses and stood looking out over the chaos of ice floes tumbling downstream.

"We are late," Chii Tsal finally said, sighing deeply. "We should have left Came-to-a-Hill earlier. We would be across *Ch'oodèenjik*."

Khon knew there was no point arguing with his brother. He had been thinking about what to do if the river was open since they left the hill. They could not turn back to the Flat Plain without knowing if grasseaters summered there.

"We wait for the ice to clear. then we cross with a skin

boat."

"Why not stay here for the summer?" Jovan asked.

"We have not scouted the *Ch'oodèenjik* in summer," replied Khon. "We know there are grasseaters in the South Mountains."

"It will take us days to build a boat and many trips to carry us over to the other side," Chii Tsal said.

Khon nodded, pointing to the heavy thickets of willows lining the river shore. "There is wood here, and we have skins to build a boat. When the river clears we cross and make travel frames and move to the mountains. We have food enough."

"It is a long way - too far," Chii Tsal argued. "It will take us all summer to reach good ground."

"The band is strong. We cannot summer in a place we have not scouted," Khon answered. "Chii Tsal, you are our best boat maker. We have skins and there is enough willow wood here to make the frame. How many days to build the boat?"

Chii Tsal went down to the river edge and surveyed the channel, assessing the current and the distance across. He shrugged and headed into the willows, rubbing his thickly calloused hands on the smooth bark while the band unloaded the sled and prepared camp.

Left Behind

Blue's hunger is growing as he paces the willows behind the den. Broken-Tail watches her father preparing to hunt as he moves in and out of the shrubs. A little later she hears him howling somewhere down the river. Then he is back, pacing the meadow and howling, announcing his departure. Broken-Tail joins his howling, bringing Grey-Eye and the curious pups out from the hole in the ground. She stretches, yawns and finds the pups are already wrestling with Broken-Tail, nipping at her feet and pulling her tail. Other wolves are scattered at the edge of the meadow, enjoying the shade out of the warm sun. They stand and grow excited, knowing there is to be a hunt. Moments later the whole pack is barking and howling. Blue walks to the far end of the meadow and disappears. The five pups scramble behind Grey-Eye as she follows Blue. When she reaches the willows she stops and nudges them back, growling clear instructions to stay.

Broken-Tail arrives and herds the pups back toward the den. She finds her favourite resting place and lies down as they climb over her back, chewing playfully at her neck and legs. After a while the pups tire of wrestling and wander around the meadow in search of Grey-Eye, but she is nowhere to be found. They return to chewing on Broken-Tail until she pushes them down into the den, where they fall asleep, exhausted.

By evening, Broken-Tail's hunger overwhelms her pup-caring duties. She slips out of the den and disappears into the shrubs on the scent of her pack. The female pup emerges from the hole and sits whimpering at the entrance. The dusky meadow is silent except for the thin song of a lone grey-cheeked thrush: "Wheeoo-titi-wheeoo phreu."

A Warning

The men went to work splitting the hard willow trunks and shaping the gunnels, thwarts and frame while the women stretched and sewed the skin covering for the boat. The children collected wood and speared fish in pools along the shore as the ice continued to run.

Kazan and Aron stood above a deep, dark pool with forked spears, waiting to add another grayling to their catch of fish. Behind them the sound of stone axes rang out. A shadow darted out from under the ice; Kazan thrust his spear down but missed the large fish. Aron moved along the shore, his spear ready to stab at anything he might frighten out into the pool. As Kazan waited with his spear poised, he heard footsteps.

Naali was walking along the shore, carrying a load of firewood. She did not notice Kazan or Aron, although Kazan was easily seen. She seemed distracted as she turned into a stand of willows where Khon was cutting ribs for the boat.

Kazan heard them talking, but he was too far away to hear the conversation. He thought a meeting between Khon and Naali was odd. A sudden splash turned his attention back to the fishing. Aron was smiling, a pike twisting on the end of his spear. Kazan nodded to his cousin and readied his spear.

The band had finished the evening meal and were gathered outside around the fire to hear Chii Tsal's report on the boat-building. The main frame had been lashed together with heavy rawhide strips, the bottom ribs were in place, and the large skin cover was sewn and ready to be fitted onto the frame. Tomorrow the seams would be sealed with spruce pitch. Chii Tsal said the boat would be ready in two nights, when the ice should begin to clear from the river. When Chii Tsal was finished, Khon raised his hand to speak.

He began by thanking *Vadzaih* Spirit for coming at a time Wolf Band was most in need of meat. He went on to describe

Came-to-a-Hill Hunt, celebrating the skill of the hunters. He thanked the women who had worked throughout the nights preparing the many skins and drying meat. Then he asked if anyone else wished to speak.

Jovan told them he had seen a caribou milling on the opposite shore but the animals did not enter the ice-choked river. Teekai and Gilgan said they were making milk, and both babies, Jak and Yukaih, were healthy. When no one else raised a hand to speak, Khon looked to Naali. After a few moments she stood and brushed her black hair from her face.

"I am *Shih* Band," she said quietly, "a grateful guest of Wolf Band. I ask permission to speak." It was not customary for children to address a meeting of the band, but no one objected. Khon nodded for her to continue.

Naali swallowed hard. "There is spirit trouble in this place."

It had taken her all day to find the courage to speak. A young girl talking about spirits sounded strange to anyone's ears.

"I feel the spirit trouble here, on this ground. I do not know what spirit is troubled." She was looking into the fire. "I feel it grows stronger. I say this as a warning that we should leave."

The band looked at Naali and then at each other, perplexed and surprised.

"Tarin spoke of a bad spirit at Long-Nose Camp," Khon said. "He warned us the ground was bad. We did not listen, and Yogh and Tarin were killed by lions." He turned to Naali. "Why is the ground bad?" he asked, already knowing the answer.

"Bad spirits come."

"Did you dream this?" Chii Tsal interrupted, his voice unable to conceal his doubt.

"No. I feel it - something is coming."

"Is the river to flood? Should we pack now?" he asked mockingly as he kicked the dirt beneath his feet. "Should we leave the boat, leave the river and run?"

Naali answered him calmly. "Something comes. I do not

140

know what it is or where to go."

"If we all spoke when we had a bad feeling, our tongues would never stop wagging," Chii laughed, looking around the crowd for support. He paused as he considered his next question. "Do you claim to be a medicine woman, a shaman who can see what will happen before it happens?"

Kazan sat listening to Chii Tsal, growing more distressed with his rude tone and questions. It was bad luck to ask someone about their medicine power. It was proper to only listen to the words. Before Naali could answer, Kazan stood to speak.

"Naali dream-travelled. She found grasseaters and brought them to Came-to-a-Hill," he exclaimed, his voice much louder than he had meant. He looked to his father, hoping he had not spoken out of turn, but Khon did not seem concerned by his sudden interruption.

"Naali told us grasseaters were coming," he stammered, "before we could see them." He suddenly felt uncomfortable. He was interrupting Chii Tsal, a respected hunter, his uncle. A boy did not interrupt a hunter while a hunter was talking. As Kazan's face turned red, his father joined in.

"Naali came to Kazan and I the morning of Came-to-a-Hill Hunt," said Khon. "Kazan speaks the truth. She told us grasseaters were coming. We saw nothing there on the Flat Plain. No tracks, no grasseaters. That same day grasseaters came. Many." He waited a few moments. "Naali dream-travelled grasseaters and brought them to our darts and spears. I do not know of a shaman with such dream-travel power. But I believe Naali if she feels there are dangerous spirits here."

Assan stood and glared at Chii Tsal, her lips drawn tight. "If we do not believe in signs, then Wolf Band will not live. If Naali says she dream-travels, who can question her? Are you a dream-traveller, Chii Tsal? A shaman? Do you see things that will happen? Do you know her warning is false, or do you only hope it is so?"

Assan's voice softened. "Spirit knowledge knows no age,"

141

she said to Naali. "I believe your warning. I believe you dream-travel."

Barik sat enthralled by the unexpected conversation. Of course! His sister had medicine! How could he not have realized it? He had seen her speak to a lion, the most powerful of the animal spirits, and make it sleep. And she dream-travelled a herd of grasseaters to Came-to-a-Hill! He raised his hand to speak.

Khon turned to him. "Barik wishes to speak."

"I am *Shih* Band. I ask permission to speak." He did not wait for an answer. "Naali has great power. She has spoken to lions," he said. There was sudden silence. "The day we met Wolf Band, we met the lion that killed your two men. Naali spoke to the killing beast and it lay down with their bones and let us pass safely."

Chii Tsal's disbelief grew. "How does a girl-child speak with lion and dream-travel grasseaters?" he asked, exasperated.

Barik did not wait for Naali to answer. "It is in our blood. Our mother was a medicine woman. She taught Naali and I her ways. I have medicine but not as powerful as Naali's," he added. "We used our power to escape the bushman and cross the Flat Plain in winter. How else could we have lived?"

Naali was stunned.

This is not how my warning was meant!

She had had a disturbing vision the moment she arrived at the river shore. When she told Khon about it, he said the band should hear her warning. Her mother was not a medicine woman! Barik was the furthest from a shaman she could imagine.

Why is he lying? It is untrue. Saran did not teach me to dream-travel. It happened. Barik is not a dream-traveller. Why is he saying this?

Naali realized there was a purpose behind Barik's words, but she did not know what it was. He was still speaking, sounding much older than he was. "I dream-travelled and found your camp on the Flat Plain. That is how we came to you."

142

Naali had to say something. "I do not know why I have medicine!" she declared, staring at Barik. "I do not know why the lion listened to me. I do not know where the words came from or if it was my voice speaking the words. I know that the lion let us pass unharmed." She paused, unable to look at Barik. "We did not dream-travel and find your camp on the Flat Plain. My brother has never spoken to me of his power." She wished for the meeting, the difficult questions and Barik's unexpected lies, to be over.

"Something comes," she said. "I speak this warning because you are generous friends to Barik and I, and I do not wish any harm to come to Wolf Band." She did not look up as she walked away.

They began talking all at once. Chii Tsal leaned over to Khon. "She is a girl. She is too young to dream-travel. There has never been a child who knows dream-travel. Dream-travellers are not children." Khon did not hear Chii Tsal. He stared at the tent wall, a deep chill in his heart.

Assan sat back, her mind shutting out the excitement around her. She could feel the girl had powerful medicine. It shone from her eyes - blue and clear. Khon had told her of Naali's dream-travel at Came-to-a-Hill and of her warning about bad spirits in their camp by the river.

She had the courage to speak of the warning, and the words were of someone older and wiser. Was Eyak's spirit in this young girl watching over them? She wished Eyak was sitting beside her now. She would know what to say. Assan had felt a sudden and disturbing loss when Naali walked away; it was as if an ancient spirit had left.

The discussion to stay or leave continued through the evening. Chii Tsal argued they should not leave. He would need only two days before the boat was worthy, enough time for the river to clear of ice. The frame was finished and only the skins needed to be sealed and cured. After more discussion, some band members decided Naali's dream was confused and would not

143

come true. In the end, all but Khon, Assan, So'tsal and Kazan agreed with Chii Tsal. Kazan knew the boat was important, but he had felt a deep foreboding when Naali left the meeting. He waited a while and followed outside, where he found her sitting on a boulder. She did not look at him when he sat next to her.

"What should we do?" he asked.

"I do not know."

"Is it the river? Is it dangerous to cross? Will the boat sink?"

"I do not know rivers and boats."

"I believe you. You dream-travelled grasseaters to Came-to-a-Hill."

"The others do not believe," Naali said.

"How do you know the spirits are dangerous?"

"I feel it."

They sat together for a while in the waning evening light, watching the river flow by. When Kazan went back to camp and slid into his bed, he could hear Chii Tsal outside, describing in detail the crossing of the *Ch'oodèenjik* in the boat.

Killicki

Kiikiikiikiiii...kiikiikiikiiiii.... kiikiikiikii.

One-Eye heard his name being called from high above. He looked up to see the screaming bird plunging down the cliff face at him. He ducked as the falcon broke out of its swoop just above his head, screaming out over the ice-filled river. He had not heard his name for a long time, not since he was a boy - not since the bad thing happened. The jarring screech of the hawk made the memory come rushing back.

He is walking with a group of boys along a different river, under a different cliff. A mother falcon is screaming sharply - Kiikiikiiikiiikiii - as they pass below the rocky ledge where her young are resting. The boys stop and look up, spotting the blue-grey hawk perched on a spire of rock high on the cliff.

"Ch'ichèe calls Killicki," one of the boys says, laughing at the rhyme. 'Ch'ichèe dares Killicki to take one of her young." He points his spear to the white nestlings high above, laughing loudly.

Killicki laughs with the boys and defiantly waves his spear at the flying bird, thinking the challenge is only a friendly jest. He is younger than the others but much bigger and stronger. They are continually after him to prove his strength. As he laughs they surround him, chanting his name, daring him to climb the rocks.

They are pumping their spears and shouting, "Killicki, Killicki, Ch'ichèe dares Killicki" until he is up on the steep rock face, his fingers wedged into the cracks. He is halfway to the nest when the falcon appears out of nowhere, screeching by only inches away, narrowly missing his face with her outstretched feet. She sails out over the river, furiously beating her wings as she climbs high above the cliff. She swoops and comes at him again and again, just missing his head each time she passes. He presses his face into the rocks, her deafening scream so loud he is shaking, sweating, imagining what will happen if she strikes him. He looks down at the rushing water below. He thinks it too dangerous and

145

he should climb down, but he sees the boys are standing on the shore dancing and shouting his name.

The falcon's attack pattern is always the same. She swoops straight down a vertical cliff face, dips behind a rock outcrop and blasts by above his head. She is so fast he does not see her, feeling only the sudden rush of wind in his hair. He begins to time his climb, scrambling up a few feet and pushing his face against the rocks until she passes and is ascending again. He is relieved when he finally reaches the nest. The thin ledge is in the open and there is no cover above him. He is badly shaken and wants to leave. He looks down to see the boys throwing stones in the river. They have lost interest in the challenge. He will show them.

As he pulls himself onto the narrow ledge, the white nestlings begin to scream and flap their wings excitedly. He snatches one by the back as it thrashes its thick talons and pecks at his hand with its beak. He is turning to show the boys, holding the bird out, when something smashes into his face.

They told him he fell from the cliff and hit the river. The water had saved him. He was unconscious and would have drowned but for the boys hauling him to shore. There was a deep gash across his face. His left eye was gone, plucked out by the falcon's talon.

When Killicki woke, his face was bruised and disfigured and his head throbbed with excruciating pain. He was unable to speak. His mother cleaned his wound and nursed him, but his voice never returned. His father refused to see him, afraid that his voiceless son was a portent of bad luck. In time a thick scar formed across his empty eye socket, leaving him disfigured and ugly.

As time passed the pain in his head did not go away. On bad days, he raged and struck at anyone who came near him. The other boys taunted him and made fun of his scarred face. When he caught one he beat him fiercely.

With only one eye, he could no longer focus well at a distance. He had trouble hitting a target with a throwing dart - an

146

essential skill for any developing hunter. As he grew older, the band began to shun him - an angry, half-blind mute who would never be a hunter. He grew increasingly distant as the years passed.

He was permitted to live near camp but was not welcome in their tents or to take meals with them. For a time, his mother brought him meal scraps, but eventually even those meagre offerings stopped. He lived in a rough lean-to covered in discarded skins and survived by snaring grouse and hares. When the band moved to follow grasseaters he would follow behind, until one day they were gone and he was alone on the tundra-steppe.

The falcon screamed as it dove over One-Eye and flew over the ice-jammed river, jogging him out of his daydream.

Killicki.

He tried to form the name with his tongue but no sounds would come. He felt a deep longing, a pining he had not felt for a very long time. Long ago he had lived with humans. He had a band, a name, a mother and a father. He vaguely remembered them but could no longer see their faces or recall their names.

Killicki felt the uncontrollable anger taking hold again. It did not matter what his name was. It had vanished when they left him alone on the tundra-steppe. He was a bushman, *nanaa'in*, shunned and feared by humans. They had called him *Ch'ihlak Ch'índèe* - One-Eye - and looked away from his disfigured face in disgust. He hated people. He needed no one. When he caught them he used them until they slowed him down or were no longer of use. Then he killed them. He would kill his mother and father if he ever found them.

One-Eye continued working his way up the river, passing through ice-choked willows and flooded meadows. Slabs of fractured ice rushed past in the muddy river. He moved quietly and quickly, stopping often to watch for grasseaters swimming the river or listen for them walking the shore.

He crouched behind a boulder and waited, the sound of ice grinding and scraping against the bank. A little later a caribou floated by on an ice floe. He stood and raised his hunting dart, poised to throw. He could easily hit the caribou, but it was too far out to bring it safely to shore. He lowered his arm, pulled his hood up and waited for something else to kill.

Hunger

Blue rubs his nose into the bison track, smelling the freshness of prey. He has led the pack onto a high ridge overlooking a wide plain. There are many prey, and he can smell the young ones. He follows the trail to a rounded rise and lies down, but Grey-Eye is walking behind anxiously whimpering her distress. Hunger pulled her from the den, but now her milk-swollen teats are aching; she is being drawn back to the den and her new litter of pups. Broken-Tail walks past her and lies down next to Blue. It has not occurred to Grey-Eye that Broken-Tail has abandoned the pups to hunt. The will to return to the pups is becoming too much to resist. She waits for Blue to follow her back to the den by the river, but her mate is sound asleep. She finds a warm patch of open ground and settles down but cannot sleep. After a while the pack is on the move again. Grey-Eye stands and stretches and licks at her swollen belly, uncertain which direction to follow. Blue is leading the pack onto the low plain.

She is about to turn around and head back to the den when the fresh scent of bison fills the air. Bulls are feeding near a small lake in the distance. The pack is moving toward dark horns flashing in the dusky evening light. Grey-Eye runs and catches up to them, the lure of hunger and the hunt overwhelming all other thoughts.

No Birds Are Singing

Naali woke from the nightmare, her bed wet with perspiration. She stared into the ceiling for a long time, trying to calm her beating heart. Pulling on her clothes, she got up and carefully stepped around the sleeping bodies. As she went outside, she paused and looked carefully around camp, afraid the spirits were waiting for her.

The early morning light shone through the grey, leafless shrubs. Downstream, a robin briskly sang and others answered from the willows behind her. Somewhere across the river ravens were calling, their raspy voices lost in the din of rushing water and grinding ice. Far off she could hear the honking of swans.

Chii Tsal was sitting by the outside fire. He looked at her briefly and then stirred the smoking embers with a stick, lost in thought.

He does not believe.

Naali looked around and listened. There was nothing. The world was peaceful - normal, like any morning. Perhaps she had been wrong: the nightmare just another dream with no meaning; the ground did not hold bad spirits. She went behind the tent and relieved herself.

She turned back to camp and was looking at the boat when the blackness struck. Dark shapes swirled around her. Human cries and shouts filled her ear, so loud and clear the screams she turned to look for them. Spirit shapes - some human, some animal - collided in a commotion of leaping, writhing shadows as hot points of light streamed by her eyes, plunging through the willows and racing out over the river.

Naali looked to Chii Tsal, certain he must be seeing the dark chaos that had descended on the camp, but he was sitting calmly by the fire drinking tea.

He does not see them!

The darkening grew, the reeling shapes becoming more

chaotic, moving faster and faster, surrounding her, shredding the light. The centre of the disturbance was above the boat. The frame was violently shaking, slamming up and down on the shore ice. The skins rippled and shimmered as if the boat were a living, breathing animal. High bird-like cries radiated from all around it. Then she recognized the voices.

People are screaming!

The sky filled with black clouds as the screams rose and thunder filled her ears. Naali sensed something coming toward her. She turned her back, afraid of what she might see. A voice suddenly ended the dark vision.

"Naali? Naali."

It was Barik. The vision unravelled as the shapes dissolved; the wind stopped and the sky turned blue and cloudless again. She heard the birds singing, the rush of the river, the fire crackling, her heart beating.

"Are you dreaming?"

"No." Her voice was weak and frail. She was not certain if she was awake or still dreaming. Her eyes focused on Chii Tsal, who was standing by the fire, looking at them perplexed. Barik took her by the arm and moved her away from the camp until they were out of hearing.

"You were dreaming. What did you dream?"

Naali rubbed her eyes. "Dark spirits." She was trying to clear the frightful vision. She wanted to cry.

"Are they here now? The spirits, are they here now?"

"I do not know."

"What did you see?"

"I do not know their shapes," she said, lowering her voice. "Something dangerous." She was unable to shake the screaming voices out of her mind.

"Is it the river? Will it flood? Will the boat sink? Was it a killing beast?"

"It is coming." She was beginning to panic. "I feel it!" Tears

151

welled in her eyes.

When she looked up she saw there were others awake, collecting around the fire and drinking tea. Water was heating in spinning bladders over the high flames and Karun and Assan were slicing dry meat. Khon and Jovan were drinking and talking. Korya was chasing her young brother, Aron, along the shore, laughing playfully. Kazan was coming out of the tent, his spear in his hand. It was a morning like any other morning. There was nothing else.

"Think. What did you see?" Barik asked, growing impatient.

Naali had to get away from her brother to clear her mind. She moved to the fire, where someone handed her a steaming cup. She sat down, barely aware of the bustling life around her. Barik followed her to the fire and sat far from her, his expression brooding and distant.

Kazan woke to the sound of birds singing and a stream of sunlight shining through the walls of the tent. He came out of the tent and searched for Naali in the crowd. She was by the fire cradling a cup, looking downcast. He was standing at the edge of the crowd when she stood up and shouted, "It is coming!"

The band fell silent and turned to her. Naali's blue eyes were wild, her face fierce. "It is near!"

Kazan stood at the rear of the crowd, listening to Naali. He heard a soft splash upstream and turned to look at the shore, expecting a caribou or elk to appear. A bird flashed out of the willows, chirping an alarm call. Then another splash, soft and quiet.

Too soft. Not a grasseater hoof...

He peered into the shrubs. Two robins flew out, calling out a distress signal.

The birds.

He shifted his eyes to where he had seen the first robin take flight. As he stared into the dense thicket he imagined every budding willow leaf was an eye looking at him. Then a shadow shifted. To his left he heard a faint sound like a breath exhaled.

152

Jovan had turned and was watching the shrubs, his spear raised in defence. He lifted his hand high in the air and closed his fist so everyone could see.

A baby cried and someone whispered. The men moved to their spears as a flock of swans passed over camp, their loud staccato calls breaking the eerie silence.

"Hoo-ho-ho, hoo-ho-hoo."

The lions erupted from the willows like clouds in a windstorm and came at the band so fast there was no time to call out. One flew past Kazan's spear, knocking him down. The noise came all at once: yelling, screams, shouts, roaring, crying.

Dazed, Kazan fumbled for his spear and climbed to his feet. He was surrounded by people screaming. Women were running, shielding babies. Men were stumbling backward, their spears flashing and jabbing at lions leaping and roaring around them.

Lions!

Kazan heard a deep wail and turned to see legs kicking beneath the stooped body of another lion.

"No!" He shouted, watching in horror as the great beast lifted Karun off the ground, still alive and kicking. It turned and carried her off into the shrubs.

There was a great shouting, and Kazan turned back to watch a wall of spears driving for the lions.

"Get behind the spears!" It was Jovan. Women scrambled past Kazan and ran behind the men.

"Spears!" someone shouted. Kazan turned and raised his spear, his hands shaking so hard he nearly dropped it. As he nervously jabbed out, a lion snatched the spear from his hand. Chii Tsal charged, driving his spear into the lion's face. Bloodied, the wounded lion retreated to the edge of the willows, roaring fiercely. Kazan picked up his spear and scrambled back into the line of defence. The cat was joined by another and they paced back and forth, watching the stinging spears swaying dangerously.

"How many?" someone shouted beside Kazan.

Kazan's mind raced - two and one that had taken Karun. "Three!" he shouted. "There are three!"

"Jovan! Where is Jovan?" It was Khon. "Has anyone seen him?"

"He went down!" Dat'san shouted.

"Where?"

"By the fire."

"Can you see him?"

"No."

Khon move quickly to the fire, only to find a thick blood spot by the hearth. As he scrambled back the lions came at them again. As one cat was driven back the other paced behind, waiting for an opening to attack. The band had backed up to the edge of the river where a jumble of shore ice blocked any escape upstream. Women and children were crying. Kazan could hear Assan soothing them, imploring them not to panic. Downstream the boat stood perched on the shore.

Khon glanced over at it and shouted, "No, hold the shore!" Their only hope was to stay in a tight group and defend themselves with their four spears. A lion charged, but Dat'san caught it in the side, turning it back in a fit of pain and rage. Behind him a woman screamed in panic.

"Hold!" Khon shouted again, but it was useless. The defence was unraveling. Chii Tsal shouted something and he and Dat'san broke for the boat. Grasping the bow, they shoved the stern hard into the river.

"Get in!" Chii Tsal shouted at the band. "Get in!"

Kazan was ready to race to the boat, too, when he heard his father.

"No!!" Khon screamed. "Stay!"

Chii Tsal gathered Korya and Aron toward the boat. "Karun!" he screamed, his eyes darting everywhere for her. As he turned, he saw the boat had filled with people. "No!" he shouted.

154

"There are too many!" The overloaded boat spun out into the icy current. Dat'san jammed his spear onto the shore in a desperate bid to hold the boat from capsizing. Chii Tsal looked at Khon, waving his hand frantically.

"Khon!" he yelled as the boat slid into the crushing rush of ice.

An ice pan slammed into the stern, shattering the upstream gunnel like kindling. Wood snapped and cracked as ice skated over boat, instantly driving it and its passengers underwater. People scrambled for shore but it was too late. Kazan watched in horror as the huge ice block slammed into the shore and spun out into the roiling current. Everyone was gone except Barik. Kazan watched him leap off the bow just as the boat slipped under the ice. He fell onto the shore, scrambled up the bank and ran downstream. Kazan looked back to the river and saw heads bobbing in the rushing torrent. He heard shouts and screams as people floated away into the rush of ice. His spear swayed as the shock finally struck.

They are drowning! Bad spirits... Naali said bad spirits would come.

"Kazan!" Khon shouted. "Hold!"

Assan, So'tsal, Dèhzhòo and Naali stood behind them, their feet in the river. A lion charged, but Khon drove it back with his long spear. Kazan thrust his spear wildly at the retreating cat but his aim was off. The confusion and shock of the sinking boat had overwhelmed him.

Khon shouted again. "Two spears! Work with mine!" Another cat attacked but Khon pushed it back. As it turned, Kazan managed to find the lion's back. Another charge and then another charge. With each attack, his confidence grew. The lions did not know the pain of spears. They were hesitating.

"Strike hard," Khon shouted. If two lions charged together, they would not be able to defend. "Follow me!"

They rushed out, driving the lions back to the edge of the willows. When they retreated to the shore Kazan saw the women

155

were gone. He glanced up and down the shore for Assan, So'tsal, Dèhzhòo and Naali and checked the river, but they were not there.

Where are they? They were just here!

Then he saw someone running down the shore.

Naali!

She was a few steps behind Barik, who was jumping onto a large moving ice pan.

"Go! Go! Follow her!" Khon screamed, pointing downstream.

Kazan hesitated. He could not leave his father! The lions were pacing, moving closer.

"Run!" Khon shouted, this time so fiercely he startled Kazan. "I will follow!"

Kazan ran. The shore ice was slippery and he nearly tumbled into the river. Ahead, he saw Naali and Barik sitting on an ice floe as it spun out into the river. He had one chance. He leaped, his arms and legs flailing to stay above the muddy river as long as possible. He slammed down onto the ice floe and slid into the water.

"Watch out!" Naali screamed, pointing behind him.

Kazan glanced back to see a lion sliding to a stop on the shore. It looked at the racing current and ran along the shore, following the ice floe downstream. Suddenly it leaped into the river. With a great splash, it landed just behind Kazan, who was holding onto Barik's hand.

"Get on!" Naali shouted as she and Barik pulled Kazan up onto the floe. The lion swam to the edge, gripped the ice with its claws and lunged at Kazan's legs as he kicked his way out of the water.

"Kill it!" Barik screamed, pulling his legs up to his knees.

Kazan realized he had not dropped his spear. He turned to face the lion and, at that moment, all fear and shock disappeared. He screamed at the top of his lungs, driving the spear deep into the lion's snarling mouth. The cat screamed and roared, unable to

156

avoid the flurry of the sharp spear. The lion released its claws from the ice pan, slid back into the water and swam for the shore. Climbing out of the river, the lion stood shaking its soaking fur and watched the three children disappear into the jumble of ice floes in the middle of the river. They held onto the ice as it rocked and spun in the current. Kazan suddenly remembered his father and looked back expecting - hoping - he would see Khon running along the river beside them.

Khon was on the shore, but he was not running; his lifeless body was under a feeding lion. Beside Khon lay a second lion, his long spear sticking up from its side.

Ice Riders

One-Eye stepped out of the shrubs just as a flock of swans glided over the shore in preparation for landing on the river. The lead swan saw him and veered away at the last moment, its wide white wings flapping above the water like a billowing cloud. One-Eye threw the dart, but it fell short as the flock rose into the air. He retrieved the dart and inspected the point for damage.

As he moved upriver he stopped to listen for the sounds of grasseaters: a clatter of hard hoofs on rocks, a splash, the soft swish of hair brushing a willow, the snap of a branch.

He was standing in a thicket, listening, when he heard human voices. He turned back to the shore toward the sounds. When he reached the river he saw three people on an ice floe rushing downstream. They disappeared around a bend in the river, their voices lost in the pounding crush of ice and water. He looked in the river and saw the shattered remains of a boat with a body bobbing in it. Another body was floating behind the boat, long black hair streaming along the surface.

One-Eye watched but nothing more came, and he moved again. Stopping at a small pool, he dipped his hands into cool clear water and took great gulps. As he wiped his hands on his stained parka, he heard roaring not far upstream. He pulled up his hood and moved toward the sound.

Finding *Zhòh gii*

The ice floe was slowly breaking apart underneath them as it bumped and rocked downstream. It submerged completely a few times, soaking Naali, Barik and Kazan in the river's icy grip. Each time they managed to stay on the twisting ice pan. Finally, the river made a sharp turn and the block slammed into shore, splitting apart. The impact threw Kazan and Naali onto the bank while Barik was knocked into the river. He was about to be sucked into the current when Kazan reached into the water, grabbed Barik's jacket and pulled him, sputtering, onto shore, where they collapsed soaked, frozen, exhausted.

Kazan lay on the ground, barely conscious, with visions of lions roaring and people screaming and shouting. The sudden ambush... Karun alive in the jaw of a lion... his band swarming into the doomed boat... Assan, So'tsal and Dèhzhòo vanishing before his very eyes. He was running, jumping... Naali pointing... his spear jabbing jabbing jabbing... Khon lying dead. He could hardly comprehend the gravity of what had happened. His band was gone! Everyone was dead. Without his family, his band, he was lost. Kazan slipped in and out of consciousness, shock and cold dulling his mind.

"F-f-f-fire," stammered Naali. She was standing over him, her voice chattering. "F-f-f-fire... freezing."

Kazan opened his eyes. He tried to move; his arms and legs would not move. His fingers were frozen shut. He rocked back and forth until he managed to flip up on his side. Pressing his arm down he staggered to his feet, wobbling as he gained balance. Naali had already collected a pile of driftwood and was kneeling over a bundle of dry grass. Kazan fumbled at his coat for his firesticks, found the pouch, pried it open with his mouth, pulled the flint out and fell to his knees. He piled on more dry grass and struck the flint until sparks ignited a fire large enough to add small piece of kindling. His fingers slowly thawed and, as he stood, he

159

saw Barik, naked, holding his wet clothes over the flames. Kazan did the same and Naali took off hers. Soon the flames had dried their clothes. No one spoke, each lost in their thoughts. Kazan looked at the river and realized they had landed on the other shore from camp.

Naali ended the silence. "Some may be still alive."

"We are the only ones," said Barik.

"Assan, So'tsal, Dèhzhòo - did you see them?" Kazan asked as he pulled on his pants. They shook their heads.

"Your father followed you. He killed the first lion. He turned and jammed the spear into the ground and waited. The spear went through the running lion. He had only his club for the other one," Naali said, feeling terrible she was the one to give Kazan details of his father's death. "I saw no one else."

"They fell in the river with the rest of them," said Barik. He reached down and picked up Kazan's spear lying by the fire. Kazan watched in surprise as Barik's hand closed around the handle.

"It is my spear!" Kazan shouted, reaching to take it back.

Barik pulled it away from his hand. "I should carry it. I am older."

"But you lost yours! You cannot take another hunter's spear!" Kazan looked at the weapon, the last thing left on earth that was his. "Give it back!"

Barik raised the spear and twisted it in his hands; his eyes darkened like a winter storm.

"Stop!" Naali shouted. She was walking upstream. "Some may have made it out of the river," she said. "We must go back and see."

In her heart she knew there was little hope anyone had survived, but she kept silent. The boys separated and followed behind her without speaking. Soon Kazan forgot the spear as he searched the far shore for signs of human life. At each bend he looked for a fire, someone walking or lying on the shore, but each time his hopes were dashed. They were moving through high
160

willows near the river shore when Naali suddenly stopped.

"*Shih*," she whispered as she crouched and pointed to a sloping meadow beyond the shrubs. She touched her finger to her nose.

Kazan smelled it too - bear! They crawled through the shrubs to the edge of the meadow and saw the freshly dug soil in the centre.

"A wolf den," Barik said, trying to keep his voice low. They looked around the meadow and stayed hidden in the shrubs until they were sure there were no wolves or bear around. Walking onto the meadow, Kazan could see the den had been dug out. He looked inside the deep trench and saw the small bones.

There were three tiny skulls still wet with blood. There was no torn hair or fresh blood, no sign of a struggle. "A bear killed the cubs," he whispered. "The wolves are gone. When they come back they will be mad."

"We must go," said Naali. It was then Kazan saw the wolf pup running across the meadow.

"*Zhòh gii!*" he shouted. He caught it before the pup could reach the willows. As he grabbed the twisting handful of fur, it turned back and nipped his hand. Kazan held it firmly by the neck as it squirmed to break free. With a faint smile on his lips, he showed it to Barik and Naali.

"Let it go. The wolves will be back," Barik said stiffly, showing no interest in a ball of fur. Naali was looking intently at the pup, her eyes soft and yielding.

"If you take a wolf you bring the pack," Barik said sharply. "Leave it here."

But something told Kazan he must keep it. He had lost Wolf Band. Here was a wolf that had lost its littermates. The pup was good luck. It was meant to be his.

Naali turned the pup over and inspected the belly. "A female *Zhòh gii*. Look."

"Let the bear have her," Barik said.

161

"No!" exclaimed Kazan. "She is mine. Wolf Band is gone. They are all dead but me!" Tears filled his eyes. "She is mine! I will take care of her."

Before Barik could protest again, Naali slipped her hands under the wriggling pup. *Zhòh gii* suddenly stopped squirming and relaxed.

"I will take care of *Zhòh gii*," she whispered as she wrapped the pup inside her jacket.

"She will bring bad luck!" Barik griped as Naali headed back to the shore. By the time they reached the river, *Zhòh gii* was already fast asleep in the warmth of Naali's jacket.

Assan Meets One-Eye

The lion pushed its head between the huge tilted slabs of ice. It stretched its foreleg into a crevasse and tore at the ice with its long claws, but it could not reach the prey below. Something struck its paw and it roared out in pain. As the lion licked blood from the wound, the prey suddenly seemed not worth further effort when there was fresh meat nearby. It moved through the camp and circled the tent. It found the door and stepped inside, remembering the smell of the place. The lion had once killed a human inside the skins. It stepped over a pile of furs, sniffing the human scents everywhere. Ignoring the empty skins, the lion walked to a half-eaten carcass, gripped the torso in its jaws and carried it through the willows to a small opening. Settling the body on the ground, the lion licked the face with its rasp-like tongue until the skin was gone.

Assan wiped the blood from the point of her blade. She had made three quick stabs into the lion's paw. She knew two were deep cuts when it roared so loudly she had to press her hands against her ears.

They were jammed into a narrow crevasse in a tumble of ice slabs on the shore of the river. So'tsal and Dèhzhòo were remarkably quiet despite their fear. The lion had reached down to kill them, but they were too deep in the ice. A few inches less and the lion would have raked them with its razor-sharp claws and pulled out their shredded bodies.

"Is it gone?" So'tsal asked.

Assan raised her finger to her lips. "If the lion cannot hear it will forget," she whispered.

Jammed between the icy walls they waited in silence. Once a shadow passed above and then nothing moved for a long time. As evening fell, Assan felt the cold take hold. So'tsal and Dèhzhòo were freezing, but they stayed still and quiet, their arms wrapped around each other.

Finally, Assan told them to stand. She propped herself against the ice and stepped onto their shoulders but was still too short to reach the top of the ice. She signalled So'tsal and Dèhzhòo to push her up until she was looking at the camp. There were no lions in sight.

How many?

They had come so fast it was hard to know. Assan rolled out of the crevasse, her knife clenched in her hand at the ready.

Ready for what? To kill a lion?

Assan nearly laughed in despair. The tents were still standing. The fire was cold. Above it a skin bladder swung in the wind. Skull cups were scattered everywhere. Far off, a lion roared and another replied. They are feeding, she realized in horror. She suddenly felt sick and fell to her knees vomiting. I do not want to know, she thought, gripping her stomach.

She walked through the camp, careful not to make a sound. She found the blood spot where Karun had fallen. The second spot she did not know until she saw Jovan's spear lying by it. She picked it up and moved to the shore where the boat had been.

Downriver she saw the body of a lion with a long spear sticking from it. She moved to it, listening to the lions roaring.

Khon's spear!

That was all she needed to see. Pulling it out, she stared at the bloody shaft.

Khon… it cannot be.

She found the blood trail and followed it a short distance into the shrubs.

It cannot be.

Assan bent down and touched the cool blood, rubbing it on her lips, tasting him.

Kazan and Naali? Where are they? Did they reach the boat?

Assan walked along the shore but found no blood. Then she remembered the words she had heard in the crevasse, the last

164

words Khon spoke - *Run, to the girl. Run.* She had not understood what he had meant. Now she knew. The words were for Kazan. Had Naali run? Had Kazan followed and escaped? She went farther down the shore until there were no tracks or sign of humans. There was only one possibility. Her heart sank as she stared into the ice-choked river.

Kazan has drowned - and Naali. They are both dead.

Her heart sunk in despair.

So'tsal and Dèhzhòo and I - we are the last of Wolf Band.

As she turned to walk back she saw a man standing by the tents. He was huge, a head taller than Khon - the biggest human she had ever seen. He carried a spear, a quiver of hunting darts and a large skin pack. His jacket was darkly stained with dried blood and animal grease. A thick scar angled through his empty eye socket. Under his raised hood, there was a tangle of long black hair matted with sticks and leaves. She knew who he was instantly.

One-Eye!

Naali had described the bushman many times. Assan recoiled, looking for a place to run; there was nowhere. The giant motioned her to give him the spears. She knew it was useless to fight, so she tossed them down. Spears in hand, he moved through the camp, checking the tents. When he reached the fire pit, he snatched a bladder of water and drank it down. Then he waved her forward. She thought of So'tsal and Dèhzhòo in the crevasse.

Do not make a sound.

He motioned again. She shook her head. He rushed at her, striking her face with his open hand. She buckled to her knees and cried out. So'tsal and Dèhzhòo heard her and called out from the crevasse. He cocked his head toward the sounds. As he approached the ice, he peered down and they screamed. He glanced back at Assan, raised the two spears and pointed them. She scrambled to her feet.

"No!" she said, rushing by him. She could not lose them too. She could not bear it. She pulled off her waist belt and dropped it down in the crevasse, pulling So'tsal and Dèhzhòo out one at a time. She held them both and turned to face the bushman. He was standing next to a tent, hardly interested in them. He pulled the tent down, wrapped the skins into a bundle, gathered the poles and tied them together with a rawhide rope. Lifting the skins on his back, the bushman pointed to the poles and grunted.

Assan motioned So'tsal and Dèhzhòo into the tent, where they found sleeping skins and packs. Then she ran to the fire, collecting whatever she could find: skin bladders, stone knives, bone scrapers. They were lifting the poles onto their backs when a lion roared downstream. The *nanaa'in* put his finger to his lips and they followed him without a sound.

Returning Home

Grey-Eye sits on the high ridge, her stomach heavy with bison. The others are sprawled around her, sleeping. She is growing restless for her den and the comfort of pups. She nudges Broken-Tail and Blue. Neither wolf wakes. She barks, eventually rousing her mate. He stands and stretches, urinating against a boulder. The rest of the pack wake up, assemble around their parents and wait. Grey-Eye heads off down the slope toward the river, her pack following close behind.

As she slips through the shrubs along the shore she smells bear. Following the scent along a small creek, Grey-Eye tracks it over wet boulders and into shrubs. She stops at the edge of her meadow, her apprehension growing. The scent of bear is strongest here. A light breeze blows another scent – humans. She crosses the meadow heading for the den but it is gone, replaced by a wide-open trench. Fresh soil is scattered everywhere. She jumps into the trench and finds the pup bones. The smell of blood and bear is everywhere. She is suddenly overwhelmed by a sense of loss. The pack approaches the pit. She is whimpering, her nose pressing a tiny skull. As her despair grows, she frantically sniffs the scents.

She follows the scent of the female pup to the back of the open chamber where it ends. She digs down, following the pup, dislodging gravel and small rocks, until she reaches an immovable rock. Leaping out of the trench, she finds the fresh scent again crossing the meadow and follows until it ends at a ground-squirrel hole. She moves to the edge of the meadow and picks it up in the shrubs, mixed with the heavy scent of humans. She follows her pup to the river, where the scent disappears. Confused, she returns to the meadow where her pack is already sleeping. Grey-Eye drops into the trench and sniffs the pile of pup bones. A little later she walks off the meadow and howls. Broken-Tail wakes and joins her mother. Soon the pack is howling their mournful chorus along the river.

PART 4

SHIN: DAYS OF LIGHT

Swan Eggs

The three children stood on the riverbank across from the camp. The river was no longer running ice. The willows had leafed out, making it difficult to see any detail on the far shore. There was no fire burning and one of the tents was down. They had been watching for some time, looking for any sign of human life.

"They are all dead," Barik said.

Kazan was kneeling beside him. His last hope of finding anyone alive had vanished. It had taken five days to walk back upstream. On the way he found a long willow to make into a spear, hardening the tip in the small fires they built each evening to keep warm. He had not spoken to Naali or Barik during the trek, his thoughts only on his family and band, now gone.

As he looked across the rushing water he realized there was no hope. He replayed the lion attack many times in his head as he walked. Karun was dead: he had watched her die. And Khon. He had seen his lifeless body on the shore beside the dead lion. He tried to remember who was in the sinking boat. He could not be sure; it had happened too fast. He could see heads bobbing in the water. Everyone had been swept out into the current except Barik. Then Khon had shouted and turned back to face the lions, the last cries of Wolf Band disappearing in the noise of the river.

Kazan cast his eyes on the place he last saw his father. He could see Khon was gone, but the dead lion was there. At least some of it. A mob of ravens was feeding on it, squawking and calling noisily. He was suddenly struck by something: Khon's spear

168

was gone. He moved down the shore to get a better look, careful to stay out of view of any lion. He could not see Khon's spear. Kazan walked back to Barik and Naali, who were hiding behind a boulder.

"Khon's spear is gone. It was stuck in the lion when we drifted by. I cannot see it."

"It must have fallen," Barik said. "Or a lion knocked it over."

Kazan thought a spear sunk in a dead lion could not have fallen over. He was about to say so when Naali spoke.

"What are we going to do?" she asked. "We have eaten only bird eggs. We need food." She stroked the wolf pup in her arms. "*Zhòh gii* is growing."

Kazan moved back from the shore. "Where can we go?" he asked, his voice filled with despair. There was no hope — three children, with no food, no tent or beds, one spear between them.

"Quiet," Naali whispered. She was looking across the river, her hand raised.

A lion appeared near the tent, walked toward the shore, slipped down the bank and took a long drink from the river. Then it raised its head, sniffing at the air. It suddenly roared and Kazan realized they were upwind.

It smells us!

They lay behind willows watching the lion move further into the river. Then a second lion appeared near the tent. Suddenly the tent was ripped down and the two lions roared. Kazan crouched and watched. He had not been careful. The lions had their scent.

"Go!" Barik shouted as he stood up.

They raced through willow stands and across open meadows toward a low ridge that ran along the river. They arrived out of breath on the ridge top and looked back, certain the lions were coming.

"Is it coming? Did it see us?" Kazan asked, but Naali and Barik were already running again. He glanced toward the river. A lion was sprawled on top of the collapsed tent, but he could not see the one in the water. He caught up and passed Naali and Barik, finally stopping at the shore of a small pond, where they fell exhausted to the ground.

Kazan stood up and looked back watching for any movement. "It would have caught us by now. It must not have crossed the river." Naali and Barik stood and scanned the horizon for the lion. After a few minutes they all relaxed and sat down.

"Where is Shih Band?" Kazan asked. "We need to find other humans."

"I do not know," Naali answered, pulling the pup from her parka. "We were downstream from here, near the Ch'oodèenjik, when One-Eye took us." She looked to the south and pointed. "Shih Summer Camp must be there." She looked at Barik. "Do you know?"

It took Barik a few moments to answer. "There," he said, pointing in the same direction. "It is far away. I have never walked this ground. I do not know how many days to walk there."

Kazan was looking out across an ice-covered pond. In the distance, they heard the musical whistle of swans and the honking of geese. The edge of the pond was open water. A muskrat swam close by and dove when it spotted them. A fish jumped noiselessly and then disappeared. Suddenly Kazan felt faint hope. He remembered seeing a few ponds when they had first looked down upon the ice-choked Ch'oodèenjik from the other side of the valley.

"The ponds will have duck eggs and fish and muskrat to kill. If we follow the ponds we can collect food. We stay moving south and hope you will remember Shih Summer Camp." Kazan snapped off a willow branch and rolled it in his hands. "We have no skin for shelter, but there are shrubs enough for fires."

"The mountains are filled with grasseaters - horse, caribou, elk and bison. Shih Band will be there." Naali tried to
170

sound hopeful, but her thoughts turned to the question that had bothered her since the bushman killed her father and took their family.

Why did the Shih band not come looking for us? A band is one. So why has no one come looking for us?

They kept moving south, skirting around ponds for the rest of the day. Once, a group of elk crossed a small lake in the distance, but they had disappeared by the time the children reached its shore. While they walked they found three swan nests, collected the large white eggs, cracked the shells and eagerly swallowed the thick contents. Naali held some out for the pup, pouring it slowly into *Zhòh gii's* ravenous mouth.

In the evening they made camp. Naali collected small branches and wove a rough frame for a night shelter, covering it in moss and grass. They each ate a swan egg by the fire, watching the Arctic sun move high along the west horizon. The sun would not set for many days. *Shin* had come - it was summer. Naali pulled her wet mukluks inside out, inspecting the worn soles. They would not last the summer.

One by one, they slipped into the makeshift shelter, pressing close together for warmth. They sprawled on top of each other but there was no escape from cold. *Zhòh gii* slipped down beside Naali, licking at her ear, searching her mouth for food. Kazan barely slept, rising often to feed the fire. Each time he crawled from the shelter, he scanned the horizon for lions.

In the morning, they woke to a familiar drone. It was the sound of *Ch'ii* - the sound of millions of mosquitoes waking after a long winter; and the promise of endless torment, bloody bites and constant harassment for the season. Soon they would be covered in welts and bloody skin.

Kazan sat up. "*Ch'ii* are awake," he said almost casually as he crawled out of the shelter.

As Barik stood, a mosquito flew onto his hand and he slapped at it. "*Ch'ii*," he said, wiping it off the back of his hand.

171

Naali did not relish the thought of spending sleepless nights in makeshift shelters, fighting off clouds of mosquitoes. "We need shelter," she said. "Skins. We cannot live during *Shin* in the open with *Ch'ii*."

With nothing to eat they headed off, glad to move and escape the first onslaught of the biting insects. By the end of the day, they were approaching a creek that emptied into a small lake. In the distance they could hear splashing but could not see beyond the high shrubs bordering the creek.

They lay down, expecting an animal to appear out of willows at any moment. Kazan signalled to Barik to move forward with him. His sharpened stick could not kill an adult grasseater but it might be strong enough to take a calf. As they approached the creek, the splashing got louder. They slipped through the willows and saw what had been making the sounds. The shallow creek was teeming with spawning fish, some as long as their arm.

Barik leaped up, shouting "*Altin! Altin!*"

He drove his spear into the water and plucked out a pike, tossing it behind him. Kazan joined in, stabbing into the chaos of splashing fish. Naali arrived and jumped into the water, flipping a fish out with her bare hands. They whooped and shouted with joy as the pike piled up behind them. Soon a few dozen *Altin* lay dead in the grass. Naali, Kazan and Barik stood looking at each other, breathing heavily and smiling.

"*Altin!*" Kazan said, embracing both of them. They had found fish - plenty of fish. They laughed and jumped up and down, not caring what might hear them. They had found food, on their own, with no hunters to show them.

They spent the next day slaughtering pike, filleting the thick white meat into long strips. Naali hung the strips on a rough willow rack above a smudge fire. The boys collected wood while Naali pulled out willow roots from the ground. She washed the roots in the creek and wove three baskets to carry the dry fish. They feasted on fresh fish, stuffing the oily meat into their mouths until

172

they could not eat another bite.

That evening they slept in the open beside the fire. As Kazan fell asleep, he heard the rasping "*Analuk, analuk, analuk*" as long-tailed ducks glided onto the small lake. High above a flock of cranes flew over, calling "*Kar-r-r-r-o-o-o.*" The final sound he heard was a wandering tattler's sharp whistling from a nearby meadow.

Kazan woke and found his arm wrapped around Naali. The morning fog was so thick he could not see the lakeshore. *Zhòh gii* woke suddenly and her ears pricked up. Kazan quickly sat up, listening to soft sound of something approaching through the fog.

Cliff Camp

Assan watched the bushman sleeping, his matted hair with its tangled sticks looking more like a bird's nest than a human head. He was at the far end of the tent sleeping soundly. She wondered what he dreamed; if he dreamed. He had not spoken a word since they left Lions-Came Camp. She soon realized he could not talk. His commands were rough grunts, or he simply pointed instructions to them. If they did not understand, he would strike them with the flat of his hand, sending them sprawling to the ground. They soon learned how he wanted the tent positioned, how much wood and grasseater dung to collect, how warm to keep the fires, how hot he liked his food and drink. When he pulled the tent down each day, he expected everything to be packed up before he bundled up the skins. If they were not finished with the packing, he struck them all. He was leading them away from the river to the north toward a low plateau that rose to ice-capped mountain peaks - a land Assan had never travelled.

The bushman was a remarkably strong traveller. He carried the tent bundled on his shoulder. On his back was a quiver of hunting darts and a backpack jammed with an assortment of stone blades, bladders, rawhide thongs, flaking tools, hammerstones and skin clothes. He seemed to not notice the weight.

They followed him every day, carrying their beds, tent poles, food and bone utensils for cooking. Most days they could not keep up to One-Eye's pace, falling behind as soon as he disappeared over the horizon. They would find his camp late in the day, a spear propped by the bundled tent and visible from a long distance. He would be hunting and they would hurry to make camp. He rarely returned without something: a brace of ptarmigan, a caribou or elk calf, a foal. Assan would cook the meat, boiling it in a skin bladder over the fire.

His appetite was so great that when he was finished eating there was little left for them. He ate like a wolf, snapping bones to

174

suck out the marrow. They were allowed a small ration of meat but it was never enough, so they scavenged whatever he didn't eat, scraping off whatever meat they could from his discards. Assan began to hide meat from him; otherwise they would not have the strength to keep up.

Each morning they broke camp and moved. Then one day, in the middle of summer, caribou began to appear on the tundra. In the evening the bushman's load was waiting at the base of a low rock cliff in front of a small cave. The hole in the rock was barely high enough to erect the tent, but they managed. He returned that night with two caribou calves. When he had eaten his fill, he fell asleep, leaving an entire calf uneaten. For the first time they feasted.

Early the next morning, Assan woke and looked at the bushman from her bed. He was asleep with his back to her, his spear propped against the tent. She eyed the weapon, judging the distance.

I could kill him.

She considered her chances for a moment. She would have to reach over him. It was impossible. The spear would be in his hands before her fingers touched it. Then he would kill her and So'tsal and Dèhzhòo would be alone. She would have only made their desperate lives more miserable.

Assan looked at them sleeping. She hoped they were dreaming good thoughts. Her own dreams were filled with lions and ice and rushing water, children crying, women screaming; and always Khon's voice: "Hold, hold." But the spears broke and it all had happened so quickly — the boat suddenly disappearing in the river, the screaming, falling into the crevasse.

We should have stayed with Khon and Kazan. At least we would have died together.

It was Khon who pointed to the crevasse on the shore. He had pushed So'tsal and Dèhzhòo down so he could defend them better. Now death seemed more fitting than the hopelessness they

175

faced. Their lives meant nothing to the bushman.

Suddenly, he was standing over her bed. As he kicked her, he pounded the end of his spear on the floor skins, pushed open the tent flap and was gone. Assan understood.

We are staying.

Avii

In the dream Naali is walking. Thousands of small brown animals are parting ahead of her, each scrambling to avoid being stepped on. Lemmings. There are so many it is as if the ground is alive. Some climb up her mukluks as she shakes them off. The boy is there, just behind her. He is gently shoving them away with a spear as he walks, careful not to hurt any.

"Have you ever seen so many?" Kazan asks. His voice is nervous.

She tells him she has never seen so many.

"What can we do?"

"Nothing."

"They will strip the grass and shrubs; they will eat everything," he says. "Grasseaters will starve without grass, and we will starve without grasseaters."

Soon there are so many they are wading knee deep into the mass of squirming brown bodies.

"Only one animal can help us," she tells him.

He is becoming deeply troubled.

"What animal - wolf, lion, bear, wolverine?"

"None of those. They will become bored with killing."

"I know," he says confidently. "Long-Nose can step on them. Let us call mammoth."

"Not Long-Nose. She does not like the feeling of dead things between her toes."

He thinks again. "Ch'izhìn - eagle!"

"Not Ch'izhìn. She can carry only one in her talons. It would take her a lifetime and she would still not be finished killing." By now the sea of lemmings reaches their thighs. Kazan is becoming more agitated.

"What animal, then? What beast can we call?" He is sweeping away the lemmings with his spear.

Suddenly they hear screaming. It is the lemmings. The

177

sound is so loud they must cover their ears. A small animal
appears, its long tail tipped in black. It is covered in blood, leaping
from lemming to lemming, biting each in the neck until there are
none alive.

"Avii!" Kazan smiles. "Weasel will save us."

Naali could still hear Kazan's voice ringing in her head as she woke. She shivered in the makeshift shelter, remembering the vivid dream but unsure what it meant. Outside, the air was shrouded in a thick fog. As she was about to fall back asleep she noticed Kazan was sitting up, listening. And the pup was no longer snuggled in her jacket, warming her skin.

Ch'ii

There were four wolves, their yellow eyes fixed on the strange shelter on the lakeshore. Broken-Tail froze in mid-step, suddenly aware of the scents of humans, fish and smoke mingling in the cool fog. The pup whimpered and Kazan instantly woke.

"Wolves," he whispered as his hand pressed on Naali's shoulder. A thick lump formed in his throat. Barik raised his head and saw how close they were.

The wolves and the humans did not move, each caught in the surprise encounter. *Zhòh gii* had slipped from between Kazan and Naali and was scrambling toward the four wolves when Barik snatched her behind her neck.

"The pup is yours," he said, sending her tumbling at the wolves' legs. *Zhòh gii* yelped as she rolled to a stop by Broken-Tail's foot. Broken-Tail vaguely remembered the pup's scent but everything was out of place. The scent reminded her of a den - not here. Her muscles tensed but she did not move. The other three wolves stepped back, disappearing behind the fog.

Kazan was about to stand up when Naali's voice stopped him. The sound from her mouth was higher pitched and sounded strange to his ears. He did not understand what she was saying.

"We are Wolf Band. The pup is ours. *Shih* killed the other pups in the litter. We found her and took her from the den so she would not be killed by the bear. *Zhòh gii* is safe." Naali peered deep into Broken-Tail's eyes. "Are you *Zhòh gii's* mother?"

"No. Her mother is my mother," Broken-Tail replied.

"Then leave us. The pup is safe. You cannot help her."

From the shelter, Kazan watched the wolf's eyes soften, her nervous stance melting as Naali spoke.

She is speaking wolf tongue!

Barik slowly raised the spear at Broken-Tail.

"No," Naali warned him, but it was too late. The wolf melted into the whiteness. *Zhòh gii* followed Broken-Tail a few

179

paces, stopped and sat on her haunches, whining softly. Moments later they heard the wolves howling.

Barik turned to Naali. "We need skins," he said sharply. "I could have killed the wolf."

"Never touch *Zhòh gii*," she replied. "She is with us. Our band."

"And what band is that?" Barik chortled, not waiting for her answer. "Wolf? Bear?" He clenched his fists. "We have no band. We are three children - a wolf pup does not make us a band." His voice rose as his eyes darkened.

He turned to Kazan, his mouth twisted in anger. "And you, Willow Boy - *K'àii Chyaa!* You think you are a hunter. But I hold the spear and you hold a stick!" He waved the spear at Kazan. "A hunter would not give up his spear. You are not a hunter. You are a willow branch, tall and weak - *K'àii Chyaa.*"

Kazan's face turned red with resentment. "You lost your spear - and then took mine. You hold it but have yet to hunt a grasseater. Hunt with the spear!"

Barik laughed. He went to the drying fish and poked the spear into a fillet, hanging it over the fire to roast. "I would rather spear fish," he said, smiling hard.

"You will not kill grasseaters by arguing," Naali interrupted. "There is one spear. You are both hunters. Find a way to hunt together. We need grasseater skins for shelter." She walked into the willows to relieve herself. Barik ate his fish as he watched the pup follow her into the shrubs. Ashamed, Kazan clenched his fists and walked into the fog along the lake, pretending to search for firewood.

They spent a few days drying fish, rarely exchanging words. Naali finished weaving the carry baskets. They filled the baskets with dried fish and struck off under the constant swarm of stinging mosquitoes. As they walked they swung willow branches in front of them, but the relentless insects inevitably found a way into hair, down shirts and in eyes. Without a proper shelter, the
180

evenings were the worst. They huddled beside a smudge fire, barely enduring the swarm until morning. They travelled this way for five days, becoming increasingly agitated by the constant harassment.

On the sixth morning, Kazan woke first. He built up the fire, walked to a hill to look for grasseaters. As he was scanning the lakeshore, out of the corner of his eye he saw a movement, and slowly turned his head. A cow caribou staggered, passing by only a few paces away, heading toward the camp. She stumbled down the hill barely able to stay on her feet, her emaciated body shimmering oddly in the early morning light.

Naali had woken and was by the fire, her back to the caribou. Without as much as a glance at her, the cow stumbled into the water and instantly sank. She surfaced for a moment, thrashing weakly, then went under again. Kazan ran down the hill, hardly believing their luck. Naali was already in the water, reaching for the cow; Barik was running to the shore.

"Hold on to her," Kazan shouted as he flew into the lake and grabbed the cow by the antlers. Twisting her head, he swung it toward Naali's and Barik's outstretched arms. After they hauled it up on shore they looked down, hardly believing their eyes. The cow's skin was shimmering, alive with thousands of mosquitoes still feeding on her blood.

"*Ch'ii!*" Naali whispered, recoiling in disgust.

They slapped at the cow's skin until they had killed every blood-filled insect. Kazan looked down at his red hands and smiled. "*Vadzaih* meat and skin," he said excitedly, rubbing his palms clean on the neck. Barik rubbed his hands on Naali's drenched pants and they laughed.

"It is a good omen," Barik said, standing up. "*Vadzaih* has given us a gift!"

"*Chii* has given us a gift!" Naali replied heartily.

Kazan was already turning the cow over and pulling his stone knife from his belt. When he cut into the belly the wonderful aroma of grasseater guts wafted up, filling his nostrils and reminding him of his father.

They stayed by the lake drying meat and scraping the caribou skin clean. Naali tended the fire while the boys went off hunting. Kazan and Barik were on the far shore, moving through a broad stand of shrubs. They had followed fresh elk tracks along the lake and saw the band of cows and calves in the distance. Barik was leading, holding the spear. Kazan followed close behind, wishing he held the spear instead of the sharpened stick. As they neared the edge of the shrubs, the elk suddenly appeared and the boys fell to their knees. Kazan nodded to Barik as they crawled through the shrubs on their bellies. On signal they sprung to their feet and were running into the meadow when the elk spotted them. The calves spun away, following their surprised mothers. Kazan was nearly upon the calves, his sharpened stick at the ready. Suddenly Barik's spear flew past his head, glancing harmlessly off the back of a calf. Kazan saw his chance and picked up the spear without breaking stride. The herd climbed a low hill and turned to watch him. The cows raised their heads, sniffing at the air, but there was no wind to bring scent. Barik arrived, breathing hard. Kazan did not look at him, his eyes fixed on the elk.

"Give me the spear," Barik said, reaching his hand out.

Kazan hesitated a moment, passed Barik his stick and sprinted hard for the herd. Kazan remembered the words his father had taught him since he was big enough to carry a hunting dart.

Run like a wolf. Stop when grasseater stops, wait and move when grasseater moves. That is how wolf hunts; that is how a hunter hunts.

When the elk stopped, he stopped. He raised his arms up over his head and swayed back and forth, mimicking an antlered bull as he moved slowly closer. When he was nearly within range, the elk ran again and he followed. The game went on until the animals moved into a large stand of willows. As the cows hopped over the low shrubs, their calves fell farther behind. Kazan saw his

182

chance. He ran for the closest calf, spearing it as it collapsed in a tangle of shrubs. He caught up to the second one and killed it and found the third caught in a thicket of willows. He watched as the herd disappeared over a ridge a few hundred feet away, the success of the hunt slowly sinking in.

Three calves! I chased them like a wolf and caught them.

Barik arrived as Kazan was butchering the last calf. "Good hunt," he said, his tone friendly. Kazan nodded his thanks, but his smile disappeared when he saw Barik had picked up the spear and was aiming the stone point at his head.

"Never touch my spear!" he growled. He seemed larger, his face flushed with anger.

Kazan stood up and faced him. "It is my spear, not yours."

Barik was suddenly on top of Kazan, driving his fist into his face. Kazan fell to the ground and raised his arms to protect himself from the blows.

"Never touch it," Barik panted furiously as he kicked his back. Kazan slowly stood and faced him.

"I made the spear. I carved the handle to fit my hand. It is not yours."

Barik came at him again, but this time Kazan dodged and landed a punch on the side of Barik's head. Barik grunted with rage as his fist flew into Kazan's stomach, sending him to his knees gasping for air. Then he swung the spear shaft, hitting Kazan on the shoulder.

"I killed two elk calves," Barik said, kicking at the dead calf at his feet. "Tell my sister I killed two. You killed one!" He lifted the calf onto his shoulder and disappeared into the willows.

Tears filled Kazan's eyes as he rubbed his shoulder.

I am a boy, not a hunter. I let him take the spear twice. He struck me with it. A hunter never uses his spear for anything but hunting grasseaters.

For the first time he realized the danger lurking within Barik.

He will kill me.

A Wounded Nose

The foals are running, bolting out from under pounding hooves, moving as fast as their mothers. Broken-Tail is alone behind the herd, her eyes fixed on a small one following its mare. She has not been able to separate them.

A foal breaks to her left, a slick stream of saliva flying from its mouth. Before Broken-Tail can turn it, the foal finds its mother and disappears in a flurry of hooves. Tufts of grass and dirt fly up from the beating hooves, blinding her. Broken-Tail stumbles, pitches headlong into a cushion of heather, rolls to her feet and is running again.

Ahead the foals are tiring. Two are falling behind, but still matching her step for step as they trail the herd up a long ridge. She hurtles over the grass, ready to follow the first foal that breaks away. As she reaches the top of the ridge, the closest one hesitates as it looks back. Broken-Tail snatches the small head in her jaws, instantly breaking the foal's neck. Without slowing she drops it and twists around, grabbing the second foal by the hind leg. As it crashes down, Broken-Tail bites down on its back, sending a fountain of blood into her mouth.

Broken-Tail is panting. She lies down in a shallow pool, lapping up the murky water in deep gulps. She moves to a snow patch above the meadow and lies there, cooling her body and collecting her breath.

She falls asleep as the sun circles high in the summer sky and is awakened by the rapid tinkling call of a dusky shorebird. She walks to the nearest foal, snips open the gut with her front teeth, eats the gut filled with creamy milk curds and moves off in search of her pack.

She finds them as she moves up the valley onto a plateau. They are resting by a rock outcrop near a jumble of rotting skins and bleached bones scattered across a grassy meadow. She nudges at the decayed carcass of a fox and finds another one a few feet away. The wind changes, bringing with it the familiar scent of human.

Broken-Tail follows the scent to the rock outcrop, where she finds Blue standing in a dim cave looking at a hole in the rock. Blue has followed the smell to the hole and is cautiously sniffing the rock, sensing danger. But the scent is too much for Broken-Tail to resist. She pushes her head into the hole and instantly receives a sharp blow to her face. She leaps back in surprise, yelping and barking as blood spatters everywhere. She runs out of the cave and collides into Blue. He follows Broken-Tail racing away, her frantic barks muted in the brisk wind.

Dèhzhòo Tells a Secret

Assan was thinking about One-Eye as she scraped the flesh from an elk-calf hide.

He is a man-child. So'tsal and Dèhzhòo are old enough to be mated but he is not interested in either of them.

One-Eye was a skilled hunter, the best she had known. He hunted alone and brought back as many animals as any band of hunters. The growing cache of skins and sacks of dry meat were proof. Such a hunter would be prized anywhere. But hunting was all he knew. He was a child in every other way. Assan wondered how he had become a bushman.

Stories about *nanaa'in'* were always the same. They were humans who refused to share or follow the laws of humans. They were driven away and, if isolated long enough, turned wild. Assan remembered *nanaa'in'* stories she had heard as a young girl. They roamed the tundra-steppe in summer, raiding from human bands and stealing their food and women. When One-Eye had captured them, her first fear had been that he would rape them. She had waited for One-Eye to take So'tsal or Dèhzhòo that first night, but he did nothing. He showed no interest as they slipped into their beds. She watched him fall asleep with his hand resting on his spear.

He behaved as a child - a huge and dangerous child, Assan thought. His disinterest in them was troubling. They would be slaves. Their lives meant nothing else to him.

But he did touch them with his fists. His anger often flashed without warning. He struck them for the smallest violations: the fire not ready, not hot enough, or too hot; his food cold or too hot; or looking at his disfigured face a moment too long. At first he beat them every day, leaving bruises on their faces and arms. Now, after a full change in the moon had passed, they had learned his ways, and the blows fell less often.

They realized One-Eye lived and breathed to hunt. The

moment he woke he took up his spear. It would be in his hand until he fell asleep. Each morning he ate his meal alone, never looking up at them. Each day Assan packed him a sack of dried meat and a bladder of broth and then he left, taking his quiver of hunting darts, spear and antler club. Each evening he would return with a butchered elk or caribou calf slung around his shoulders, and one of them would stay up all night by a smudge fire, drying the meat.

They set up a skin lean-to beside the tent where they cooked meals, dried meat and tanned skins. So'tsal and Dèhzhòo were sitting beside Assan, the sun beating down off the dark rock face behind them. They were quietly stripping sinew through their teeth, making thread for sewing.

"What will happen to us?" Dèhzhòo asked her in a whisper.

Assan was removing fat from a caribou skin with a bone scraper. "We will stay for the summer and put up dry meat, make a new tent skin and sew his new winter clothes," she answered calmly.

"Then where will he take us? Will he take us to his den? To a hole in the ground to spend the winter?" She looked worried.

"I do not know." Assan tried to sound optimistic and not frighten them. "We will have dry meat and a new skin tent before the snow comes."

Dèhzhòo pulled a string of sinew from her teeth and licked her lips. "You make his winter clothes. He will have new mukluks, mitts, parka, skin pants - but we make nothing for ourselves. We will need winter clothes. It is already growing cold at night." She raised her foot, showing the patched soles. "These will not last to winter. If he is going to take us with him, we should be making boots and clothes for all of us."

So'tsal joined in, her voice becoming excited. "Naali and Barik escaped from One-Eye. We could do the same. It is summer and easy to travel. He is off hunting everyday. We could run."

187

"To where?" asked Assan. "Barik and Naali ran and were lucky to meet us before the bushman found them. We have no one to run to." Assan suddenly felt a hopeless desperation. She had thought of escaping many times since he took them, but she knew it was not possible.

"They had winter darkness and snow to cover their tracks," she said. "He will find us before we make our first camp. You know his tracking and hunting skills. You have seen how fast he moves across the tundra. Naali was a dream-traveller: she spoke to lions. We are not the same. We know sewing, net-making, bone-carving, tanning skins, cooking food. We are not dream-travellers. We cannot tell a killing beast to let us pass." Assan shrugged as she turned to them.

"We need him to live. Without a hunter, we will die. If we run, he will kill us. We must stay until we find other humans. Then we run."

A little later Dèhzhòo followed Assan to the stream to clean the cooking gear. Assan pulled out a handful of goose grass and began scouring the skull cups clean, handing them to Dèhzhòo to dry with a piece of horsehide. The young woman had grown quiet in the past days, and Assan sensed something was troubling her. She tried striking up a conversation, but the young woman hardly spoke until they were ready to head back to camp.

Dèhzhòo slowly turned to face her. "I am with child," she cried, raising her hands to her mouth.

Assan dropped the kitchen sack on the ground.

"I… I think I am with child," Dèhzhòo repeated.

Assan heard but did not believe. "You cannot be," she whispered sharply. "How could you be with child?"

Dèhzhòo looked away. Tears welled in her eyes.

"How could you be with child?" Assan repeated, her heart suddenly pounding.

"I have not bled for two moons." Dèhzhòo turned and looked at Assan, waiting for her to say what she so desperately needed to hear — *No, you are not with child.*

Assan knew the answer before she asked the next question. "Did you lie with Khon at Lions-Came Camp?"

"Yes. But it was only a few days after my bleeding stopped."

"Have you been sick?"

"Yes. A few times."

Assan gripped the young woman by the arms. "You cannot be with a child. Not now!"

Dèhzhòo collapsed onto the ground. She buried her face in her hands and sobbed deeply.

"Stop! He will not have it. He will not let you have a child," Assan hissed. "He is a bushman. He will not have a child - not Khon's, not any man's!

"Then end it!" Dèhzhòo cried as her head fell between her knees. "End it."

Assan bent down and raised the young woman's face up to hers. "I cannot end it."

"There is a way, there are medicine plants. Make it. I will take it."

Assan stood and took a few steps toward the creek, her fists clenched.

"There is no medicine. It was left at Lions-Came Camp. The herbs are known only to *Shanaghàn.*"

"But you are an old woman. Eyak must have told you," Dèhzhòo implored.

"I am not Old Woman yet," Assan replied firmly.

"Then what do I do?"

Assan paused and then looked at her, suddenly struck by how small she seemed lying on the ground.

"Nothing. There is nothing to do. You must hide yourself from him. Wear loose clothes. Do not get sick when he is near. Do not get sick in front of So'tsal. She must not know. No one can know."

"What will he do?"

"He will kill you. If he finds you are with child, he will kill you. Do you understand?"

Assan paced back and forth, thinking - searching for an answer. She lifted Dèhzhòo and stood in front of her. "You must keep this secret from the bushman and So'tsal until we meet others. It is our only hope. You must hide it from him until we find others."

"What will happen if we do not meet humans?"

Assan picked up the sack and slung it over her shoulder.

"What will happen if we do not meet other people?" Dèhzhòo repeated. Assan turned and walked toward camp, and did not answer.

Little Weasel

Shih Summer Camp was abandoned. Naali removed her pack and walked behind Barik and Kazan into its remnants. The collapsed tent skins were shredded, the poles scattered over the grassy meadow. All around them the ground was strewn with broken skull cups, torn baskets and shattered bones. *Zhòh gii* walked among the remains, sniffing at the debris.

"Dead," whispered Naali as she gently nudged a human skull with her foot. She wondered who it was. It was small, the size of a woman or a boy. "There is no one here. What happened?"

Barik walked through the camp, pushing aside the rotting tent skins. "We must count the dead," he said. They spread out, collecting as many bones and skulls as they could find; most in the pile had been gnawed or shattered by scavengers.

"How many were *Shih* Band?" Kazan asked, looking down at the heap of skulls.

"Twelve adults, six walking children, one infant," Naali said, "including our family."

"There seven big skulls and two small ones," he said, pointing to the collection.

"Wolves or bears or lions could have carried others away," Barik said.

"There are no weapons anywhere - no spears, no hunting darts," Kazan answered. "Some *Shih* have gone."

Naali and Barik began sorting through the skulls, trying to identify who they might be, when a chorus of ground-squirrel alarms sounded behind them. *Zhòh gii* was walking across the meadow, her nose pressed to the ground, following a scent, heading toward the rock outcrop not far away.

"What does she smell?" Naali asked as she followed after the wolf. Barik and Kazan fell in behind her. As they passed a colony of ground-squirrel burrows, Kazan noticed the snares. He bent down to inspect the sets, rolling the freshly braided sinew through his fingers.

These are new. Someone is living here.

He ran to catch up to Naali and Barik, who were about to enter a cave in the outcrop. *Zhòh gii* was inside, sitting by a hole at the back of the cave.

"There are new snares in the meadow," Kazan said as he followed them inside.

"We played in this cave," Barik whispered, pointing to the hole. "Small children could fit inside the hole. There is a smaller cave farther in." He knelt down, raised his hand for silence and listened. Something was moving inside the rock. He nodded slowly, pointing at the hole.

A spear suddenly flew down, jabbed into dirt and then was gone. Naali looked at the hole. She had never been able to fit in it.

Who is small enough and strong enough to use a spear?

She moved closer and called softly, "Avii Tsal. Little Weasel?"

The spear jabbed again and disappeared.

"Avii Tsal - it is Naali. Barik is here. Come out, it is safe."
They waited but there was no response. "Your mother and father,
where are they?"

If they were alive, she would not be hiding in this hole.

They stood and waited patiently until two small nervous
brown eyes appeared. A little later a thin figure slid out of the rock
and knelt beside the hole, gripping a spear.

"Little Weasel," Naali gasped, her heart falling at the sight
of the emaciated girl before her. She was completely covered in
dirt and grime, her long hair matted with sticks and leaves. Her
face was so blackened with grease she looked more animal than
human. She was so thin - half the size of the girl Naali
remembered. Naali extended her hand, but the girl moved back,
pressing against the wall. Her chest rose and fell as her small eyes
darted around the cave. She was shaking. When she saw the wolf
pup in Naali's arms she recoiled, shaking the spear at *Zhòh gii*.

"*Zhòh gii* is not dangerous," Naali said reassuringly. She
turned to Barik. "We are cousins. You remember Barik?" Kazan was
standing behind them. "He is called Kazan. He is a friend." Little
Weasel looked fearfully around before she slipped back into the
hole.

"She is afraid," Naali said. "The hole is too small for a
killing beast. Even wolverine cannot reach her without feeling a
spear."

Naali pointed around the cave. "There is no fire. The floor
is covered with ground-squirrel and hare bones. She has lived in
the hole without fire."

"How could she live without fire?" Barik asked.

Naali shrugged. "We can ask her."

But Little Weasel did not come out the rest of that day.
Naali waited by the hole, coaxing her with offerings of food.
Eventually, the boys left to salvage what remained of the camp,
retrieving strips of tent skins, bone utensils and a sack of flint for
making points and blades.

Naali built a fire at the entrance of the cave while Barik collected firewood. Kazan went to a nearby creek and filled skin bladders they had made from the elk-calf stomachs. The creek passed near the outcrop through a series of small ravines and canyons before dropping into the valley below.

On his way from the creek, Kazan found a dead ground squirrel in a snare. Naali burned the hair off it, skewered the carcass on a stick, roasted the meat and placed the offering in the hole. While she waited, she chewed up the heart and liver, spitting out the mush for Zhòh gii, who devoured it.

After a while, a small hand appeared and vanished back into the rock with the ground squirrel. They waited for her to return, but Little Weasel did not appear.

"We could build a fire," Barik suggested. "Smoke will drive her out."

Naali answered her brother with a glare.

That evening, they slept in the cave wrapped in the decaying shreds of tent skins. It was the first comfortable sleep since Lions-Came Camp.

Naali woke the next morning to the sound of the pup growling and the sight of the heaps of animal skins scattered across the floor. Little Weasel was squatting behind a pile, one hand on her spear and the other cradling a small doll. Naali stood slowly, careful not to frighten the girl as she looked at the remarkable treasure of animal skins. Her hands brushed bison sleeping beds, caribou-skin parkas, mukluks, sheepskin pants, fox and wolf hats, bison mitts and raw grasseater hides.

Naali nudged the boys awake, holding her fingers to her lips for silence. They both saw the furs but did not move. Avii Tsal was about to break for the hole when Naali reached out and touched her on the shoulder. The girl shifted toward the hole. "No," Naali said softly. "It is safe." She picked up a thick bison fur, rubbing the soft curly hair across her cheek, nodding to the girl.

Barik began to get up, but Naali shook her head and he

194

lay back down. She reached for Little Weasel's hand; this time the girl did not pull away. The girl's small fingers caressed the doll. Naali remembered how she had watched Avii Tsal's mother, Jutta, make the doll one winter night. It was made of the split hide of a calf elk. The figure was of a girl, the head trimmed with a patch of wolverine hair tied behind the neck. The doll's eyes were two discs made from the leg of a bird, and the mouth was a twist of hide dyed with ochre.

"You call her Calm Day," Naali said. Avii Tsal nodded.

"Your mother named her because the wind stopped blowing when she finished it. I had a doll. Do you remember it?"

The girl nodded.

"Do you remember the name?"

Little Weasel glanced around the tent and made a hoarse sound in her throat.

She cannot talk.

Naali smiled and nodded. "Her name was Little Bear. My mother named her for the stars high in the sky. Do you share these skins with us?" she asked.

The girl picked up a caribou-skin parka and handed it to Naali.

"Can we touch the skins?"

Avii squatted back down and pushed a pair of mukluks toward Barik. He began lacing the mukluks around his feet while Kazan stepped through the skins, his hands brushing the luxuriant furs.

"Clothes, beds - enough skins to cover a tent," he whispered with excitement.

Barik slipped a parka over his head and patted it down, checking the fit and remembering the owner. "You have many skins," he said to Avii Tsal. "This was Cut Knife's, my uncle." She looked away anxiously.

"We thank Little Weasel. We have few skins," Naali said.

The girl slipped back into the hole and moments later

195

spears and hunting darts clattered onto the floor.

"Hunting weapons!" Kazan exclaimed, hardly believing his eyes. He picked up a long spear, a wide smile lighting his face. They were different sizes, all tipped with sharp stone or ivory points. The hunting darts were as long as he was tall, made from willow with foreshafts of ivory or elk antler, each tipped with a sharp stone point. Kazan picked up a throwing board and slipped a dart into a notch. Raising the board, he looked down the dart shaft as his heart soared.

With throwing darts they could kill grasseaters from a distance. They did not have to spear them! Barik joined him, picking through the weapons. They looked at each other and laughed. Naali motioned to the girl to sit by the fire and began to cook the morning meal.

As they ate, Barik asked, "How did *Shih* Band die?" Avii Tsal's eyes suddenly shifted, looking for Naali.

"Did they starve?" Barik looked at her. Little Weasel shook her head.

"Is your mother dead?"

She nodded, casting her eyes down.

"Your father?"

Avii nodded again.

"How did they die?"

She looked at him and made a guttural sound. "*Naaaaa....*"

"*Shih* Band - are they all dead?" Barik asked. Little Weasel shook her head, trying to say something. "Who lived?"

Avii Tsal moved her mouth up and down, searching for words that did not come.

Naali looked at her. "Nod when I name the ones who live."

When Naali was done listing the names, Barik said, "Yong and Jila and their two children, Stone and Yellow Tail. And Kural, our uncle." He looked at Little Weasel and saw the tears. "Where

196

did they go?" She shrugged her shoulders, looking more desperate. "Did they leave you behind?" Naali asked. Avii Tsal began to shake.

They left her.

Naali gently wrapped her arms around the girl's shoulder, suddenly aware of her thin frame. She soothed her with comforting words, gently stroking her head.

"*Neegoo* sickness," Kazan said. "There are fox bones scattered in the camp." He looked at Avii Tsal. "*Neegoo... Neegoo*. Is that what you are trying to tell us?"

Avii Tsal's eyes fell to the ground and she began to sob.

"Fox sickness?" she asked. "Did *Shih* Band die of *Neegoo* sickness?"

Avii Tsal buried her face in Naali's coat.

"She was sick and they left her behind," Barik said. "No one lives with the sickness." He looked at Little Weasel. "But you lived." His voice had suddenly turned flat and distant. "She will bring bad luck."

Naali looked up. Disbelief turned to anger. "She is not bad luck! She has given us these skins, spears, throwing darts! She brings good luck!"

"They left her because she was a bad omen," Barik repeated, pointing to the pup. "The wolves left that one behind. They are both bad luck."

Naali stood and faced him, unable to contain her rage. "If Little Weasel is a bad omen, why is she alive? She has lived the winter alone with these furs to keep her warm. Now she shares them with us. She is a good omen!"

"She took the skins from the dead." Barik was growing angry, losing control. "And what has she fed on in the hole? The bones of the humans cannot speak!" His words seemed to hang in the air.

Kazan stood up. To accuse Little Weasel of eating human flesh was the worst charge someone could level.

197

"How else could she have lived?" Barik hissed.

"She has given us skins and spears!" Kazan shouted. He pushed his foot into a pile of small bones. "Ground squirrel, hare, ptarmigan. This is what she has eaten."

"She crawled out of the hole because she needs us." Barik stared at Kazan, his eyes growing darker. Suddenly he lunged and drove his shoulder into Kazan's gut. Kazan spun sideways and thrust his knee into Barik's shoulder, sending him headlong into the wall. Barik's head glanced off the rock as he fell into the dirt. Rolling onto his knees, he screamed with rage, a thin trail of blood streaming from his forehead.

"No! Stop!" Naali roared, but Barik was already moving. He swung his fists into Kazan's face without connecting. Kazan stumbled back, fending off the punches.

Suddenly Barik was waving the spear. Kazan's heart raced. Spears were for hunting! He dropped his head and slid under the shaft, slamming his head into Barik's chest. They fell to the ground and rolled across the cave.

"No!" Naali shouted, but Kazan heard only his pounding heart. Barik ground Kazan's face into the dirt, trying to turn him on his back. In a surge of strength, Kazan heaved up and flipped him off. They choked and wheezed as their grips tightened. Naali reached for a spear, shoving the shaft between them. "Let go!" she shouted, twisting it with all of her strength. They both released their grip and rolled away.

Naali was crying. Little Weasel had retreated into her hole. The pup had disappeared outside. She looked up at them, her eyes pleading. "Why do you fight? We are three children, alone. How can we live if you fight?" she muttered through a stream of tears.

Barik snatched the spear up and stared across the cave at Kazan. "I will kill you!" he shouted as he left. Kazan brushed the dirt from his clothes, unable to look at Naali. She moved to the hole and coaxed Little Weasel out. She sat stroking the girl's head, hardly believing her brother's words.

To kill another human is unthinkable! To accuse Avii Tsal of eating another human is unthinkable! What is happening? Barik has always been strange, but he has never spoken this way before.

Kazan knelt down beside them, touching Avii Tsal on the shoulder. "You are brave," he said. Then he went outside and walked to the ruins of *Shih* Summer Camp.

As he looked over the remnants, he imagined how it had ended. He had seen foxes with sickness, their mouths foaming as they staggered to their deaths. Once, when he was young, a sick fox had approached camp. The women killed it with rocks and burned the carcass until there was nothing left but smoking ash. He knew about humans with the sickness. They died suddenly, writhing in great pain, vomiting - but Avii Tsal had not died. She lived while others died around her. Kazan suddenly felt a deep bond to the girl. He, too, had lived while everyone in his band had died.

He turned to walk back to the cave when he noticed Barik sitting on the top of the outcrop, watching him approach. He did not understand him. One moment he was friendly to Little Weasel, the next he was accusing her of eating the dead.

He said he will kill me.

As he passed under the rocks, he could feel Barik's eyes following him into the cave. Slipping inside, he thought he heard Barik's voice. Then a gust of wind muffled the sound.

A Conversation

"He will take her."

Barik glanced around the rock outcrop, looking for the speaker of the words.

"The tall boy. Kazan. He will take her."

Barik recognized the voice - the same one that came at night in the darkness. But it was daylight. The sun was shining. The voice had never spoken to him in the light. Below, he could see Kazan in the meadow moving through the ruins of *Shih* Summer Camp.

"They are bad luck: the wolf, Little Weasel, Kazan. She will leave you behind."

"She will not leave me. Naali is my sister. She needs me."

"You think you are wise, but anger fills your mind. Now they are angry at you for speaking badly of the girl, accusing her of eating the dead. And you threatened to kill the boy. You know both acts are unmentionable."

Barik shifted uncomfortably on the rocks.

"There are ways to make them leave. But you cannot lose their trust. Have patience. There will be a time. Then you will have her back."

Barik saw Kazan leaving the ruins and walking to the cave, his eyes downcast.

"Look at him. He does not trust you. He is stronger than you think. And dangerous. If you let him become strong she will leave you. She will go with him."

The wind began to blow. Barik turned his parka hood up.

"Be patient. They will make mistakes. Then she will be with us."

A Broken Arm

One-Eye held his arm against his chest as immense pain radiated from his shoulder. He had strapped on the handle of his club to stabilize his shattered upper arm, but the pain was still excruciating. As he staggered toward Cliff Camp, he was barely able to find his way. When he finally stumbled into the tent, he did not hear the woman gasp as he collapsed unconscious at her feet.

He woke as something cool and wet touched his forehead. He was suddenly overwhelmed by panic. He tried to move his feet but something held them down. His eyes shot open. He was lying on his back. The older one, Assan, was staring down at him, wiping his face. So'tsal, the girl, was slowly waving a willow branch over him, brushing away mosquitoes. He tried to reach for them but he could not move. His arms and legs were lashed to wooden stakes in the ground. A lightning bolt of pain shot through his body and he screamed out in agony. Someone was pulling hard on his shoulder. He twisted around to see Dèhzhòo sitting behind, her hands wrapped around a heavy rawhide cord. She was leaning back, pulling with all of her weight on his fractured arm. He roared, as much from helpless frustration and rage as from the stinging pain.

"We are setting the break," Assan said. He roared again then fainted before he could find her face. Slipping in and out of consciousness, he recalled how it had happened.

He had been stalking a group of bison, using shrubs along the creek for cover, when two cows separated from the herd, their small red-skinned calves following behind. One calf made the mistake of crossing the creek near him. He flew from the shrubs and hit it with a hunting dart. As it was dying by his feet, he looked up to see a cow moving away. He thought it was the mother. Gripping the calf by the leg, he pulled it into the shrubs and hid. Suddenly he heard something thundering at him from behind. Before he could turn, the cow slammed into his side, launching him into the air. Crashing to the ground, he heard his arm shattering. It sounded like an antler club smashing into soft bone.

The cow could have trampled him to death but she circled the dead calf, waiting for it to get up. One-Eye lay still there for hours until she finally walked off, snorting and snuffling. When he staggered to his feet he knew he was badly broken. He gutted the calf with one hand and slung the carcass over his good shoulder. When he reached camp he dropped the calf at someone's feet. And that was all he remembered. He woke to the woman's voice.

She raised her hand, spreading out her fingers and thumb. "Five nights for the bone to set. You cannot move your arms or legs. You are tied to the ground so you will not move the arm."

He turned and saw his arm splinted between two leg bones. His hands were lashed to willow stakes to keep his arms immobile. He kicked and struggled in a futile attempt to get up, roaring when he found his legs were staked, too. He felt utterly vulnerable and powerless.

Why has she not killed me? She could spear me or smash my head in with a club.

Assan lifted a skull cup to his lips, dribbling a stream of cool water into his parched mouth. Then she brought him warm broth, spooning it slowly into his mouth. "If you move the arm it will heal wrong. I will break it again if it is bent. Do not move. You cannot move for five days." Then she was gone.

He saw he was in a low skin shelter on the tundra, a smudge burning nearby to keep away insects. He wrenched at the stakes, sending a pulsating pain through his entire body. He gave up struggling and slept, waking to the muffled sound of voices behind him.

"We could kill him. We could kill him and leave. His spear is right here."

"We cannot live without a hunter. We are women, not hunters."

"We could learn to spear and throw darts."

"Without a hunter, a lion or bear would kill us."

There was a long pause.

"He will kill us when the snow comes. He will have dry meat and winter clothes. He will kill us and then climb into his hole for winter."

"If we run, we will die. Our only hope is for him to heal. The break is not his throwing arm. We stay with him until we find others. Then we run. That is our only chance."

One-Eye thrashed and struggled furiously against the rawhide straps, and then he began to slowly relax. To heal the bone, he needed to be still. She had told him - five days. Then he would be strong again. He would hunt again. As he stared into the skins rustling in the wind above his face, his wildness won again and he suddenly erupted. He fought the straps like a snared beast until he was exhausted, collapsing into a restless sleep.

Training a Wolf

Avii Tsal was outside the cave, watching the pup. Naali had tied a mouse skin to a long rawhide lace and was dragging it in front of *Zhòh gii*, making a squeaking sound. At first the pup did not respond. Naali tried again, this time pulling the lure closer. On the third try, the pup followed the dead mouse a few feet and caught the scent. The next time, *Zhòh gii* snatched it in her teeth. Naali rewarded her with a piece of raw meat.

Little Weasel clapped her hands, motioning that she wanted a try. Naali handed her the skin lure and watched. Each time *Zhòh gii* caught it, Little Weasel rewarded her. Soon, the pup was full and lost interest in the training game.

The next day, Avii Tsal caught a live mouse in the recess of the cave. The first time the mouse was dragged, *Zhòh gii* snapped the neck, instantly killing it. Naali cut open the gut and pushed out the bloody entrails at *Zhòh gii*. The pup devoured the mouse before retiring to the cave to sleep.

As the pup grew through summer, Naali gradually introduced her to larger, more difficult prey, starting with young ground squirrels, graduating to flightless ptarmigan and finally progressing to young hares.

Little Weasel supplied all the victims. She fixed snares along the creek and through the ground-squirrel colonies that surrounded the rock outcrop they had named Hole-in-Rock Camp. To live catch victims, Little Weasel tied small knots in the snares so the sinew did not close too tightly around the necks. Most days she returned with a hare or ground squirrel squirming in her sack.

With the fast hares, Naali tied sticks to their legs, finding the right weight to slow the victims just enough so the pup would have to run fast to catch them.

Naali was sitting atop the rocks, surveying the late-summer tundra-steppe. The meadows were a mosaic of yellow, orange and red with splashes of gold. The willows along the creek had turned, the yellow leaves scattering onto the open tundra. The mountain peaks showed the first apron of new snow.

Naali watched flocks of cranes pass high overhead, filling the air with their loud, musical call. Summer was ending. The sun that had not set for many moons had dropped below the horizon a few days ago. Stars now sparkled in the dark night sky. Morning ice formed on the edges of the ponds. The relentless attack by mosquitoes had ended with the first freeze.

Zhòh gii had grown quickly. She now stood above Naali's knee. She was becoming a hunter, able to catch a wild hare in open pursuit.

The pup was sleeping on the rocks next to Naali, enjoying the warm rays of the afternoon sun. Naali was watching for grasseaters. Yesterday she had spotted a band of elk, but the boys were hunting elsewhere and had missed seeing them. As she scanned the horizon, she saw Barik and Kazan returning from hunting. Their gait was smooth, meaning their packs were empty. They were walking far apart as they approached Hole-in-Rock Camp. As they neared she saw they were still avoiding one another's company. Naali climbed down the rocks, went to the cave entrance and waited.

They have not spoken for many days. How will we share a winter camp?

Barik arrived first. He did not greet her as he pulled off his pack and leaned his weapons against the rock. He took a sliver of dry meat from the rack and gnawed on it.

"This place is bad luck. We have not killed a grasseater for a moon," he said, scowling at the wolf pup chewing on a hare leg. "The pup eats meat we should be drying for winter," he complained, kicking the leg across the floor of the cave. *Zhòh gii* bolted away and hid in the shadows. Barik settled onto the floor and stared blankly at the rock wall.

Moments later Kazan arrived, followed by Little Weasel, who had returned from checking snares. When she pulled the two hares from her pack, he felt both relief and a little shame. "Little Weasel feeds us again," he said, trying to sound pleased. He took a piece of dry meat and leaned against the rock wall.

No one spoke. Kazan could see Naali was upset with her brother. He had his own reasons to be angry at him. They had found a band of elk grazing in a broad meadow. They crawled for hours in the open and were finally within dart range. Then Barik lost patience. He stood up and charged before Kazan could ready his dart. Barik's throw went wide and the elk thundered off. Kazan chased the band for a long way, but they disappeared into willows. The elk were the first grasseaters they had encountered since coming to Hole-in-Rock. They had not put up enough dry meat for winter.

"Unless grasseaters come, we will have to search for them," Barik said.

"We could travel with a small camp and hunt. Then come back with meat," Kazan said. "There is no better winter camp than this cave."

Naali listened, suddenly aware the boys were talking to each other. Little Weasel grunted, realizing they were talking about leaving Hole-in-Rock. Naali reached over, smoothing her hand on her shoulder. "Your snares are far from here," she said. "It is becoming dangerous for you to check them alone."

"We can hunt grasseaters before the snow falls and return here with dry meat," Barik said, nodding at Kazan. "It is a good plan, Kazan."

Kazan had not heard a compliment from Barik before. He did not know if he should respond.

Little Weasel vigorously shook her head. She did not want to go anywhere.

"We will come back," Barik said, his voice friendly and patient.

Kazan glanced over at Naali, surprised by sudden Barik's attention to Little Weasel. He had hardly spoken to her since they

206

had come to Hole-in-Rock.

"Where are grasseaters?" Barik asked Naali.

She looked at him and replied, "I do not know."

"You have not dream-travelled for a long time, not since Came-to-a-Hill. Have you tried?"

"Dream-travel comes. I cannot ask it."

"We need to find grasseaters. Winter is coming. We need meat and skins."

Kazan had been thinking the same thing. He knew that whatever happened, they could not leave the cave. It provided safe shelter and protection from winter winds. To make it through winter they needed to find grasseaters and return to Hole-in-Rock before the snows came.

"We cannot go far. Summer is ending. We must return before the snow arrives," Kazan said. "You said the bushman found your family near the river. How far is the *Ch'oodèenjik?*"

Barik raised his hand and spread his fingers. "Four days, but we hunted and picked berries on the way. If we travel fast, we could make it in three days."

"Did you see grasseaters at the river?"

"No," Barik replied. "But we have found little to hunt here."

Naali listened to the conversation between Barik and Kazan, the first friendly exchange they had had since they met. Maybe they had realized they must trust each other to be successful hunters. As she turned to look for Little Weasel, Naali saw her disappear into the hole, pulling her sleeping bed behind her.

Hunting Hare

Blue walks beside the stand of willows in the middle of the meadow, startling a flock of yellow warblers from the shrubs. When he reaches the end of the thicket, he stops. Hare scent fills the air. Suddenly he is charging into the willows. Branches snap and whip at his face as hares rush out from under the shrubs. One panics and swings toward Blue, running under his legs. He snatches it by the back, killing it instantly. Ahead, others are twisting, turning, stopping or backtracking, desperately seeking a way to escape. Blue kills two more as he charges ahead. The willows are thinning and the hares in front are running onto the open meadow, breaking in all directions.

Grey–Eye is waiting with her pack at the edge of a creek wash. As the hares near, she charges, scattering the approaching hares. She snatches one in her jaws as it tries to dodge around her and kills three more before they can reach the wash. Blue arrives and turns a group back toward the willows, running down four before they can reach the safety of the shrubs. Then, as quickly as it began, the hare hunt is over.

Scores of dead hares are strewn over the meadow. The wolves spread out and start feeding. They spend the night sleeping along the creek, but Grey–Eye is uneasy. She wakes often, remembering the den. She had bonded with her new pups, and their absence is still distressing.

In the morning she leads the pack up the creek toward a high mountain. By midday they are rounding the shore of an alpine lake when they are stopped by a chorus of howls. Grey–Eye howls back, recognizing the voice of Black–Foot, her sister. Across a low incline fresh holes are scattered among a series of depressions and mounds. Grey–Eye knows the place. She was born here. She walks into the denning area, remembering where her own mother nursed her, the collapsed hole now filled with dirt and covered in shrubs.

Black-Foot is lying near the lake surrounded by her mob of playful pups. Grey-Eye stops, sensing she must wait for her sister's invitation to approach closer. She waits until Black-Foot greets her. They circle until they are both satisfied neither poses a threat. The rest of the wolves cautiously sniff rumps and nudge together, growling mutual greetings. The half-grown pups jostle into the crowd, moving around strange legs, eager to make friends.

Broken-Tail appears from behind a low mound. She has been gone from Grey-Eye's pack since they abandoned the den. She is an adult now, two years old and ready to have her own pups. Her posture is wary and defensive, as if she does not recognize her mother. Grey-Eye circles, sniffing and exploring her new scents. Grey-Eye suddenly turns away, but Broken-Tail follows her through the den.

Grey-Eye's pack continues to visit until evening when Blue, having lost interest, begins to howl, signalling his departure. As his pack follows him along the lakeshore he stops and looks back, noticing Broken-Tail is following them at a distance. Grey-Eye has stopped and is looking toward the den. By the time they reach the creek and head down the mountain, Broken-Tail has turned back and is howling. Grey-Eye answers, sensing something is missing from her pack.

New Skins

One-Eye lay strapped to the ground for five frustrating days. Dèhzhòo brought him food and water while So'tsal kept a smudge fire burning inside the shelter. Assan rubbed grease on his wrists and ankles to keep them from chafing, and she checked the splints for tightness. On the last day she pulled down the shelter and released the straps from the wood stakes.

"Do not bend the arm," she said as he tried to sit up. His senses swirled as the blood rushed from his head. She held his elbow as he leaned back. "You must wear the splints for a moon. You cannot hunt until the bone is set." He sat for a while, gathering his strength. Finally, he stood up, swaying awkwardly as he gained balance.

Assan was wearing a new caribou-skin parka and a new pair of mukluks. She had tried to disguise them by smearing the clothes with grease and grime to make them look old. She had taken a huge risk making the clothes and feared his reaction. She waited for the blow, but he did not appear to notice. Encouraged, she called to So'tsal and Dèhzhòo. They emerged from the tent wearing their new parkas. Dèhzhòo's was loosely cut, hiding her condition. One-Eye paid no attention as he gazed out over the land. A little later he walked away, disappearing over a nearby ridge.

Assan knelt down to stoke the fire as she spun a bladder of water over the flames. "When he hunts again he will need us to dry meat."

"He did not notice our clothes," Dèhzhòo said.

"He noticed," Assan replied. "Now he is only thinking about hunting. Be careful. We are not used to him being in camp all day. He will become angry as he heals but cannot hunt. Make sure you do not get in his way."

For two weeks One-Eye wore the splint as he paced the camp like a wolf, staring out on the plain with growing impatience.

Herds of caribou and elk appeared, adding to his frustration. But despite his immense irritation he did not strike at the women. He slept much of the day, and they changed the order of their chores to avoid waking him.

Then one morning his bed was empty. It was nearly dark when he returned, carrying half an elk on his back. The splint was gone and he did not appear to be favouring his arm as he unloaded the carcass. Assan pointed at his shoulder. He shook his head lightly and then turned away. She brought him hot broth while Dèhzhòo and So'tsal stripped the carcass. As he drank, Assan watched him from the corner of her eye. He had changed since the accident. He no longer moved through the camp as if they did not exist. He had let them make winter clothes. She wondered if they would be with him through the winter - and the next summer. Would they still be alive? She glanced over at Dèhzhòo and felt all hope vanish.

She will show soon.

The Ravine

Little Weasel was filled with anxiety as she pulled the last few snares from the willows in the ravine. They were moving: Naali, Barik - the angry one - and Kazan, the friendly one. They were back at the cave preparing to leave. She would go, but she was unhappy and nervous to be leaving her hole. Naali had promised they would come back to the cave - to the hole - for winter. They were moving to find grasseaters but would come back. Little Weasel was to close the snares while the others packed camp.

She stood at the edge of the ravine, the rock outcrop in the distance. She could see them loading skins onto a travel frame. The last snare was down in the ravine, in a willow thicket close to the creek. A long-billed snipe exploded from the grass near her foot, sending her heart racing. As she watched the small bird fly into the ravine, she heard something. A light breeze blew, rustling the leaves. Far off, a raven called. High above, geese were honking.

Wind.

Little Weasel scanned the shrubs, listening to the rumble of the flowing creek as she walked into the ravine. She heard a familiar scuffle and knew she had caught something. Bending down, she gripped the snared ground squirrel by the back and broke its neck with a sudden twist of her wrist. She heard the noise again. As the wind shifted, she smelled it, and she froze.

Lion!

Avii Tsal dropped the ground squirrel, slipped behind a boulder and listened. She knew the stink of lion. One had come to her hole and pushed its head inside. She had struck it in the ear with her spear, and it had disappeared in a roaring fit. The scent was blowing up the ravine. She looked across the narrow creek but could not see anything. Reaching into her parka, Little Weasel pulled out the bone whistle hanging from her neck. She wanted to blow it - hard. She wanted them to come running with their spears

212

and darts. The small spear in her hand felt useless.

She hesitated. Maybe it had not smelled her. She slid around the boulder and inched her way out the ravine, her eyes fixed on the creek when she heard the soft splashing. It was following her. Her mother's voice suddenly came to her:

If a lion comes do not run. Do not look away.

Her instinct was to turn and run. If she blew the whistle, they might see her if she could make it to the open meadow. Had the killing beast seen her, smelled her? Was it waiting for her to move, waiting for her to run? She would never get out of the ravine. Lowering the whistle, Avii Tsal stood perfectly still.

She could hear something and imagined a pebble shifting under a thick padded foot, hair brushing a branch, a soft breathing. It was moving closer. She held her breath and did what her mother had told her to do. Little Weasel stepped out from the rock and looked straight into the eyes of the lion. The beast stopped in midstride, its bright yellow orbs locked on her. It stood twice her height, its broad head wider than her small body.

She nearly screamed in terror. It was a few steps away. Fear rushed through her, compelling her to run - to turn and run for her life. She had heard stories of lions attacking humans and she fumbled, trying to remember what to do.

Do not look away! Do not run!

The lion was staring at her, every muscle in its trembling body straining to be unleashed. Little Weasel moved slowly, backward, toward the meadow. With each step she held her eyes on the lion's.

Watch its eyes.

A stumble, a missed step, and it would attack. Tears streamed down her cheeks but she did not cry - although her terror was growing. Panic was creeping into her thoughts. She remembered her mother's advice:

Make yourself big. Take off your coat. Wave it. Growl, roar.

She slowly pulled off her parka and raised it up on her

213

spear. As she waved it, she roared with all of her strength. The lion lowered its head.

Do not run!

The lion followed her out of the ravine until they stood in the meadow looking at each other. She raised the whistle to her lips.

Naali was packing the travel frame with her back to the ravine. She was cinching down the straps, but her mind was elsewhere. She had dream-travelled last night, the first time in some time. In the dream, there was a river filled with swimming *Vadzaih*. She saw the river as if she were a bird flying high above it - and that was what confused her. She saw three people in a camp.

There should be four. Someone is missing.

She had woken from the dream feeling raw and exhausted. The grasseaters were a good sign. They would have a hunt. Naali told Kazan and Barik about the dream, but she did not mention the three humans.

Am I the one missing? Can I see myself in my dreams?

She was unsure. Naali watched Kazan tie himself into the harness she had made him. He and Barik had built a light travel frame from two tent poles that formed a V-shape. It was the first thing they had worked on together since their fight in the cave. In the centre of the V they lashed shorter poles, forming a platform to carry the camp.

At first Little Weasel refused to follow. Naali saw she was deeply afraid of leaving the cave. The hole was her safety, her home. In the end, it was the pup that convinced her to come. Over the summer, Little Weasel had become attached to *Zhòh gii*. The pup often followed her to the snares and was rewarded with raw meat.

"*Zhòh gii* wishes you to come with her to the river," Naali had told her. That was all that needed to be said. She packed her things, brought them from the cave and went to close her snares.

The high-pitch scream of a bone whistle shattered the

morning stillness. Naali's heart leaped as she searched for the location of the sound. Kazan and Barik were running, looking in all directions. A second blast sounded, echoing off the rock outcrop.

"Avii Tsal!" Kazan shouted. "Where is she?"

"The ravine!" screamed Naali.

Barik, Kazan and Naali ran toward the creek, blowing their whistles, shouting her name. But there was no reply, no answering whistle. Naali's heart sank.

Blow your whistle, Avii Tsal. Blow it!

They stood facing the creek. Naali listened, but there was only the sound of the water rushing through the ravine.

"She might be hiding," Kazan said.

"Hiding from what?" Naali asked. She suddenly felt helpless. Little Weasel was in the ravine. What was in there with her?

"Here!" Barik shouted from behind. They turned and saw him pick up Avii Tsal's parka. He picked up her spear and silently raised it.

"Blood," Kazan pointed to a dark spot on the ground and saw the huge claw print. "Lion," he whispered.

"She could be alive!" Naali answered. "She is smart. She would not make a sound. She is hiding!"

"We should go," Barik said as his nervous eyes scanned the creek. "It is waiting for us."

Naali was numbed by shock. "Why did I not dream this? I did not feel this happening. We must find her. We cannot leave her! She may be alive!" She walked toward the ravine, her spear pointed ahead. Kazan joined her, but Barik waited a safe distance behind on the meadow.

"You will bring it out! Leave her," Barik hissed at them as they disappeared into the creek.

They moved slowly, their eyes on the rocks around them, watching for any movement. Kazan's hand brushed a boulder and he felt a sticky wetness. He raised his hand and pointed to the blood smear. At that moment the air trembled as a low menacing

215

growl rumbled from the other side of the boulder. Kazan raised his spear. He could see the top of lion's white back moving only a few steps away. Suddenly it sprang across the creek into a heavy thicket carrying something.

It is warning us.

He moved carefully around the boulder and looked down. Naali was about to follow him, but his hand stopped her.

"Is she there?" she asked, her eyes imploring Kazan.

Say yes, she is here, alive, unhurt.

"Do not look," he whispered as he pushed her back. Somewhere down the creek the lion roared. It was moving off. Their eyes met.

"She is dead," Kazan said. "We must go. There is nothing we can do."

As Naali walked her legs felt like stones. Kazan was speaking, but she did not understand anything he was saying.

Stunned by Little Weasel's sudden death, they returned to camp and sat by the travel frame in gloomy silence.

Kazan was the first to speak. "I should have been careful."

"She checked the snares many times," Naali replied. "I did not think it dangerous." She looked at the boys. "Why did I not see it happening?" Her voice shook. "She is a little girl. I should have protected her!" Naali broke down, sobbing miserably. "What should we do now?" Naali was nearly hysterical with grief.

Kazan looked at Barik and Naali. "We should leave. We are packed. Move to the river. There is nothing we can do here." Kazan felt Little Weasel's loss deeply. They had become like brother and sister. "I should have been more careful where she set snares."

Naali, badly shaken, was of no use for breaking camp. Barik loaded the travel frame while Kazan gathered the skins they would leave behind. He tied them to a rope and stuffed them into Little Weasel's hole to retrieve when they returned. When he was done, he stood staring at the rock wall. Naali entered the cave and came to his side.

216

"I promised I would not leave her," she whispered. Reaching into her parka, she pulled out Little Weasel's doll.

"It is time to go," Kazan said, touching her gently on the shoulder.

Naali stuffed the doll inside her parka and followed him out of the cave.

Barik Decides to Change

The harness traces bit into Barik's shoulders as he pulled the travel frame through the shallow creek. Beside him, Kazan lunged forward in his harness and the load slid over the rocks and onto the meadow. Barik could hear his sister splashing through the water, coaxing the wolf pup to follow.

Since they left Hole-in-Rock, he had decided he would change. Little Weasel's death shook him more than he showed. It could have been him killed by the lion. They had all hauled water from the creek, checked snares and collected firewood from the ravine. The lion killed the girl, but it could have been him. Since they had left the river, a gnawing loneliness consumed him. Nearly everyone in *Shih* was dead. If any had lived, they were of no help. Kazan was the only survivor of Wolf Band. Little Weasel was the only other living human they had met. Naali was devastated by her loss.

Kazan did not trust him. Barik saw it in his look and heard it in the short way the boy spoke. His own anger was driving away the only humans left in his life.

He was exhausted from travelling but slept little. The loneliness had crept into his dreams. When he did sleep, the dream was always the same. He was standing on the plain. It was snowing. He could see blurred shapes moving in the storm. He shouted to them, but they kept moving away until he was alone. He had to change or he *would* be alone. He heard Kazan in the harness beside him.

"We can rest."

They stopped and took off their harnesses. Barik unslung a water bladder from his shoulder and passed it to Kazan. "Here," he said.

Kazan nodded and took a long drink, passing the bladder to Naali.

"One more day," Barik said, pointing to the dusky bluffs in

the distance. "The *Ch'oodèenjik* is close. There is a shallow crossing somewhere ahead. The bushman took us across the same shallows. Grasseaters will know the river. It will be a good place to hunt."

As he pulled the travel frame over the tundra, he thought about Kazan. He would become his friend. He would pull until Kazan tired, even though his body was screaming to stop. He would hunt with him, slaughter grasseaters, make hunting points with him - become a hunter with him. He had grown up watching hunters; good hunters worked together. And Kazan was already a fair hunter. He could run faster and longer than him, and his skill with throwing darts was developing quickly. He needed Kazan. His thoughts turned to his sister.

She was becoming as skilled as women twice her age. She could process meat and bone swiftly, tan skins and sew rough clothing. But her real worth, her real power, was spirit medicine. She was a dream-traveller who could speak with caribou, wolf and lion, the greatest of animal spirits. She had visions of the future - warnings, premonitions. Her power was worth more than a band of skilled hunters. Barik knew his life depended on her and he had resented her for that. But there was something else that held her close to him. Since they escaped One-Eye, he felt a growing possessiveness toward Naali. At first he thought it was simply a brother protecting a sister. But as she revealed her power, he knew he wanted to be part of it, to share it, to feel it himself. But he had been moving away from her, not closer. He needed to gain back the trust and friendship of Naali and Kazan. But there was something within him - a darkness, a voice - that told him he would fail. Naali would leave, and he would be alone.

The River

They reached the river, passing scattered groups of caribou and elk in the distance. As they approached the shore the air became crisp and cool. The darkening sky was filled with flocks of cranes and geese and other waterfowl. The land would soon be covered in snow, and the open tundra plain would be no place for humans.

They set camp beside the river shallows and waited. The first morning, Naali's dream came true. They woke to the sound of a large herd of caribou stumbling through the middle of the camp. They killed two cows with spears before the herd ran off. The shallows had been the right place to hunt. Each day, a steady stream of grasseaters swam to them: elk, horse and caribou. They used their spears, afraid they would lose their hunting darts in the river. When animals reached their shore the boys charged, shouting and hooting as they leaped into the water. In three days, they had killed more grasseaters than Naali could process and dry.

Naali saw that Barik had become surprisingly enthusiastic about his hunting partner. He offered to touch spears after a kill. He whooped and shouted when they killed a grasseater, embracing Kazan in celebration. At first, Kazan was suspicious of the sudden change in Barik. But he became caught up in the excitement of the hunt and gradually began to trust him. While they hunted, Naali built more drying racks and collected wood for drying fires. Whenever she looked out over the river, she watched for humans. As the crisp autumn days passed, she lost all hope they would ever meet another person.

Barik Dreams

Naali is beside him. They are together flying high over the plain, their hands touching. Barik is filled with intense, complete joy. Ahead, animals are beginning to appear. Suddenly, he and Naali are on the ground, surrounded by mammoths. As they approach, the beasts look up, swinging their ivory tusks and long trunks. Naali is speaking Long-Nose - and he understands her. She squats down and begins telling them a story about how all living things were saved from the flood. "What I have heard, I will tell you," Naali says, looking up at the great beasts. "It is an old story, as old as the land." The mammoths stand still, listening.

"Long ago, people and animals lived together and shared knowledge freely. One day, people came to a flat plain that stretched as far as their eyes could see. The grasses were green and thick and the land was covered with all grasseaters: mammoth, horse, saiga, bison, caribou, elk. There were so many grasseaters they darkened the land. For a long time, people and grasseaters lived together on the great flat plain.

"Then one day the water came. It kept rising and the land was flooded, until all living beasts stood together on the last patch of dry land. As the water rose, the ground became smaller and smaller, until there was no room to move. People and animals were frightened. They did not know what to do, where to go. The humans asked their most powerful medicine man what they should do. He called down Raven from the sky. Deetrù' called the people from their tents. They were sick with worry. Raven changed and spoke human."

The pitch of Naali's voice shifts. Barik is thrilled he understands everything.

"'Why do you all look so worried?' Deetrù' asks.

"'We do not know which way to go,' the people said, pointing at the rising waters.

"Deetrù' saw a boy standing in the crowd and called to

him. 'Come. See with your eyes.' Raven turned into Eagle and picked the boy up. They flew over the great water. In every direction, there was nothing but water, except for a long ridge that disappeared where the sun rises.

"Deetrù' and the boy flew back down to earth. The people came around them and asked. 'Boy, what did you see?'

"The boy did not want to scare them, so he told them, 'There is a dry trail going from here to where the sun rises. Follow grasseaters. They know the way.'"

Naali stops and looks at Barik. She wants him to continue the story.

He is ready. "All animals walked together: mammoth, saiga, elk, bison, caribou, horse and wolf, lion, bear — and people," he says. "They walked together through valleys and mountains until they came to mountains they could not see beyond." Barik stretches his arms as wide as he can reach.

"As time passed, grasseaters and people lived here together," he says, picking up a handful of grass. "This is the ground all living beasts share."

The dream is so vivid, he has imagined he is the boy on the back of eagle - the boy who finds land and saves all living beasts.

Suddenly the mammoths are gone. He and Naali are standing on the shore of a rushing river.

He turns to her. "What is his name, the boy who flew with the eagle?"

She turns and points toward the river. "There. That is him."

Kazan is wading out of the river surrounded by a herd of caribou bulls. A shadow suddenly passes overhead and a great eagle glides down and lands beside them. Kazan climbs onto the bird's back, pulling Naali up with him. The bird spreads its huge wings and they fly away. Barik calls for them to come back, to take him with them. But they are gone.

Barik woke shouting, his arms flailing, his heart racing.

223

"You are dreaming," Kazan said, as he held him by the shoulders.

Naali was kneeling over him. "Barik, wake! It is a dream!" He tried to strike them but Kazan held his arms down. "It is Naali and Kazan! Wake up!" Kazan said.

Barik woke, but he was spinning down into a hole of blackness.

"You left me!" he growled, his eyes flashing at his sister.

"We are here. We have not left you. We are all here."

"Let me go!" he shouted as he shrugged them off.

Kazan released him and sat back on his own bed.

"What did you dream?" Naali asked quietly.

Her face was twisted, unrecognizable. He was sinking deeper, to where the voice was waiting.

"I do not remember," he said, settling into his bed.

"You said we left you."

"I do not remember." He turned away and buried his face in his bed. A darkness was engulfing him. His heart filled with fear and apprehension. He waited in silence until they went back to sleep. Then he was alone, and the voice spoke again.

The Hunt

Naali woke to the sound of the fire crackling and saw Barik was already up, feeding kindling to the flames. She slipped out of her sleeping bed. The sun was just beginning to rise. *Zhòh gii* scrambled out of the bed and went outside the tent.

"You woke early," Naali said, rubbing the sleep from her eyes. She thought it was strange - her brother was always the last one to waken. She pulled on her jacket and went to the fire. "You had a hard dream last night?"

"A dream? I do not remember," he said cheerily, then he turned to Kazan still in his bed. "It is our last hunt day. Kazan, wake up! There are grasseaters to hunt. You will sleep the day away!"

Kazan woke, surprised to find Barik and Naali already drinking tea. He crawled out of his bed and slipped outside to relieve himself. The sky was overcast, a dull grey. The *Ch'oodèenjik* was enshrouded in a thick white fog. Ravens were circling the camp, eager for another day of meat-raiding.

Kazan and Barik ate their morning meal planning the hunting day. They gathered their packs and struck off downstream while Naali tended the camp. They settled down along the shore behind a thicket of shrubs and waited all morning, watching the fog slowly lift and the river flow by. Then a large group of caribou appeared on the far shore, their thick white manes flashing in the sunlight. The leading bulls stepped into the river and began to swim across. The river was shallow and the current fast, and the boys saw the herd would reach the shore somewhere downstream. They ran down the shore, reaching a small backwater where they thought the bulls would land.

Kazan crouched behind a willow thicket, the thrill of the hunt pounding in his chest. They had guessed the landing right. As the caribou swam into the shallows, he and Barik burst from cover at the same time. He was a few feet ahead, his arm cocked and ready to plunge his spear into a bull climbing out of the river.

225

Leaping into the shallows, he sunk the stone tip deep into the animal's side. The bull bellowed in shock, coughing up a cloud of bloody mist and reeling back into the river. Behind him he heard Barik shouting. Suddenly something hard struck his head, and everything went black.

Naali had spent the morning filling skin sacks with dry meat and cleaning the last of the skins. She collected firewood, fed Zhòh gii a mash of caribou meat and made herself a hot tea. The fog had lifted from the river and the afternoon sun had broken through the low clouds. Along the shore, blueberries were ripening in the handfuls. Naali took a small sack and began picking them, the pup following close behind.

She saw the caribou appear on the far shore and watched with growing excitement as they swam out into the river. Downstream, she saw Kazan and Barik moving and knew they had also seen the Vadzaih. When they were out of sight, she stepped out on the shore for a better view of the hunt. The current had taken the animals well downstream. They were heading for shore. She heard the shouts and she smiled to herself. There he was - Kazan — leaping into the water. She could see his spear flash and the bull was rearing back into the river. The rest of the herd was turning back into the current. Then Barik appeared, swinging his club. She watched in disbelief as he struck Kazan.

Kazan crumpled and fell into the river. For a moment she thought it was an accident. But as he lay face down in the water, Barik struck him again and again. Naali could not believe her eyes. She started to run to help Kazan, but something made her stop. Barik stood on the shore casually swinging his club, watching Kazan float into the river with the escaping caribou.

It is no accident!

She lost sight of Kazan among the brown bodies and swaying antlers. As she slipped into the shrubs the horror of what had just happened struck her. She fell to her knees and vomited.

He has killed Kazan! He said he would kill him!

Her heart was racing as she stood up and peered through a space in the willows. Barik was facing camp, holding something in his mouth. The shrill blast of the bone whistle stunned her.

What is he doing?

Suddenly she knew. She snatched *Zhòh gii* in her arms and turned back to camp, sprinting through the bushes. Behind her Barik's whistle blew, getting closer. Naali reached camp, pulled out her whistle and blew it as loudly as she could. Her mind raced, trying to think of what to do. She could hear Barik shouting her name between whistles. She waited, breathing in the cool air, trying to stop her chest from heaving.

He cannot see I know!

He suddenly came running up from shore, looking distressed.

"Kazan!" he shouted, stooping over to catch his breath. "He has fallen in the river!"

He cannot see that I know.

"What happened!" she exclaimed, certain he could see the disbelief and fear in her eyes.

"We speared a bull. He tried to club it but it kicked him in the head. He fell in the river. I tried to reach him but he was too deep in the river."

There is a tear in his eye.

She concentrated, pretending to be surprised and shocked. Her hand flew to her face. "Oh, no! Is Kazan dead?"

"I do not know," he answered. "He may have floated to shore. Come," he shouted and ran to the river. "Come!"

Naali tossed *Zhòh gii* into the tent, closed the flap and followed. As they passed the dead bull, Barik gasped, "He fell here!" They dodged through shrubs, running along the shore, but there was no Kazan. Barik stopped and looked at Naali. "He is drowned." Tears welled in his eyes and his mouth quivered. "It is my fault. I should have helped him." Naali stood staring out over the blue rushing water.

He has trained his whole body to lie.

He reached for Naali, wrapping his arm around her stiffened shoulders. She wanted to recoil - to hit him, to scream "You killed him!" But something told her he could not know she had seen everything. She softened and let him hold her. Then she cried.

The Swimmers

He vaguely remembers grasseaters approaching in the river, their velvet antlers swaying, a caribou skin draped around him, hooves rattling in his hand, an antler tied to his head, white smoke billowing at his feet... Vadzaih coming...

I am Vadzaih.

The dream becomes a chaos of freezing wetness. His lungs are filling with water as he rises from the blankness only to be cast back under again. His body shudders and he coughs, spitting water and blood. His face is pressed against a moving roughness - hair grinding against his cheek - caribou smell so strong he can taste it. He is vaguely aware of heavy breathing as his head bumps against a lurching body. Then icy water fills his mouth and nose and lungs again, and he is sinking into the darkness. Suddenly his eyes fly open as his lungs scream for air.

I am Vadzaih.

He woke and knew it was not his heart he heard. His arm was stretched, caught on something, wrenching at his shoulder. Everything was shifting from black to grey to black - wet, cold, wet, cold - black to grey to black.

A struggle for survival began in his body. His lungs were filled with water. His throat was closed. The blackness pulled him down. Then light came back and the struggle began again. His lungs screamed for air. With monumental effort, he lifted his head out of the rushing water. His throat convulsed as icy water spewed from his lungs. He coughed and vomited, his mouth sucking at the air.

He was floating on his back, his arm - and his life - attached to a swimming caribou - her dark eye inches from his. He propped his head on his outstretched arm and gulped in air, pulling his face out of the rushing current. Above, the sun was spinning in circles.

He remembered the spear, how the bull swung its head

229

back in a bellow. Then nothing. He stretched out his neck and saw the antlers silhouetted against the spinning sky. He pulled hard and felt the sleeve of his coat caught in an antler tine. With his free hand he reached up, his fingers grasping for the tine. He pulled again and heard the sleeve ripping. He stopped as panic struck him.

I cannot swim!

He tried climbing higher on the back of the bull as he shook his head and kicked. The shore raced by, too far away to reach. He slowly relaxed as the freezing water numbed his senses. Kazan slipped in and out of consciousness, waking suddenly to the sound of gravel grinding under him. The bull was grunting and wheezing, dragging him onshore. His weight was too much and the bull fell over, pinning him under his flank. He felt his arm wrenching from his shoulder and he screamed into the water. Suddenly his arm was free and the bull was trying to stand, pummeling his back with a flurry of stunning kicks. The bull pushed off him and scrambled away into the shallows.

He lay on the shore for a long time, barely conscious. The taste of blood startled him awake. He reached behind his head and felt the wound at the base of his skull. Soaked and shivering, he checked for other injuries. His arm was tender but not broken. His thigh was bruised from the pounding hooves. He pressed his hand

230

down on his head to stop the bleeding and noticed he had lost a mukluk in the river but his club was still strapped to his waist. He trembled and shivered with cold as he pulled a flint from his jacket and managed a small fire, trying to remember how he came to be dragged in the river by a *Vadzaih*. As the first wisp of smoke rose he realized what had happened.

Barik! He clubbed me!

It was the only explanation. The bulls were in front of him, Barik behind him. His fingers touched the wound - the thick lump was as large as his hand.

Where am I? How far have I floated down the river?

Nothing was familiar. As the flames grew, Kazan realized he was in grave danger.

The fire! He will see it.

He kicked the fire into the river, hoping the smoke had not been seen. A gust of wind blew across the river, chilling him to the bone. He needed warmth or he would freeze to death. Stumbling along the shore, he found a small creek filled with river debris. He crawled under a low bank and pulled dead branches, leaves and dirt over his shivering body. He lay there as the cold slowly overwhelmed him. He trembled, waiting for the sun to set and for darkness to fall. There was no choice. He would die without fire. A little later he was sitting beside a small fire, drying his clothes between brief fits of sleep. He ripped the sleeve from his jacket and wrapped it around his bare foot. When the sun finally rose, he doused the flames and kicked the charred wood into the river. Then he moved upstream.

Moving

It was nearly a moon since One-Eye's accident and the summer was quickly waning. The dim evening light was gone and the night skies were dark again. His arm had healed and the strength was slowly returning. He hunted every day, filling the drying racks with grasseater meat.

Today, the hunting was good. He was kneeling over a horse foal, field-dressing the carcass. His hunting dart had hit the foal below the shoulder and the stone point had driven clear through its lungs, knocking it off its feet. The mare swung around but stayed well out of range as she watched him butcher her only young. When he was done, One-Eye noticed the dark clouds building on the afternoon horizon. The air had turned crisp: a sign the weather was changing. He slung the foal on his back and headed for camp. As he neared the cliff, he saw the women in the distance standing by the fire. He knelt down to watch.

They wear their new clothes.

He pressed his hand on the caribou-skin coat Assan had made for him. He had noticed her sewing, hiding her work from him. She had used his caribou skins for their own clothes. He was going to stop her but realized they needed new clothes to move camp; theirs were worn and tattered. As he watched them move around the fire, his anger rose.

He had heard them talking of running. He knew they would try. They all tried to escape. He would keep them until he no longer needed them. Then he would kill them. They could not go back to humans and tell stories of the bushman; others would come looking for him - and kill him. He would decide what to do with the women when he reached Winter Camp.

He rubbed his hand over his healed arm. Assan knew medicine. The arm was good. She dried meat, sewed him a new skin tent and sleeping bed, and made him winter clothes and mukluks. She did not kill him while he was on the ground. The

232

others had wanted to, but she did not. He would keep her until the winter ended. The other two he would not need.

As he watched Assan stoke the fire, he was reminded of his own mother - her face vague, her name no longer remembered. She had cared for him after the hawk took away his eye and tongue. But, like the others, she had left him, ashamed of his injuries. These women were the same. They stayed because they needed him to hunt and keep killing beasts away. He had heard them. They would leave when humans came. It did not matter. He would kill them before that happened.

As he approached the camp he noted the women stopped talking. The young ones shunned him, turning their backs and pretending they were working. Assan received the foal, laid it by the hearth and brought him a hot tea. He grunted quietly and she looked at him in surprise.

One-Eye woke to the soft patter of snow hitting the tent dome. Crawling from his bed, he opened the flap and peered out over the grey plateau. The snow was falling in thick wet flakes and the ground was covered in a white carpet. He kicked the women awake and they scrambled to the outside fire. Soon, the rich aroma of boiled horse filled the morning air. He ate in silence and then disappeared into the tent. Moments later their sleeping beds and skins flew from the tent and the structure collapsed. Assan frantically filled sacks while So'tsal and Dèhzhòo bundled the skins and furs. One-Eye hoisted his pack onto his back and struck off in the falling snow.

We are moving again, Assan thought wearily.

Where is he taking us?

She lashed together the travel frame and tied on the bundles. By the time they were ready to leave, his trail was already filled. Assan prepared the load and glanced at So'tsal and Dèhzhòo as they strapped on their harnesses. They wore their new caribou-skin parkas and matching pants. New mukluks were lashed around their legs. She wore the same.

233

How long will we wear these winter clothes? Will we be alive when the Dark Days come?

"We must move quickly," she told them as they hauled the camp through the deepening snow. They followed One-Eye's trail as the storm increased. Suddenly, he appeared through the snow. He snatched Assan's harness and pushed her aside, roared at So'tsal and Dèhzhòo and pointed to his trail. The travel frame shot forward. Assan snatched a handful of snow and filled her mouth as her eyes followed the bushman.

Where is he taking us?

Banished

Barik stood, stretched his back and glanced around before he disappeared again. Kazan had been watching for an hour. He could see Barik's spear propped against the shrubs.

Where is Naali?

As he wondered, Naali appeared from upstream. She walked to the dead bull and stood while Barik filled her pack. Then she was gone, heading back to camp with her load. Kazan moved back from the shore until he reached a low ridge. Crawling to the top, he found a viewpoint where he could see camp and Barik. He closed his eyes as the pain pounded in his skull. When he opened them again, Naali was returning for another load with *Zhòh gii* trailing behind.

Kazan saw his chance. He slipped down the hill and headed for camp. As he arrived, a horde of ravens lifted up from the drying racks, scolding him for interrupting their feast. He found his pack in the tent, pulled out a spare mukluk and lashed it around his foot. Then he grabbed a spear and headed back to the hill to wait, watching as Naali moved back and forth with her loads. It was early evening when he moved back toward the kill. The sun was blood red, about to sink below the horizon. He could hear Barik talking to her.

"Go. I will finish and follow."

Kazan's heart was pounding as he heard her moving off. Moments later he heard water splashing - Barik had moved to the river, away from his spear. Kazan crouched for a better look, hesitating.

Now! Take the spear!

Kazan was flying through the shrubs, his eyes fixed on the shaft. Leaping through the last of the willows, he landed on the shore and had it.

Barik was kneeling by the river with his back to the shore, washing his bloodied hands. When he heard the noise, he gasped

235

and spun around. Kazan was facing him, a spear in each hand.

"Kazan!" he shouted. "You are alive!"

Kazan dropped the spear he had taken from camp into the willows. He was holding his own spear and the familiar feel of the shaft gave him confidence.

"You clubbed me," he said sharply, aiming the spear at Barik. "You tried to kill me."

"What? What do you mean?" Barik fumbled for words. "Why would I kill you? We are a band of three: Naali, Kazan, Barik." He stood up and smiled weakly. "I was trying for the bull after you speared it but I stumbled." He moved forward a step, eyeing the spear at Kazan's feet.

"My club struck you by accident. I tried to bring you to shore but the grasseaters were everywhere. Then you were floating away. We thought you had drowned. Naali and I - we looked for you. Ask her. We ran down the river but could not find you. We thought you were dead. She will be happy you are alive," he said, stepping toward Kazan. But Naali's voice stopped him.

"It is not true!" she said sharply. "I saw. You struck Kazan - not the *Vadzaih*. You clubbed him again when he was in the river." She paused. "You tried to kill him." She was standing in the willows, holding a spear, her eyes fierce.

"To kill a human is unthinkable." She leveled her gaze at her brother. "You tried to kill Kazan. Why? Why do you want him dead?"

"You are wrong, sister! It was an accident. Why would I hurt Kazan? He is a hunter and my friend."

"You said you would kill me!" Kazan exclaimed. "You have pretended friendship."

A look of deep hurt spread over Barik's pallid face. "I spoke out of anger. I did not mean it. A human cannot kill another." He walked slowly toward them, his hands outstretched. His eyes suddenly flared and he snatched a fist-sized stone and hurled it at Kazan's head. He was charging at Naali, reaching for

236

her spear. Kazan sidestepped the stone and swung his shaft hard, catching Barik's shoulder. Barik keeled over, swooning in pain.

"Stay down!" Kazan shouted, waving the spear in his face. He reached behind Naali and pulled a rawhide thong from her pack. Jamming his foot down on Barik's neck, he lashed his hands together behind his back.

"It is broken," Barik wailed. "You broke my arm."

Kazan pushed the point of his spear on his neck. "Then you will die with a broken arm!"

"No! Do not kill him!" Naali shouted. "You cannot kill another human!"

Kazan's anger rose. "He will try to kill me again!"

"Banish him!" Naali pleaded. "Banish him. Do not kill him. It will bring bad luck to you for the rest of your life. You know this to be true. We all know this!"

"If we banish him he will come after me!"

Barik shook his head. "Banish me. I will go! I will not return!"

Naali's heart was torn. The words she had uttered suddenly struck her. This was her brother. They had grown up together in *Shih* Band. They had watched One-Eye kill their father and mother. He had run with her across the Flat Plain. Together they had joined Wolf Band, escaped the lions on the river and found Hole-in-Rock.

But there was something strange about him. Since the bushman had taken them, he had grown angry, dark. He had accused Little Weasel of eating humans. He had tried to kill Kazan. Barik was her brother, but she could no longer trust him.

She looked down at him squatting on the ground. "Let him go, Kazan. Banish him." Her eyes met Kazan's. "If you kill him I cannot live with you. You will be bad luck."

"Yes! Bad luck will happen to you if you kill me," Barik shouted, twisting his neck away from the spear.

"He will die if we banish him," Kazan said. "He cannot

survive the winter alone."

"Leave him a camp: tent skins, a spear, darts, dry meat. If he dies it will be his choice - not yours, not mine."

Kazan contemplated Naali's proposal. The wound on the back of his head was throbbing - a bitter reminder of how he could never trust Barik again. He lifted the spear and ordered him to his feet. "Where do we banish him? He will come back."

Naali's eyes darkened. "You are banished to the other side of the Ch'oodèenjik. If you return to this shore, it will mean you have come to kill Kazan."

Barik looked at the far shore. "I will go. I will leave my sister to you."

"I am no longer your sister," she snapped.

Kazan spun him around and checked the bindings on his hands. "Go," he said, pushing him toward camp. Kazan looked at Naali. She was staring out across the river. She waited until they were out of sight before she gathered the pup in her arms and followed. She had believed nothing her brother had said.

Crossing Over

When they arrived in camp, Kazan pushed Barik to the ground as Naali grabbed Barik's pack and stuffed in a bag of dry meat, a bag of flint and chert, winter clothes, his bed and mukluks. Kazan gathered up skins for a tent cover and wrapped them in a bundle. When the camp was ready, Kazan stood him up and looked into his eyes as Barik spat in his face.

"Bad luck will follow you," he screamed. "Bad omens will be with both of you! You have wrongly accused me. If I had wanted to kill Kazan I would have done it. Wolf Leg!" Barik laughed. "You are not a wolf! You are Willow Boy. You blow like a willow branch in the wind."

"And you!" he shouted at Naali. "You choose him over your own blood. You banish your own blood, *Shih* Band blood!"

Kazan took a spear, walked to a boulder and jammed the stone point down, snapping it off. He stuffed the point in Barik's pack and tossed the spear at his feet. Then he took a single hunting dart and shoved it into Barik's quiver.

"Go," he said, turning Barik around. He untied his wrists and stepped away, his spear at the ready, but Barik did not move.

"I will not go. You are no chief. I do not listen to a boy. I will not cross the river."

"You will! It is not your choice!" Kazan looked at Naali, but her back was turned.

Barik shouted, "I did not try to kill him!" He called Naali but she refused to look. "I no longer know your names!" he finally screamed as he pulled on his pack. Then he waded into the river.

"Stay in the shallows," Kazan shouted. "Use your spear to keep your feet under you." His advice seemed hollow in his own ears. They were sending him to his death. No one lived alone except bushmen. Barik was a boy, not a bushman. He had no chance.

He turned and faced them, the water flowing above his

239

knees. "When we meet again, I will kill you, Willow Boy," he said ominously.

They watched him wade into the shallows. At times the water was above his waist but he managed to stay upright in the swift current. When he made it to the far shore he turned and looked at them before he disappeared into the shrubs.

Kazan and Naali broke camp in silence. They had sent him to his death. He would never survive alone. But Kazan knew he could not live with Barik again. He was dangerous, and he would keep his word - "I will kill you, Willow Boy." When everything was tied to the travel frame, Kazan put on his harness and the poles skidded ahead. Naali carried a bag of skins on her back and followed with *Zhòh gii* alongside.

They walked all day without speaking and made camp by the small river they were following. After eating in silence, Kazan looked over at the pup asleep beside the tent. The sky was clear but for a thin wisp of cloud passing below the half moon on the horizon.

"*Zhòh gii* is growing," he said, opening a conversation.

Naali looked up but did not reply.

"She will be big enough to kill grasseaters soon," he said, moving to refill his skull cup with broth.

Naali looked at him. "He would kill you at his first chance. He is jealous of my medicine, my spirit medicine. He does not want to share it."

Kazan sat down. "I do not understand. Why would he not want us to stay together? The more spears the better chance we have to survive."

Naali paused. "It is not my choice that I am a dream-traveller. He does not want to share my power with anyone. There is a darkness to him. There has always been, but never like this." She moved over to the wolf, dropping some food at her feet. *Zhòh gii* ate it and looked up at Naali's hand for more. "I did not know this until my eyes saw him strike at you." She knelt by the fire, feeding it a handful of kindling. "You are becoming strong. He
240

believes my medicine power is his own. He will not share it with you or anyone else."

She came around the fire and sat down next to him. "Do not wish him dead. If he dies it will have been his choice. It is bad luck to wish a death on a human."

Kazan picked up a tuft of grass and cleaned his skull cup. Then he refilled it with steaming tea. "He is your brother. Barik will not live long."

Naali looked at him. "He has no name." She moved to the tent. "I am tired," she said and went inside. Kazan stayed and stoked the fire until it was roaring hot. He tried not to think Barik's name.

Zhòh *Chooses*

The distant sound of ravens breaks the morning silence. Grey-Eye is walking on a steep ridge running alongside a small creek. She has been following the fresh scent of humans since she cut the trail early in the night. She stands gazing out over the dark creek, her nose lifted in the air, her anticipation building. The smell of smoke wafts along the ridge, irritating her nose. She becomes more curious about the scent she is following. She slips down the ridge toward the camp. As she passes near the tent, she recognizes the smell of her pup - the female. She recalls the last place she smelled the scent, high in bushes by the den.

A human is asleep inside the skins. The head is down and making low breathing noises. Suddenly, the pup scrambles out of the skins and is standing facing her. She is half her size, with long, gangly legs and broad feet. Grey-Eye sniffs the air, confirming the scent of her pup. She waits, watching the sleeping human, ready to bolt at the first sign of movement.

Zhòh gii approaches Grey-Eye, drawn by a primordial urge she does not understand. She does not know she is the same form as the animal standing in front of her. In her mind she is human, like the one that has raised her since her memory awoke. Still, the smell of the animal at the edge of the light draws her, kindling a vague recollection of milky darkness. Grey-Eye steps back, waiting for the pup to approach, but Zhòh gii sits down and watches her.

Naali woke suddenly, instantly aware of something outside the tent. She peered out and saw the wolf standing in the dim light. She was about to wake Kazan when she noticed *Zhòh gii* was not beside her. She looked outside again and saw the pup at ease, squatting near the big wolf. A cascade of images flooded her mind: the destroyed den... pup skulls piled in a heap... soil scattered everywhere... the fresh smell of bear. Naali looked into the wolf's eyes and knew she was *Zhòh gii's* mother.

242

"What is it?" Kazan asked sleepily.

She raised her finger to her lips. "Wolf," she whispered. Then a vision came in a swirling jumble of vague and formless shapes until the figure she sought appeared and she heard her own voice speaking. She was standing outside the tent, facing the wolf.

"Welcome, Mother Wolf - you have found your pup. I took her to keep her safe. She has been away a long time. You have not forgotten her."

Grey-Eye hears in the voice a reluctance to give up the pup.

"Wolf pup, look to your mother," Grey-Eye says. Zhòh gii does not hold the wolf's gaze long. "I am Mother Wolf. I made milk for you. Bear killed your brothers. I have been looking for you to fill an emptiness."

Zhòh gii whines softly but does not move.

"If Zhòh gii is still yours, she will follow your path." Naali kneels down. "Follow Mother Wolf if that is your choice, Zhòh gii. She will teach you wolf ways. If you choose to stay you must know you are wolf and not human."

Zhòh gii is confused and looks at the girl. "You are wolf shape - the same as Mother Wolf. You live with humans but you will always be wolf. You must choose who to follow. It is Zhòh gii's choice."

Grey-Eye moves away in an attempt to draw the pup toward her. "Come, pup. I am Mother." The pup takes a few steps and then stops. "Follow the way of the wolf," Grey-Eye says, but the pup is already turning back.

By the time *Zhòh gii* reached Naali, Grey-Eye had already disappeared over the ridge.

"What tongue did you speak?" Kazan asked as he came out of the tent. "Was it wolf tongue?"

Naali did not answer. Her mind was still wolf-dreaming, draining every bit of strength from her body. She stared at the ridge, knowing Grey-Eye would appear and howl her sadness to the world.

Kazan heard Naali whisper strange sounds, then Grey-Eye was standing on the ridge howling. Naali cupped her hands to her mouth, tilted her head back and answered.

PART 5

KHAIINTS'AN': GETTING DARK

Winter Comes Early

Barik left the river to follow a string of hills that led to a high, open plateau. He spent the first night huddled under his shelter made from animal skins, waiting for the snowstorm to pass. As he moved north the snow melted, and he met a steady stream of grasseaters moving south. He saw wolves and bears, but the killing beasts were interested in grasseaters, not him. As he moved, he searched for signs of human life - broken shrubs, tracks, fire rings, smoke in the distance - but he saw nothing.

His supply of dry meat dwindled. He chased bands of grasseaters but failed to make a kill. The closest he came was a small herd of bull elk. He had managed to crawl across the open tundra, out of their sight, until he was within darting range. His only dart glanced off the back of a bull and became fixed in the animal's long antlers. He followed the herd for days, waiting for the dart to drop. Then one day he was looking down on the *Ch'oodèenjik* in the distance. When the dart finally fell he took it as a sign of good luck, that it would lead him to something.

His luck did turn. He managed to kill a calf elk. He dried the meat, hoping someone might see his smoke. His luck held until he reached the *Ch'oodèenjik* canyon.

He stood on a high bluff looking down into a narrow, incised gorge. The river was a torrent of cascading rapids and holes, impossible to cross. Small creeks formed side canyons lined by steep cliffs and filled with willow thickets, and he decided to search the labyrinth of canyons for a winter shelter.

After a few days of searching, he saw dark clouds forming

245

in the south. The air suddenly chilled and he knew summer was ending. As he scrambled up into the headwaters of a small canyon, he felt a gnawing desperation. To survive the winter, he would need to find a cave. Wet snow began to fall and wind began to bluster; the snow turned into a driving sleet. He raised his hood and crawled under a willow thicket. Bending the branches down, he formed a crude frame to support his skins. He sat in the makeshift shelter and waited for the storm to pass. It blew all night and the next day.

When the snow ended he climbed out of the shelter and looked down the narrow canyon. The creek bottom was covered in a heavy blanket of snow. His heart sank. Winter had arrived. His luck had run out. He tried not to think about Naali and Kazan in the warm tent at Hole-in-Rock. If the bad dream had not happened, he would be with them - he would not have tried to kill the boy. But the dream was clear. They had flown off together on the back of the eagle, leaving him alone. He had called to them to come back, to take him with them. He wanted to fly, to see what she saw, to share the power of her dreams. But they did not come back. He had tried to stop the darkness. He had tried to block out the voice. But the blackness came, and the voice told him what he must do. He knew the consequences.

Banished.

If she had not seen him strike Kazan, if the boy had floated away, he would be at Hole-in-Rock with grasseater meat, warm skins and the most powerful dream-traveller on earth.

Barik shivered as a gust of wind blew up the canyon. He had to find shelter. His decisions now meant life or death. As the rosy-fingered sun climbed across the top of the canyons, he trudged through the snow and saw the gaping cleft in the rock.

Dèhzhòo is Discovered

Assan, So'tsal and Dèhzhòo hauled the travel frame over the tundra, skirting to the north of the Flat Plain. Each evening they would find One-Eye's load on the tundra and ready the camp before he returned from hunting. He seemed to grow stronger by the day while they were becoming exhausted from the pace and began to slow. Dèhzhòo lagged behind on the most difficult days.

As they swung west to the mountains, Assan began to recognize the landscape where Wolf Band had spent the previous fall vainly waiting for grasseaters to come. One day they passed by a low hill and she recognized Mountain Winter Camp. The fire pits and the tent rings were still visible in the meadow. She unstrapped her harness and walked into the campsite. Standing in the centre of a tent ring, she was struck by an overpowering sadness. This was the ground where they had sat in their tents debating, discussing and arguing whether to leave as the snow piled up around them. The memories of their desperate journey overwhelmed her. Eyak, kneeling in the snow, choosing her place to die. Tarin snatched from his bed by a lion. And Lions-Came Camp. The last time she had seen Khon and Kazan, their backs to the river. The girl had warned them to leave, but they did not listen. They had not believed a girl could see the future. Assan heard footsteps and saw So'tsal and Dèhzhòo approaching.

"It is Mountain Winter Camp, Dèhzhòo," So'tsal said as she walked into the tent ring. "This is where our *nèevyaa zhee* stood." She bent over, touching the ground. "My bed was here, beside Kazan. You were there, near Khon." She walked to Chii Tsal's tent ring. "They are gone," she said quietly. They walked the camp, remembering when they had lived as a band.

"I cannot travel like this," Dèhzhòo said. "I need to rest. We move too fast."

"We must stay together. No one falls behind," Assan replied.

"He is taking us to a hole in the ground," So'tsal said.

Assan walked up the hill toward the travel frame. "Come, or it will be dark."

They found One-Eye standing on a grassy rise watching the sun disappear on the horizon. He was sniffing the air pensively, looking at the cloudless sky, obviously disturbed. There was no wind and the plateau was silent except for a ptarmigan calling from the top of a nearby knoll: *"Tuk, tuk, tuk, tuktuktuk…'*

Assan could smell a change in the air. A light wind began to blow.

A storm comes.

It was dark when they finished erecting the tent and began preparing the meal by the fire. One-Eye was not back from his hunt. Dèhzhòo stoked the fire and sat with her tea, her back against the tent, while Assan and So'tsal braised strips of caribou. They moved around the hearth in silence, exhausted from hard travelling. When One-Eye came into the tent, they could feel his anger. He snatched a bladder of water and drained it. By now, they had all endured his beatings for the smallest infractions. They turned away and avoided looking at him.

Assan offered him tea. He shrugged and struck her hand, sending the skull cup flying across the tent. With lightning speed, he flew at Dèhzhòo, snatching her roughly by the hair. She screamed as he dragged her from the tent. Assan dove for her legs but One-Eye kicked her away.

"What is happening?" So'tsal screamed. "Where is he taking her?"

Assan crawled on her hands and knees out of the tent. Dèhzhòo was screaming, kicking and beating his arms as he dragged her away.

He knows! How could he know!

"No!" Assan screamed into the darkness. "Leave her! She has done nothing." She picked up a rock and threw it with all of her strength, narrowly missing his head. He stopped and turned, moonlight reflecting in his fierce eye.

So'tsal flew from the tent, shrieking. Assan grabbed her and held her tight.

"Where is he taking her?" she wailed. "What has she done? Is he killing us?"

"No," Assan gasped. They fell to the ground sobbing. Assan wrapped her legs around her daughter and covered So'tsal's ears.

"She is with child," she whispered. They lay together for a long time, weeping. Assan helped her into the tent and wrapped her in her bed. She built a large fire and sat beside her daughter until she was asleep.

Assan heard him coming back and braced for the beating. Her despair was so complete she did not care if he killed her. He slipped inside the tent and threw Dèhzhòo's coat and pants at her. She looked at him, filled with rage. "Have you killed another woman?" she hissed. "Have you killed a woman and a child? You keep what you need and kill what you do not!"

He stared back, his fingers on his club; then the bushman crawled into his sleeping bed and turned his back on her. She looked at his spear for a long time before she fell into a fitful sleep.

When Assan and So'tsal rose at dawn, he was already gone. Neither spoke as they broke camp. Assan gazed at the horizon, imagining where Dèhzhòo lay. She helped So'tsal into her harness and they headed for the marker stick the bushman had placed on a hill to show his direction.

They found Dèhzhòo's frozen body not far from their trail. She was naked, curled up, her head bent over on her knees, her face hidden. Her black hair blew in the cool wind.

"Do not look!" Assan told So'tsal.

"Why did he kill her?"

I should have known. We should have slowed and waited for her.

"A child slows travel," Assan replied, as she braced into her harness and pulled.

The wind came during the night but the dawn was cloudless. By midmorning it had begun to snow. Soon the snow was too thick to see any distance ahead. A little later it was up to their knees. They flipped the travel frame over, dragging the skin load over the snow like a sled. The storm grew and One-Eye's trail disappeared.

"Can you see his tracks?" Assan shouted as she pulled down her parka hood.

"No!" So'tsal replied as the wind howled around them. "The snow is too deep. I cannot pull the load."

"You must," Assan shouted. "There is no shelter! We cannot stop." She pulled hard on the traces. So'tsal strained beside her as the sled inched forward. Soon the snow was too deep. They cleared a trench for the sled and the load staggered forward.

So'tsal collapsed in the snow. "I cannot go farther!"

"Get up! We cannot stop here!"

"I cannot pull. It is too heavy!"

Assan dragged her to her feet. "Pull!" she shouted into her daughter's face, leaning into the harness with all her strength. The sled slid forward a few inches. They kicked a snow path and pulled again, and again.

They found One-Eye facing into the storm holding an empty caribou bladder at his waist. When the sac was pointing directly into the wind, it bulged out like a balloon. He stepped forward, kicking a trench for the sled until the bladder deflated. Then he shifted his body slightly until the sac popped open and he moved again.

As they followed him into the blistering wind, their clothes became caked in snow and ice. That night they dug snow tunnels to escape the freezing wind. Assan collapsed into her bed, too tired to think about Dèhzhòo. Now she had only So'tsal to watch over and protect. Her heart sank.

I cannot bear to see her die before me.

Dawn came and the sun rose in a cascade of pink and

yellow light over the snowy plain. They crawled from their snow caves and ate a few handfuls of dry meat as they prepared to move. Assan was loading the skin sled when she heard So'tsal whisper behind her.

"Lions!"

The Lioness

The ravens tear at the carcass, flying off in every direction with chunks of bison meat, caching their prizes under snowdrifts and shrubs before flapping noisily back for more. The lion cub is hiding behind a snowdrift. He crouches and inches closer to the carcass. Suddenly he rushes at the black flock covering the dead bison. The birds wait until the cub is nearly on them. As he leaps in the air, they casually flap their wings and are lifted safely above his outstretched claws. The cub tumbles over the bison and into the snow. The ravens dive down onto the cub, scolding him. A few brave birds strike him on the head and back with their beaks as he retreats. Rumpled and disappointed, he returns to his sleeping mother.

He rubs the top of his head on her chin and settles down beside her, leaning affectionately into her broad chest. Then he rolls over on his back, rubbing his snowy face against her forehead. His head is pressed to her shoulder as they both fall asleep.

In the morning, they are startled by roaring. A large male lion is approaching. The lioness answers the challenge with her own blood-curdling reply. Her ears are turned back, her narrow eyes compressed to slits and her lips raised in a menacing grimace. She turns her head to the side so the male can clearly see her intimidating array of yellow teeth.

She knows him well. He has driven her from other kills. The cub struts confidently for the intruder, oblivious of the danger. His mother grunts and he quickly retreats, understanding the clear warning. She raises her muzzle and, with eyes and ears relaxed, roars before abandoning the kill.

She leads the cub across the tundra until she crosses a snow trail filled with strange scent. She does not recognize it as prey and quickly loses interest. The cub, though, is curious and follows the tracks. She grunts sharply, ordering him back, but he does not listen. She reluctantly follows the cub as snow begins to fall, her interest in the scent slowly growing. She overtakes him as the snowstorm builds. They spend the night huddled together under a willow thicket as the snow covers their sleeping bodies.

When the cub wakes he finds his mother sitting on a hill watching shapes moving in the brilliant whiteness. He wades through the snow and stands alongside her, rubbing his head on her shoulder. He feels her muscles tense as she walks down the hill toward the strange forms.

The Cub

"Lions!"

Assan turned around quickly to see two lions standing a short distance away. One-Eye was already walking toward the cats. He let out a huge roar and waved his spear, stamping his feet in the snow and shouting, but the lions did not move. He came back and motioned to Assan to pull the sled as he broke a wide trail through the snow. As Assan and So'tsal pulled, they glanced back, but the two cats were nowhere in sight. By mid-morning, One-Eye was well ahead of the women, barely visible against the brilliant white of the snowy plateau. As they entered a small basin, Assan caught sight of movement beside her. The cub was leaping down the slope through the snow, heading straight for them.

"Lion!" she cried out. Not far behind, the lioness came plunging into view. "They are curious!" Assan shouted. "Keep pulling. They will leave!"

But the lions did not leave. The cub grew bolder, coming closer as his curiosity and courage increased.

Assan snatched a spear from the sled. "Go!" she screamed, waving the spear. The cub's interest intensified as he circled the sled, his tail snapping back and forth with excitement. The tension was becoming too much.

"It is going to attack!" So'tsal screamed. Assan quickly untied herself from her harness.

"Untie your harness!" she cried. "Stay behind me. Do not run!" She turned to face the cub. "Make noise, scream!" She waved the spear over her head and yelled at the top of her lungs. So'tsal joined in, making the shrill sounds women use to drive off killing beasts. The lioness was approaching, her head low in a menacing posture. She roared and the cub spun around. Assan looked for One-Eye, but he was not in sight.

"Behind the sled!" she shouted, motioning So'tsal to follow her.

254

Suddenly she saw One-Eye running down the slope behind the lions, his spear on his shoulder. The cub turned just as the stone point slammed into his chest. He roared in shock, his claws raking the air as he fell back. One-Eye unslung his club and pounded the cub's skull until it was a bloody mass of shattered bones and skin. Pulling the spear from the cub, he charged at the lioness, his shrill cry shattering the morning silence. She retreated and stopped a safe distance away. He held his club in one hand and the spear in the other, cracking them together as he roared and screamed. She slowly moved to the top of a hill and sat watching them.

"Go!" Assan shouted at So'tsal as she strapped on her harness. But One-Eye pushed So'tsal aside and took her harness; his powerful legs dug into the snow and the sled lurched ahead as So'tsal pushed from behind. As they moved down a long slope, the blue water of Porcupine River slowly appeared in the distance.

It was nearly dark when they neared the river. The lioness had not followed them and they had slowed. They were above a rocky canyon, the far-off roar of the river echoing through the chasm below. Assan smelled the smoke before she saw the wisp of white rising from the canyon. One-Eye stood on the rocky rim, his nose lifted in the air.

Vengeance

She watches the cub sprawled in the snow. He is not moving. A light wind carries the scent of his blood and triggers alarm. She walks down the slope until she is standing over him. The face is gone. His legs are splayed wide. She growls softly, nudging at his bloody shoulders with her thick muzzle, but he does not stir. He is covered in the strange scent. She deeply inhales, locking it into her memory. Filled with anxiety, she lies down next to the cub and lets out a long, low moan. He has always been with her. Since the day he was born, he has followed her every step. Now he will not move.

She stays beside him for the rest of the day, slowly realizing he is dead. Then the mother–offspring bond begins to unravel. She paces back and forth, circling the cub as an enormous distress overwhelms her. The human scent that is everywhere suddenly grips her and she moves over the snow trail. A menacing growl rolls from deep in her throat. She follows the scent and, with each step, the smell of vengeance grows stronger.

Bitten

Kazan and Naali watched as the storm built in the south. The air cooled quickly and the wind increased. They broke camp before sunrise and made Hole-in-Rock Camp just before the heaviest snow fell. Kazan was untying his harness when three foxes bolted from the cave, passing so close to the travel frame he could have touched them.

"*Ch'ich'yàa!*" he shouted as the foxes raced past Naali and *Zhòh gii* and disappeared into the falling snow. In the cave they found their furs scattered across the floor and skins spilling out of Little Weasel's hole. Gripping the leather rope, Naali hauled out the furs they had wedged inside. As the contents collected into a pile at her feet, a fox fell out, wrapped in a parka sleeve. It squirmed until it untangled itself, dodged around Naali and ran straight into the pup. *Zhòh gii* yelped as the fox bit her in the neck and bolted from the cave. Naali reached for the pup, but *Zhòh gii* would not let her touch the stream of blood. Naali looked at Kazan and saw concern spread over his face.

Fox sickness! No, it was too quick. Sick foxes are slow.

Anything bitten by a sick fox would die in a few days. Every child knew about the frothing mouth of the sick ones, the staggering vacant look and the sudden urge to bite anything that moved. They were both thinking the same thing.

"Was there white coming from the mouth?" Kazan asked.

"No. It ran too fast to be sick."

Kazan nodded, but he was not certain. Animals in the early stages of sickness did not show symptoms. He had not had a good look as it ran from the cave. It had all happened too fast. If it had the sickness, *Zhòh gii* would die quickly, but it would be a few days before she showed the first signs.

They spent the next two or three days setting camp for winter, constantly watching the pup for indications of sickness. The tent was placed at the mouth of the cave with the chimney

257

expelling smoke to the outside. Thick animal skins covered the tent floor, dry wood was stacked behind the tent inside in the cave, and sacks of dry meat and berries hung from the cave roof, safe from scavenging foxes. They had everything needed to winter: meat, spears and darts, skin bladders and bone tools for cooking, sewing materials, flint and chert for making points.

Four days and no sign, Naali thought.

Each day she had watched *Zhòh gii* for any change in behaviour. She noticed how much the wolf had grown. Her legs were long and her face was lengthening into an adult's. Her canines had nearly fully descended and were long enough to grip the skin of a grasseater.

On the fifth day, Naali woke to find Kazan kneeling by the fire. The wolf was not in the tent.

"Where is she?" Naali asked nervously.

"Outside," he said as he stood and left the tent. Moments later, he was back inside. "Her tracks lead behind the outcrop."

Naali laid a handful of kindling on the fire. "*Zhòh gii* has grown," she said, opening a bag of dry meat and dropping a handful into a steaming bladder. "She is not a pup. Her name is no longer *gii*. She is *Zhòh* - wolf."

Kazan nodded agreeably. They ate their meal, discussing where to hunt for the day. As they readied their gear, Naali began to worry about the wolf. They went around the outcrop, following *Zhòh's* snow trail.

Kazan stopped suddenly and raised his hand. "There," he said, pointing to the creek. She was coming out the ravine carrying a ptarmigan in her mouth.

"*Daagoo!* She has killed a ptarmigan," Naali said, smiling. As *Zhòh* walked toward them they could see there was something wrong. She was limping and weaving sideways.

"Fox sickness!" Naali whispered, gripping Kazan by the arm. The wolf stopped and sat down. They could hear her whimpering as Naali walked toward her.

258

"No! Stay!" Kazan said. "I will get the spears." He ran back to the cave and returned with two. *Zhòh* was lying down, her chin resting on the ptarmigan.

"She has not moved," Naali said as he handed her a spear. They approached together, carefully watching the wolf. As they neared, *Zhòh* got up and staggered toward them, leaving a small blood spot in the trail.

"Her foot is bleeding!" Kazan exclaimed. "It is her foot!"

Naali held out her hand as she knelt and reached for the wolf's leg. *Zhòh* pulled back nervously but then let Naali raise the foot to inspect the thick pad. A small stick was embedded between the toes.

She stood and looked at *Zhòh*. Greatly relieved, Naali embraced Kazan. "She is not sick," she said as she wrapped her arms around his waist. Kazan immediately blushed with surprise, his hands slowly touching her shoulders. She was crying.

"There has been so much bad luck," she sobbed.

He held her, tightening his embrace, not wanting to let her go.

"*Zhòh* is not sick," he whispered. "It is good luck." She nodded and let him go. They walked back to Hole-in-Rock followed by the limping wolf.

An Unexpected Reunion

Barik moved to the narrow cleft in the canyon wall, trying not to make a sound in the deep snow. He rapped the rock softly with his spear point and was met by silence. Gathering his courage, he slipped inside into complete darkness. At first he could not judge the size of the cave, but from the sounds he sensed it was large. As his eyes adjusted to the dimness, he saw the round ring of stones on the floor where a skin tent had once stood. He walked into the ring, touching the floor with the end of his spear. Only a small tent could fit inside it.

Soon he had a large fire burning outside the entrance, lighting the back recesses of the cave. High on the roof was a large bag suspended by a leather rope tied to a stake at the rear of the cave. He untied the rope and lowered the heavy sack to the floor, opened it and hauled out the contents. There was a tent, thick sleeping bed, assorted clothes, a bag of chert, flint, bladders, a sack of dried cranberries and some dried herbs. He unfolded a large, grime-stained parka twice the size of his own. As he stared at it, he slowly realized whose camp he had stumbled upon. Outside the fire erupted, snapping and hissing as the flames ignited the wet wood. The wall of the cave swirled in shadow and light, and his heart pounded. He dropped the coat.

It is the bushman's cave!

He thought of his sister's warning as he was banished.

Bad luck will follow me.

He moved to the entrance and picked up his pack. He could not stay here. He could feel the walls, the roof closing in on him. He put on his pack, walked out into the snow and surveyed the steep canyon. There was plenty of wood, a creek to draw water and ice - and a cave with a narrow entrance he could defend alone. The cave had everything he needed but meat.

It is good luck to find the cave! Safer than a tent on the open plain. It is One-Eye's camp, but he is not here. Why should I leave?

He went back inside and dropped his pack on the cave floor. A little later he had gathered a stack of dry willow. He worked until early evening, erecting the tent and securing it to the ring of rocks in the centre of the floor. Then he unpacked his small camp, took a few handfuls of dry meat and berries from his supply and hoisted the sack to the ceiling. Standing in the cavern, he surveyed his home. It was a good winter camp. His main worry was killing beasts getting in. He looked at the entrance and decided he would gather boulders to make it even smaller. He thought of Little Weasel's hole.

She lived the winter in a hole. I can live the winter here.

Picking up a bladder, he filled it with water from the creek, deposited dry meat, suspended it over the roaring fire and waited for the broth to heat. He was staring into the flames when he heard snow sliding somewhere up the canyon.

Melting snow, he thought, but something was wrong. Suddenly a shadow was running toward him. He scrambled back in the cave, grabbed his spear and swung around, his heart racing.

A lion? Bear?

The beast roared as it entered the cave and Barik's legs turned to jelly - but the roar was not lion or bear.

A spear flashed at the entrance as he recognized the grunting snarl.

One-Eye!

Barik dropped his spear and scrambled to the back of the cave. With his back to wall, he slid down to the ground and prepared to die.

One-Eye Remembers

One-Eye saw the human running from the fire into his cave. As he followed him in, he raised his spear and roared. He stopped when he saw his camp scattered across the cave floor. His parka and sleeping bed were lying at his feet, his tent was standing.

He looked in the tent for the human. Something moved at the rear of the cave, and the bushman jumped over the tent towards the sound. He aimed his spear point in the direction of the human's sobbing, driving it into the rock as the wood shaft splintered in his hands. Roaring in disbelief, he reached into the darkness but found only the rock wall. Suddenly a shadow ran past the tent, scrambling for the cave mouth. He caught the screaming being by the leg and, with his free hand, unslung his killing club. As he raised it over his head he recognized the horrified face looking up at him.

He was confused. He had killed everyone he had captured. How could he know this face? He looked down, and he remembered. It was the boy who burned his winter tent - the one with the girl with eyes the colour of the summer sky. He strained to remember the name she called him - Bar... Bari... Barik. That was the name. But they were both dead. He remembered the half-eaten skull at the end of the lake in the storm, and the lion. It was her skull. How had this one lived? His mind ached, trying to understand. He had sworn to burn them alive when he caught them.

The club hovered for a moment and then slammed down beside Barik's head, spraying his face with dirt. Barik screamed, waiting for the next blow to kill him. But he was suddenly being rolled over, his arms and legs tied together. Then the bushman hoisted him onto his shoulders, walked out of the cave and tossed him into the snow next to the fire. He went back into the cave, returned with an armload of wood, threw it on the fire and watched the flames rise.

Barik screamed, wrenching at the bindings, trying to turn his face away from the searing heat. He was being lifted over the flames, his face turned to the moon rising over the canyon. He screamed, and then another scream answered up in the canyon - a woman's scream.

"Lion!"

As One-Eye looked down on the roaring fire, his grip on the boy shifted.

The shout was nearer. "Lion! She is coming!"

Another voice, shrill and loud, filled with fear. "She is coming!"

As Barik fell, the heat enveloped him. His hair ignited as he landed in the flames on his back. He screamed and twisted instinctively, kicking his bound legs and rolling his shoulder until his face was out of the flames. There were more shouts, and then someone grabbed his feet and dragged him through the snow, pounding his back, throwing snow on him, beating his legs. He opened his smoke-filled eyes and saw he was back in the cave. A lion roared so loudly he was certain it stood over him. Turning on his back, he saw humans, yelling and shouting, thrusting spears from the cave entrance.

"It is afraid of fire!" A woman's voice.

One-Eye was there, roaring and stabbing at the beast moving just beyond the fire. Someone knelt down and untied his bindings. He looked up into the face shimmering in the firelight.

"So'tsal," he gasped.

"Barik!" she shouted, pulling him to his feet. "It is Barik!"

Suddenly he was holding a spear and being pushed to the mouth of the cave. One-Eye was standing beside him, oblivious of his arrival.

"Keep her out!" It was Assan. "Keep the fire burning!" She pitched more wood onto the flames. The lioness retreated out of the firelight and continued to roar as she moved away into the canyon.

"You are alive!" So'tsal whispered. "We thought you had drowned."

Something struck his head, sending him reeling into the rock. A huge hand held him down as the other hand tied his arms.

"No! Do not kill him!" Assan shouted, her hand reaching to Barik. "He is a spear - another spear. He is a hunter. We need him!"

One-Eye paid her no attention and continued binding Barik's hands.

Assan moved to the cave entrance. "You must kill me," she screamed. She raised her spear and held it front of her, knowing there was no hope of touching the bushman.

He looked at her, more perplexed than angry. He could kill her anytime he wanted. Why did she want him to kill her now? The others all wanted to live. They begged him. He glanced at the boy. She would die for the boy?

A hunter?

He hesitated. He had faced many killing beasts. He had never before felt fear as he did now. This lion was different; more dangerous than any killing beast he had encountered. He knew it when he looked into her eyes on the trail, the dead cub lying at his feet. Killing the cub was bad luck. She had followed them all but she had come for him. She would not give up until she killed him.

Another spear? The boy was another spear. Assan had called him hunter. He kicked Barik on the back, untied his hands and pushed him toward the women as he collected his skins and clothes from the floor, constantly glancing back at the entrance shining in the firelight.

"You are alive," Assan said quietly. She looked into his eyes, but her mind was suddenly back at Lions-Came Camp. Barik nodded, his mind racing for answers to questions he knew were about to come.

"You did not drown. What happened? You were in the boat."

264

"I jumped off and climbed on an ice floe. I nearly froze in the river, but I had good luck and made it to shore. How did you and So'tsal escape?" he asked, biding time, working out the detail of his story. "I thought all were dead but me."

"We hid in the shore ice. Dèhzhòo, So'tsal and I. He found us." She nodded at One-Eye, who was busy rolling up his skins. "He was bringing us here. The lion and her cub followed. He killed the cub."

"Why has the lion followed you here?"

"I do not know," Assan replied. "She is angry with the bushman. She followed us a long way." Assan braced for the question she wanted most to ask him. "And what of Kazan? Naali?"

"They drowned," Barik said sadly. "I tried to help, but they went in the river." He hoped she had not seen them running for the ice floe.

Assan's looked at him in numbed silence, tears welling in her eyes. Kazan was dead. "Khon and Kazan were holding back the lions when we went down in the ice. Khon told him to run, to follow Naali. He must have run." She looked at Barik. "And you saw them in the river?"

"Yes. A lion drove them into the water as I was carried away on the ice floe. I tried to reach them." A tear rolled down his cheek. His story had no challengers. Khon was the only one who had seen them reach the ice floe, and he was dead.

Barik looked at them. "Khon was killed by a lion. No others lived. I thought you were all dead." He paused. "Dèhzhòo - what happened to her?"

Assan was silent for a long time. Her hands were shaking. "He killed her."

"Why? What had she done?"

Assan glanced over at So'tsal and their eyes met. "He is a bushman. He kills for nothing."

"I grieve the loss of Wolf Band," Barik offered.

"Wolf Band is not lost," Assan answered wearily. "So'tsal

and I still live." She touched her daughter's hand. Barik nodded, but he saw no hope for them. He had watched the bushman kill his father and mother. One-Eye had just tried to burn him alive. He would kill Assan and So'tsal.

When the lion is dead, he will kill me.

Somehow Assan had saved him. He was another spear. But there was something else. How had she changed the mind of the bushman so quickly? Somehow she was able to control him. Barik began to understand. Woman. He remembered Saran, his mother, could convince the bushman to change his mind, to not hit them. Assan had done the same, except she had stopped One-Eye from burning him alive. Woman - but not any woman. Mothers! Barik had wondered why the bushman showed no interest in touching Naali or his mother.

He is a child in a giant body.

Barik knew that if Assan had not interfered, he would be dead. What had she said? *"You must kill me."* But he did not kill her. He wanted her alive. The way to One-Eye was through the mother. The way to survive was through Assan. She could never know about Kazan and Naali.

Killing Bison

The old cow bison moves cautiously onto the river ice, testing the thickness. She hesitates as it sags under her heavy weight. She moves downstream where her broad hooves find thick ice, and her trust grows. The rest of the herd is moving along the shore, watching her as she walks out on the river. A second cow swings her broad horns toward the river and follows the old one. Soon, hundreds of bison are on the ice, moving in single file, headed for the other side.

From his resting place on a low bluff, Blue watches bison feeding on the opposite shore, their broad heads sweeping snow from the shrubs. As they begin to cross, he becomes interested in hunting. He walks down the bluff, waking Grey-Eye and five yearlings sleeping in the willows below. They fall in behind Blue as the pack moves onto the river ice.

The old cow is halfway across the river when she hears the sound of rushing water beneath her. She stops and snorts nervously as the thinning ice creaks and sags. The other bison stop and wait, their senses on high alert. She shifts sideways and finds good ice again as she spots the loping wolves approaching. She instinctively turns to retreat but is met by a wall of her own kind.

At the end of the line, the last bull is stepping onto the river when he senses something rushing at him from behind. Black-Foot's pack is charging through the shrubs, heading straight for him. The bull panics and collides into the bull in front of him. They stumble, lose their footing and bump into the next bison. A wave of alarm rolls through the herd as the two wolf packs close in from both sides of the river.

Bison are spreading out on the river as Blue watches for a limp or a stagger that will help him choose which one to hunt. The line quickly unravels and the herd splits in all directions, shaking the ice under him. He charges ahead, his claws digging into the smooth ice. Grey-Eye quickly overtakes Blue and cuts out a calf from the big ones.

Suddenly there is a loud crack and the ice breaks, sending a large group of bison tumbling into the fast-moving water. The current pushes the mass of bellowing beasts against the shattered ice shelf. Calves that are not crushed slip out into the deeper current and disappear beneath the shelf. The bigger bulls manage to grind their hooves into the gravel bottom as the icy current flows over their backs. They lift their heads and bawl frantically as they scramble to escape. Two bulls lift their forelegs onto the ice; the shelf collapses before they can climb out. They turn into the current with the others, bellowing at the sky.

On the other side of the river, Black-Foot charges into the mob of snorting bison. She is reaching for the flank of a cow when she slips and skids out of control. The cow swings her horns, catching the wolf under her belly and foreleg and flinging her into the air. As she crashes down on the ice there is a loud crack. She tries to roll up, but her foreleg is broken. She yelps out in pain as Torn-Ear, Broken-Tail and the rest of her pack leap

onto the cow, tearing into her side. The sheer weight of her attackers drives the cow to her knees. She swings her horns at them, snorting and bellowing, but cannot hook a wolf. Each time she tries to stand she collapses and more wolf teeth rip into her hide. Torn-Ear releases the cow's neck and moves to the belly, tearing into the gut. The bison is sliding into shock, no longer aware of what is happening as she watches herself being ripped apart. She dies as her head finally sinks down onto the bloody ice.

Torn-Ear stands and scans the river. Bison are scattered up and down both shores. Blue's pack is feeding on a calf in the distance. His mate, Black-Foot, is limping on the ice, dragging her leg. Panting with the exhilaration of the kill, he shoves his head into the cow's gut, snatches a piece of liver and devours it in a few bites. His pack is snarling and jostling to feed. Broken-Tail pushes her nose into the gut. Torn-Ear drops his head down and snarls, sending her scurrying back.

Black-Foot hobbles to the kill, watching them feed. She is in immense pain, although she makes no sound. Swaying on her three good legs, she does not challenge for feeding rights. She limps away and finds a quiet place on the ice to lie down.

As night falls, the two wolf packs rest together but do not visit the other's kill. Broken-Tail walks past Grey-Eye, showing no interest in her mother. She heads to the open pool and skirts around the trapped bison that have fallen silent. A bull slowly raises his head up and grunts at her as she leaves.

Grey-Eye is woken in the morning by the arrival of the ravens. A white mist rises above the pool. She walks to the icy rim and looks down. Two bulls stand in the neck deep water, their mouths barely above the current, their backs caked in a blanket of frost. The bulls' vacant eyes stare into the moving water as if in a trance. Grey-Eye circles the pool and returns to the wolves.

Black-Foot and Torn-Ear are lying together away from their pack. Torn-Ear stands and stretches, but Black-Foot is not interested in moving and turns away, resting her head on her paws.

Soon the sky is filled with circling ravens. Some have landed on the ice, watching the wolves, waiting for their chance to steal meat. A bird hops toward the cow carcass and squawks loudly. Broken-Tail rushes at it but the raven is already safely in the air. Behind her, another raven lands on the rib cage, slices off meat and flies off before Broken-Tail can turn and chase it off. The two ravens play this feeding game with her until they are full.

The wolves spend another day on the ice feeding, visiting and wandering the shores. In the morning, Grey-Eye takes her pack upriver. Torn-Ear also has the urge to move. He paces through his sleeping pack, communicating his interest in leaving with his whimpers. Black-Foot hears him, but her leg is too weak, so she watches her pack leave. Later, she limps slowly after them, leaving behind the raucous din of ravens and the shallow breathing of the last bison alive in the pool.

The Eye of the Lion

She waits patiently, watching the dark canyon below. Nearby a fire burns, casting yellow light across the cliff walls. The lioness drops her head on the snow, her dead cub and the human scent consuming her every thought. She has followed the scent of the one that killed the cub. She will kill it. That is where her thought begins and ends.

The first sound comes with daylight: the soft shuffle of something moving below through deep snow. It stops. She cannot see it, but knows it is not prey she has listened to her entire life. It is moving differently – with hesitation. She listens carefully and hears the shuffle of two animals. As they near there is the sound of skin gliding over snow and broken breathing.

Now they are under her. She stops breathing, listening – instinctively calculating the attack distance. A low growl rumbles in her throat; she cannot suppress it. Her muscles coil, ready to spring. She must see the animal before she attacks. She inches ahead, stretching her neck out to see over the canyon rim.

Barik was behind One-Eye. They were moving slowly up the canyon to retrieve the sled the women had abandoned the night before when the lioness attacked. One-Eye could see it in the shadowy dark. They were almost there. One-Eye took a few steps and then stopped and listened. He heard the growl, barely audible, somewhere above the canyon. He stepped back, his eye fixed on the rim. His reaction instantly filled Barik with anxiety. He raised his spear as the first golden rays of dawn struck the top of the canyon. He could not believe he was with the bushman, walking into the shadowy chasm filled with fresh lion spoor. But he had had no choice. One-Eye had pulled him from his bed, slapped a spear in his hand and pushed him out of the cave. The bushman had a look of desperation and fear that Barik had never seen before.

He fears it.

As Barik surveyed the high rim, he saw her. Stepping back, he heard the fire crackling behind them as he stumbled into a drift and lost his footing. Suddenly the canyon erupted in an avalanche of snow and an ear-splitting scream.

The lioness exploded off the rim and landed next to One-Eye in a great shower of snow as his spear plunged into her shoulder. She roared as he rolled away, colliding into Barik and knocking the boy's spear out of his hands. Panic-stricken, he swept his hands through the snow, searching for the weapon. He found it and turned to see One-Eye running for the cave, the lioness behind him. The bushman turned to look at her, his eye filled with fear. Scrambling through the deep snow, he was almost at the mouth of the cave when a burning stick flew from the entrance; more followed. The lioness jumped back as a firestick bounced off a boulder, showering her in a cascade of sparks as she raked her paws at the burning light. Barik watched One-Eye disappear into the rock.

He is inside the cave!

Barik stood in the canyon with the lioness between him and the cave. She was pacing back and forth and roaring, her eyes fixed on the burning fire.

He tried to run up the canyon but his legs were locked in panic. More burning sticks flew from the cave. The lioness screamed and retreated, snapping at the flying sparks as one hit her on the shoulder. She loped effortlessly through the snow, moving back up the canyon, her eyes locked on him. There was no use running. He was about to die. He closed his eyes and waited. He could hear her thick breathing as she neared. He waited. Then snow slid from the canyon and he turned; she was already gone.

Barik Makes a Plan

"The lioness followed One-Eye. He has killed the cub. She has come for him." Assan whispered low so the bushman could not hear. They were huddled in back of the cave, the light from the fire casting shadows across their faces. One-Eye sat at the entrance, watching the canyon. "Now he has wounded her. Wounding a lion, the greatest of killing beasts, is the worst curse." Assan looked at Barik squatting beside her. His head was down and he was not listening. "She knows his scent and she will not leave until she kills him."

Barik looked up, realizing Assan was talking about why the lioness passed him in the canyon - why she had not killed him - why he was still alive.

"Then let the bushman die," So'tsal whispered. "Let her kill him. Then they both will be gone." She glanced at Barik, her tone suddenly confident. "You are a hunter. You will protect us. We do not need a bushman."

Assan glanced over at Barik, who was still lost in thought. Assan knew he could not protect them. He was barely a hunter. He could not provide for the three of them; he was too young and inexperienced. And there was something about him she did not trust.

She had felt it the moment they found Barik and Naali on the Flat Plain. He was different from other boys like Kazan, who yearned to be a hunter. He had announced he had spirit medicine. She remembered Naali's reaction. He did not have the power to see the future, to dream-travel. So how had he escaped the lions and found his way to the cave? There was something wrong about his story of escaping Lions-Came Camp. He had hesitated in telling her, as if he were waiting to see what she knew of that day. His explanation too simple, too easy. How had he survived the summer, alone? He had come with a small camp, little food, a spear and a single hunting dart. Yet, they had found him in the

273

cave, alone and alive. It made no sense. How had he survived, a boy barely a hunter?

"If the bushman lives, we live. If he dies, we die," Barik said in a hushed voice. "The lioness will not quit until she kills him. When she is done, she will kill all of us." Barik knew his spear would never be enough against such a powerful killing beast. A lion was feared by the best hunters. Wounding the lioness had cursed One-Eye. He was terrified, his confidence withering. Barik looked over at One-Eye's dark frame silhouetted against the fire. He had never seen the bushman so afraid.

The lion-wounding is draining his strength. He is wilting. Soon he will be of no help.

As they talked, Barik had been devising a way to kill the lioness and keep One-Eye from burning him alive. It was a dangerous plan. If he failed, the bushman or the lioness would kill him. For the plan to work he needed luck; but mostly he needed Assan.

"Snare the lioness," he whispered, shifting to look directly at So'tsal and Assan. They stared back in disbelief. "A heavy snare, much heavier than a grasseater snare." He had never heard of such a snare, but he continued. "Make it as long as the cave and as thick as your hand. It must be strong enough to hold a lion."

"No one has snared a lion!" Assan whispered. "There are no stories. Lions are too large, too dangerous. It is not a grasseater. She will tear a snare apart."

"Not if it is around her neck." Barik looked up to the roof of the cave, pointing to a section of broken rock above the entrance. "We pass the snare through the rocks up there and drop it down in the entrance. When she puts her head into the noose, we pull the snare tight." He stopped for a moment and swallowed. "When she is hanging, we kill her with spears."

Assan shook her head and laughed nervously, certain the bushman must have heard them. She glanced at One-Eye and saw he was still watching the canyon. "We do not have the strength to

274

hold such a beast," she hissed.

"No, but One-Eye is strong. He will pull on the snare until we kill her." He looked at Assan.

"We are to kill a lion? A woman and a boy who is barely a hunter? I know nothing about spears! I sew, make dry meat, cook meals!"

"You know the tip of a spear. There is no other way. Look at him. He is losing his strength. The lioness's curse is draining him. He cannot kill her - not alone." Barik was beginning to believe his plan might work.

"The fire will keep her away," So'tsal said. "The lion fears flames. We need only to keep the fire burning. She will grow tired and go." As she spoke, they heard the far off roar of the lioness. They looked at each other.

Barik bent closer. "Fire is not enough. We do not have enough wood to burn a big fire all winter. We are trapped in this cave." He looked at Assan, rubbing his hands together. "He will not listen to me. You must tell him. You must convince him."

"No," Assan said tersely. "It will not work." She stood up and moved toward the fire. "Come, So'tsal."

The lioness came that night. They were all asleep except for One-Eye. He was by the fire feeding wood to the flames. Suddenly she was standing at the edge of the firelight, snarling so deep and low it shook the walls of the cave. Assan woke in a start, shouting the alarm. The lioness was moving for the cave. One-Eye stumbled back to the entrance, blindly thrusting his spear around the rock as wood flew from the cave onto the fire.

"Wood!" Assan shouted. "More wood!" The fire suddenly erupted. The lioness roared, and One-Eye's scarred face flinched as he gripped the spear with shaking hands. The big cat paced around the fire, roaring. Suddenly she was gone and the canyon fell silent.

Assan fetched a bladder of water and slung it over the roaring flames. Spinning the bladder, she went to the stack of skins, selected a thick elk hide and handed it to So'tsal. Gripping her

275

daughter's hand, Assan lifted three fingers.

"Cut the strips this wide," she said, squeezing So'tsal's fingers gently. "Braid three strips together and make the snare as long as the cave." Assan took the steaming bladder and poured tea around. When she handed Barik his bowl she whispered under her breath, "The spears must be strong and sharp." One-Eye was lost in thought and did not hear her.

The Hanging Beast

Barik climbed the rock and fed the heavy snare through cracks in the cave roof. He tied a loop in one end and let it hang free in the entrance at waist height. Assan smeared grease along the snare until it pulled easily through the cracks. Barik adjusted the noose until he was sure it would catch the lioness at the chest and around the neck. At the rear of the cave, he drove a piece of wood into the dirt and wrapped the end of the snare around it.

One-Eye watched the snare setting with disinterest. When they were done, Assan nodded to Barik and brought the bushman a hot tea. He took it from her and drank it down. Barik and So'tsal waited for her to speak.

"We will snare the lioness," she said matter-of-factly. "Come. See."

He grunted, obviously confused by the device.

"Here is the noose. It is strong - three thick rawhide cords braided together. Barik made the snare. He will kill the lioness and take away her wounded spirit."

One-Eye's fist struck out at Barik with no warning.

"No!" Assan shouted. "He wants to help One-Eye! The lioness will not stop until she kills you - you killed the cub and wounded her. The snare will kill her and take away the bad luck!" The bushman roared at her, then went outside and shouted into the canyon. When he came back in, he snatched the snare and examined the noose.

"It will work," Barik said. "She will come inside the cave for you." He went to the back of the cave, pulled on the snare and watched the noose pull closed.

"Her neck will be in the noose. You pull the snare hard and stand her up. Barik and I will kill her with spears," Assan said, not believing her own words.

One-Eye roared as confusion spread across his scarred face. His eye followed the length of the snare to the back of the cave. He swung his head back and forth, as if he was clearing his mind.

Barik watched as Assan calmed him. She was speaking so quietly Barik could not understand what she was saying. The bushman went to the end of the snare and pulled it.

He is like a child. The mother speaks and the bushman listens.

They waited three nights before she came. Each night, the lioness approached but did not come closer than the edge of the fire. On the final night they let the fire die down and waited, crouched in the shadows, as the moon rose into a clear, starry sky. A little later northern lights began to shimmer with tubes of twisting red and green spread across the sky, suddenly turning into rolling ribbons of pale green that dimmed even the brightest stars.

Yukaih - northern light - is a good-luck sign, Assan thought, squatting with her back against the cave and a spear in her hand.

I am to spear the lioness. A woman who has never killed anything larger than a hare.

Barik sat across from her. They were waiting to kill the fiercest beast on Earth. So'tsal was in the shadows behind him, holding a third spear.

Since Lions-Came Camp, Assan had been ready to die. She lived only for So'tsal. Each breath she took was so her daughter would live one more day. All the humans she loved were gone: Khon, Kazan, Eyak, Tarin, Yogh, Teekai, Yukaih, Chii Tsal, Karun, Korya, Aron, Dat'san, Gilgan, Jak, Jovan, Anik, Naali and Dèhzhòo.

How does one live when all those you love are dead?

Assan had been badly shaken by Dèhzhòo's murder. She was barely showing child and she had taken care to hide the change to her body. They were talking, happy even, when the bushman grabbed her. What future did So'tsal have with him? She closed her eyes and asked Khon to help guide the spear into the lioness's heart - and then she would turn it on the bushman. In her
278

hand, she held a piece of kindling, ready to throw it when the lioness slipped into the noose. It was the signal for One-Eye to pull the snare hard, before the lioness sensed the trap. They had practised it many times: she threw the stick and he pulled, wrapping the snare around the stake; she and Barik jumped up and plunged their spears at the heart of the imaginary lion hanging in the noose. It was an impossible plan, Assan thought. Her confidence drained with every moment that passed in the dark cave.

The fire had burned down to flickering embers when she finally came - so silently Assan could hardly believe the cat was standing there. She made no sound, emerging from the dark canyon only a few steps from the cave, walking so slowly it seemed she was floating on snow. Assan watched the noose shudder slightly as the lioness's neck grazed the snare. Then the great beast stopped in mid-stride.

She sees it!

Assan was hidden against the rock wall. She raised her hand ready to throw the stick. The lioness turned and sniffed the noose; then her head swung back and she looked into the cave.

She sees me!

The noose began to slowly slide down, and Assan knew she was coming in.

The stick seemed to sail forever through the dark cavern, finally clattering against the rock wall as everything exploded in a din of shouts, screams and roars. Assan lunged for the lioness, her spear shaking like a willow in the wind. The roar was deafening, splitting her ears. What she saw was not an animal but a writhing shadow of raging madness framed against the moonlit sky. Her massive head snapped back and forth as she raked the rock walls with her claws, tearing blindly into the darkness. Her body rose and she was swaying on her hind legs, roaring, unable to reach the thing that held her by the neck.

Assan stood in front of the raging beast, too frightened to move. Barik suddenly appeared beside her, his spear waving

279

frantically. He was shouting. For an instant she saw the target in the dim light of the cave.

The belly!

She plunged her spear at it but as she was about to sink it into the gut, a paw flashed, knocking the spear from her hand. Barik was frozen, his spear poised there, waiting.

"Spear it!" she screamed.

One-Eye roared from the back of the cave and the lioness lifted off the ground. Assan fell down, blindly searching for her spear in the dark. She was rising to her feet when someone suddenly snatched it from her and knocked her into the rocks. As her face struck the wall, she heard the most remarkable noise - a gagging screech that shook her to the core of her bones. The noise became unbearable. Then someone fell on her and she lost consciousness.

A Killing Lesson

Kazan followed the fresh snow trail, stopping now and again to ponder the strange track. On one side of the trail he could see the hoof prints of the elk; on the other was a wide, sculpted trail, as if the elk were dragging something. Pulling his visor on, Kazan squinted into the narrow slits, following the trail on the sun-drenched tundra until it disappeared behind a ridge. He kicked the ice from his mukluks and ran quickly, knowing the elk could not be far ahead. As he raced through the snow, his excitement grew.

The cow was below the ridge feeding on the grasses surrounding a frozen pond. He saw what had made the strange track. A thick ball of snow was frozen to the elk's lower leg. Kazan watched her drag her heavy snow-crusted leg along the shore of the pond. It would be an easy hunt. He took a dart from his quiver and slipped it onto the tail of his throwing board. He was about to go down when he thought of Zhòh and turned back for camp.

As he approached Hole-in-Rock he shouted, "Naali! Bring the wolf!" She came out of the cave carrying her spear, followed by Zhòh.

"What is it?" she asked.

"A hunting lesson!"

Zhòh was soon well ahead of them, moving in the direction of the elk. When they crossed the cow's trail, Kazan pointed down. "Her leg is covered in ice. Zhòh has already found her." They reached the crest of the ridge and looked down. The cow was facing Zhòh.

Naali and Kazan ran down the hill and circled the elk, waiting for her to make a move. She slowly turned with them, her eyes carefully watching them.

Zhòh began pacing, anticipating a hunt. Kazan positioned a throwing dart and aimed it carefully so the shaft struck the cow flat on the back. She grunted in surprise and bolted.

"Hunt!" Kazan shouted as *Zhòh* ran. She made a cautious charge but lost her confidence at the last moment, breaking off a few paces from the running elk. Kazan caught up, hurling a second dart. The point plunged into the cow's shoulder, held briefly and fell out, leaving a thin stream of blood on the snow. *Zhòh* lunged up, grabbing the cow by the neck. The elk tried to swing around and shake the wolf off, but the ice ball slowed her turn. *Zhòh* hung on, pulling down on the neck until her weight was too much for the cow. She stumbled and fell.

Zhòh released her grip on the neck and instinctively reached for the elk's nose. The cow rolled but *Zhòh* kicked free, still holding the nose closed. The cow tried once more to shed the wolf but failed. She dropped her head and blew a cloud of red mist. Kazan and Naali watched with growing anticipation as the wolf slowly suffocated the elk.

"Where did she learn to do that?" Naali asked.

Kazan rushed toward the dying elk, shouting, "She killed it. A cow. *Zhòh* killed a grasseater!"

Suddenly the wolf turned, bared her bloody teeth and snarled an ominous warning. Kazan stopped, but *Zhòh* was already charging for him. He had become so used to the wolf's presence he had forgotten her wildness. As she sprung up, Kazan raised his hand in defence. Her teeth brushed by his hand as she turned away at the last moment and clamped her jaws shut. Kazan stood completely still as the wolf ran back to the cow and stood over it, defiantly claiming the kill. *Zhòh* tore into the gut and fed as if she had never eaten flesh, all the while watching Kazan and Naali with suspicion. A little later she carried off a piece of the heart and bedded down with it.

Kazan and Naali moved carefully to the carcass. He lifted the ice-bound leg, broke the ball apart with his knife, revealing a deep wound weeping a thick sticky pus. He showed it to Naali and then flipped the dead caribou onto her back. It was bad luck for a girl to be part of field butchering, so she moved away, careful not to step on the bloody snow.

"A hunter cannot speak to a girl while he butchers a grasseater," Kazan said, smiling. He raised his spear and their points touched.

The Lion's Skin

Assan woke to the sound of water splashing. As she opened her eyes, she saw the bloody skin of a lioness hanging from the cave entrance. Her head was pounding. She raised her hand to her forehead, feeling the thick swelling. As her eyes adjusted to the daylight she saw So'tsal scrubbing the rocks, and the memory of what had happened slowly returned.

"Mother - you wake!" So'tsal whispered as she moved to her side. She gently pressed her hand on her shoulder. "Do not get up."

"What happened?" Assan asked as she glanced around the cave. "Where are they - One-Eye, Barik?"

"The lioness is dead!" So'tsal declared, pointing to the skin. "It happened as Barik told us." Her voice was triumphant. "They are out hunting. I worried you might not ever wake." She paused and kissed her mother's fingers softly. "I am glad you have woken. You have slept two days."

Assan rested on her bed as So'tsal told her what happened. The last thing she recalled was someone snatching her spear and the deafening screams.

"When you threw the stick, One-Eye lifted the lion up until the snare choked her, until she was hanging in the air. The noise was terrible. Then he ran to the entrance and pushed you aside and took your spear. Barik and the bushman stabbed her many times and her blood was everywhere." She waved her hand around the cave excitedly. "Barik said to wash the blood from the walls, to take away her bad luck."

Assan nodded, her head pounding now. "It is good to wash the bad luck away."

"The lioness's foot struck Barik on the shoulder. I cleaned and bound the wound as you have taught me." So'tsal's tone was proud. "It is not the throwing arm. He is out hunting with One-Eye. A herd of *Vadzaih* passed close by yesterday. Killing the lioness
284

brought good luck! Barik says that the lion meat will bring us good luck!"

Assan was surprised with this news.

One-Eye tried to burn Barik alive. Now they are out hunting - together. He is a bushman. He hunts alone.

A dull, thudding pain racked her forehead. She lowered her head back to the bed. When she woke again, it was night. The fire was roaring outside and she could see the shadows of Barik and One-Eye moving around the flames. Assan suddenly felt famished. She sat up and called for So'tsal, who brought her food and drink. As she ate, Barik came into the tent and squatted down beside her.

"Your face is as ugly as the bushman's," he joked.

"The snare worked."

He nodded and pointed to the lion skin. "I skinned it," he said with obvious pride. "One-Eye will not touch it. I hung it as a warning to other killing beasts. So'tsal is drying the meat."

"You hunt with him."

"I follow him and carry back meat like a good hunter," he said with a hint of scorn.

"Your shoulder - is it bad?"

"The wound is deep. So'tsal has dressed it."

"The snare," Assan said. "It was good. No human has snared a lion."

"Barik, the Lion Snarer," he said sighing. "I will be the Lion Snarer to only you and So'tsal. No one else will ever hear the story."

He stood and went to the fire. The bushman was resting against the rock. Barik offered him a piece of caribou and One-Eye took it. Assan saw Barik had changed. His confidence had grown.

The snare worked. A snare that even Khon would not have thought of. I will have to stop thinking of Barik as a boy.

Still, something about him disturbed her. She watched him sit down across the fire from One-Eye, their shadows shrouding the walls of the cave in darkness.

PART 6

KHAII: DARK DAYS RETURN

Raven Steals the Sun

The Dark Days: the day sky lit by only a dim sliver of dull grey beneath the southern horizon. The sun had lost its grip and slipped under the world, plunging the tundra-steppe into darkness. It was too dark to hunt and too dangerous for Naali and Kazan to leave the cave for long. They spent long hours chipping away at Avii Tsal's hole until it was wide enough for Naali to climb into. They wedged a sleeping bed inside, furs and a sack of dry meat and berries. If a killing beast came into the cave, that would be Naali's escape. Kazan could not fit and would have to fend for himself.

Naali thought of her brother. Where was Barik now? In her heart she hoped he was alive, but that seemed impossible. Humans did not survive on the tundra-steppe alone, especially in winter. Where was he in the darkness? Dead? Guilt tightened her throat. She had banished her brother for trying to kill Kazan. She knew he could not be trusted. Killing another human was punished by banishment. But knowing this did not make it any easier.

Khaii - the Dark Days - would last more than a moon. It was the time when band children would be safely among their families. Naali had never felt such gnawing loneliness. She longed for the cramped and smoky skin tents filled with people. Inside the warmth of the tents, people kept busy making weapons and tools, sewing skins, making fire, boiling tea and cooking meat. The tents hummed with the sound of voices: talking, laughing, crying, shouting. In the darkness, the men planned hunts, discussed where grasseaters would be when the sun returned, argued when the
286

snow would melt and endlessly described what they knew of grasseater behaviour. Women talked skin-tanning and sewing clothes, shared advice about sickness remedies and gave the children their daily chores.

But it was the nighttime stories that Naali and Kazan missed the most - stories they had listened to every night, their eyes gazing into the safe glow of the tent fires. There were funny stories, sad stories, animal stories and spirit stories. *Googwandak* from long, long ago, when humans and animals spoke the same tongue. Lesson *googwandaks* that warned children of what happened when they strayed from camp, or when a human turned against the ways of the band. There were stories about first hunts, the passing of elders and travelling to new places. The stories kept the knowledge of human beings, and Naali and Barik missed them badly.

Naali stretched out in her bed. *Zhòh* was sprawled at her feet, basking in the heat of the fire. She and Kazan had traded stories back and forth to pass the evening and now they were both staring into the shifting flames. He had told *Blind Man and the Loon* and *Young Man and Bear*. Naali recounted *Smart Woman and the Nanaa'in* and *Ch'ataiiyuukaih Fixed Bad Animals*. She waited for Kazan to tell another tale, but he was already dozing.

"Kazan! I cannot sleep. Tell another story!" She thought for a moment. "*Raven Steals Back Sun from Bear*. Tell the story of how Raven Tricked Bear!"

Kazan suddenly woke. He loved listening, but he was new at telling a *Googwandak*. He cleared his throat and began, hoping he would tell it right.

"This is a *Googwandak* about *Deetrù'* - Raven - how he stole the sun from Bear and gave it back to humans. Long ago and in another story, Grebes got mad at Raven and took away the sun. For a long time, the land was dark and humans saw they could not live without light, so they went to Raven, who was smart and had magic. They asked him to steal back the sun. *Deetrù* knew Bear had taken it from Grebes and hidden it in his cave. So Raven changed into a baby and joined Bear's family. One day the baby cried until Bear came to ask what was wrong. The baby - who was really *Deetrù* - asked Bear if he could play with the bright yellow light. The yellow light was the sun stolen by the Grebes... that Bear stole from Grebes."

Naali smiled silently. He will learn to tell stories, she thought, stifling a small laugh.

"But Bear said no, he could not guard it from others who would come and take it. The baby cried until Bear was sick of the whining. He said he could play with the ball as long as it stayed inside the tent."

He paused and looked at her. "Remember. The baby was Raven in disguise, the Trickster."

"Yes!" Naali exclaimed. "I am not a child hearing my first *Googwandak*! Tell it right or I will finish it for you!"

Kazan continued. "Baby rolled the sun around the floor as Bear watched. Then Bear fell asleep and forgot the sun. When Baby pushed it outside it flew into the air and back to its place in the sky. Then Bear woke. He saw he was tricked, but he was secretly happy to see the sun back in the sky. He missed the light too. Raven tricked Bear not just for humans to have the sun back. Raven needs the sun because he cannot fly in the dark. That is the story *Raven Stole the Sun Back from Bear*." Kazan sipped his tea, staring into the flames as fire crackled. "My father's mother told him this *Googwandak*. He told it to me."

Naali clapped slowly. "Good, Kazan but the stories need to be longer and more exciting if we are going to make it through *Khaii*." She raised herself in her bed and looked at him. He was already sleeping. Naali fed the fire and gingerly lifted a warm rock from the hearth, slipping it into her sleeping bed. She pressed her hare-skin socks onto the stone and rolled over on her side, feeling the warmth. She was disturbed by something and tossed and turned for a long time before she finally fell asleep. The dream that came was darker than any *Khaii* night.

The noise comes out of the blinding snowstorm, from the darkness, moving closer. She is sitting, her mitts gripping the slick ice, trying desperately to hold herself from being blown away.

Scraping and thumping. The sound is getting closer. She reaches for her brother's hand, but Barik is gone. He was beside her only moments ago! She pulls back her hood and stretches her arm as far as she can, hoping to touch him, but the darkness is complete. She sees nothing beyond her outstretched hand.

The scraping sound is nearer... she buries her face in her arm. A mukluk glides over the black ice, sliding past her. Suddenly, she knows.

It is One-Eye!

He has found her. She turns her face away, waiting for the spear to sink into her back, ending her life. The howling storm is driving ice crystals against her cheeks. She pulls her hood down and covers her head with her mitts - listening, waiting to die. But nothing happens.

The sound is moving away.

Naali peers into the dark, the wind buffeting her back. She is alone. She rolls onto her elbows and is nearly blown away by a gust. Then she senses something is wrong, terribly wrong. Someone is watching. She can hear the soft breathing, the scuffle of leather boots on ice.

"She is here." The voice rises to a shout. "Come back. She is here." It is Barik.

Naali knew she had screamed because the wolf was barking and Kazan was shouting.

"Naali! Naali!" He gripped her by the shoulders and held her tightly. "You are dreaming!"

She watched the wolf scramble under the tent door and disappear into the dim grey light of morning. Naali's whole body shook.

"It is a dream," Kazan was saying. "Do not move. I will make a fire and make a tea. Do not get up."

289

The flames blazed, and soon water was boiling in a bladder. He poured two skull cups and nodded to the door, awkwardly attempting to strike up a conversation. "*Zhòh* will come back." Naali wrapped her shaking fingers around the cup and slowly sipped the drink.

"You called for Barik," Kazan said matter-of-factly. He set an armload of wood onto the fire.

She lied. "I cannot remember." She knew he would want to know what she dreamed. Everything she dreamed would happen, whether she wanted it to or not. She was powerless to stop it. It was her power - her curse. Shaking her head, she said, "I do not remember the dream." She wondered if her voice gave away the lie.

"If you do not remember, you will not have to forget." He looked at her, smiling weakly, but she would not look at him. "I will get *Zhòh*," he said, feeling awkward. He slipped out of the tent.

As his eyes grew accustomed to the soft light of dawn, he saw the wolf sitting on the snow nearby. With practised eyes he scanned the plain for subtle movement, any change in the shape of the horizon. He had searched so often he knew every dip and rise of land as far as he could see. In the dimness, Kazan could see nothing out of place.

We have had good luck wintering in this place.

A few lions and a wolf pack had come close but had left without bothering them. One night, *Zhòh* had barked and growled into the blackness beyond the cave. The next morning Kazan found where a lion had skirted by the cave but had not lingered. He had silently thanked Wolf Spirit for the good luck.

The wolf stood on the snowy tundra and walked toward him, keeping her distance. *Zhòh* would never let him touch her, but she had become attached to him. She went out hunting but never hunted with him. She had quickly learned how to kill. Since her first kill - the elk with the ice ball - *Zhòh* had taken a yearling caribou and an elk calf. He and Naali had scavenged the kills, eating the fresh meat of winter.

290

He glanced back at the tent. Smoke was billowing from the chimney. Naali was speaking to the wolf in the soft tones she reserved for *Zhòh*. In his daydreaming, he had not noticed the wolf had slipped back into the tent.

She does not forget a dream. She called his name. Naali dreamed her brother. What did she dream? Kazan thought about the banishment. He knew sending Barik away was the hardest thing she had ever done. Before he went back into the tent, he searched the skyline a last time. At the seamless fusion of grey sky and windswept land, he saw ravens approaching. Moments later, the air was filled with raucous calls as they passed over Hole-in-Rock Camp, disappearing somewhere behind the outcrop. Then there was only the sound of the wind.

Black-Foot Rests

The ravens skirt around the rock where a thin column of white smoke rises. They pass over the human; the face wrapped in thick fur looks up as they pass. Ahead there is a patchwork of open ground and snow. Somewhere ahead, under a thicket of shrubs, is the meal the birds discovered before roosting last night.

Black-Foot is curled up under shrubs, looking very much alive. The ravens circle the thicket and see they are not the first to arrive. Standing beside the still wolf are two adult ravens. The flock squawks and calls down, scolding them for claiming the food.

Suddenly the two big birds are beating their way into the air. In a frenzy of dives and dips, they drive off the young flock, clacking their heavy black bills. A young bird makes a wrong turn and loses a patch of its back feathers. The aerial skirmish changes when the flock retaliates, driving the two adults to the ground, where they take cover under a willow thicket. There are too many young birds. Eventually, the adults slip from under the branches and fly off, pursued by only a few of the bravest ravens.

The flock of young ravens circles above the wolf, calling loudly until many more arrive from all directions. They land on the snow near the wolf, their wary eyes watching for any movement. A sudden gust of wind sends them hopping backward. They are not certain the wolf is dead. There is no blood, torn hair or bloodied tracks on the snow.

They patiently watch the carcass for a long time, summoning their courage to approach. Finally, a bird hops forward, stretches its long beak and pokes and tugs at Black-Foot's thick fur. A little later many birds are stabbing their powerful beaks into flesh. Before the brief light is gone, they have completely stripped the carcass of flesh. One by one, the birds flap into the air, catching the evening wind that takes them back to their night roost.

The ruckus of the ravens attracts a fox. It drives off the last of the straggling birds and goes to work on Black-Foot's carcass, gnawing at the last of her flesh as falling snow covers its back in a blanket of white.

Assan Remembers

Assan coped with the Dark Days by staying busy. She spent her waking hours smoking and tanning hides, making baskets, splitting stone for points and knives, checking and re-checking the supply of food and preparing the meals. *Khaii* always dragged So'tsal down. This winter was no exception. She was sleeping longer and she was becoming irritable and impatient - still helpful, but less inclined to initiate her tasks, and rarely with her characteristic pleasantries. Neither spoke of how much they missed Wolf Band and the friendly commotion inside a winter tent.

Assan remembered when she was a young mother and So'tsal was learning to walk. Assan felt the oppression of the endless dark and the cramped, awkward confines of the tent. The small fire, where she spent most of the day, was always jammed with other women preparing meals. They talked while they worked, jostling around each other to find a skin bladder or bone utensil or to add wood to the fire. There was never privacy; always someone in view, and the talking - someone always talking. Children endlessly cried, laughed and sang. Stories filled every evening, sometimes not finishing until the dim light of dawn. Yet, somehow, Assan had learned to cope, even enjoy most days. She had to. It was the way of a band. It was how humans coped with the Dark Days. She longed to hear Eyak, Khon, Kazan and the rest of Wolf Band that now lived only in her memory.

Winter cold had forced them to move from the roomy cave into the tent positioned at the entrance. Assan and So'tsal spent their days inside the tent, the only relief coming when One-Eye and Barik left to hunt. One-Eye seemed unaffected by the constant dark. His temper had not lessened, but his violent outbursts were fewer. He reserved his blows for Assan and So'tsal. Since the lioness, he had come to tolerate Barik. Sometimes when Barik spoke to him, One-Eye even nodded a wordless reply.

Barik had grown more sombre with the absence of light. He was changing from a boy to a man, just as So'tsal was blossoming into a young woman. His prowess as a hunter had risen sharply since he had snared the lioness, quickly endearing him to So'tsal. Assan quietly watched as Barik played her, openly courting her interest and then feigning indifference. As she watched the familiar mating ritual, her heart sank. Was this to be their new life if they somehow survived One-Eye's rages - Barik married to So'tsal?

Barik and One-Eye had left the tent, slipping out into the dark and down the grey canyon. It had been weeks since they had killed anything. Assan was beginning to worry about their food supply. She had carefully measured the meals in the sack and calculated that there was not enough to make it to spring. The snares outside provided few hare or ptarmigan. She could only hope that when the sun returned, the hunting would improve and they would have meat so she would not have to ration the dwindling supply even further. The hunters returned that evening without a grasseater, both in foul moods. Neither spoke as they gnawed on dry meat and drank a thin broth of boiled elk bone.

"I am hungry," Barik complained, draining the last of his broth.

"That is all there is. There is not enough to spring," Assan replied as she sipped her broth.

Barik went over to her, snatching the skull cup from her hands. "We are hunters. We need food." He drank it and handed the empty cup back to Assan. Her hands shook with anger.

"Then bring me a grasseater," she said acidly.

Fuming, he sat down. Assan saw One-Eye was watching them over his steaming broth. She suddenly realized how dangerous her words were - *There is not enough food to spring.* Why had she talked about food? The bushman would kill them - all of them - if the food was low. Her heart raced as One-Eye slowly stood. He walked past her, slipped out of the tent and went to the back of the cave. She waited nervously by the fire. He returned carrying his club and a leg bone, sat down and pounded the bone until it cracked. He picked out the marrow fat from the bone with his knife and gulped it down as he watched her.

The Voice

It is the same dream but more vivid and disturbing. Barik is watching Naali and Kazan fly away on the back of the eagle. He calls out, but she does not turn. Kazan looks back and smiles mockingly. He runs after them, shouting to them to take him, until they disappear and he is standing on the river shore, alone in the dark.

He hears the familiar voice and is struck by a mix of joy and fear. The voice is strong and confident.

They have left you.

"*No, they will be back.*"

I saw the boy smile. It was goodbye.

"*No, she will be back.*"

She is gone. She shares her power with the boy. Not with you, her brother. You are alone.

"*I have the bushman and Assan and So'tsal.*"

I am always with you.

"*No. I do not want you bothering me. You bring bad luck.*"

Then why do you call to me?

"*I do not call you; you come.*"

You call me to me. Do you want her back?

"*Yes.*"

What will you do?

"*Anything.*"

Then kill the boy.

"*I tried. You saw — I tried.*"

Then do it right this time. Kill him.

"*But they banished me.*"

The river is frozen. Walk across. Kill him.

"*I cannot kill him alone.*"

Then take *him* with you.

"*Take who?*"

297

The bushman.

"He will not follow me."

He will follow.

"Why?"

Think. What has Kazan got that he wants?

"But he will kill her."

Think. His mind is a like a child. You snared a lioness and took her bad spirit away. Let him kill the boy. Then think how to keep her. Think.

PART 7

SREENDYIT: GETTING LIGHT AGAIN

The Future Unfolds

When Assan and So'tsal climbed to the rim of the canyon to sing the *Sun Welcome* song, Assan felt no joy. She felt none of the hope for the coming summer, as she had when her band stood with her every winter. She was missing Khon and Kazan and Eyak deeply as the words came to her:

From down under the sky,
I come to earth shining,
Light that ends Khaii and brings warmth to the earth.
Sree shares her light so snow will melt and grass will grow,
And Wolf Band will grow strong on the flesh of the land.

Unable to finish the last line, her voice trailed off into So'tsal's singing, the hope glowing in her daughter's sunlit face. Assan saw that she did not understand that nothing had changed. They were the bushman's slaves and he would kill them when he no longer needed them. She had measured the food before the others woke in the morning: barely enough for another moon. Would he kill them then, or today? She did not look at So'tsal as she turned her back on the sun and went down into the shadowy canyon.

Barik's Plan

Two weeks had passed since the sun had returned. One-Eye had killed a calf caribou from a small group crossing the river, but it was nearly gone. Assan had rationed the meat carefully, giving more and more to One-Eye and Barik as the days passed. They were hunting farther from camp, sometimes spending the night away. One day they spotted a group of bison crossing downriver. As they approached the herd, the skies darkened and a blizzard struck. Barik and One-Eye huddled together in a ravine for two days, wrapped in skins. When the storm passed, the bison were gone. They returned to camp with a single ptarmigan. As they approached the cave, One-Eye stopped and looked up at the lion skin swaying above the entrance. He drove his spear up into it, slung it to the ground and stamped on it.

A few days later, they found a bison carcass frozen deep in the river ice. As they were approaching the blood-stained ice, a wolverine scrambled out of a hole and disappeared into the shrubs. The bushman stood over the icy tunnel as if measuring it. He looked at Barik and pointed. Barik removed his pack and slid down the wolverine's hole without protest.

The darkness was filled with such a sour rankness of rotted death that he nearly vomited. Beneath he could hear the rush of the river. It took a while for his eyes to adjust to the dimness. There was little left except for hide and bone. Barik severed a thick leg bone and crawled out.

"Only bones," he said.

One-Eye pointed and Barik went back down the putrid hole, retrieving more. When he was done, Barik looked up and down the trackless shore while One-Eye filled their packs. The bushman slung his pack on.

Barik pointed toward the distant range of snow-capped mountains and Hole-in-Rock. "My sister is alive," he said, "the one with the strange eyes. She burned your winter camp. She lives."

One-Eye stopped and looked at him, his dark eye narrowing to a dangerous slit. Barik had expected anger but the speed and force of the assault surprised him. The bushman rushed at him and he fell, protecting his face with his hands. He was flying through the air, slamming down on the ice, rolling into a ball as One-Eye kicked and beat at him with the flat of his spear. He stood above Barik, his spear pressed down hard on his chest.

Barik twisted his face and looked up. "A cave with furs, darts, spears, wood and meat," he said hoarsely. "Three days - there is food and skins and shelter. I know the way - three days."

The spear slowly lifted from his chest. He waited until the bushman stepped back before he stood.

"There are two of them: my sister and a boy." One-Eye looked at him. "He is nothing. A boy. We take their camp. You can do what you want with her. I will kill him."

One-Eye was listening intently, carefully studying Barik.

"We escaped the lions on an ice floe," Barik said blankly, shrugging his shoulders. "I stayed with them for the summer but I tired of them."

One-Eye snatched Barik by the throat and lifted him up until their noses touched.

"They banished me," Barik stammered.

One-Eye grunted and threw him to the ground.

"I took away the lioness's bad spirit. I made the snare. Why would I lie? We are hunters."

One-Eye gazed toward the south, twisting the spear in his hand.

"Three days," Barik said. "The woman cannot know."

When Barik and One-Eye returned to camp with the bones, Assan sensed something was wrong. She had noticed a change in them the moment they entered the cave. Barik, normally talkative, offered no greeting. He sat by the fire and stared blankly into the flames as she prepared a broth from the bones. The bushman was inspecting the harness traces. She wondered if they were planning to hunt away from the cave.

"Are you hunting away?" she casually asked Barik. One-Eye glanced up at her and went back to checking harnesses.

Barik shrugged. "I do not know the bushman's plans."

Assan glanced at One-Eye. He was unravelling another harness.

We are moving.

She woke in the darkness. Barik stood over her, his face barely visible in the dim glow of the fire.

"Get up. We are moving," he said.

"Where?"

"I do not know." His voice was distant and unfriendly. "Make the meal. We will leave. You follow with a small camp."

She pulled on her jacket and shook So'tsal awake.

"We are moving," she told her. "Roll up the beds and tie floor skins in a bundle."

"Where? Where are we going?" So'tsal asked sleepily.

Assan shook her head. "We are moving."

"In winter! Why?"

"I do not know. Hurry. Pack."

They broke camp before sunrise, the sled skimming down the canyon. Assan looked back at the cave as they moved out of the gorge and onto the river. Her anxiety rose as she remembered the great struggles and many deaths on Wolf Band's winter journey. They followed Barik and One-Eye's trail up the *Ch'oodèenjik* and then off the river south onto the windswept open tundra.

"Where are they going?" So'tsal asked.

"I do not know," she said, looking up the broad valley leading to mountains in the south. They followed a small river, their sled pulling easily over the smooth ice. Late in the day, they found the two hunters on the river shore butchering a calf caribou. They built camp and collected kindling for a fire while Barik and One-Eye disappeared upriver. They returned dragging a freshly killed cow. They butchered it and piled snow over it.

302

"How many *Vadzaih* are you hunting?" she asked. "We have enough fresh meat to feed us through winter."

"There are more up the river."

"We have taken two," Assan said. "We should return to camp."

Barik shrugged. "I do not know what a bushman thinks."

The next day the women continued upriver and found the hunters with another cow. They made camp. Assan was certain they would turn back for camp the next morning. Surely they had killed enough grasseaters to feed them until spring.

When she woke, One-Eye and Barik were already gone. The fire was cool and they had not taken a meal.

Hunters do not leave without a hot meal.

She went outside and climbed a hill as the sun rose over the horizon. Assan spotted their trail weaving up the river and onto a high plateau. There was something moving in the distance near the river. Caribou slowly appeared.

How could they miss the herd? The grasseaters are next to the river.

They were not hunting, she suddenly realized.

Where are they going?

Somewhere upstream Assan heard wolves howling. She walked to the tent but did not say anything to So'tsal.

Entangled

The wolves walk down into a valley filled with the smell of prey. Grey-Eye presses her nose down on the soft caribou dung, raises her head and sniffs the cool morning air. As they reach the willow-lined river, they cross a trail of humans. Grey-Eye sniffs the tracks briefly but loses interest. Fresh caribou scent is coming from every direction. The herd is scattered up and down the river. As the wolves approach, the caribou raise their heads, instantly aware of the approaching danger.

The pack spreads out through the low willows along the river, waiting for Grey-Eye to begin. A few bulls prance toward the wolves, their noses in the air, while the rest of the animals start walking away, heading for higher ground. Grey-Eye watches from behind her pack, waiting. Suddenly she runs for the herd, quartering across the slope, driving the caribou back toward the river. She spots something in the commotion of churning legs and flying snow: a bull is limping as he weaves in and out of the stampeding animals. She quickly closes the gap, leaping over shrubs as she tries to cut him out of the herd. He swerves away from the river and heads for a steep hill, but she cuts him off, driving him onto the river ice. She is gaining, about to lunge for his leg, when the bull staggers trying to avoid something on the ice. He leaps and crashes down.

Grey-Eye sees the sled too late. As she jumps, her leg snags in a harness trace. She lands hard on the ice, sliding into the struggling bull. She tries to grab the bull by the neck, but something is holding her. She rolls and kicks at the harness until she is completely entangled. Then something is pushed into her neck.

Release

Assan heard the thundering of hooves approaching from upriver. She tossed her tea and bolted out of the tent as the leaders passed a few steps away, their eyes wide with panic.

"*Vadzaih!*" she shouted to So'tsal.

Hundreds more came, splitting around the tent and the sled on the ice. A bull saw the sled at the last moment and leaped over it, snagging his rear legs in a harness. He slammed down on the ice, breaking his neck as the sled cartwheeled behind him. The next instant a leaping wolf landed in the tangle of harnesses on top of the bull.

"So'tsal!" she shouted as caribou continued to stream by.

"Come! Now!"

The entangled wolf was twisting and rolling, biting at the leather rope as it wound around its body until it could not move. Assan reached for a spear and pressed it down on the wolf's neck.

"No!" So'tsal shouted. "You cannot kill her!" She pointed to the wolf's swollen underbelly. "It is a mother! We are Wolf Band!" Her hand gripped Assan's arm. "She cannot move! We must release her!"

The bull drew its last breath and died beneath the wolf. Assan hesitated, uncertain what to do. "It is too dangerous!" she shouted. If she released the wolf, she would certainly bite her. Her mind raced, imagining what a hunter would do. She needed a way to hold her head down. Assan glanced around camp and saw the other spear under the upset sled.

"The spear," she said to So'tsal and pointed. "Bring it and tie a strip of rawhide above the point. Then wrap the other end to my spear." When So'tsal was finished tying the spears together, Assan drew a stone blade and handed both spear shafts to her.

"Now push down hard on her neck with the spears. Hold her tight. Do not let her up. Keep her face on the ice. She is nervous. She will bite!"

So'tsal pushed down across the wolf's neck, jamming the two stone points into the ice. Grey-Eye snapped and growled, kicking in vain as Assan settled down on top of her. Holding the wolf by the back legs, she began cutting the harness traces until she reached the wolf's shoulder. Grey-Eye was growling fiercely.

"What will we do if she breaks free?" So'tsal asked in a shaky voice.

"You will hold her!" Assan commanded. "When I cut the last traces on her neck, I will move back. Push down with all of your strength. Do not let her stand until we are both ready."

Assan slid the stone knife under the leather harness. As she cut the rope, the wolf's unblinking eye followed her shaking hand. "The last one," she said as she cut around the face. "Now! Hold her!" she shouted, grabbing the shaft of a spear as she jumped back. They pushed down hard, pinning the wolf's head to the ice.

"Hold!" Assan said as Grey-Eye thrashed and kicked, trying to get to her feet. Finally, the wolf collapsed, panting heavily.

"Slowly," Assan whispered. They released the spears and stepped back. Grey-Eye's chest heaved as the cool air filled her lungs. She slowly raised her head and stumbled to her feet. She barked at them, not knowing she was free of the harness. Downstream Assan heard wolves barking and howling. Moments later Grey-Eye was running down the river.

"You are brave," she said, reaching for So'tsal's hand.

"She will have her pups," So'tsal said and squeezed her mother's hand. Without another word they turned their attention to the dead bull on the ice.

They are Coming

Naali started to worry about Kazan when the sun set and the snow began to fall. He had told her he would return from hunting before night fell. He had left with Zhòh, leaving Naali behind for the first time in many hunts. As the light faded, she built a large fire in front of the cave, hoping he would see it and find his way to Hole-in-Rock. She tried not to imagine all of the dangers beyond the firelight. She began to fear the worst had happened.

Lions. Had they met lions? Bear? It was late winter when bears were coming out of their dens. Or wolves. Had they met a hungry pack?

She squinted, hoping to see them on the tundra, but the snow was falling heavily.

Zhòh hunts with him. They have killed a grasseater. He is bringing it back. Zhòh will show him the way back.

As she heaped wood onto the fire, she was suddenly struck by a vision that sent her crumbling to her knees.

Barik is holding a long harness in his hand. At the end of it is a one-eyed beast. It is a great bear with its hump swaying in the moonlight. No! It is a ghost-white lion, its yellow eyes searching the dim light. Naali is on her hands and knees, paralyzed with fear as she hears his voice: 'Come back. She is here.'

Suddenly the beast is no longer animal. He is towering above her. Barik pulls on the leash, snapping One-Eye's head back. The bushman roars.

"She is here."

Naali climbed to her feet and stood staring into the darkness as the bonfire burned behind her. Then vision struck again.

Kazan is running, his mukluks slapping on snow. A bear as black as night is snapping at his heels. The huge jaws are about to bite into his foot when the shape shifts. It is One-Eye chasing him, his spear ready to plunge into Kazan's back.

Suddenly she is dreaming Zhòh - her eyes are the wolf's.

She is running hard. Kazan is sitting on the ground next to a hole in the ground. A bear is charging, nearly upon him.

The vision ended and Naali woke instantly. She kicked snow over the fire. Running for the tent, she slipped under the skins and slid into Little Weasel's hole. She exhaled, cramming herself into the tunnel until she was the hidden cave. Climbing into the furs, she waited, listening to her heart pounding in her breast.

They are coming! Barik and One-Eye. Where is Kazan? Where is Zhòh?

The Boy and the Bear

Kazan lay on the ground helplessly watching the charging sow grizzly. Everything was moving in slow motion, every detail of her powerful body sharp and clear. He tried to move, to cover his head, to roll, to scream - but he was frozen. The sow's mouth opened wide. A long skein of milky saliva flew from her yellow canines. Then something was flying through the air, grazing the sow's snout.

Zhòh!

Time suddenly sped up as the bear turned away and charged after the wolf.

Up! Get up!!

Kazan tried to stand, but his brain and body seemed to be disconnected. He stared at his feet, willing them to move, to stand. He rolled onto his knees to push himself upright and found he was sliding, tumbling down the knoll. When he reached the bottom he saw his spear by the boulder and the long ridge of broken cliffs ahead. Somehow the spear was in his hand and he was running up the steep ravine, the ground quaking behind him. His legs were churning through the gravel and snow. He slipped, each time scrambling back to his feet, only to fall again. The strength was draining from his legs. He saw the black cliff ahead. A loud roar erupted behind him, filling his ears.

Shih!! He could smell her rancid breath.

Gravel spilled around him as he stumbled for the rocks. He dropped his spear and leaped, his right foot catching a narrow ledge. His hand reached up to grip a boulder. With surprising strength, he held on, swinging his left foot to a higher ledge. He climbed, but every move seemed impossibly slow. Glancing down, he saw the sow lunging for him just as he raised his right foot. A searing pain burned at the back of his ankle as her teeth tore the heel of his mukluk. He screamed, expecting to be ripped off the rocks. Then - impossibly - his foot was free and climbing again.

He did not dare look down. Reaching a high ledge, he jammed his face against the frozen rock. He spread his arms, wedging his fingers into cracks, and held his balance. He was sobbing, tears streaming down his face.

The sow roared. Kazan looked down to see Zhòh lunging at her. The bear turned and swung her powerful foreleg, but the wolf was too fast. All of a sudden, Zhòh was behind the bear, slashing at her open flank. The bear twisted and spun in the gravel, unable to parry the wolf's lightning assaults. She roared in frustration, shaking her head at the elusive wolf.

The sow charged, but Zhòh spun sideways, easily dodging the great jaws. Each time the bear attacked, the wolf slipped around her, biting into her side and back. Finally, the sow ran into the ravine, up the knoll, and disappeared.

Kazan shifted his fingers, hoping the attack was over. He craned his neck, only to see the bear had reappeared and was charging down the knoll at a terrible speed, heading for the cliff. Bounding up the steep slope, she launched at the boy, but Zhòh was already there, cutting off her attack. The bear stumbled into the gravel as the wolf slashed into her back leg. The sow roared, slamming her feet down at the circling wolf. Then she looked up at Kazan perched on the rock and roared again.

Moments later she was back at the top of the knoll and facing Kazan. The boy, wolf and bear silently watched each other. Kazan's feet were cramping on the narrow ledge; his toes and legs ached fiercely. His fingers were turning blue, and he realized his hands were bare. He pulled on his mitts and watched the sow circle her den. When the sun dipped below the horizon, he heard the faint cry of a bear cub. Then the sow disappeared down in the den.

He waited on the ledge until the first slice of the moon appeared and his eyes adjusted to the twilight. He was freezing, and he knew he had to get down or he would fall. He climbed down the rocks carefully and retrieved his spear, then scrambled uphill to the top of the long ridge, continually checking for the bear. When he reached the top he bent down to inspect the damage to his ankle. The back of his mukluk was ripped away, revealing a dark bruise the size of his thumbprint. There was no wound, no bleeding and little pain. He had been bitten by *Shih* but he was not only alive, he was unhurt.

Zhòh suddenly appeared on the ridge, startling him.

"Zhòh," he whispered. "You have saved my life. I thank you." The wolf was already moving. Kazan checked the stars, found his bearings north and ran for Hole-in-Rock and Naali.

Kazan and the wolf moved swiftly over the moonlit tundra. Soon clouds appeared and snow began to fall. The wolf was ahead, looking as if she were floating on white clouds.

He had been bitten by a bear, unhurt but for a small bruise on his ankle. *Shih* was a powerful spirit, the most powerful of all animals. He was carrying Bear Spirit.

He turned his attention to the passing landscape. As he ran, he felt a new awareness, as if he had been reborn. His mukluks kicked up a shower of snow behind him. His arms propelled his body through the cool night air. Snow pelted his face, melting on his cheeks. His breathing was even and measured. He glanced at his moon shadow alongside him.

I am Zhòh vitth'àn, Wolf Leg.

He stopped to look around, etching into memory the shape of each ridge, hill, valley, gully and creek. His father had taught him this when he was very young:

"Know where you are, where you have come from and where you are going. Look around and remember. Imagine seeing a place from every direction, how it looks in day and at night, in storm, in bright sun, in fog. Remember the shape of the land. You will survive if you know its shape."

He looked back from where he had come, remembering the detail of the passing landscape.

"Breathe it in," Khon had told him. "The land smells different everywhere. Learn the smell of a creek, a meadow and a

311

lake. Listen. A sandpiper will announce its marsh before you see it. Know how the wind blows and always travel into it; never walk with the wind at your back. Always watch grasseaters. Know how they travel, how they use wind. The path of the grasseater is always the same; only the ground changes.

"Watch how wolves move, how they hunt. Wolves taught humans how to hunt grasseaters. Run like one. Stop when grasseater stops, move when grasseater moves."

A familiar ache wrenched at the Kazan's heart. What would Khon think of him? He was alive, living with a girl and a wolf. He was growing into a good hunter. Still a boy, but a hunter.

The snow ended and the sky began to clear. He saw Naali's fire shimmering on the plateau in the distance. He was at the end of a sloping ridge and about to drop down into the valley when Zhòh stopped. She was looking toward camp, whimpering softly. He peered into the night, watching for movement. All of a sudden the fire was gone. As his eyes adjusted to the darkness, he spotted shadows moving toward Hole-in-Rock.

A Conversation of Lies

Barik and One-Eye moved toward Hole-in-Rock until the snow began to fall heavily. They waited until the storm passed, striking off through the new snow. Barik climbed a ridge that overlooked the darkened plateau. He tried to make out the rock outcrop, but it was too dark.

One-Eye was below, waiting impatiently, when Barik saw flames suddenly appear. Surprised by his good luck, he pointed to the fire.

"There," he said, with confidence. "Hole-in-Rock." One-Eye climbed the ridge and pushed by him, heading for the fire in the distance. As they neared the outcrop, the sky was clear and the moon was rising over the horizon.

"Wait," Barik whispered. One-Eye turned to him, his eye burning with impatience.

He will kill them both.

Barik motioned him closer. "The girl... she has a great power. She is an animal-dreamer. Her dreams will show us the way to grasseaters. Her eyes see the future. She will keep Bad Spirits away... away from One-Eye." But the bushman was already moving for Hole-in-Rock.

Barik scrambled to catch up. "Leave her to me," he said. "Kill the boy. There is wolf. Kill it. Leave my sister to me." One-Eye continued as if he had not heard him. They were at the bottom of a low rise when the fire suddenly went out.

"They have seen us!" Barik hissed. One-Eye ran for the smoke. He disappeared into the cave. Barik arrived moments later, expecting to find them all dead. The tent was empty. One-Eye was standing in the centre, his head bent, his face grim. He raised his hand, motioning for silence. Reaching down, Barik's fingers touched the warm coals.

They heard us. Where are they?

One-Eye went back outside. Barik looked at the two beds

313

spread out on the floor.

They are both here.

Then he noticed the back skins of the tent were pulled away, as if someone had crawled under. As he was about to slip under himself, a wolf howled. He scrambled from the tent to see One-Eye standing in the moonlight, looking at two figures of the tundra. It was Kazan and the wolf.

"Who are you?" Kazan shouted, his voice flat and unfriendly. "What do you want?"

"Kazan! It is Barik! I have come for you and Naali. I found *Shih* Band and have come for you. To bring you back. I found their winter camp across the river. It is a good cave, safe and warm. We have food, skins."

"You are banished from here. You are not welcome." Kazan pointed his spear at the bushman. "Who is this with you?"

Barik saw One-Eye was bristling. He was slowly fixing a dart onto his throwing stick.

"He is Kural of *Shih* Band, my uncle. We have come to bring you back." Barik waved his arm, beckoning to Kazan. "Come closer."

Kazan sensed something was wrong. He had seen how they had approached the camp in the darkness. They had not waited for an invitation to enter. He looked at the big man beside Barik and his confidence wavered. He was huge.

"Where is *Shih* Winter Camp, Kural? How far have you come?" Kazan asked. There was no answer.

Barik's reply was swift. "Three days." He took a few steps toward Kazan but stopped when he heard the low growl from *Zhòh*. "She has grown," he said in a nervous tone.

"Kural!" Kazan shouted. "You left Avii Tsal to die. That is not how a human treats another." He could feel the bruise where the bear had bitten him. It burned, but not with pain. His strength surged, his fear was waning.

Bear Spirit. I call on you.

314

"Why did you leave Little Weasel to die?" he asked again. The big man showed no response. "If you are Kural, wave your spear."

One-Eye did not understand. His name was Killicki, One-Eye. He did not raise his spear.

Barik's patience was fading. He decided to shift the conversation. "Where is Naali?"

"Dead."

Barik bit his lip, thinking.

Two beds in the tent. He is lying. She is here. Alive.

"Naali dead!" he said, feigning shock. "How? How did my sister die?"

"You are not her brother." Kazan watched the big man's feet shifting, sensing his impatience and anger.

"I have come to take you back to *Shih* camp."

There was a long silence. Then Kazan answered sharply, "You are banished and unwelcome!"

Barik stood motionless, his back rigid with anger. He turned to One-Eye. "Kill him," he hissed.

The bushman came so fast Kazan barely had time to turn. He had never seen anyone move so quickly. In his panic to escape, he stumbled. As he fell, he saw the flying dart just in time and turned his back. The point glanced off his back and knocked him to the ground. He scrambled to his feet again and ran. Kazan glanced back and saw the man's scarred face and single eye.

One-Eye!

Naali had described the bushman to him many times. It was him! Kazan's confidence crumbled. The bushman had run down bull caribou - how could he outrun him? He reached a slope and headed up it, slowing with every step.

The bushman was closing in. As Kazan crested the hill, he glanced behind and saw another dart glinting in the moonlight. His feet pounded along the ridge, kicking up a shower of snow as he ran. He focused on the ground ahead, waiting for the dart to slam into his back and end his life. He no longer felt Bear Spirit with him. One-Eye waited until he was on the hill before he threw the second dart. As it launched from his throwing stick he knew it would fall short. The boy was moving so fast he was already out of range. He knew he could not catch the boy, but he could wear him down. The boy would tire like all the others. Then he would catch and kill him.

Barik watched One-Eye and Kazan disappear into the darkness. The bushman would kill Kazan, he was certain. He went back to the tent and lifted the skins. The rear of the cave was completely dark. He pressed his spear along the rock wall, feeling for Naali.

"Come out, sister," he whispered. "I will not hurt you."

Then he realized she might be waiting in the shadows with a spear. He pulled the tent skins high and built a large fire to see to the back recesses of the cave. Naali was not anywhere. As he was about to drop the skins, he remembered the hole.

She is in Avii Tsal's hole.

"Naali," he said loudly. "Come out. It is Barik. I found Kural, Yong, Jila, Stone and Yellow Tail. Their camp is across the *Ch'oodèenjik*. We have food and skins, a warm cave. I have come to bring you back. Come out." He waited, but there was no reply.

Naali did not move. Earlier she had heard *Zhòh's* howl and muffled voices but could not make words. Then the voices stopped. Her mind raced to the dream. Barik had come. She knew One-Eye was out there with him. There could be only one reason.

He has come to kill Kazan and take me.

Smoke began to fill the hole. Moments later she could not breathe. She held her breath until she began coughing uncontrollably. Her eyes burned, and she knew she would suffocate if she did not leave the hole. She closed her eyes and slid down through the thick smoke, choking and coughing.

Barik snatched her by the arm and lifted her to her feet. "I did not want to do this, but you made me. You do not listen to me,"

316

he said darkly. She coughed until her lungs cleared.

"Where is Kazan?" she wheezed, rubbing her eyes.

"Kural is looking for him."

"Kural is here?"

Naali listened to her brother's reassuring words and knew he was lying. It was One-Eye in her vision, not Kural.

"Why have you come?" she asked.

"We have come to bring you back to *Shih* Winter Camp." He reached out to touch her on the shoulder, but she shrugged him off.

"I will not leave," Naali said firmly. "Kazan will not go with you." She stepped back and faced him. "You were not to cross the river."

"You left me!" He shouted. "You left me for him! You left me to die. I have come to take you to *Shih* Winter Camp. It is close."

Naali paused. "Kural is not with you." She looked hard into his unblinking eyes. "It is One-Eye."

Calling *Zhòh*

Zhòh watches the human run at them. She reels, leaping back and barking in surprise. At first she thinks he is playing. She swings back toward him, but there is no play in the face. A dart flies and Kazan falls.

Kazan is on his feet and running, so she follows, racing past him. His breath is hard and uneven - she can smell fear. He is not watching her. He is moving like prey and in the excitement she has the primordial urge to grab him by his neck, to drag him down. But something stops her. In her mind she is a human. Attacking her own kind is not possible.

When she reaches the top of a hill she stops, waiting for Kazan to pass. A dart whizzes by and sinks into the snow.

Suddenly she hears the girl, her voice clearer, sharper, full of fear. She is calling to her.

"Zhòh! Come! Come! Run to my voice! Run! Run!"

Wolf Leg Tires

Kazan bent over and sucked air into his heaving lungs. He could not be sure, but the bushman seemed to be getting closer. He drew in more air as he searched around for the wolf. She was his only chance. She had saved him from the bear. Now he needed her again. But she was gone. As he scanned the moonlit landscape, he recognized the small hills on his right. He was running toward the den, toward the bear.

He looked back again, breathing deeply. The bushman was gaining. Kazan turned and ran on. He was tiring. His mukluks felt like stones moving through the snow. One-Eye was getting closer - still out of dart range, but closing. He tried conjuring Bear Spirit, but he felt nothing.

I have fought lions. I have been touched by a bear and I have lived. I am not afraid of One-Eye.

But he was afraid - very afraid. The bushman was more dangerous than any lion or bear. A killing beast might give up the chase, but the bushman would not. He had chased Kazan all night. Dawn was breaking, and Kazan saw his trail leading from the den. His strength was ebbing with every step. As he ran toward the light on the horizon, he thought of Naali.

Where is she? Where could she run to - into the creek? Barik would track her in the light.

Then he remembered the nights he sat in the tent and laughed as she rolled under the skins and disappeared into the hole. She had practised the move many times, as if she knew she would have to hide there one day.

"If you were not so big, you could hide with me," she had laughed.

Naali Chooses

"Why have you brought the bushman?" she shouted. Barik did not answer. She knew the perilous silence of his anger. He brushed at the fire with his spear, turning over the glowing coals.

"You have special medicine, power. You see things that will happen."

"No!" she whispered. "I do not know how this will end."

"It will end with you coming with me." He walked to the tent door, lifted the skin and looked out into the darkness. When he turned back he did not look at her. "We have Assan and So'tsal. If you do not come, he will kill them. That is your choice."

Naali was stunned. "Assan and So'tsal are alive? How can that be? Everyone was killed. We saw. No one lived!"

"They hid in the ice. One-Eye found them." Barik sounded excited. "I found his cave. He brought them there and tried to kill me for burning his camp." He scowled at her. "He tried to burn me alive. I warned you not to burn it. If you had listened, none of this would have happened! But you never listen to me."

He kicked at the skins on the floor. "He killed a lion cub. Then he wounded the mother who came to kill him. He was filled with her bad luck. I made a snare and killed her. I took away the lion's spirit." He paused, catching his breath. "No one has snared a lion. Now there is a story, a *Googwandak* - Barik, Lion Snarer."

"Where are they? Assan and So'tsal?"

"In the cave across the *Ch'oodèenjik*."

"Kazan will not believe you; he will not go."

"No," Barik said. "He will not go." He paused a moment, took a piece of kindling and dropped it into the coals. Naali understood.

"You have brought One-Eye to kill him."

"He is dead. When One-Eye returns he will kill you... unless I tell him not to. You burned his camp. For that he will kill you. He is simple, but he does not forget."

"Our camp," Naali exclaimed, "not his camp! Have you forgotten? He killed our father and mother! Now you travel with the *nanaa'in'* who killed them!"

"What choice do I have! I am banished! You banished me! My own sister. You left me for him, for Willow Boy!" He swung his spear and she raised her arm just in time to deflect the blow. She staggered and fell. He lunged down, shoving the spear on her chest.

"You will come or I will kill you here!" he screamed. His voice was strange, distant.

She looked at his twisted face and knew he would do it. Her eyes closed as she fell into a trance.

"Zhòh! Come! Come! Run to my voice! Run! Run!"

Snow is flying beneath her feet. She is Zhòh, or the wolf is her - she cannot tell what form she has taken. Dawn is coming. The rock outcrop looms ahead in the grey light. Her heart is pounding.

"Run to my voice," Naali whispers. Then her eyes roll back into her skull and she hears a voice as clear as river ice.

"Zhòh is coming."

The Chase

One-Eye saw the boy was faltering and nearly in darting range. He would catch the runner. He always caught them, even the strongest ones. The boy would pay for the long chase. He pulled his hood down, his face drenched with perspiration.

The runner was moving on top of a ridge that curved around a high knoll. Suddenly, he stopped and disappeared. One-Eye reached the spot and looked down. The boy was at the bottom scrambling through deep snow, heading for the knoll in the ravine. He was shouting something. The sound echoed around the ridge.

"Shih! Shih! Shih!"

One-Eyed plunged down the slope, sliding past small cliffs and through steep scree. When he reached the bottom he walked toward the knoll. The boy was halfway up, struggling in the deep snow. The bushman followed up his deep snow trail. He pulled his club. He would not need the spear.

Kazan was on his hands and knees, climbing through the powder snow, still shouting *"Shih! Come! Shih!"*

As One-Eye raised the club, the morning sun broke over the hill, blinding him with its brightness. He raised his hand to shield his eye. The boy had turned and was facing him. His spear was pointed in a final, desperate defence. He was still shouting, but One-Eye paid that no attention. The boy's face was hard and calm. One-Eye charged. A wall of snow suddenly blotted out the rising sun, then a great weight hit him, driving him off his feet.

The Pup Calls

Grey-Eye spends the day walking alone, disturbed by the encounter with the humans. She can still smell the breath, the dark eyes watching as something hard moved along her back, biting through the traces. Then the tightness stopped.

Her pack is howling down the valley. Blue's deep howl is searching for her reply. She howls a few times and continues moving up the valley as the daylight fades. Snow begins to fall, settling on her back. She circles, scratching out a snow bed, and lies down on a ridge. Pressing her nose into her shoulder, she smells where the human touched her fur.

Sometime later in the night, she wakes to the sound of her approaching pack. She stands and shakes the heavy blanket of snow from her back. Blue circles and lies down close to her. She settles back into her bed as the wolves dig in around her. As she is about to doze off, she hears a voice, sharp and clear:

"Zhòh! Come! Come! Run to my voice! Run! Run!"

She jumps up and lunges through the snow down the hill onto a wide, moonlit plateau. Her pack follows in her trail, uncertain where she is taking them.

Zhòh Attacks

"What happened? Your eyes turned into your head, you made strange sounds."

Naali opened her eyes. Barik was standing over her, the spear pressed to her chest. He looked at her with suspicion. "What did you see?" She heard fear rattling in his voice.

Naali swallowed hard, collecting her thoughts. "Let me stand," she said. Barik stepped back. She rose to her feet, her eyes shining in the firelight. "Something is coming."

Barik shifted uncomfortably and glanced at the door. "What? What is coming?"

"You must leave here. If you stay you will die."

"No," he said. "You have seen Kazan's death, not mine."

"Leave. I do not wish you dead." Her voice was flat, detached.

Then Barik heard the voice inside his head.

She is lying. She has seen nothing.

She sees the future. She has not lied before.

The bushman comes. It is him she fears.

I saved One-Eye from the lioness. He will listen to me. He will not kill her.

He has forgotten the lioness. He will not listen to you. He will kill her. Then you.

No! He needs me!

What do you have that he wants? The women do his work. You have brought him to Naali. He will kill her. Then he will kill you. You are nothing to him.

No! That was not my plan! He kills Kazan and we bring Naali back. She has medicine, power. With her, So'tsal, Assan - we will be a band.

What use is a band or spirit power to a bushman? He will kill everyone. Then he will be alone. That is the bushman way.

Then what do I do?

He is coming. She wants you to leave so she can hide in the hole. Look at her. She banished you. She left you for the boy. She is trying to save herself. If you want to live, kill her.

Barik looked at his sister standing by the fire, her face hidden in shadow. Her hand was reaching out for something. In the dappled glow of the fire he saw the spear against the tent wall. His spear hit Naali across the head, driving her to the knees. He kicked her until he was straddling her, the stone point resting on her chest. He raised it and drove down. She rolled to her side and the point glanced off her chest and sunk into her forearm. She screamed out, shielding her face as he raised the spear again.

A low growl vibrated throughout the tent. Barik turned toward the door. *Zhòh* was standing there, her head down and her teeth bared. She jumped, slamming into Barik. His hands flew to protect his face as her powerful jaws sunk into his shoulder. The wolf shook her head, tearing through his parka. A deep moan rose from his throat as he crashed against the tent skins. He kicked at *Zhòh* but her teeth sunk further into flesh and bone.

"Get her off!" he screamed, pounding at the wolf's head. His shoulder bone shattered and his eyes rolled back in agony. "Get her off!" he moaned, and then he fell unconscious.

Naali staggered to her feet in shock. She glanced down at her wound. The stone point had cut deep into her forearm, exposing the bone. She swooned and nearly fainted. She had to stop the bleeding. She found a blade by the fire, cut the arm off her jacket and cinched it around the wound. She sunk to her knees, trying to clear her mind. Blood was spattered on the tent wall. Her brother was on the ground in front of her. *Zhòh* was on top of him, tearing into his neck. As she watched the bloody scene, Naali gradually regained her senses.

"*Zhòh!*" she shouted. "Let him go. Let Barik go!" The wolf growled defiantly and held on as blood poured from her jaws. "Let him go! He cannot hurt me now. Let him go." The wolf's jaws remained clamped on his neck.

Naali reached for *Zhòh* and touched her on the back. "Let him go," she said softly. The pain in her arm was so intense she nearly fainted. *Zhòh* turned her head slightly and looked at Naali. "Let him go."

Her jaws slackened. She was panting heavily and looking down at Barik. Blood covered her face and neck. She went to Naali's bed and lay down, her eyes staying on Barik's body sprawled by the fire.

Naali tried to quell the blood rushing from Barik's wounds. There was so much blood. His eyes fluttered as she pressed down on the shredded mass of muscle, shattered bone and blood. He suddenly came to. His eyes were vague and unclear. A deep, wet moan rattled in his throat as he struggled to get up.

"No," Naali whispered, pushing him back down. "Lie down. You are bleeding. It is bad. I will wrap it." His eyes showed no recognition. His lips quivered and he moaned something inaudible. Then he stumbled out of the tent. *Zhòh* stood up and growled as he left.

Naali followed him outside as he staggered aimlessly through the snow. "Come back," she cried. He fell a few times as he stumbled toward the ravine, then disappeared around the outcrop. Dawn was breaking. Her throbbing arm screamed in agony. She went into the tent. *Zhòh* was already asleep.

The Battle of Giants

Kazan turned to face the bushman. He raised his spear, but his strength was all but gone. He tried to stand but could not.

"I have been touched by *Shih* and I am alive," he shouted out. "I have fought lions and I am alive. I will fight you!"

He felt the ground shudder around him. Suddenly, he was being carried down the slope in an avalanche. As he rolled in the showering whiteness, a dark shadow passed over him. His face came out of the snow for a moment and he saw the bushman tumbling down the knoll, his spear flung in the air.

The snow stopped moving. Kazan was buried, his mouth filled with snow. He tried to clear the snow from his eyes but his hands would not move. He could not tell if he was upright or upside down. He saw dim light above and pushed his head up, breaking the surface. He gasped as air filled his lungs. Crawling from the snow, he wiped the snow from his eyes and looked around. Below, the bear and One-Eye were locked in battle. The bear had sunk her teeth into One-Eye's side and she was shaking him. His club slammed down on her skull. She released him. With lightning speed, she swung her giant paw at his head, ripping away his ear and half his scalp. One-Eye screamed as he slammed his club into her face. She snapped at it but missed. He roared, pounding her bloody face again and again.

One-Eye staggered backward, blood streaming down his face. He was feeling for something in the snow when she charged. *The spear! He is searching for his spear.*

His club smashed into the side of her skull but she did not slow down. She bellowed, seized him by the shoulder and drove his head under the snow until Kazan could see only his kicking feet. A spear flew out of the snow and plunged into the bear's neck. She shook her head and roared. The spear flashed again, sinking into her throat. She caught it between her teeth and snapped it in two.

One-Eye climbed from out of the snow and swayed, no longer looking human. His disfigured head and face were caked in snow and blood. His scalp hung from his skull. He swung the club blindly. The sow lunged and fell upon him.

Kazan suddenly realized he was in grave danger. He crawled across the slope, trying to stay out of sight. Below he could see the bear's humped back moving up and down. When he reached the bottom of the knoll, he slipped into his own trail and crawled toward the ravine ridge. Moving up the slope, he slipped behind any rock he could find. When he reached the ridge top, he looked back. The bear was burying One-Eye in a mound of blood-soaked snow, her neck glistening red in the sun.

A noise drew his attention to the top of the knoll. Two cubs were walking outside the den, wailing for their mother. The sow heard them and weakly stumbled up the hill. As she neared the top, they ran to greet her. She suddenly stopped, fell onto her back and slid down the knoll, her still body coming to rest near the mound. He watched, numbed by what had happened. The bear that had tried to kill him that morning had saved him. *Shih* had heard him shouting. Now she was dead. Buried beside her was the bushman - dead. Then he remembered Naali - and Barik!

He will find her in the hole!

He ran.

Sleep

Naali stoked the fire until it was blazing. She heated water to near boiling, removed the bandage carefully and wiped away the blood. Pulling back the flap of flesh, she inspected the wound. All her fingers moved. The bone was not fractured. Catching her breath, she cut a clean piece of hide and placed it in a bladder until the water was steaming. She removed it, let it cool for a few moments and then quickly bound her arm again. She collapsed onto her bed beside the wolf, exhausted. Where was Kazan? Had the bushman caught him?

I have not dreamed your death! Do not let him catch you. You are a fast runner. Run!

She thought of how Barik looked as he staggered from the tent.

His eyes were already dead. His wound is great and he has lost much blood.

She reached for the wolf and touched her ear. "You saved my life," she whispered. *Zhòh* shifted her head and went back to sleep. Naali remembered the most dangerous part of the vision.

One-Eye! He will come!

She crawled under the tent skins and into the hole. She squirmed up the narrow tunnel, the pain in her arm almost too much to bear. Somehow, she found herself in Avii Tsal's hideaway, lying inside a sleeping bed.

I will not look at his scarred face when I die. I will die in Avii Tsal's hole.

Good Hunt

As Kazan approached Hole-in-Rock, he noticed a bloody trail leading around the outcrop. His heart raced as he ran for the cave. He flung open the flap, his club ready, but the tent was empty. The fire was cold, two spears were lying on the floor and the walls were spattered with blood. He recognized Barik's spear and picked it up. The stone point was covered in blood.

"Naali!" he shouted as he ran from the tent. He followed the trail toward the ravine. In two spots there were bloody impressions where someone had fallen in the snow.

He reached the ravine, following the trail across the creek through a willow thicket to a small meadow. Something moved ahead. *Zhòh* was sitting next to a body sprawled face down in the snow. His heart sank.

It is Naali!

He fell to his knees and reached for the parka.

The mukluks are too large... The parka is dark brown... Hers is light-coloured...

He gripped the back of the parka and turned the body over. Barik's snow-caked face was frozen in a death grimace, his teeth tightly clamped. His shoulder was a bloodied mess of flesh and bone. Kazan turned to *Zhòh*. She was whining softly.

"Is this your kill?"

Zhòh circled through the snow. Her neck and face were covered in blood.

"Good hunt," he whispered.

Where is Naali?

He ran for camp, scrambled under the tent skins and called into the darkened hole. "Naali, it is Kazan! Come out!"

There was no answer. He pressed his head closer. "It is Kazan. It is safe. Come out."

He heard a faint movement inside, and his heart soared. The reply was soft and weak. "One-Eye is coming."

"No. He is dead. One-Eye is dead."

Her voice was a little stronger. "Barik. He is badly wounded. Help him...'

Kazan paused, thinking what to say. "He is gone. Come out. It is safe." Moments later, she slipped down the hole and sat slumped in the tent, holding her bloodied arm.

Kazan knelt down and embraced her. His lips touched her ear as he whispered, "You are hurt." She wrapped her good arm around his waist, pressing her face into his neck. Tears wetted his skin. She cried silently. Then her shoulders began to heave. He tightened his embrace, kissing her forehead.

They sat in silence until he led her to her bed and built a fire while she stared into the flames. He made a tea and held the cup while she drank from it. After she finished, he inspected her wound. He cut a fresh skin compress, boiled it and carefully wrapped her arm.

She slept the whole night while he sat beside her, feeding the fire. Once, she woke and called for *Zhòh*. She muttered something he did not understand, and then she fell back asleep.

The Visit

The wolves skirt around the rock outcrop in the moonlight, keeping well away from smell of the camp. Blue crosses the human trail first, scenting the fresh blood. The yearlings mill around, their noses pressed to the snow. Grey-Eye takes the lead and follows the tracks into a rugged ravine. She crosses a frozen creek and catches the scent of wolf. It is her pup, the one that did not die in the den. As Grey-Eye enters the meadow, she sees the young wolf standing over something. She leaves the trail and slowly circles the pup.

Zhòh watches the wolves enter the moonlit meadow. Instinctively, she recognizes the subtle postures of the lead wolf as friendly. Raising her nose, she smells a familiar scent but has no memory of the place or circumstance. Blue arrives and everything changes. Zhòh is growling, claiming the body as hers. Blue stops to assess the threat. He has no interest in the human. He circles around the meadow and heads back out on their trail. The yearlings follow him, leaving only Grey-Eye. She circles once more, whimpering an invitation for Zhòh. As Grey-Eye leaves the meadow, Zhòh is struck by an urge to join her. She catches up to the pack as they leave the ravine. Grey-Eye glances back and continues walking.

A light wind is blowing as the pack moves over the plateau toward high hills. The wolves settle down behind a large boulder, digging night beds. Zhòh lies down near Grey-Eye but feels anxious. Her interest in her mother's scent is fading. As the wolves sleep, she rises and heads back on the trail. The pack does not notice her leaving.

Burial

Naali woke from a deep sleep, her bed wet with perspiration. The fire was burning strong and hot but the tent was empty. A throbbing pain shot from her arm. She vaguely remembered Barik spearing her in the arm and *Zhòh* attacking him, but Naali could recall nothing after that. She examined the compress around her arm. Someone had tied it neatly with rawhide cord. She heard footsteps approaching and panicked. Kazan came into the tent with an armload of wood. He laid the sticks down beside the fire and knelt close to her.

"You are awake," he said. "Your arm - how is it?"

"How are you here? Barik… One-Eye… where are they? They came…'

"They are gone," he said, uncertain how she would take the news.

"I remember *Zhòh* came into the tent and then nothing more. Where is Barik?"

He decided to tell her all that had happened. When he finished, she looked up, showing no emotion.

"They came to kill you and take me," she said. "I would not go." She looked into the fire. "Kazan, there is something to tell."

He waited. There was little that could surprise him now.

"Your mother and sister live."

Kazan's eyes widened. "Alive?" he asked.

"One-Eye took them from Lions-Came Camp."

"No one lived. We saw the camp! Everyone was dead."

"He found them hidden in the ice and took them. Assan and So'tsal have been with him since summer. My brother lied about many things, but I believe he told the truth about Assan and So'tsal. They are three days away in a cave near the *Ch'oodèenjik*. Three days."

Kazan paced around the tent. "Three days!" He looked at Naali. "But you are wounded. We cannot travel. You must heal

333

first."

"No, we must go," Naali said. "I cannot pull, but I can wear a pack and carry a spear."

Kazan's voice grew excited. "Can you leave so soon? Your arm?"

She gently touched her forearm. "Make a small travel camp. We will go to them and bring them here."

Kazan was beaming with anticipation. He looked at her and his voice softened. "We must bury your brother. He is in the ravine. I will take you."

Zhòh was waiting in the meadow when Kazan and Naali arrived. She moved off as Kazan dug the snow from around Barik's frozen body. He lifted Barik onto the cleared ground, pried up loose boulders and carefully placed them on top. After they covered him with the rocks, they piled on snow. Kazan took Barik's spear and pushed it into the mound.

"It is your spear," she said.

"It belongs with Barik's spirit," Kazan said as he stood it straight, marking the grave. There was nothing more to say.

As they left the ravine, Naali suddenly stopped.

"*Dinjii kat,*" she said pointing to two humans in the distance pulling a sled.

Reunion

Assan's suspicion grew as they waited for One-Eye and Barik to come back. When they did not return that night, she organized a light travel camp including the tent, sleeping beds, a ration of dry meat and a small kitchen. She and So'tsal would move up the valley and search for them. If they did not find the two hunters in two days, they would return, retrieve the butchered caribou and head back to the *Ch'oodèenjik* cave.

In the morning, they cached the fresh meat in a snow pile along with a sack containing Barik's and One-Eye's belongings. By midday, they were near the headwaters of the river, about to climb onto the plateau where Assan had last seen their trail. So'tsal came to a halt. Something was moving along the river. Assan's eyes had weakened since summer and she could no longer see distant details.

"Wolves," So'tsal said nervously. "Coming this way."

They took spears from the sled and stood behind it. There were eight wolves strung out in single file coming down the river. Assan recognized the leader as the female they had released from the harnesses. She continued walking toward them while the rest of the pack slipped into the willows a safe distance away. As Grey-Eye neared, her eyes met Assan's; neither wolf nor human blinked.

"Hunt well, wolf mother," Assan whispered as she watched Grey-Eye join her pack down river. She looked at So'tsal and saw her smiling.

Late in the day, they camped at the base of a long ridge near the river. There was no sign of Barik and One-Eye. The next morning, they hauled the sled to the top of the ridge and looked over a broad plateau covered in fresh snow. So'tsal saw smoke.

"Look!" she exclaimed, pointing to the thin white column rising from a rock outcrop in the distance. "There is a cave!"

Assan was filled with apprehension. "What are they doing? Why did they not come back for us?"

So'tsal did not answer. As they hauled the sled onto the

plateau, two figures appeared and walked toward a small canyon.

"I see a tent." So'tsal said, turning to her mother. "Barik and One-Eye do not have a tent."

"Who are they?" Assan asked.

"I do not know. They are too small for the bushman to be one of them."

They stood on the hill watching until the humans reappeared out of the canyon with a wolf following in their trail.

"A wolf!" So'tsal gasped. "A wolf is following them!"

Assan could make out only indistinct shapes moving in the distance. "Is it not Barik and One-Eye?" she asked, still not believing.

"No," So'tsal said. She pulled off her hood and raised her hand to block out the sun in her eyes.

"Do they see the wolf?" Assan asked.

"The wolf is running with them," So'tsal shouted. "Look! They have seen us. They are running to us. They see us!"

Assan squinted hard to make them out, but they were still too far away.

"It cannot be!" So'tsal said, her voice quaking. "It cannot be! It is Kazan!" She turned and gripped Assan by the shoulder, screaming "Kazan! Kazan! Kazan!"

Assan looked at her in disbelief. "How... how can it be Kazan?" she asked, her voice like a dream.

"Naali. It is Kazan and Naali!"

Assan leaned on the sled, the strength draining from her legs. As they got closer, she recognized Kazan by the way he ran. Like a wolf - slicing though the soft snow, the long loping gait. He was bigger now, more sure in his stride.

He runs like his father.

Then Assan heard her name being called. She staggered and fell to her knees.

EPILOGUE

A mob of ravens swarms through the ravine, waiting for their chance to feast on the two bodies sprawled at the bottom of the snowy knoll. Scores of the black birds land on the partially eaten bear carcass, jostling to snatch a share of meat before they fly off. The snow mound with the human body is untouched as waiting birds peck at the bloody snow, cawing excitedly. A brisk evening wind carries a tuft of bear hair up the slope to the top of the hill, settling in the mouth of the den.

Two bear cubs stumble out from the den and waddle their way down the slope, bawling constantly as noisy clouds of ravens rise in their path. Black wings pump and slap the air as the birds climb in the air, circling the two intruders.

The cubs are starving. Climbing onto their mother they find no milk, no warmth, no life. The cubs move to the snowy mound, stepping on a mukluk. They scramble over the top of the mound, sniffing at the face covered in snow and ice. Finding no milk, the cubs clamber up the knoll and drop back into the den, bawling the entire milkless journey. The ravens return to the bear's body like a dark cloud, scrambling to claim flesh. As daylight wanes, a bird cautiously approaches the snow mound.

Parts of the human are exposed - a finger, a foot, a leg, the top of a head. The raven is wary of how the human lies covered in the bloody snow, the face and eyes hidden. Gathering courage, the bird hops forward and stretches its feathered neck toward the end of a dark finger sticking out of the snow. It snaps its beak, grazing flesh, but suddenly the raven pulls back and hops sideways, cawing excitedly as its black eyes watch the finger with growing suspicion. Spreading its wings, the bird finds an upslope breeze until it is circling high over the knoll, waiting to feed one more time before darkness falls.

Afterword and Acknowledgement

In his book *The Naïve and Sentimental Novelist* (2010), Orhan Pamuk writes "Novels are second lives...we hope this second life will keep evoking in us a consistent sense of reality and authenticity." When writing *Zhòh* I tried to call to mind an authentic tundra-steppe landscape 14,000 years ago, fill it with interesting human and wolf characters, and tell a story to draw the reader into a second life, at least for a time. With the help of some talented people, I hope I have told the good story.

The novel setting is ancient Beringia, a vast un-glaciated land covering much of Siberia, Alaska and the Yukon through the Ice Ages. To conjure a believable landscape, I am indebted to Dr. Grant Zazula, Yukon paleontologist, who reviewed drafts and provided new fossil evidence of what the vegetation was like and what Ice Age mammals lived in the Yukon long ago.

Evidence for how ancient people used the land is based largely on human cultural material unearthed by archaeologists. I thank Grant Zazula, Greg Hare and Ruth Gotthardt of the Heritage Branch, Yukon government, for their thoughtful review of drafts and for their candid and spirited debates about weapon and tool technology and nomadic hunter-gatherer lifestyle at the end of the Pleistocene epoch.

A most compelling challenge was summoning an ancient nomadic culture in a place and time where humans had never walked before – so I chose the closest real culture I could find. The Vuntut Gwitchin First Nation, on whose Traditional Lands the story is set, have lived in the north Yukon for many thousands of years. The Heritage Committee agreed to review drafts for cultural consistency and language use. I thank Megan Williams, Robert Bruce Jr., Mary Jane Moses, Marion Schafer and Jane Montgomery for their insightful comments about cultural and spiritual concepts of the Gwitch'in People. I also thank Jeffrey Peter and Shirleen Smith for additional literary advice. It is unlikely the Gwitch'in language existed as far back as the novel setting. I chose to use it to give the culture and characters a spirit of authenticity. Any inconsistencies are entirely mine.

Much of the wolf natural history is from my experience as a Yukon wolf biologist, and many scenes are drawn from real events my colleagues and I saw during our field studies. I thank Steve Cooper and Lu Carbyn for their observations of wolves hunting bison.

I am very thankful to Patricia Robertson, my writing coach and editor for her supportive comments and generous advice which improved the book greatly. I thank Erling Friis-Bastad for allowing me to include his poem *Collaboration*. Special thanks to Joanne Haskins for her remarkable copyediting and Bruce Chambers for proofreading an early draft. Barrie Hayes provided line drawings, maps and charts in the same style as *Wolves of the Yukon*, our first book collaboration. Regine Zimmerman designed the book and coordinated production. Ulrich Wotschikowsky and Franz Windirsch coordinated book printing and shipping from Germany.

Special thanks to Caroline Hayes, who suggested important changes to the novel. She is a good reader, editor and my best friend. Last but not least, I thank Ava Milner, who was the first to say she really liked the story. As the book evolved, Ava gave constant advice about the plot and characters. I think there is no better judge of an adventure tale than an 11-year-old reader.

Last I would like to thank my 'Band' for their support and encouragement: Kelly, Chris, Ava and Molly Milner; and Aryn, Aidan, Pippa and Elias Madley.

Thank you for supporting independent writing.

Glossary of Gwitch'in Words and Terms

Gwich'in word	Meaning
Altin	Pike (fish)
Analuk	Long-tailed duck
Avii	Weasel
Ch'ich'yàa	White fox
Ch'ichèe	Falcon
Ch'ihlak ch'indèe	One-Eye
Ch'ii	Mosquito
Ch'izhìn	Eagle
Ch'oodèenjik	Porcupine River
Chihshòo	Whitefish
Daadzaii	Loon
Daagoo	Willow ptarmigan
Dachan	Wood
Daii	Break-up
Danach'l'	Old Man
Deetrù	Raven
Dèhzhòo	Snow on branches
Dinjii kat	People
Dinjii khehkai'	Chief
Geh	Snowshoe Hare
Googwandak	Stories
Jak	Berries
K'àii chyaa	Willow Boy
K'àii'	Willow
Khaii	Winter (Dark Days)
Khaiints'an'	Autumn
Khehkai	Chief
Nanaa'in'	Bushman
Nanh	Earth
Nantsaii	First clan on the land

Natl'at	Cranberry
Neegoo	Fox (check)
Neekai	Two
Nèevyaa zheh	Round tent
Nehtr'uh	Wolverine
Nilii	Meat
Nin	Animal
Njàa	White-winged scoter (black duck)
Shanaghàn	Old woman
Shih	Bear
Shih tri'ik	Female grizzly bear
Shin	Summer
Sik-Sik	Ground squirrel
So'tsal	Evening star
Sree	Sun
Sreendyit	Spring
Tr'iinin	Two
Troo	Wood
Ts'ìivii	Spruce
Vadzaih	Caribou
Vyah	Caribou snare
Yahkee	Dawn
Yukaih	Northern lights
Zhòh	Wolf
Zhòh dinji	Wolf people
Zhòh gii	Wolf pup
Zhòh vitth'àn	Wolf Leg

Bob Hayes

Bob Hayes landed in the Yukon wilderness in 1976 and spent a career studying ducks, falcons, wolves and other wildlife. After retiring, he wrote the narrative non-fiction book *Wolves of the Yukon* that won acclaim for the easy, non-science writing style. The book was translated into German, and sold out its first printing. He is a believer in quality self-publishing, recognizing that working with a team of talented editors, family and friends is the most rewarding element of publishing. Zhòh: The Clan of the Wolf is his first work of fiction.